"WONDERFULLY IMAGINED . . .

Campbell's deeply sympathetic, ecumenical, and unsparingly honest book will not comfort racists in their disease nor victims in their passivity; but it will open up a new kind of discourse, in fiction at least, where writers work harder to create understanding for the characters they, the authors, are most unlike."
—*Raleigh News & Observer*

"Campbell has a strong creative voice. . . . She writes with simple eloquence about small-town life in the South, right at the start of the great social upheaval of the civil rights movement."
—*The Washington Post*

"This contemporary historical novel, spanning four decades, connects civil rights times in Mississippi with the Chicago that many African Americans escaped to. . . .Moore illuminates the inner struggles of men and women trapped in the heritage of slavery and racism, and she provides a window both into history and into the minds of all participants."
—*The Seattle Times*

Purchased book at Chapters after I've seen it advertized in magazines. It's good — not the best story but an enjoyable read.

By Bebe Moore Campbell
Published by The Ballantine Publishing Group:

SUCCESSFUL WOMEN, ANGRY MEN
        Backlash in the Two-Career Marriage
BROTHERS AND SISTERS
YOUR BLUES AIN'T LIKE MINE
SWEET SUMMER
        Growing Up With and Without My Dad

YOUR BLUES AIN'T LIKE MINE

Bebe Moore Campbell

ONE WORLD BOOKS
BALLANTINE BOOKS • NEW YORK

A Ballantine Book
Published by The Ballantine Publishing Group
Copyright © 1992 by Bebe Moore Campbell

All rights reserved under International and Pan-American Copyright Conventions. Published in the United States by The Ballantine Publishing Group, a division of Random House, Inc., New York, and distributed in Canada by Random House of Canada Limited, Toronto.

http://www.randomhouse.com

Library of Congress Catalog Card Number: 93-92551

ISBN 0-345-40112-3

This edition published by arrangement with G. P. Putnam's Sons.

Manufactured in the United States of America

First Ballantine Books Trade Edition: September 1993
First Ballantine Books Mass Market Edition: August 1995

10 9 8 7

I thank God for enabling me to write this novel.

I also want to thank some helpful people who extended to me the love and support I needed to complete this book. My husband, Ellis Gordon, Jr., was not only supportive but inspirational, and his suggestions were always thoughtful and important. My mother, Doris C. Moore, read my first draft and gave me the essential input I needed in order to improve my novel. When I wanted to relax, my daughter, Maia Campbell, and my stepson, Ellis III, took my mind off this book with their slightly bizarre, although always upbeat, humor.

I began this project with one editor, Adrienne Ingrum, and completed it with another, Stacy Creamer. I thank Adrienne for her vision and faith. I thank Stacy for her insight and invaluable skills in strengthening my original story. Her expert judgment and critical analysis were invaluable. In addition, I would like to thank Marjorie Horvitz for superior copyediting.

Finally, I'm grateful to my agent, Lynn Nesbit, for her guidance, enthusiasm, and hard work.

To Ellis

1

The music was as much a gift as sunshine, as rain, as any blessing ever prayed for.

Lily woke up when the singing began. She lay quiet and still in her bed until her head was full of songs and the strong voices of the fieldworkers from the Pinochet Plantation seemed to be inside her. Part of the song was soft like a hymn; then it would rise to the full force of vibrant gospel and change again to something loud and searing, almost violent. The music was rich, like the alluvial soil that nourished everything and everyone in the Delta. Lily began to feel strong and hopeful, as if she was being healed. Colored people's singing always made her feel so good. Much too quickly, the song was over, without even leaving an echo to keep her company. Years later, she would fight to hum even a scrap of the notes that floated to her from the Pinochet Plantation that day, but by then the song had seeped into the land like spilled blood, and its vanishing echo was just another shadow on her soul.

As Lily lay in bed looking out the window into the wee hours of that Mississippi morning, it seemed as if someone had drawn down a heavy black curtain on the world. She felt lonely and adrift in the sudden quiet. Daylight was at least an hour away, and she couldn't fall back asleep. She groped in the dark toward the still body of her husband, who was lying next to her.

With movements as quick and furtive as a thief's, Lily pressed her breasts into Floyd's bare back; she wanted him to wake up feeling the tips of her nipples against his skin, the slight undulating movement of her groin rotating against his behind. It was like the ticking of a clock, the way her crotch burrowed into him: a small relentless movement. He'd been gone for nearly ten days and had returned earlier that evening. She felt frightened and weak when he was away from her. It was as though she didn't exist when he was absent. As she pressed into him, rubbing his shoulder blades with the tips of her nipples, she thought of how excited he would be when he woke up. She smiled, thinking how she could make him want her, remembering the times he even begged. Maybe he would plead with her this time. She might yawn a little and act uninterested, which would only make him hotter. She gently stroked his behind with her thigh, over and over again. Lily squeezed her small, white body against Floyd's back and rested the side of her face on his shoulder blade. She kissed his spine and thought: *If I can get him to give me three dollars, I'll get me another Rio Red lipstick; ain't had a lipstick in going on three months. I might can buy me some Evening in Paris and a scarf too. And maybe some rose-colored nail polish.* The thought of the lipstick, the bottle of perfume, the scarf, and the nail polish made her breath come heavy and fast. She calmed herself, because the trick was to wake Floyd softly, to let him discover her squeezed against him, to make it seem coincidental that the front of her nightgown was undone, her breasts exposed. Wanting her had to be his idea; he didn't like it the other way around. Floyd said only whores acted that way.

Looking out the window, Lily could see that a soft, drizzling mist was coming down. It had rained almost the entire time that Floyd had been gone, a hard, driving rain that rattled the tin roof and leaked into the pots and pans she placed strategically throughout the house. Not that it made a dent in the September heat spell they'd been seeing in Mississippi, Lily thought. Probably just fatten up the old mosquitoes and breed new ones. She wondered if her husband would ever fix the roof.

Lily's body was soft and slightly damp, like the weather. She could smell the musty odor coming from between her legs and clamped her thighs shut to keep the scent away from Floyd. When they put in a bathroom, she would take baths every night. Bubble baths. Beneath the thin sheet, she could feel her husband's first waking movements. She wrapped her arm around his waist and squeezed his belly, thinking as she breathed softly into the nape of her husband's neck—which was speckled with dirt he hadn't bothered to wash off—about the $67.58 in his pants pocket, pay for a week of construction work in Louisiana. Then, just seconds before he woke up, she fell away from him, so that only her nipples grazed his back. It was easy to let her mouth fall open, to push a soft, sleepy moan from her lips. She thought: *I can make him do what I want now.*

Lily opened her eyes slowly when he touched her. Fully awake, they admired each other. They were beautiful in similar ways; the people in the town used to mistake them for brother and sister. They both had glossy, dark curls, the same full lips and bright green eyes. They were a pair, all right. Lots of folks told them that they were the best-looking couple in the Delta.

"You are a pretty thing," Floyd said. He put his hands on Lily's breasts, then wriggled down in the bed and began sucking one of her nipples, gently at first and then with growing force. He pushed her gown up, then grabbed her hips, pulling her into his groin; he put his fingers between her legs and pushed up inside her. Lily felt a sudden fire there. She wanted to cry out, "Harder!"—she often wondered what the harm in that would be—but she said nothing. As Lily closed her eyes, bright colors swirled around her head. She could feel herself opening up in sweet anticipation.

Floyd slid into her too fast, then began rocking and pumping and pressing, his fingers grabbing and kneading all the wrong places. Lily opened her eyes. Disappointment gripped her shoulders like an old friend. She wanted to cry out, to tell him to stop, that nothing he was doing felt good, but she kept quiet, realizing that her power was gone, that she would have to ride out the storm. Go numb.

She had learned to do that years before.

She bit down on her lip and threw her arms around Floyd and held on as tightly as she could until she felt his shudders and hard spasms; then she closed her eyes and let out a practiced moan. When her last sigh faded, she fell away from him with relief.

Floyd smacked her on her behind, then reached for a pack of Winstons that lay on a rickety table next to their bed, and leaned forward, lighting two. He handed her one. "You know what?" Floyd said, blowing out smoke. "You know what? I'm taking you to Memphis."

She turned to Floyd. Words bubbled in her throat but wouldn't come out. Finally she managed, "For true? Memphis! Lordy!" Her disappointment, her pain, was pushed aside. Memphis!

"We gon' go for a week, after I come back from Little Rock. 'Round November or December. Be nice weather then. Cool. Couple of these boys around here owe me some money, and they'll pay up once the cotton's in. We can stay with some of my people. I got first cousins in Memphis. That make you happy?"

She flung her arms around him, grinning. He moved away from her and stretched. Frowning a little, he turned to her and said, "That girlfriend you useta set such store by, what's her name?"

"Corinne," Lily said carefully.

"She gon' take you to Memphis?"

"No, Floyd." Lily hadn't seen Corinne for months. Her old schoolmate no longer came around, and neither did anyone else, except Floyd's family.

"And you sure can't take yourself."

"No, Floyd, I sure can't. I need you to take me. I need you for everything."

He didn't try to hide his pleasure. "I want to go by the pool hall later and check on things," he said, smiling.

Lily measured her words so they sounded casual and spontaneous. "Can I come with you? Keep you company? Maybe on the way back we can run to town and stop at the drugstore. I need me a couple of things."

Floyd gave his wife another quick swat across her behind. "Fix me some corn bread this morning, will you? I got me a taste for corn bread."

After Lily got up, Floyd went back to sleep. She was hoping she could get breakfast cooked before her baby awoke, but just as she got a fire going in the stove, she heard Floydjunior's cries. She cooked with the boy on her hip, holding his bottle. "You hush now," she hissed in the child's ear as Floyd came in. She scurried to the table while her husband washed his hands and face at the kitchen sink, which had the only running water in the house. By the time he sat down, she had finished putting the food on his plate.

After breakfast Floyd and Lily walked down a dirt road that ran in front of their house. The air was scented with jasmine as they walked to his brother's home, passing houses that resembled their own: shotgun clapboards set up on cinder blocks, where the gardens in the back were haphazard affairs and the chickens and guineas were likely to wander into the front yard and even into the road. The string of homes owned by the poor whites in the area faced a long stretch of hedges. Behind the hedges was a dump and, in back of that, the Quarters, a compound of rented two-room tarpaper shacks where the field hands and sharecroppers who worked the nearby plantations lived, surrounded by yards full of Johnson-grass and buttercups and an occasional neat clapboard that some enterprising Negro had managed to erect.

They borrowed Floyd's brother's truck and left Floyd-junior behind, heading for town, driving across land that was perfectly flat, punctuated only by acres and acres of Pinochet cotton, occasional splotches of rice, soybeans, and milo. They reached the city limits of Hopewell and were about to park where they could see the banks of the Yabalusha, which washed up along the east side of the delta town near the railroad tracks, when Lily said, "Floyd, please drive through the Confederacy." She held her breath until the truck turned down a wide street, shaded by huge oaks and stately magnolias.

Even better than looking in the store windows, she liked driving through the Confederacy, an area composed of General Lee Boulevard, General Jackson Road, and General Longstreet Avenue. On these streets, half hidden behind a bank of towering magnolias, were large brick two-story homes with screened-in front porches and meticulous lawns where the shiny black faces of sculpted jockeys in red jackets and white pants were frozen in perpetual grins while inside, their living counterparts were equally accommodating. Lily often daydreamed about how it would be to live in one of these houses, the finest she'd ever seen. Of course, the sprawling plantation mansions of the Settleses and Pinochets, reminiscent of the antebellum splendor that was part of the region's mythology, were grander. But who could even begin to imagine living in one of those?

Lily didn't come into town very often, and the sight of the paved streets and the stores made her eyes open wide with expectation, even though the city was small, its business district no more than three or four blocks sandwiched between the two gins—both owned by the Pinochets—that made up the north and south boundaries. As they drove down Jefferson Davis Boulevard, the main downtown thoroughfare, she craned her neck in hopes of glimpsing the Chinaman and his family who ran the town's laundry and Chinese restaurant. Or maybe the Jew who owned the small department store would pass by. She yearned for something wild to touch, see, or feel. Some excitement.

In Burke's Drugstore, Lily was flipping through movie magazines when someone tapped her on the shoulder. She smelled the lilacs before she even turned around. Mrs. Purdue, the woman who had taught her English when she was in eleventh grade, was standing in front of her. "I thought that was you, Lily. How have you been, my dear?" she said, smiling at Lily with a look of sincere interest on her face.

"I been fine, Mrs. Purdue. I got me a little boy now."

Her former teacher nodded at her. She was holding some books and magazines in her hand. "Are you keeping up with your reading, Lily?"

"No, ma'am. I ain't got much time for reading," Lily said.

"Well, my dear, you find the time. Reading broadens the mind. You take care of yourself, Lily," she said, as she left.

"I will, Mrs. Purdue." Lily watched the older woman as she walked down the street. She laughed to herself. Mrs. Purdue was still trying to get her educated.

Lily was sixteen when Floyd asked her to marry him—they'd been boyfriend and girlfriend since she was ten—and when he looked into her eyes and said he didn't want to wait, she quit school one day, and that afternoon they borrowed his brother's truck and drove to Greenwood and came home husband and wife. The next week she was stunned as she watched him pack his things for an army base in northern California, from where he would ship off to Korea for eighteen months. She hadn't realized that a war was going on; neither her daddy nor Floyd had told her anything about it.

She was sitting on the front porch of her parents' house, a weathered clapboard with a tin roof and four rooms placed one right behind the other, when she looked up from the doll she was holding on her lap and saw Mrs. Purdue climbing up the broken steps. Her En-

glish teacher was tall and flat-chested, the only woman
Lily knew to wear glasses all the time. Once, she'd
seen her reading a newspaper with a scrunched-up intensity in her face that Lily thought odd. And she talked
funny. Not quite like a Yankee, but almost. She was
from Washington, D.C., but had married a man from
the Delta, who died only two years after they got
married. Mrs. Purdue had to work for a living, which
Lily thought was a tragedy beyond belief. She had been
in Hopewell so long that sometimes people forgot
where she came from until she reminded them. Mrs.
Purdue sat in the empty chair beside Lily and was quiet
while she caught her breath. Finally she said, "Lily, I
heard your husband has shipped out to Korea. Is that
right?"

"Yes, ma'am." Lily had always liked Mrs. Purdue
and had loved when she read *The Scarlet Letter* to the
class in her soft, almost Yankee accent. One of the test
questions was: What was Hester Prynne guilty of? Lily
thought about that for a long time after the test was
over.

"Well, I was thinking that maybe you'd be interested
in coming back to school. Graduating. I could arrange
that. You were a fine student."

Lily could smell the soft scent of lilacs, the perfume
the teacher always wore, as Mrs. Purdue fanned her
neck with her hand. There was not a speck of polish on
her nails. "Oh, no, ma'am. I can't do that. I'm married
now."

The teacher put her bony fingers over Lily's hand.
She spoke softly and slowly. "Yes, I know, dear, but,
well, education is precious. And you're so very bright."

"But I'm married now." Lily said this as gently as
she could. She didn't want to hurt Mrs. Purdue's feelings.

"A girl, a woman, needs to have an education to fall
back on," Mrs. Purdue said clearly.

"Ma'am?"

"Look at what happened to me."

The teacher returned several times that summer to ask Lily the same question, and each time Lily felt surprised and then sorry that she'd made Mrs. Purdue so unhappy. But really, she thought, she was married, and she and Mama agreed that going back to school didn't make no sense at all.

Lily almost skipped to the truck. Floyd had bought her a lipstick, some nail polish, a scarf, and, best of all, a bottle of Evening in Paris. "Thank you, Jesus," she said softly, as she climbed into the cab. She was grinning when Floyd sat down beside her. "What are you so excited about?" Floyd asked.

"I don't know." She looked at Floyd hesitantly. Maybe he didn't like her acting so happy. She pressed her lips together and sat quietly. But inside, inside she felt the way she did that time Floyd took her to the drive-in in Greenwood and they saw *High Noon*. As they took off for the pool hall, Lily smelled her wrist and looked at her red lips in the tiny mirror she carried. Every time she smelled herself and saw her face, she felt fluttery and almost crazy, as if she was getting ready to go to the drive-in.

Armstrong Todd bent over the cue stick, taking aim at the eight ball. He'd get it right in the pocket, he thought. He was a tall colored boy whose skin matched a lemon wafer. With his muscular body, he appeared older than his fifteen years. His hair was wiry and rust-colored, and his face was sprinkled with freckles that gave him a mischievous look. When he wasn't smiling, his eyes seemed darker and sad. Drinking in his certain victory, Armstrong paused to stare down his opponent. He held his cue upright in his left hand and leaned against it, while stroking his chin with his right thumb and forefinger. "Boy, I'm gon' beat you like you stole something," he said.

Darnell, a short, fat, brown-skinned boy, who was

about to lose the last of his dimes to Armstrong's superior skills, said nothing, but the men lounging along the walls laughed so hard that their shoulders shook.

The pool hall Floyd Cox owned was little more than a shack. The paint had long ago peeled off wooden planks that had buckled and splintered from so many rains and from relentless sunshine. Inside, newspaper was stuck between the cracks in the wood to keep out the heat and cold, and the linoleum floor was almost as wet and slimy as the waterlogged dirt road, so full of ruts and gullies, that led to it from Route 49E. In the middle of the small room stood a battered pool table; four cue sticks were propped up along the back wall. In one corner an ancient jukebox blared a scratchy Louis Jordan record; the drone of what seemed to be a battalion of mosquitoes ready for combat competed with the music to be heard, and the insects, strong and bloodthirsty that summer from so much rain, were clearly in the lead.

Not that weather conditions would deter any of the black men watching the game from coming to the pool hall; in fact, because the rain had cut the workday short, the twenty or so regulars had come early, the gumbo mud clinging to their brogans. There was a grocery store owned by a colored family that they all frequented. Occasionally they played a game of checkers or swigged down a Jax beer there, but there wasn't another pool table in the Delta for fifty miles where coloreds could stand around and shoot the breeze, and it would have taken much more than the light rain that had begun to fall to keep them away.

After the eight ball ricocheted off the corners and sank into the side hole, Armstrong put down the cue and held out his palm to his friend and laughed when the thin dime fell into his open hand. "Just too good for you, boy," he said, grinning so hard that Darnell had to laugh. The room was hot, and the sweaty bodies of the men created a curtain of musky funk that clung to the air. Armstrong's victory made his spirits soar. To-morrow he'd be leaving Hopewell and his grandmother, a sharp-tongued cotton picker named Odessa Daniels, to attend school in the eastern part of the state. *Be glad to say goodbye to all these country fools,* he thought. "Now, in Chicago, they got some pool players," he announced to the room. He deliberately made his voice loud and condescending, so that everyone understood that he was a Chicago boy, born and bred, city slick and so cool that nobody better not mess with him. And anyway, he told himself, as soon as his mother saved enough money to get a larger apartment, he'd be going back to Chicago; that was for damn sure. His mama was gonna send for him; it was just a matter of time.

He looked at the men along the wall. Armstrong liked the feel of their eyes upon him. They recognized that he was way above them, he told himself. What he didn't realize, as the men reared their heads back in laughter, was that among themselves they declared that Chicago couldn't have been all that great, seeing as the boy's mama sent him down to Hopewell.

When he saw the men were silently watching him, Armstrong launched into yet another description of the wonders of the Windy City, embellishing his limited sightseeing—he'd been no farther than his mother's South Side neighborhood—with the imagination and alacrity of a born liar. He looked at Darnell as he spoke and was gratified to see his friend's eyes widen in admiration. The sharecroppers and field hands had drawn in closer around him and were laughing loudly as he described his exploits. The boy's blunt crowing about the fabled city so many miles north of them was part of their entertainment. The more they laughed, the more Armstrong lied.

But from the corner of his eyes, Armstrong could see big Jake McKenzie watching him with a cold expression and an angry mouth. Jake was strikingly ugly, with a large bald head, a nose that stretched across his face, a bright pink bottom lip that hung down like a pump handle, and skin as black and shiny as an eel's. "Black Jake. Ugly as a snake!" the children from the Quarters sang out whenever they saw him. Armstrong knew that Jake stood behind the sagging counter and sold colas and bologna sandwiches because that's where Floyd Cox told him to stand. If a white man told Jake to jump off a bridge, that black fool would jump, Armstrong thought. *That's what's wrong with the colored people down here; they're so scared of these crackers. Well, I ain't. I ain't scared of no crackers.*

"Boy," Jake said, "Chicago ain't nothing."

"How would you know?" Armstrong shot back. "They don't let no ugly people in Chicago. They got guards at the border, and I know they sent you back."

Behind the counter, Jake shifted his rat-colored eyes but said nothing. He turned his head when he heard the men laughing.

"Voulez-vous danser avec moi ce soir? Vous êtes belle, mademoiselle." The words pranced out of Armstrong's mouth like so many high-stepping show horses. His father, who had served in France during World War II, had taught him a few French phrases, and he liked showing them off. "Yeah," he said, breaking into English again, "I'll be going back to Chicago to live soon. I'll be glad to leave this place. What I wanna stick around here to go to school with some redneck crackers next year?"

"You better watch your mouth, boy. Don't tell me Delotha and Wydell done raised a jackass," Jake said.

"You know my daddy?" Armstrong was surprised.

"Yeah. I know that fool," Jake said.

Uneven laughter rippled around the room. Armstrong gripped the cue ball so hard he thought he was going to break it. He felt as though someone was ripping a bandage off his bleeding sore. He said loudly, "I ain't seen the fool in so long I wouldn't know him if he knocked me down." He looked at Jake and laughed. "Darnell, let me hold a cigarette, boy." He felt stronger, cooler as he inhaled the smoke. "It was in the newspaper," he said loudly. "The Supreme Court said last year that the schools hafta integrate. But me, I'd rather sit next to northern crackers. Not these poor-white-trash people down here." The men lined up along the walls gaped, while Armstrong laughed.

"You better watch your mouth," Jake repeated.

"Voulez-vous danser ce soir? Qu'est-ce que c'est que ça . . ."

Armstrong was still spouting French phrases when he turned his head and there was the white woman, pretty like a doll. Red, red lips, that's what he saw first, and then the blue scarf tied around her neck. The fingertips that caressed it were as bright as flowers. Her smell was like dim lights and slow-drag music. She was standing at the door, peeking inside the poolroom with the exhilarated, frightened look of a girl sneaking her first drink behind a barn. The woman stepped inside, smiling at him as he spoke his French phrases, and then she raised her hand and smelled her wrist and started laughing. Armstrong laughed too. The look in her eyes said that she'd done it, had the drink and not gotten caught. Then she paused in the middle of a giggle, looked over her shoulder, and stepped outside.

He heard the woman say, "We need to hurry up and go get Floydjunior." She said the words quickly, tossed them lightly, as though they didn't mean anything.

A man said, "Thought I told you to stay in the truck."

The men began clearing out as Floyd walked in. He took a quick look around, surprised that so many were leaving so early in the day. "How y'all doin'?" Floyd asked the room. The remaining men grunted out their replies. He nodded to Jake, who began grinning as soon as he saw Floyd. "Jake, come on over here," he said.

"Yassuh, Mr. Floyd." Jake followed him into a small room that adjoined the pool hall.

The French phrases drifted into the space where the white man and the black man stood talking. *"Voulez-vous danser avec moi ce soir?"*

"What the hell is that?" Floyd asked.

"French, he call it," Jake said. He added, "Suh."

Floyd paused for a moment. All the niggers he'd ever met spoke English, and most of them didn't do too good with it. "Never heard of that."

Jake's words bubbled up like poisonous gas. "Mr. Floyd, he was talking it to your wife."

Floyd's head jerked around. He walked toward Jake. "She come in here?"

Jake stepped backward. "Well, uh, suh, she come just to the doorsill."

"Talkin' French to my wife?"

Jake's eyes gleamed. "Yassuh."

Purple fanned out from the base of Floyd's throat and traveled slowly over his face to his hairline. Just as suddenly, he started trembling. For a moment he stood motionless, trying to decide what to do, because if the boy had talked crazy to Lily, he had to do something. Should he just holler at him? Should he go in that room and beat him with the pool cue? Knock him down? Just how angry was he supposed to get? If John Earl was here, Floyd thought, pounding his fist into his palm, he'd know just what to do. His brother always knew how to take the lead in any situation; that's what his daddy told him often enough. He could hear his father's proud voice saying, "John Earl is a natural-born leader." With a sudden savage burst of energy, Floyd spun around and strode into the room where Armstrong was bending over the pool table. The men who lined the walls looked up when Floyd stalked in, and their eyes glazed over with fear. Darnell's forehead became bright with sweat, his mouth drawn as he saw the rage in the white man's flushed face. Floyd hesitated for a moment, then took a deep breath and grabbed Darnell by the shoulder, spinning him around to face him. "Nigger, what's all that voully voully dance? You say something crazy to my wife?"

"Mr. Cox, I—I—I ain't said nothin' crazy," Darnell protested. "I ain't said nothing to your wife."

Confused, Floyd turned to Jake, who ran his hand over his mouth and held his hand out to Floyd in a way that made the gesture, which had the appearance of begging, seem involuntary. Then Jake said, "Where you learn that ole funny talk, Armstrong? Hey, you with them damn spots on your face. I'm talkin' to you." He slammed his fist down on the thin wooden counter, and a jar of pickles crashed to the floor. The harsh odor covered the room like a sheet.

Floyd stood before the boy and suddenly realized how tall and strong he was. Silent eyes bored into him like nails. They could all kill me, he thought. Just come at me and tear me apart, and that'd be the end of that. Floyd crooked his head to the side and peered at Armstrong; he felt his fingers trembling, and he shoved his hands behind his back. His words came out soft and weak. "You get your black ass outta here. I don't wanna see you 'round here no more."

"But Mister—" Armstrong began.

"Nigger, I don't wanna hear nothing you got to say. Just get your ass outta here now."

Floyd watched as Armstrong, followed by Darnell, left quietly.

None of the remaining men said anything; nobody moved. *I shoulda hit that boy,* Floyd thought. *You always gotta hit a nigger what steps outta line; keeps the other ones respectful. What was I thinking of? Lord, I don't want this getting back to Daddy and them.* He said to the silent, averted eyes, "I'm trying to be a Christian."

He looked out the window and saw Lily sitting in the truck, her face serene and composed, her lips so red that from a distance they looked bloody.

2

Jake tried not to inhale the sour odor as he wiped up the
pickle juice with a wet rag. Out of the corner of his
eyes, he studied Floyd, although he didn't appear to be
watching him at all. He could see that the white man
appeared perplexed and that hidden within the confusion in his eyes was fear. He stared at Floyd's trembling
hands. *Just let me be a white man,* he thought, *I
wouldn't be scared of nothing. He up there thinking
about whether he done right. Shiiit. Shoulda knocked
that smart-talking Chicago boy right on his ass. Teach
him a lesson, with his yella, freckle-faced self. Floyd
Cox is scared! Just plain scared! Like some of these
sorry mens gon' do something to him. Anybody could
tell how fast they lit outta here that them some sorry
niggers.* Jake almost laughed aloud.

Looking up at Floyd, Jake could see a deepening
frown settling in the middle of his forehead. Jake's
voice pierced through the silence, pouring out like
syrup from a bottle. "You handled that boy real good,
Mr. Floyd. You told him just right." Floyd looked at
him, his face as blank as an empty field, his hands fluttering by his sides. Jake made his eyes wide and
scratched his head. "You give him a warning. Lotsa
mens ain't that . . . fair."

This last comment seemed to have a soothing effect;
at least Floyd's hands stopped shaking.

After Floyd left, Jake was alone in the empty poolroom. He knew that no one would come in that eve-

ning; by now word would have circulated that Floyd had put a colored boy out of his place, and the others would feel uneasy. Scared. There hadn't been trouble between colored and white in a while, not since the year before, when one of the sharecroppers tried to leave the Settles Plantation owing money. Business would be slow for a day or two.

He walked out the back door to a persimmon tree and urinated, humming the whole time. The sky was vast and purple, and under it the land spread out like a green blanket. A mockingbird was singing, and for a moment its sweet chirps were the only sounds in the world. The rustling in the bushes startled Jake, and he whirled around just in time to see four little ashy feet scampering down the road. Childish, singsong voices screamed, "Black Jake. Ugly as a snake!"

He clapped his hands over his ears. "You little black bastards!" he shouted, over and over again. Only when he was sure that their taunts and laughter had ended did he take down his hands and pull a small dark brown case from his hip pocket. It snapped open, and he retrieved a harmonica and began playing a soft, mournful blues tune that seemed to rise up from inside him. He played for a while, and then he held the harmonica in his hand and sang. "There's trouble all around me, and the night is cold . . ." As the words floated above him, he imagined being in Chicago, standing on a big stage, performing his songs, a crowd stomping and cheering for him.

"Have you ever been lonely? Have you ever been blue?" Lily sat in the truck, looking over the flat landscape around her and swaying a little as Patsy Cline's sweet soprano trilled from the radio. The rain had made the cotton good and high. By the end of November the land would be stripped, and the men around Hopewell, both black and white, would take to the woods, staying for days at a time. *Floyd'll be out there hunting with his daddy and John Earl, and I'll be stuck at home with Floydjunior*, Lily thought, yanking at some threads on her dress. But then she remembered that she and Floyd were going to Memphis. She closed her eyes and imagined being far away from Hopewell, walking down a street with a sidewalk, wearing a pretty new dress, her nails painted a vivid red.

The slap caught her by surprise; it was heavy-handed and so full of meanness and rage she couldn't even cry. Lily was stunned. Floyd had hit her before, but she always knew when the blow was coming. "I thought I told you not to go in there," Floyd said, his voice quivering, his hand gripping the back of her neck. He had opened the door on her side and was leaning in, his mouth close to her face. She could feel his breath on her cheek.

"I only went to the door," Lily said, coming to her senses, whimpering a little and rubbing her face so he'd feel sorry for her and not hit her again. What had happened? Who had told him that she'd been inside? Why was he talking so softly?

"What'd that boy say to you?"

"What boy?" But as soon as she asked the question she knew which boy and what Floyd was angry about. Her thoughts collected like bits of steel being pulled toward a magnet; she had to protect herself. If she said she was sorry, it would be like admitting that she'd gone into the pool hall to look at a colored boy; Floyd might hit her again. If she told him what the boy had said (what had he said? what?), Floyd might hurt him.

"What'd that boy say to you?"

Lily cried, even though the pain had disappeared. She knew how to extend her tears. "I don't rightly know. Talked like a foreigner. I was just curious, Floyd."

"You don't go in there no more, you hear me?"

"Yes, Floyd."

He stroked her cheek. "Did you hurt yourself?"

Floyd walked around to the driver's side and slid into

the front seat. As he was backing out, he said, "You
don't let on about what happened. You know how
Daddy and them are."

3

Clayton Pinochet sat crouched over the copy he was editing for the next edition of the *Hopewell Telegram*. The stories spread before him on his desk were the same old rehash of births, weddings, and deaths that were the staple of his semiweekly paper. He could write them in his sleep. Next to the pile of articles was a letter from Taylor McIntyre, his former editor at the *New York Bulletin*, where he had worked for nearly ten years. Taylor's note had arrived several weeks earlier; it asked him to write an article on how Mississippians were responding to the Supreme Court decision favoring integration of public schools. He had put off his response long enough, he told himself; today he would write back and inform Taylor that he just didn't have time to do the story. It was a plausible excuse.

Clayton was sipping coffee when he opened a drawer and glanced down and saw the face of Dolly Cox staring at him from a photograph. A sound came out of his mouth, a blended moan and gasp. He'd forgotten that he'd slipped the photo into his drawer; it had run in the obituary section of the paper three months earlier, on the occasion of Dolly Cox's death. He wished he'd thrown it away. She was still beautiful in the picture, the Dolly of old, not the weather-beaten, blowsy woman she became. The family gave no explanation of her death, but even the colored people around town knew that she drank herself into an early grave. Clayton hadn't gone to the funeral; he knew he wouldn't be wel-

21

come. Sitting at his desk, studying the face of the Dolly of his youth, he suddenly flung the photograph across the room. He didn't need reminders of her. What he needed was a way to forget, a way to quell the wave of disgust that rose inside him when he thought about Dolly and his cowardice. And he couldn't think of one without the other. *Why did I ever come back here?* he thought.

He glanced at his watch. Where was the boy? He had hired Armstrong to clean his office every evening, but he'd come to depend upon him for much more. Armstrong made him laugh, with his silly stories and quick wit. And the boy was bright. He'd shown such an aptitude for newspaper work that Clayton had taught him how to set type. He'd even made Armstrong a kind of roving reporter, with instructions to contact Clayton at the office if Armstrong heard or saw anything newsworthy. Once, the boy wrote a story of his own about a traveling carnival that had come to town. Except for a few misspellings, the article was perfect, and Clayton had run the piece under a pseudonym, warning Armstrong not to tell anyone.

Clayton pushed back his dark, spiky hair. He was of medium build, with eyebrows that formed a bridge across his nose and deep-set gray eyes. His body was hard and strong-looking, but his shoulders were rounded from constantly bending over copy and there was a weakness about his chin; he had to remind himself to hold his head up.

"What do you want to go up there for? Living with Yankees! You won't be fit for anything," his father had said years before, when Clayton told him his plans to move to New York. He might as well have said he was going to live on the edge of the sun. His father had stared at him, his dark eyes searching the young man's face, his lionine head and square jaw held high and unwavering as he sat behind his exquisite handmade walnut desk in the library. He was a big man, who appeared then as he always had: strong and in control, a man incapable of breaking or bending, of even aging, because that would have implied weakness. And there was nothing weak about Stonewall Pinochet, as everyone called him. Clayton remembered how rubbery his knees felt as he stood before his father that day; his entire body shook. But then, he'd been frightened of his father for as long as he could remember.

He wasn't even eight years old the summer day he watched his father's farm manager horsewhip one of the black laborers, a man named Jim, who sometimes told him stories. Even now he could taste his eight-year-old passion. "Stop it! It's not right!" he screamed, flinging his small body between the two men. Suddenly he was lifted up, and then he was momentarily airborne, before he landed on the ground with a thud. When he looked up, his father's body loomed over him. Stonewall Pinochet's face was contorted with rage and venom as he shouted, "If you ever—ever—try to save a nigger again, I'll . . ." He stalked away. The day Clayton knew he wanted to rescue colored people was the day he became afraid of his father. And the fear never left him.

So Clayton escaped from Hopewell, the one independent act of his life. And when he returned he found the Delta crueler than it had ever been and emptier, because Etta was dead.

Even now, as he sat in his own office, he couldn't believe that the old colored woman was gone. Etta, who lifted him from his mother's arms right after he was born. She wiped the blood and mucus off him, then nursed him from her own breasts and raised him, until the word "mother" became synonymous with coffee-brown skin and rough, crinkly hair, and the white woman who bore him was relegated to being a bystander in her own son's life. Etta, his mammy. He sighed and could feel a fist beating within his chest. Tears welled up in his eyes but refused to fall. Deep inside him, some secret code always prevented him from mourning Etta. He was a Pinochet, and Pinochets didn't cry when a colored person died.

But he hadn't come home because of Etta. He came because of a telephone call in the middle of the night, his father's voice, harsh and unwavering, on the other end: "You've been away long enough."

"I don't belong there anymore," Clayton said.

"You belong where I say you belong."

What his father didn't say, because he didn't have to, was that if he didn't come home, the Fifth Avenue apartment, the trips to Europe and South America, the abortions that his careless girlfriends always seemed to need, the extravagant dinners and Broadway shows that his journalist's salary couldn't begin to cover would no longer be funded. He would have to stand on his own, without the Pinochet name to support him, and he'd never been strong enough to do that.

Clayton got up from his desk when he heard the strong knock on the door. He didn't realize how glad he was to see Armstrong. He hoped the boy had some jokes for him, some funny stories. Clayton found that when he listened to Armstrong, the twin emotions of shame and disgust, always with him, seemed to fall into remission. He gave the youth a big smile. "Well, Armstrong, how are you doing? Ready for school?"

"I'm okay, Mr. Pinochet." Armstrong picked up a broom and began sweeping.

Clayton was puzzled. Most days the boy talked his head off. He often looked Clayton right in the eye when he spoke to him; the other colored boys cast their eyes to the ground. Today especially, Clayton wanted to hear some of Armstrong's uproarious tales about winning money at pool, or how his grandmother couldn't catch him when she wanted to give him a beating. Thinking about Dolly and Etta had depressed him. "Why so quiet, Armstrong?" Clayton finally asked.

Armstrong didn't answer.

"Boy, I'm talking to you," Clayton said sharply. "I

guess you're not looking forward to going back to school."

"It ain't that, Mr. Pinochet."

"What, then?"

Armstrong sighed and leaned against his broom. "I think I got myself into some trouble, Mr. Pinochet."

"What kind of trouble?"

"That's just the thing," Armstrong said, his voice rising. "I didn't do nothing. That man didn't have no reason to—"

"What man?"

"Floyd Cox."

Clayton looked at him with a blatant dismay that Armstrong misinterpreted.

"*Mister* Floyd Cox," Armstrong said.

But it wasn't the missing title that concerned Clayton. As Armstrong told his story, Clayton became increasingly uneasy. Under the paternalistic code of the Delta, he could exercise proprietary rights over Armstrong in the face of any other white person threatening the boy's welfare. He could walk up to Floyd Cox and say, "Leave my boy alone," and that would be the end of it. Not only because Armstrong worked for him but because he was a Pinochet. That was precisely why Clayton didn't want to intercede; he couldn't face the hatred in Floyd Cox's eyes, and God knows he didn't want to see the fear. Why in the world would Lily Cox put herself in such a position? he wondered. "Don't worry," he told the boy. "Floyd Cox just likes to shoot off his mouth."

Clayton was bothered by the relief he saw swimming in Armstrong's eyes; he didn't deserve the boy's gratitude. Then it came to him: I will pay for his college education. He liked the grandness of the notion, and for a moment his high-minded intentions took hold of him and blotted out his nagging guilt. He didn't need to go to Floyd Cox; that wasn't his duty, he reminded himself. He got up from his desk and walked over to Armstrong. "Don't worry about that. Forget about sweeping up. Here." He pressed a ten-dollar bill into Armstrong's hands. "Get yourself something for school." He liked the thankfulness and astonishment in the boy's eyes, as though he had pulled him out of the water after he'd gone down for the third time. He pressed another ten into his hands. "For books. You interested in a fast game of checkers before you go?" he asked. When Armstrong nodded, Clayton went to pull down the shades. The window was open, and the air, blown by a southern breeze, was hot, moist, and as rancid as sour milk.

Armstrong whistled as he walked toward the Quarters. Twenty dollars! He thought hard. He could buy some clothes and still have money left over. Twenty dollars! He shoved his hands into his pockets and felt the two crumpled bills. Mr. Pinochet was hard to figure out. He was forever talking about things that made Armstrong think too hard, always going on and on about colored people and how badly they were treated, as though that was Mr. Pinochet's fault. And whenever he talked about colored people's misery, he shared some of his own, as if feeling sorry for colored people was just an excuse to talk about his personal blues. It was strange, Armstrong thought. In Chicago he could sit next to whites on the el and the Cottage Grove bus; in the Delta, he couldn't sit next to white people, but they often seemed anxious to tell colored people everything inside them. Of course, his grandmother didn't see it that way. She thought colored people were supposed to bow down to white folks as if they were gods. He thought about the time he and his grandmother went grocery shopping one Saturday and an old white man passed them in the street and she pulled Armstrong to her side to let him get by. When the old man had moved out of hearing range, his grandmother said, "Don't you never go ahead of no white person, hear me?" Sometimes he thought his grandmother was nuts. He wasn't scared of crackers. But he didn't mind listening to Mr. Pinochet if it meant putting twenty dollars in his pocket. Maybe he would send his mother the money and she could find an apartment, so that he could move back to Chicago! Without warning, he began to cry, silently at first and then so uncontrollably that he stopped walking and leaned against a tree. If he could just get back to Chicago with his mother, everything would be all right. And maybe, he thought, praying fervently, maybe when he got back home, his father would come around.

4

When Floyd and Lily drove into his parents' yard, they could see his mother, Mamie, and father, Lester, and John Earl and his wife, Louetta, sitting on the porch waiting for them. John Earl's two little girls, Melanie and Belva, were playing with Floydjunior in the yard. The air was clogged with the odor of jasmine and roses, which grew in thorny clumps near the steps of the sagging little house. Mamie stood up as Floyd and Lily approached. She was a small woman. Once, perhaps, she was considered dainty, but now she was wizened and hard-looking. There was no laughter in her face, and her voice was as flat and plain as the gravel in the road. "Y'all come on and eat. We been holding supper."

After the meal of neck bones, butter beans, cabbage, rice, gravy, and biscuits, the men went to the back porch to smoke and talk, while the women cleaned up the kitchen. When the dishes were put away, Mamie, Louetta, and Lily sat on the front porch, watching the children play. They were startled when they saw Jake standing in the grass. "Good evening, ladies," he said, nodding toward the two older women. Then to Lily, "Miss Lily, your husband here?"

Lily nodded, a small, nervous movement. "You got something for him? I'll give it to him."

Mamie kept her pebble eyes riveted to her daughter-in-law's pretty face. "You go 'round back," she snapped.

"Yes, ma'am. I know," Jake said, nodding vigorously as he fled from the yard.

Floyd froze when he saw Jake. He tucked his hands under his thighs so that his father and brother wouldn't notice them shaking. "Evenin', gentlemens," Jake said. "Mr. Floyd, you forgot this." He handed Floyd a piece of folded newspaper. Inside was $3.65, the day's take at the pool hall.

Floyd jammed the money into his pocket, then stood up. "All right, now. See you tomorrow." Jake turned to go, and Floyd walked into the house, slamming the door behind him. Once inside, he began to tremble. He went into the small bathroom and splashed water on his face. When he lifted his head and stared into the mirror, he could see his father's dark eyes locking into his. John Earl stood behind the older man.

"What went on over there today?" Lester asked.

"I handled it," Floyd said, trying to make his voice low and mean-sounding.

"What'd you handle?" This from John Earl.

"Some nigger said something funny to Lily. French. 'Voully voully dance.' Something like that."

John Earl's eyes tightened into tiny dark bolts. "He said that to Lily?"

"Yeah."

"A nigger talking French to a white lady? What else he say? Did that boy touch Lily?" John Earl asked.

"No," Floyd said.

"You sure about that?"

"I told you I handled it."

"Certain way you handle niggers that talk French to white ladies and say the schools is gon' integrate," Lester said, his words coming out muffled and chewed over because of the wad of Red Man in his jaw and because his four front teeth were missing.

"He say that?" Floyd knew how weak his voice sounded. He hated when his father got up close to him the way he was now. He felt he couldn't move, couldn't breathe, that there was no place for him to hide his hands.

"Handled it, did you?" his father said, spitting out a slimy wad into the commode. "I don't know about that. There's a certain way me and your brother handle niggers. That the way you took care of it? Like we woulda done? Like you was one of us?"

5

From the front porch, the women watched as Lester, John Earl, and Floyd drove off in the truck. Lily wanted to call after them and say, "Ain't nothing happened with that boy," but one look at Mamie's stern, intractable face, at Louetta's accusing eyes, and she shut her mouth. If Floyd and them were going to do something crazy and ruinous, she couldn't stop them. Going to Memphis suddenly felt like a receding dream.

Louetta turned to Lily, her round face bobbing forward, her eyes streaked with alert meanness. "Well, seems like things done got stirred up," she said. "What you think they gonna do, Miss Mamie?"

The older woman's words sizzled. "Whatever they does is menfolks' business. Us women ain't got nary to do with it." She gazed at Lily, whose shoulders jerked and shook under her mother-in-law's hard stare. "You. Miss Magnolia Queen. What'd you do to get that nigger's eyes on you?"

Lily watched Floydjunior playing with an empty box of Argo cornstarch in the middle of the porch. "I ain't done nothing," she said, bolting from her chair. She scooped up her little boy and fled across the yard. "C'mon, Floydjunior. Let's you and me take us a walk."

As she trudged down the road, Floydjunior on her hip, Lily tried not to think about Floyd, Lester, and John Earl and what they might be doing together that night. She had felt happy and exhilarated sneaking into the pool hall, like a child stealing cookies that were cooling

on the porch, but now she felt guilty, and frightened for
the boy and herself. She knew that Floyd's father had
done terrible things to more than one colored man in
Hopewell. And she knew that Floyd would go along
with anything he and John Earl suggested.

She didn't stop walking until she reached the train station. Behind it, the Yabalusha shimmered in the twilight.
The ancient depot was located at the edge of town, and
at eight o'clock every evening the Illinois Central passed
through Hopewell. The train was already in the station,
and Lily sat down on a bench marked "For Whites
Only," holding Floydjunior on her lap. "Look at the
choo-choo," she said softly to the boy. "One day you're
gonna ride away on the train, and when you come back
you'll be somebody important, Floydjunior." She nuzzled
the boy's neck. She was the only person on the white
side; the colored side was always full. She peered into
the sad clump of people at the other end of the small station. *I wonder if she came tonight,* Lily thought as she
watched the colored people waving goodbye to each
other, their faces solemn. She searched through the
crowd of brown faces. And then she saw her, a small, almost white-looking colored woman, with braids like
thick ropes trailing down her back. A small boy was
clutching her hand.

The two women had met at the depot nearly five
years earlier, not long after Lily quit school and married
Floyd, which was when she began going to the train
station. They had seen each other many times before, on
the road that led from the Quarters to the poor-white
section. They had even spoken to each other. But not
until she became a regular at the depot did she become
aware of the colored girl around her age who, like Lily,
appeared to be at the station simply as an observer. Finally one night, after the women had eyed each other
for nearly a month, Lily said to her, "What do the colored do up in Chicago?"

"Ma'am?"

"I said, what do all them colored do up in Chicago?"

"They work," the girl said.

Lily snorted. "They's plenty of work for 'em right here."

The girl spoke gently, as though trying to rouse a sleeping child. "Ma'am, don't nobody want to be in the fields. That's why people be leaving."

The discovery that colored people had dreams of a better life was the most profound and shocking of Lily's life, and so frightening that every time she saw the girl afterward she felt a fear and anger she couldn't explain or control, and at the same time she was overcome with confusion and helplessness. She always wanted to shout to her, "I ain't done nothing to you."

She didn't speak to the girl again for almost two years. Then one Friday night Lily sat on the hard wooden bench after the train had been gone for a good ten minutes; she was still straining to hear its echoes. Two days earlier, Floyd had hit her for the first time, and she stared at the bluish bruise above her right elbow as though the mark were a map that led somewhere. She glanced up, and the girl was down near the other end of the track. They were the only ones there, two small pretty women staring down an empty train track. "Sure do wish I was on that train," the colored girl called to her.

Lily stood up and looked around, then moved closer to her. "I'd tell that conductor, 'Mister, take me straight to Memphis,'" Lily said.

"Take me to Chicago. What I care if it's cold." The girl walked toward Lily; there were flames in her eyes.

Lily stepped back. Something in the girl's tone told her that she was unafraid, that she could hop a train to Chicago, alone or with a baby, and be strong enough to survive. *She don't hafta have no husband telling her what to do,* thought Lily. The idea, audacious and unspeakable, sparkled before her as bright as a Christmas ornament. She almost put her hands on the girl, almost asked her how she got to be like that, to think like that, but she stopped herself when she realized that she was standing there envying a colored person. She remembered Louetta telling her that colored women were like men, that their private parts were different from white women's. What if Floyd found out that she talked with the girl? She thought: *He ain't never gon' find out.*

The colored woman's name was Ida Long. Together they dreamed of escape.

This night, after the train left and all the colored people had gone, Lily walked down to the other end of the tracks and stood next to Ida. "Hey," she said.

"Hey yourself. What's wrong, Miss Lily?"

"Nothing."

"Something is wrong with you."

Lily took a deep breath. The air was thick and hot, waterlogged. She could still smell the rain. Floyd hadn't fixed the roof, she thought. If it rains again . . .

"What is it?"

"Nothing." She looked down at Ida's little boy, who had grabbed Floydjunior's hand. "It's just that sometimes I wish I wasn't married. Like you."

Their eyes met. "Yeah, well, I wanted to marry Sweetbabe's daddy," Ida said, "but he run off to Detroit when he found out about the baby."

"That boy probably wasn't no good," Lily said quickly. "You deserve somebody good."

"I wanted my child to know his daddy." She paused for several moments. "I don't know mine."

"I thought you lived with your daddy," Lily said.

"William been like a daddy to me, but he ain't my real father. My real father is . . ." She looked at Lily, who was staring at her.

"Is what?"

"Is a white man."

"Oh," Lily said.

"Only I don't know who he is, and William keeps saying he don't know, either. I want to know." She stared at Lily, who seemed to be studying her every feature. "Did I shock you, Miss Lily?"

"No. You ain't shocked me. My uncle Charlie had him a baby by a colored woman. A little boy, dark little chocolate, with blue eyes, like my uncle Charlie." She lowered her voice. "My uncle Charlie wasn't no good." She spread her small hands in front of her and began picking at the chipped polish on her fingernails.

"Because he got a baby off a colored woman?"

"That wasn't nothing." Lily gave Ida a hard look. "If I tell you something . . ."

"Ain't nobody for me to tell."

"He used to touch me, when I wasn't nothing but a little-bitty girl. He'd sit me on his lap and feel me and afterwards he'd give me candy. He made me promise not to tell, but I told anyway."

"What happened?" Ida said. She had her hand on Lily's shoulder.

Her tears started falling before she could speak. "I told Mama. She whipped me for lying. I wasn't but six years old. Why would I lie about that?" She began crying harder, so that her shoulders shook and her face turned red. Ida quickly brushed away the tears that had begun falling from her own eyes and patted her friend's shoulder. Lily put her arms around the black woman. "Ida," she said, leaning against her friend, "I gotta tell you something. Somebody told my husband that this colored boy was—uh, said something fresh to me today. But he didn't. I told my husband that. And everything's all right now. It's just I been a little upset, that's all."

Ida stepped back a little and grabbed her son's hand. "Be still, Sweetbabe," she told him. When she turned to Lily, all the color had drained from her face; she was almost as pale as Lily. "What was the boy's name?"

"I don't know his name."

"What did he look like?"

"I can't remember."

"How old was he?"

"Maybe about sixteen or seventeen."

"Was he tall?"

"Yes."

"Was he dark-skinned or light-skinned?"

"Darker than you. He had freckles. Never seen a nig—a colored person with freckles before. Everything is all right. I told my husband, 'That boy didn't say not one bad thing.' Everything is all right now. I'm just a little upset, that's all. Ida! Ida, where you going?"

Freckles! That simple Armstrong, Ida thought, as she ran through the Quarters, Sweetbabe bobbing on her hip. The fool was all the time smart-mouthing, and now he'd gone and opened his mouth to the wrong person. How many times had Odessa told him, had she herself told him, that he couldn't say anything he felt like saying to these crazy crackers living in Hopewell. For the first time since she'd met Lily, Ida felt nagging doubts as she raced home. Her friend—she wasn't sure she could call a white woman that—was married to a Cox, and everyone in the Quarters knew those rednecks were mean as snakes eating hot sauce. How could everything be all right? "Mama told me never to trust crackers," she said aloud. Sweetbabe looked up at her with bright sparkling eyes.

With her two braids bouncing against her sweaty back, Ida ran up the steps to Odessa's house, which was near her own. The houses in the Quarters were all in shouting distance of one another, built closer together than in the area where the poor whites lived. The shacks had a transient quality. A close look revealed that what should have been nailed was merely propped up. What should have been stored was merely put aside.

There were, of course, other settlements of colored around Hopewell. A small number of dicty high yellows, including the owner of the funeral parlor and his family, the principal and some of the teachers at Booker T. Washington School, and several well-to-do landowners, all lived near the south gin and worshiped at Bright Star AME, where, according to folks in the Quarters, the only requirement for membership was to be bright as a star.

Not that the Quarters didn't claim people of all complexions; the multicolored offspring of every conceivable race's union with blacks could be found there: Fair-skinned children of white men. Lemon- and cinnamon-shaded people with high cheekbones and hawk noses, and ebony-hued folks with straight black hair, all claiming the blood of Choctaws. Even progeny of colored women and Chinese men, who'd been enticed to pick cotton when colored workers first began fleeing north, could be seen, with their flattish faces, almond eyes, and kinky hair. These rainbow-hued children were absolute testimony that if colored women hadn't been honored, they'd certainly been desired. Although in practical terms that meant only that they and their children had been abandoned by men of every race.

Ida found Odessa on the porch, shelling peas.

"Hey there, gal," Odessa called cheerfully to her. "What's your hurry?"

Ida walked over to where she was sitting. "How you doing, Miss 'Dessa?"

"Fair to middling. Waiting on that boy to pack his clothes. How's your good-looking daddy? He come to his senses yet? I'm a whole lotta woman going to waste and ruin." She chuckled.

Odessa had been one of the women her father courted after her mother died. Because William was a carpenter and had built his own home, he was considered quite a catch. But William didn't want to remarry, and he and Odessa had broken up when she began to pressure him. "Where's Armstrong?" Ida asked.

"He in the house, getting ready for school. Mr. Hayes is driving him to Flower City tomorrow. Then I'll have me some peace around here." She grinned.

Suddenly Ida wasn't so sure of what to do. Odessa had been like a mother to her. And now she seemed so happy. She'd hate to upset her over nothing. *Miss Lily said that everything was all right,* she thought. *Besides, what could happen between the evening and the morning?* "Now, Miss Odessa, you know you gon' miss Armstrong when he go," Ida said with a little laugh.

Odessa just grunted.

Armstrong was sitting on the porch when Odessa came outside. "Boy, you finish packing?" she asked.

"Yes."

"Yes, what?" Odessa snapped.

Armstrong sighed. "Yes, ma'am." He'd be glad when he could get away from all the yes-sir and yes-ma'am shit. "Grandma, you heard from my mother? Did she say when I could go back to Chicago?"

"Your mama's working hard, trying to be somebody. That takes time. Now you just go on up to that school tomorrow and get your lessons. You ought to be glad you can stay with your cousins in Flower City. If you had to go to school around here, you wouldn't go until after the cotton was in. These white folks in Hopewell don't want black youngins fit for nothin' but the fields," Odessa muttered. "Don't worry about getting back to Chicago. Chicago ain't going nowhere."

"But every year I stay here, she's always saying this will be the year when I move back," Armstrong said dejectedly. "Then she changes her mind."

"Well, your mama's doing all she can do. If your daddy was any good, he'd help your mama with you. That Wydell's just as trifling as the day is long. Drinking liquor, that's his job. He ain't sent your mama a quarter to help keep you."

Armstrong began chewing his bottom lip. Why did she always have to talk about his old man? Why couldn't she just shut up about him? Every time he thought about his father, it was like being punched in the stomach. Now he felt that same hurt, helpless feeling engulfing him, and he hated his grandmother for causing it. He had been about to tell her what happened at the pool hall, but now he wasn't going to say a damn thing. He hated her.

"I'm going up to see Ida and them. You want to come?" she asked.

"No."

"No, what?"

He sighed. "No, ma'am."

Oblivious to the mosquitoes that were swarming as night fell, Armstrong sat on the porch, thinking about the money he'd made from playing pool and what Mr. Pinochet had given him. He could double the twenty dollars by selling sandwiches at the school. Maybe triple the money. His ruminations were jarred by the sudden barking of his neighbor's dogs.

He looked up when he heard the truck. Stood up when he heard the motor stop. The headlights revealed three men, one sort of short, the other two tall and strong-looking, their expressions fixed and hard. For a moment he sat in dazed uncertainty. Then fear, as primal as the first scream, flooded his body. "Turn them damn lights out!" he heard one of the men say. They're coming for me, he thought. He didn't realize that he'd bitten his tongue until he tasted blood in his mouth as he called, "Mama."

Without thinking, he ran. Into the yard. Toward the outhouse. In the direction of the chicken coop. His movements were wild, scattered. The faster he ran, the louder the barking became.

"Watchu running fer, nigger?" he heard one of them say. Then: "Go get him. He's yourn." It was what his grandmother's friend said when they went hunting.

"Nigger, you better make it easy on yourself," another voice said.

The three men finally caught him near the edge of

Odessa's yard. In the moonlight he saw that the old one didn't have teeth. The tallest one had a cut across his cheek. The short one was Floyd Cox. What made terror slam into Armstrong like a lash across his back was the fear he saw in Floyd's eyes.

The tall younger man hit him, a heavy, open-palm slap that struck against his head. Armstrong fell down in a daze. "What did I do?" he asked. He tried to get up, but his legs seemed to lock and then buckle. When he finally regained his balance and was able to stand, the man knocked him down again and began kicking him in his stomach, his chest, his head.

Nobody said anything. Armstrong repeated, "What did I do?" He began to cry, but the yelping dogs, their barking growing louder and more frenzied, drowned out his sobbing. He curled up like a baby, trying to avoid the blows, but then the old man yanked Armstrong's arms back so that his son could get to him. Each time the tall one kicked him, Armstrong screamed, "Please stop," but the beating only got worse. Armstrong looked down and saw that his shirt was wet with blood. "What ... did ... I ... do?" he kept repeating, gasping for breath between each word.

He watched as the white men looked at one another, each waiting for someone to articulate Armstrong's crime. His head was throbbing, and blood seeped from his nose, but he ached so badly he didn't have the strength to reach up and wipe it. Finally Floyd said, "You was talking crazy talk to my wife. That's what."

In spite of his pain, Armstrong remembered his grandmother's tutelage; her admonishments came to him in one long hope-filled wave. He would act polite and stupid. Wasn't that what white people wanted? "No, sir," he said respectfully. "No, sir. I wasn't talking to your wife, sir. I was talking to my friend, and when I turned around, she was looking at me." Armstrong managed to smile a little and even tried to nod as he had seen Jake do.

The tall one turned violently red and started hitting him again, as Floyd watched helplessly. "Looking at you, was she?" he screamed. Armstrong realized his mistake too late to call back his words. He saw the old man observing Floyd as though he wanted to beat him into the ground. "You gon' fight your own battles, or is your brother gon' hafta do it all? She's your wife. Yourn," he yelled at his younger son.

What could he do to make them stop? What did they want of him? Armstrong remembered bullies in the Chicago schoolyard where he had attended grammar school and thought of the bloodless scuffles over lunch money. And then he remembered the two ten-dollar bills in his pocket. "I have some money," he said weakly.

Floyd inched toward him as the tall one stepped aside, and Armstrong could see the rage pouring from his eyes. "You got money, nigger? You think that makes you good as me?" Floyd said.

Armstrong tried to say no, to mouth the word, but his lips were so sore and swollen he couldn't move them. They were going to kick his ass, and there wasn't anything he could do about it. One, two, three ... By the time I count to a hundred, he thought, they'll be gone and Grandma will be here and she'll fix me up. Four, five, six ... The moonlight revealed something shiny in Floyd's hand. A gun. I'm seeing things, he told himself.

The air around him was completely silent; the dogs, the crickets, the wind, were all still. He couldn't hear himself breathing; his tears seemed suspended, as though his sobs were dammed up in his chest, roiling around like furious ocean waves. "Please, mister," he managed to whisper. When he looked in Floyd's eyes he saw pain, rage, and loathing, but no mercy. "Mama," he cried.

"Get on your knees, nigger," Floyd said. He swaggered around Armstrong, waving the gun in the air, stealing glances at his father and brother, who said nothing.

Armstrong attempted to obey, but his legs wouldn't cooperate. He heard a trickling sound that seemed to come from a great distance.

"Nigger's peeing his pants," the tall one said. The terse laughter that surrounded Armstrong was as brutal as brass knuckles against his skull.

"You just gon' stand there?" the old one said.

Through half-closed eyes, Armstrong could barely see Floyd's face, the fear and loathing and monstrous rage coagulating around the set of his mouth, the cruelty in his stare. Where did all that hatred come from?

"I hate niggers," Floyd screamed, his mouth contorted. He faced his father and brother as he yelled.

Armstrong heard the click of the trigger, and he took a deep breath. He felt his bowels ripping through him, then a soft, warm mushiness in his pants. He heard an explosion; fire seared the inside of his chest. His head slammed into the dirt. Nearby, a tired dog began panting, its ragged breathing engulfing him. If only he could find the hound, he could maybe lean against its soft, warm fur, raise himself up a little. But he couldn't see anything. He pictured his father then, as the moans of pain dribbled from his lips: his father, tall and strong, coming toward him bathed in white light, his arms like steel bands, his hands stretched out for the boy to grab. As he heard the retreating footsteps in the air around him, he thought: *My daddy could whip all of you.*

John Earl took the wheel and drove out of Odessa's yard. The men's faces were stern and composed, their lips drawn together in three tight, satisfied lines. The cab of the truck was cramped, and their shoulders pressed together as they settled back in their seats. John Earl fiddled with the radio dial. There was nothing but static until he found the Greenwood station, and then they heard Hank Williams's voice, full force and pure.

"That Hank, now, he's a singer," said Lester. He opened a pack of Marlboros and passed it to Floyd and then to John Earl, and each one took a cigarette, lit it, and flicked the ashes on the floor of the battered truck. "I'm so lonesome I could cry," Lester sang, in a voice that was low and off key but contained such a thrumming heartiness that it was infectious, and Floyd and John Earl began singing too. When the song was over, Lester said, "Well, you might can't fix everything that needs fixing, but damned if you can't make some things right."

Later, when Floyd would try to forget everything else about this night, he would still recall the ride back home, the smoky air of the congested cab, the three of them pressed in close together, singing and laughing as their shoulders touched. What warmed him more than anything was the sure, true knowing that his father, at last, was satisfied with him.

6

Delotha grazed the tip of the curling iron with a wet finger, and when she heard it sizzle, she wrapped it around the lock of hair she was holding. Then, resting the curling iron on the stove, she handed the woman in the chair a mirror. Her customer smiled and gave Delotha two dollars. "Maudine. You next," Delotha called out.

It was Saturday morning, and Delotha's tiny kitchen was filled with women waiting to get their hair done. On the radio, Dinah Washington was softly crooning, and several women bobbed their heads to the music. Others were eating doughnuts and drinking coffee as they waited their turn.

Delotha managed a quick stretch before she started combing out Maudine's hair, which was thick and tangled. She'd been working since eight o'clock; the day was half gone, and she still had customers to do. The kitchen was hot. She pushed open the window and was instantly assailed by the sound of cars and buses and foot traffic on Cottage Grove Avenue.

Sometimes she thought she'd never get used to the noise of Chicago. The first time she came up from Hopewell and stepped out of the Illinois Central at Twelfth Street and walked into the cold November air—wham!—the city had slammed into her like a hard fist. There wasn't anything soft about Chicago. The Windy City was a big-shouldered, barrel-chested town, a city that drank with two fists and, when the glass was empty, beat it against its chest. She'd never known anything like the wind that blew off Lake Michigan, so frigid it drew blood. But there was fun here too. Walks through Washington Park. Baseball games at Comiskey Park. Swimming in the lake in the summer. And more colored people than she'd ever seen in her life.

But best of all, even if Chicago did have its version of the Quarters and "Whites Only" signs, she could make money here. Women in Hopewell did their own hair, but the colored ladies in Chicago were sophisticated. They'd pay good money to have their hair fixed by somebody else. Well, if Madame C. J. Walker could make her fortune frying hair, she could too. She turned away from the window and began combing out Maudine.

"You sure got yourself a nice little place," Maudine said. "How long you been in here?"

"Since May."

"That long. This place got a real bedroom?"

"Uh huh."

"And your own bathroom?"

"Uh huh."

"Well, when is Armstrong coming home? I was expecting him to be back here, now that you got more space."

Delotha frowned. Now why did Maudine have to get in her business? Wasn't none of her concern why Armstrong was still in Mississippi. "I wanted him to finish up the school term where he is."

"Well, how come you didn't bring him home for the summer?"

"I had my reasons."

"I tell you, girl, you got more nerve than I do. When I left Greenville, that was it for me and **Mis**sissippi. I don't want to see that place no more. And I wouldn't dare send no child of mine down there. Ow!"

"Did I burn you? Sorry."

Delotha was fuming inwardly. Easy enough for Maudine to shoot off her mouth: she had a husband,

who worked every day. She didn't have to explain to
anyone that she'd tried to keep her son with her. The
boy was a handful. She didn't dare leave him at home
alone while she was working or going to school. If she
turned her back on him for a minute, he'd break something or tear it up some way. And lie! Half of what he
told her he made up. He was just a hardheaded, mannish boy who wore her out. And those eyes of his. Every time she looked into those eyes, she thought about
Wydell. She sucked her teeth and yanked at Maudine's
hair as she recalled how her estranged husband used to
call up and say, "Get Armstrong ready. I'm coming to
get him." And then not show up. And then she had
to deal with Armstrong's boo-hooing, while Wydell was
out someplace acting a fool. Maudine should just mind
her business. If Mama said it was all right to send Armstrong, then who was she or anybody else to find fault?
Mama wanted the company, and Delotha sure needed
the rest.

"Ow!" Maudine hollered. "Girl, you know I'm tender-
headed."

"Oops. Got you again? Sorry."

Of course, Armstrong hadn't wanted to leave her.
That was natural. Delotha had tried to talk up the place,
but he was being stubborn that day she put him on the
train, muleheaded and vindictive, trying to make her
feel guilty. "You just don't want to take care of me," he
screamed. "That's why you're sending me away."

She hadn't meant for him to stay away so long. The
truth was she had every intention of getting her son to
come live with her. She did! She just wasn't ready quite
yet. Delotha loved Armstrong dearly, but since he had
been gone she'd learned to like the freedom of being
unencumbered by a child. And now that she had a man
in her life, well, why shouldn't she enjoy herself a little? God knows she worked hard enough. She realized
that Armstrong was angry with her for not coming

down to visit him during July, as she'd promised, but her schedule was too busy for her to get away.

It was after six o'clock when the last customer left and Delotha pulled her straightening comb and curling iron off the stove. She lit a Salem on one of the burners, then sat down on a kitchen chair, smoking and counting the dollar bills she removed from her pocket. Twenty-three dollars. Almost as much as she made for a whole week's labor at the mattress factory. When she had enough saved, she'd go to cosmetology school in the evening, and one day she would open up her own place on Forty-seventh Street, even if there were hardly any colored businesses there. She looked at her watch, then got up and quickly tidied the kitchen. Nathaniel was coming by around seven.

By quarter to seven she was out of the tub. She carefully painted her lips a dazzling red, then spritzed herself with Evening in Paris. Delotha smiled at herself in the mirror. She'd dyed her hair auburn, and it hung in curls around the nape of her neck. The gypsy hoop earrings that peeked out from beneath her hair made her feel exotic. She surveyed her form. Maybe a little too much behind, but not bad, she decided. Besides, Nathaniel liked her butt. She turned on the radio and began dancing alone in the middle of the floor, wrapping her arms around herself and moving slowly as Sam Cooke sang.

When she opened the door, Nathaniel kissed her and extended a bag with two fried-chicken dinners inside. While they ate, he blew kisses at her from across the table. "Baby, you sure look good," he said. Delotha sighed and smiled at Nathaniel. He was a little man, much shorter and thinner than she found attractive in others. He had a narrow, homely face and small, dull eyes. Sometimes when she kissed him she imagined Wydell's lips. At least Nathaniel's good to me, she reminded herself. She and Nathaniel had been going together for nearly five months, and she believed that he was going to ask her to be his wife. That thought made her a little apprehensive, because she hadn't told Nathaniel about Armstrong. She wanted to feel surer of his love before she broached the subject. Once he asked her to marry him, she would tell him about her son. And she would tell him that she was still legally married to Wydell. Nathaniel had a decent job with the post office, and he didn't drink, at least not much. If she married him, she knew surely her plans would work out. Even if Chicago wasn't perfect, the fact was that colored people could make it if they worked hard, and she didn't mind working. After a while, she would have enough money to maybe buy a house, even farther south of where she was now living. She had sense enough to know the invisible borders the city erected, the lines around white ethnic enclaves where no colored were welcome, but she didn't want to live with Polish or Italian people anyway. As long as she was getting ahead, she'd be happy living with her own kind. She thought about her life in the hateful shack that was all Odessa could afford, the days she and her mother, her brothers and sisters, toiled in the Pinochet fields, only to have nothing when they settled up at the end of the season. She shuddered. She knew that as long as she didn't have to worry about hateful crackers she would be fine. And when Armstrong came home, she'd have her own business. She blew a kiss toward Nathaniel. For the first time in the almost four years since her marriage broke up, she felt happy and serene, sure that everything would work out.

7

The flashing neon light from the Hot Spot Bar penetrated the thin shade on Wydell Todd's window, illuminating his long, muscular body, which was stretched fully clothed across a narrow, unmade bed. From the window he could hear the late evening bustle of Twenty-seventh Street. That was the thing about Chicago, he thought: no matter how cold it got, the place was always moving.

Besides the bed, there wasn't much in the room other than a dresser and a nightstand, on which there was a tumbler half full of bourbon, the last of an empty fifth, which had rolled over to the corner. Next to it was a pizza container. He could remember having a pizza a day or two earlier; he hadn't eaten anything since, and the odor of the pie's stale remains permeated the room, vying with the smell of whiskey.

Wydell Todd managed to put his hands over his eyes, but he fell back when he attempted to get up, knocking the glass to the floor. "Goddamn it. Shit." Maybe there was a corner left. He flopped over the side of his bed; his dangling fingers groped beneath the mattress for the glass. When he bent his head under the bed, he almost swooned, and he didn't have the strength to pull himself up. His eyes were dazed and unfocused, but he thought he saw something shiny and managed to get it between his fingers. Before he could bring it out, he fell over the side of the bed, and the shiny thing fluttered into the corner with the empty bottle. His neck and shoulders were throbbing after he hit the floor, and he stayed motionless in a crumpled heap, trying to focus his eyes on anything that wasn't spinning. With a lot of effort he sat up, but the room was still going around. There was a bit of brightness in one of the circles, and Wydell reached out again and picked up a piece of paper, now soaked in bourbon.

It was a picture of someone. The whiskey had erased the features from the nose down, so that only the eyes remained clear and recognizable. Wydell stared for a second at what was left of his son's spinning face, but the glare from the streetlights made the photo luridly bright, and he couldn't bear to look at it. The sobriety that flooded him was sudden and chilling. "I'm gonna call you," he said, gripping the photo. "Hear? I'm gonna call you soon."

8

Floydjunior was asleep on a pallet in the middle of Mamie's kitchen floor. Lily leaned over him and lifted the hair off the back of his neck with her fingers and wiped away the perspiration. God, it was hot! She peeked out the window and saw John Earl parking the truck in the yard. Peering into the truck's cab, Lily could see Floyd sandwiched between his father and brother; his head was bowed. The sight of her husband, folded over as though he might have been praying, frightened Lily. She had her foot on the first porch step when she heard Mamie's voice, rough as crushed glass. "Miss Magnolia Queen, when I was coming up, woman didn't ast her husband nothing that wasn't her business." Lily took her foot off the stair and sat down. She watched as Floyd walked across the yard, searching the ground as if he'd lost something. She felt her heart quicken as he got closer. There was blood on his shirt. Floyd was close enough now so that Lily could see his face, and when he finally looked up, his eyes were hollow and distracted. Looking into her husband's eyes, she felt like a foreigner visiting a strange land. *Lord Jesus*, she thought, *what's he gone and done?*

"Get the baby, Lily. John Earl's running us home," Floyd said.

Even with the kids riding in the back of the pickup, the two couples were crowded in the cab during the short, silent ride; later, after John Earl and Louetta pulled away without waving, after Lily and Floyd went inside, where stored heat rose up to beat against their tired bodies and where Floydjunior cried for a good twenty minutes before he finally fell asleep in the secondhand crib in the parlor, there were still no words.

In bed, Floyd reached for her. "I'll always protect you," he said.

Lily didn't answer, but she heard the fear in his voice, and that made her afraid too. The heat and weight of Floyd's hands on her breasts were oppressive; she pushed them aside and got out of bed. "I hafta go," she said, grabbing the slop jar, stumbling in the dark. In the tiny parlor, she placed the chamber pot on the floor and then leaned against the wall and closed her eyes.

When she returned to the bedroom, she stood next to the bed. "Floyd," she said softly.

"What?" His voice was harsh, mean. Lily reconsidered her question. What if Floyd thought she was worried about the boy?

"What?" Floyd repeated.

Lily slid into the bed next to him. She let her thighs graze his. His hot, moist hands fell on her like two rocks, and she went limp, letting her mind drift like when she used to think about the candy in her uncle Charlie's pocket while he played his game with her.

Only now she thought back to the night four years earlier when she had been crowned Magnolia Queen of Jefferson Davis High School. Her mama had made her a white dress from a fancy lace tablecloth a lady who lived in the Confederacy had given her in exchange for sewing. Lily felt beautiful, even though there was a faded gravy stain right in the center of the bodice. When she finished zipping up the dress, her mother stood back and gazed at her. She wiped at her tears and said, "Baby, all a woman has got is her looks, for a thin sliver of time. You squander your beauty, you done lost your life."

The white lace dress rustled as she sashayed up the aisle, her hands over the gravy stain. Everybody's eyes were on her, even the kids from the Confederacy, the ones who usually didn't speak to her. In that dress, nobody could dare treat her as if she wasn't good enough. The night she was crowned Magnolia Queen was the best moment of her life, even better than her wedding day. All the boys wanted to dance with her, and all the girls envied her. And when it was over, she couldn't wait to get home and describe everything to Mama.

She was sitting on the porch in the dark when Lily got back. As soon as Lily made her out in the moonlight, she rushed to her, calling, "Mama, oh, Mama . . ." She was fixing to tell her about the dancing and the cookies and the punch, when the door opened and her father came out, holding a lantern, and as he neared her mother Lily saw her face: black and blue under one eye, her bottom lip cut and bruised. And then her father's voice, like nails dragging across sandpaper: "Rose. You get in here." Her mother stood up immediately. She whispered to her, "He can't help it." Now, whenever Lily thought about being Magnolia Queen, she thought about her mother's swollen face.

Floyd's hands were pulling her into him. He had to push hard to enter, because she was like a desert inside. Next year this time, we will have us a real bathroom, Lily told herself as he began grinding inside her. And then maybe after that we can put in another bedroom for Floydjunior. She imagined the new bathroom. Bright yellow. Perhaps Floyd would agree to that. The first thing she was going to do when they put the tub in was to fill it with almost hot water and stretch down in it. Things were going to be wonderful once they got that bathroom.

Floyd clutched her and grunted hard; then they fell apart. Lily moaned a little, then was silent. She thought: *Niggers been getting their butts whipped ever since time began; what difference will one more make? That Ida, asking about the boy's age and name, his complexion, like maybe she knew him.* When she thought of Ida, she felt like screaming, "I ain't done nothing to you." She'd let Ida get too familiar, that's all. Floyd wouldn't like that. Well, she wouldn't ever speak to her again. She stared at her husband's still body. Floyd was good to her. Hadn't he bought her the Rio Red lipstick, a scarf, and a bottle of Evening in Paris cologne just to please her? If she didn't have Floyd, what would she do? Her mother and father had passed, her two brothers had moved to Detroit. She hugged herself to keep from shaking, then squeezed his shoulders to reassure herself that he was with her, that he'd always take care of her.

Floyd lifted his head and fixed his eyes on her. "What are you thinking about?" he asked.

"Nothing, darling. Go back to sleep."

Well, she knew one thing: There was no telling what that freckle-faced boy might have done if Floyd hadn't come along and saved her.

9

Ida was getting ready for bed when she heard a knock at the door and then her father's voice, low and unsteady. She ran outside. Her father and a neighbor looked up when she came out. "They done kilt Odessa's grandson," he said. There was no expression on his face. Ida's knees buckled, and her father grabbed her arm.

"When?" she asked, steadying herself.

"Just now."

"Who . . . ?" She knew.

"Some of them Coxes got aholt to him."

"Come on," Ida said.

When Ida and her father reached Odessa's yard, a small crowd of people was standing in the spot where Armstrong had been shot. The moonlight revealed blood in the dirt. Looking at the dark blot, Ida felt numb. *This is a dream,* she thought, closing her eyes. But when she opened them, she saw the same stained earth at her feet, and inside the house, she could hear Odessa sobbing. *I shoulda told Odessa. If I'd told, that boy might still be alive.*

Ida didn't want to see Odessa, so she stood on the porch alone, crying softly, while her father went inside the tiny house. While she stood there, a brand-new blue Cadillac drove up and parked on the shoulder of the road. No one got out, but she could see Clayton Pinochet inside the car, smoking a cigarette. *What do he want?* she wondered.

The car was still there when her father came outside and they walked out of the yard onto the road. She heard the white man's voice. "Say, what happened there? Somebody get hurt?"

Her father peered across the road. "Yessir, Mr. Pinochet," he finally said. "Boy got kilt."

Ida's father grabbed her hand, and as they were walking away, she thought she heard Clayton Pinochet say, "Dear Jesus."

When Ida got home, she lay down. Images she couldn't chase away swam into her mind. She kept seeing Armstrong, his head thrown back as he laughed loudly. Then he would appear to be quiet and sober, his freckles dancing, his friendly eyes following her. Then she was standing in a grand train station, and Lily was way at one end and Ida was at the other. They were shouting at each other, but both of them had their hands over their ears.

The blue Cadillac sped along 49E until Clayton came to a little road right off the highway. Turning in there, he drove straight into a grassy yard where a neat brick house stood. By the time he was out of the car, the front door was open and the woman stood just inside, waiting for him, a glass of bourbon in her hand. They didn't speak until he finished the drink. "Thank you, Marguerite," he said, handing her the empty glass. He closed the door.

"You want some more?" Her bright eyes, alert and anxious, stared into his.

He shook his head.

"You feel better now?"

Clayton looked at her. Marguerite's skin was the color of Delta soil, and her wild halo of hair seemed untamable. In his most introspective moments he admitted to himself that she looked like a young Etta, but he would not ever consider the ramifications of his sleeping with a woman who reminded him of his mammy.

And he took care of her. Marguerite was the only colored woman in Hopewell to be fully kept by a white man, the last of a dying breed. Not that white men didn't still roam through the Quarters crooning obscenities from their cars, hoping to attract willing colored lovers, but these were occasional diversions, one-night stands, with neither an emotional nor a financial commitment. Clayton wanted a steady and discreet attachment. And he was willing to pay.

Later, while they were making love, Clayton looked down and saw her tight licorice-colored legs wrapped around his thighs and felt something akin to anguish, a visceral pain that radiated throughout his body. He pulled himself out of her and sat up in the bed, remembering another pair of arms, another pair of legs. Dolly Cox.

"What's the matter, baby?" Marguerite asked.

Clayton rubbed her rough hair. "Nothing. I was just thinking about somebody."

"That boy they killed?"

"Yes. No."

"Who?" She moved closer to him and put her hands between his legs. "Some woman?" She started breathing faster, and Clayton saw a quick flickering flame in her eyes, which Marguerite extinguished with a smile.

"Yes. A white woman I used to care about."

"Why you didn't marry her? You could still have me. I know you gotta get married sometime."

"I promised her I'd marry her. But I couldn't. My father didn't approve."

"Why? She was white, wasn't she?"

"Yes, she was white. But she was not good enough."

The planter's son and the redneck daughter—such a stale Delta cliché, he thought. Cracker girls were reputed to be almost as giving as colored wenches. At least that's what the sons of the other plantation owners whispered. Except that Dolly was beautiful, innocent, and pure, and the kisses she gave him behind the north gin were the sweetest he'd ever tasted.

And then one night they drove out 49W and turned onto one of the dirt roads and parked. They made love in the back of his first Cadillac, and all the time he was inside her she cooed and twittered like a turtledove, and after that he went to her every night he could. Her body made him drunk. He gave her presents and money, and when her cooing and twittering were all that he could hear, he told her he wanted to marry her. He remembered the astonishment in her eyes. "You want to marry me?" she asked.

"I love you, Dolly. I want to marry you," he repeated. "I want to marry you," he told her over and over again, completely forgetting about the Delta code, which no one broke.

"Clayton, I'm pregnant," she told him six months later. He remembered embracing her, telling her there was nothing he wouldn't do for her. Nothing.

Only he didn't feel as brave, as sure, standing in front of his father, listening as his father told him. "Pinochets don't marry her kind. That's the end of it. Now you take her to Jackson and get the thing taken care of."

He couldn't look her in the eye when he told her, couldn't listen to her sobbing.

John Earl and Lester came to his home the next night, the outrage they felt as visible as wounds slashed across their angry eyes. They wore mud-splattered boots and carried shotguns. Clayton's father stood on the porch and talked to the men with his hands held out wide, empty. His father told him to stay inside, and so he saw and heard everything from behind the sheers at the huge windows in the living room. "You got no cause, and you got no power," his father told them. "Go on home before you do something stupid, and the next thing you know, you ain't got a friend, can't get a job in this county. You boys go home now."

"Your boy ruined my daughter," Lester said.

"Depends on what you call ruined," Clayton's father said.

"There's the law," Lester said quietly, looking toward the ground.

"Law?" his father repeated. He stepped off the porch, walking boldly toward the anger and the guns. "All this time, and you don't know who the law is around here? Your granddaddy knew. In 1862 my granddaddy paid three hundred dollars and sent yours to war in his place. He couldn't send a nigger, so he sent one of y'all." Clayton watched, the drapes partially covering his face, as his father moved closer to the Coxes, his strong jaw preceding him. "Law? Your daddy knew about the law. Who'd he beg when the boll weevil ate up half the cotton crop and any other man woulda turned him off the land? The law can't help it if you raised a whore, Cox."

They didn't say a word, just turned around and left, defeat screaming from their shoulders like a scalded cat.

Later, after Dolly had returned from Jackson with haunted eyes and memories that in time would savage her beauty and her life, Clayton's father told him, "Until you marry, you court a nice girl for show. And for the other, get yourself a nigger gal. There ain't no repercussions there."

Looking at Marguerite's lithe brown body, he wondered.

"Clayton?" Marguerite's voice was so soft he barely heard it.

He looked around the room. He'd paid for Marguerite's house and everything that was in it. And there were beautiful things in the house. He had given a colored woman lovely, lovely furniture, a car. "I treat you well, don't I?" he asked.

Marguerite touched his arm and said, "Whatever you want me to do, I'll do."

10

Early the next morning, Floyd and Lily and Floydjunior
trudged down the road to John Earl's house, a neat clapboard bungalow nearly a mile away. By the time they
were at the front door, the back of Floyd's shirt was
stained with perspiration and Lily's shortsleeve blouse
had two damp circles under the arms. Ever since he
could remember, Floyd had felt a tightening in his chest
whenever he entered John Earl's house. His brother had
two bedrooms; there was furniture in every room and
throw rugs on the floor. His brother's two little girls
slept in a bed with a chenille bedspread ordered from
the Sears catalogue. On the pillow sat a pretty, red-
lipped lady doll with a wide satin skirt. Floyd remembered the first time Lily saw that bed with the doll on it,
the hungry, aching look on her face, as if her cheek
would break into tiny shards of glass if he touched it.
And when she walked into the new bathroom John Earl
had put in, the naked longing in her eyes felt the same
as her spitting on him. When they got back to their
house, he hit her for the first time, smacked her across
her porcelain cheek with his open palm when she told
him that it was too cold to walk to the outhouse. "Ain't
what I give you good enough?" he'd screamed.

But today he didn't feel that tightness near his heart.
Today he marched through John Earl's front door as if
it was as much his house as his brother's. Today he
could look around at the Sears furniture and not begrudge his brother a single piece. He could even con-

fess that he owed his brother for advising him to go into the pool hall business. Today he didn't even begrudge his brother the love his parents freely bestowed upon him for being the strong one, the war hero, the best hunter, the best man. He had done what his brother would have done, and for the first time he felt that love too. Today what was his brother's was his, and what was his belonged to John Earl.

The two men sat across from each other at the kitchen table, smoking Marlboros and drinking the strong black coffee Louetta had poured for them. From the window Floyd could see Louetta and Lily sitting on the back porch, talking and watching the children play in the yard. He could feel John Earl staring at him as he leaned over and stubbed out the cigarette and then moments later lit another one. Floyd was enjoying the cigarettes and the coffee, the sounds of his wife and child outside. And he was loving being across from his older brother and feeling for the first time in his life that he was the equal of that man, that he had done what his brother would have done. They'd righted a wrong together. Now they shared an intimacy that surpassed what they did with their wives in the dark. Floyd felt calm and ordered and invincible. Peaceful.

"You know they found that boy? You know that, don't you?" John Earl said quietly.

Floyd felt the cup shaking in his hand, and suddenly coffee was spilling all over the front of his pants. He jumped up as the steaming liquid trickled between his legs.

"Take it easy. Take it easy," John Earl said. "Daddy always said you was the nervous type." He grinned at Floyd, who didn't smile back.

"How you know that?"

"I been to town this morning. Everybody's talking about it."

"They know who done it?"

"Yeah. Nigger was still alive when his grandma got

to him; he told her. It don't mean nothing; in a couple
of days it'll be like it ain't never happened. Ain't a man
around here wouldn't have done the same thing. It ain't
like the sheriff's gon' come around and take you to
Parchman."

"There's just some things a man ain't supposed to
stand for."

"That's right. That's right. When a nigger starts talking nasty to a white woman, well ... And when they
start talking about going to school with white children,
well, they asking for it. And see, that's another thing.
What we done, Floyd, what you done, well, it kind of
puts the whole United States of America on notice."
John Earl grinned at his brother.

"How you mean?"

"That the Supreme Court ain't gon' ram no integration down our throats, that's what. That we're prepared
to take a stand."

"Yeah. I know that," said Floyd.

On the back porch, Lily sipped the iced tea Louetta had
given her, and swatted at the flies that buzzed around
her neck. She couldn't remember a September that had
been so hot. In this heat, she yearned for a bathtub she
could fill with cold water and ice cubes; she'd lie in it
until she was numb.

"Weather like this makes you not want to move a
muscle," Louetta said, fanning herself with a scrap of
paper. "You look nice and cool, though," she added,
giving Lily a swift, envious glance.

"Oh, I'm not feeling cool," Lily murmured.

Louetta leaned in toward her sister-in-law. She'd
grown stout since she had the two girls, and the heat
and her weight made her face ruddy; she wheezed a bit,
as if out of breath, even though she hadn't moved a
muscle since they'd been on the porch. Louetta's whisper was sharp, conspiratorial, as though they were partners in some venture that bound them together. "I don't

feel not one bit bad for that little Chicago nigger. I don't! He was asking for it! And John Earl says the Supreme Court wants me to send my youngins to school with the likes of him. Well, that nigger won't be going to school with nobody."

For the first time in a very long while, Lily looked Louetta straight in the eyes. "What do you mean?" she asked.

"I mean that nigger's deader than a dried-up still."

For a moment Lily couldn't move. She began picking at the already chipped polish on her fingernails. "Dead?" In all her fearful imaginings, she'd never pictured him dead.

"Yes, honey, we got men who'll defend us," Louetta said, moving closer to Lily. "That's what a man is supposed to do for his wife. Listen, if a nigger didn't get lynched every now and then, well, there's just no telling what they'd do to us."

"Who?" Lily asked.

"Why, honey, the niggers and our husbands both. I don't care what color they are; men build up steam. And they gotta let it out somewhere. Colored men. White men. They both crazy. Honey, the point is you gotta look at it this way: A whole lotta women can't say, 'I got a man who'll kill for me.' "

"No. I mean, who killed him?"

"Oh. Well, Floyd mostly. But John Earl helped some."

I told Ida everything was gonna be all right, Lily thought in a daze. She hesitated, afraid she might appear stupid to Louetta. "Are they gonna get arrested?"

"Honey, no. Hell, don't nobody even arrest niggers for killing niggers. It's gonna be just like it ain't never happened."

Sitting on the porch, Lily could no longer recall the sound of the boy's voice as he spoke the foreign words. When she closed her eyes, she couldn't see his face. It wouldn't be so difficult not ever thinking about that boy again. She looked through the kitchen window at her husband, and he seemed taller and stronger, a man who would take care of her and protect her. Lily thought: *I got a man who'll kill for me.*

11

Delotha stared at the battered and swollen body of her son, spread out on the funeral parlor table. A strange odor she couldn't place hovered in the air. Odessa stood next to her, weeping loudly, gripping her daughter's hand. Odessa's free hand curved open and loose at her side; Delotha's was a tightly coiled fist. The director of the funeral parlor, Mr. Willie McCullum, a light-reddish man with sandy hair and the only colored man in Hopewell to wear a suit during the week, looked at both women nervously. Finally he said to Delotha, "These the coffins I have," and pointed to several wooden caskets propped up along the wall. "You need to make you a choice."

Touching Armstrong's stiff pants, running her fingers through his hair, Delotha said, "He's so little, Mama. I never should have sent him down here."

"Hush, baby," Odessa said. "You didn't know."

"It's my fault. They won't punish them Coxes. It'll be like nothing ever happened."

"It ain't your fault. If that damn Wydell had helped you . . ." Odessa began to cry.

Delotha felt a sickening churning low in her stomach; she slammed her free hand to her mouth. Too late. Vomit thick as sludge pushed through her splayed fingers.

Later, in Odessa's house, Delotha sat silent as a rock in a chair by a window, her mother nearby. Both were guarded by the women from Mount Zion Baptist

Church. Odessa's two sisters, who lived in Hopewell, had come with their husbands and children. Delotha heard whispers around her, perceived the echoes of words but not the words themselves. Gibberish floated by. Holy tongues, like in church, only there were no tambourines. Nothing made sense, least of all the screaming that suddenly filled the room. She was feeling the spirit, like in church. A cool hand lay across her forehead, above her open, vacant eyes, and she felt her body being lifted, then placed down softly.

Her life with her son passed through her mind like one long motion picture. She remembered his kicks in her womb, his tiny lips gnawing at her nipples, his first day of school—the red sweater he wore and how he cried. "Wydell," she whispered softly. "Wydell."

Odessa, thinking her daughter was calling her, leaned closer to her. "What did you say, baby?"

"I don't have a child no more," Delotha said. She sat up and placed her two hands across her belly.

"You'll always have a child, baby. You'll always be Armstrong's mama."

12

Clayton left the neat brick house early the next day. The truth was he couldn't bear sitting across from Marguerite at the breakfast table that morning; he didn't want to see her in the morning light. Or perhaps he didn't want her to see him. Before he left, he pulled five twenty-dollar bills from his wallet and placed them in a crystal ashtray on the coffee table in the living room. Some of the bills were crumpled, and with his fingers, Clayton smoothed them out and stacked them on top of one another, until it appeared as if there were only one twenty-dollar bill. He liked surprising Marguerite.

He put his wallet away and walked back to the bedroom. The door was still partially ajar, and he could see the soft swell that Marguerite's body made underneath the sheet. Her hair tumbled out onto the pillow and almost completely covered it. During the day she combed it into a smooth, fragrant bun, but at night her hair always came loose. Clayton had never felt anything as rough and springy as Marguerite's hair at night. What was her word for it? Nappy. She called her hair nappy and laughed when he told her he wanted a bedspread made of her hair. "You so crazy," she said. "You the one with the pretty hair."

Sometimes when they were making love he pulled her head down onto his stomach and rubbed her hair back and forth across his belly until he thought he'd catch fire. But now, standing at the door of the bedroom he had paid for, staring at the woman he could afford,

Clayton didn't feel fire in his belly; he felt a void too vast to comprehend.

There was a painting of a woman on the wall above the bed. As gorgeous as the art was—he'd bought the piece in Paris—Marguerite, even asleep, was far more beautiful. Looking at the painting and at Marguerite, Clayton mused that he had bought and paid for all the beauty in his life. He wanted art and beauty to insulate him against the ugliness the world presented.

The pungent odor of frying bacon and strong coffee greeted Clayton as he opened the door to the Busy Bee Café. Three old men wearing khaki work pants and faded shirts were sitting at the counter. They turned in unison when Clayton slid into his usual booth. "Morning, Mr. Pinochet," they all said.

"Morning, Jesse. Clyde. Gilroy. How y'all doing today? It's gonna be another hot one." The men had worked for his father most of their lives, and he'd always known them.

The men nodded their agreement, then resumed their conversation.

Clayton lit a filterless Chesterfield and waited until Florine appeared before him. She was an obese woman with dirty-blond hair who'd been at the café so long that she was more a fixture than a person. Her uniform had grown too small, and the top part, stained from cherry pie, pressed and flattened her breasts, which seemed to spread from her chin to her waist. When she smiled, several teeth were missing. In high school, she had been a pretty girl, Clayton recalled. "How y'all doing today, Mr. Pin'chet?" she asked jovially, handing Clayton a cup of coffee.

"I'm doing all right. How about you?"

"Fair to middling. You want your usual?"

"That'll be fine, Florine."

The coffee was black and steaming. The mug was the same chipped one that Clayton had received the last time he'd come to the café. After a couple of swallows he could feel himself becoming sharp and focused; he gulped down the first cup. He wished that he had a copy of the newspaper from Jackson to read. He hated the idea of sitting and eating alone and not having anything to occupy his mind. He prided himself on not permitting his thoughts to wander, on being controlled and well ordered.

The Busy Bee Café was located in the center of Hopewell, on Jefferson Davis Boulevard. Inside, booths were lined up next to the windows, with an aisle separating them from the counter area. The ancient counter, scarred with glass rings and cigarette burns, ran the length of the restaurant, and sitting on it were usually a three-layer yellow cake with coconut icing, a yellow cake iced in chocolate, and a variety of pies, all under glass. The pies in particular were outstanding. Sweet potato, rhubarb, and shoofly were the specialties of the house.

The "house," or at least the soul of it, was a scrawny half-Choctaw, half-colored woman named Willow Scott, whose silky, thin black braid trailed down her back and danced in the air as Clayton watched her bustle in the restaurant's kitchen. No one knew how old she was. Some people claimed that she was thirty; others swore she was fifty if she was a day. Her face didn't show age. Willow lived just outside the Quarters in a tar-paper shack she rented from one of the plantation owners. Clayton had heard colored people say that she preferred living in the woods like an Indian and that she could outshoot and outhunt any man and that she was never without a gun. They also claimed that she had slit her husband's throat in retaliation for a beating. Colored people said not to mess with her, and even white folks, who didn't usually render unsolicited opinions about Negroes, declared that she was crazy. But everyone agreed that she was the best cook in Yabalusha County. No one had ever recalled hearing Willow address white people as ma'am or sir or anything at all, and from time to time she could be heard barking orders to Florine, who responded with instant obedience. Now, as Clayton peered across the counter and into the opening in the wall that revealed the kitchen, he stared at Willow, who scowled and slammed pots and pans this way and that.

Gazing out the window again, Clayton saw that a few early birds were in the street, mostly shopkeepers who had businesses that were open on Saturday. They moved slowly, as if the gathering heat had somehow seeped inside their joints and partially immobilized them.

"Here you go, Mr. Pin'chet," Florine said, placing his breakfast in front of him.

"Thank you."

The food was hot and fragrant. He really craved a newspaper, and looked around the café to see if anyone had left one behind. As he turned toward the counter, he heard Clyde, his voice quivering with indignation. ". . . Shoulda done worse. Shoulda hung his black ass right in front of that nigger church where they make all that commotion. And let the Supreme Court know that the streets is gon' be full of dead niggers. I tell you, you let niggers get away with one thing and, by God, the tables'll turn and the next thing you know, they'll be ruling us."

Clayton tried to swallow his food and found that it clogged his throat. He looked into the kitchen. Willow was standing there, a huge iron skillet in one hand and a rolling pin in the other. Her fingers and palms were white from flour, but the rest of her was as smooth and brown as a ripe pecan. She was staring at the three men with growing agitation.

The men at the counter were talking so excitedly that they didn't see Willow as she approached them, but Clayton sat transfixed in his booth, watching as Willow's lips moved without seeming to speak, her furious eyes doing all the talking. Then she was suddenly right in front of the men, the pot at her side, her arm and the rolling pin aloft, directed. Jesse, Clyde, and Gilroy raised their eyes at the very moment that the rolling pin came crashing down, splintering the counter.

"What the hell?" said the men, in unison. They scrambled to their feet.

Willow wiped away a splattered fly with the edge of her apron; she didn't look at Jesse, Clyde, or Gilroy. She said, almost to herself, "I told that fly, Your day is coming. Yessir," and she looked at the men, who had, as if with one mind and movement, deposited their coins next to their half-full coffee cups. "Don't you think your day ain't coming."

Clayton's office was already hot by the time he arrived. The Jackson newspaper was at the door, and he scanned the headlines while he let himself inside. He went to the window and opened it a crack, pulled down the shade, and then turned on the ceiling fan, which shuddered and whirred as it churned the office air. The sound was oddly plaintive and reminded him of the singing in the fields. He stood still and closed his eyes and heard the voices, the call and response, the chanting. *My God,* he thought, *how can they bear it?*

He sat at his desk, put his paper down, and picked up the article on the wedding of Miss Vanessa Claiborne to Mr. Hoyt Fields. His eyes studied the picture of the radiant bride and groom and fell upon the copy that was supposed to appear with it. The Claibornes and the Fieldses lived in the Confederacy, and they expected comprehensive, if not extravagant, coverage of the nuptials of their children. He usually had no problems toughing out the tedious journalistic duties of a one-man shop, but today he felt a creeping malaise.

Clayton eyed the checkerboard. A quick game would be nice, he thought. Something fast to loosen me up so I can sit down and get through this damn wedding story. Wonder where Armstrong is.

Clayton got up, pushing back his chair with the heel

of his foot, and was at the front door when the memory of the previous evening flashed before him. What he recalled was as hard and punishing as a beating: the deep-red stain in the center of the boy's yard; the wailing that he heard from the small shotgun house; the sorrowful faces of the Negroes. He closed the door very gently and sat back down at his desk.

He pushed aside the photographs of the Claiborne wedding and took a clean piece of paper from a stack on top of his desk, and inserted it into the manual Underwood he used for all his stories. At the top of the page he typed: "Colored Boy Found Dead."

"A fifteen-year-old colored boy was found dead in his grandmother's front yard last Friday night. His death was the result of gunshot wounds."

Clayton's fingers hovered above the keys while he read over and over again what he had written, until the words began to blur before him. Then he typed: "His death was the result of severe hating."

He got up and went into the washroom in the back of his office and doused his face with water. He imagined what his father would say if he read what Clayton had written. He would certainly summon Clayton to the library, where he would be sitting behind his walnut desk, smoking a pipe, the paper before him. Without glancing at him, his father would lift his glasses and rub the bridge of his nose and pull his thick fingers through the shock of gray hair he had, and then he would place his huge hands squarely in front of him, and he would study those hands before he spoke to Clayton. Then he would level his dark, piercing eyes on him. *Now, son, you have to be careful what you put in print. People might think that's how you really feel. You know we've lived in this area for generations. The Pinochets have built something to be proud of here, a tradition that must continue unchanged. We've built relationships with people, folks who feel a certain way about the world. Those folks trust us because they believe that we think as they do; that's the basis for our friendship. Why, son, what you've written might be misconstrued. Our friends might think you're against them, you see, and because you're our son, our only child, they might think that your mother and I are against them, and then the next thing you know, we've got no friends. We're isolated. And let me tell you, son, I'm talking about more than getting snubbed at the Christmas cotillion, although that alone would kill your mother. Just kill her.*

But I'm talking about business, boy. Money. People just don't do business with folks they don't trust, at least not around here. Maybe in New York they do. But not around here. And where will that leave you? I'll tell you where it leaves you. Nowhere, boy. Because if you weren't pulling from a healthy trust fund every month, you wouldn't be in any position to be a roving reporter, now would you, son? If you hadn't been drawing from a healthy trust fund, you wouldn't have been able to go gallivanting with the Yankees in New York City, Mr. Liberal. Them checks you get every month—ever stop to think where that money came from, boy? Niggers. Nigger slaves. Nigger sharecroppers who rent from us and buy from us when they need a roll of toilet paper. You think we'd have a toehold in this country without them? And here you're telling people we hate them. That's a lie. We got a code down here, a way to keep things in order. Checks and balances, just like the government of the United States. That boy that died was out of order, plain and simple.

Clayton snatched the paper out of the Underwood and crumpled it into a ball. He threw it in the direction of the trash can, but it landed on the floor. He stood up and kicked the wastepaper basket. It was a thin metal basket, and the force of Clayton's foot propelled it across the room, scattering papers as it flew through the air. When he looked down, there was a photograph of Dolly at his feet. *I didn't protect her, either,* he thought.

The steamy heat engulfed Clayton when he stepped

outside his office. He locked the door carefully and looked at the building for a moment. Then he got into his blue Cadillac and didn't stop driving until he reached Greenwood.

He parked outside the Magnolia Hotel. Walking into the brightly lit lobby, he remembered how when he was younger he had brought girls to the Rebel Inn, as he and his friends called the place. They would begin the evening with dinner in the hotel restaurant, which was decorated in antebellum style, and then later he would take his date upstairs, where he had a room and a bottle of bourbon smuggled in from Memphis. But he hadn't come today for nostalgia. He was here to make a phone call.

He walked to the bank of telephone booths and went inside one and sat down on the hard wooden seat. The operator's voice sounded sleepy when he picked up the receiver. She said, "What number, please?" as though she were at the tail end of a long shift.

"I want to make a long-distance call to New York. Person to person to Mr. Taylor McIntyre from Mr. Clayton Pinochet." Clayton gave her his former boss's telephone number; he was surprised that he remembered it. He hung up the phone and waited in the booth until the operator called him back, twenty minutes later.

"I have your party on the line, Mr. Pinochet. Go ahead, sir."

"Clayton? Is that you, Clayton?" Taylor's voice sounded startled, as though he'd just been awakened.

"My God, Taylor, I never knew how much like a Yankee you sounded."

The men laughed together, and then Taylor said, "Clayton, there isn't anything wrong, is there?"

"No. Yes." Clayton put his hand to his temple and wiped away the perspiration.

"What is it, Clayton?"

"You wrote me. You wanted me to do a story about

the Supreme Court decision and how it's affecting the people down here."

"You're going to do the story? Well, that's great, but you didn't have to call me—"

"Last night a boy was killed here."

"I don't understand. What's that got to do with the Supreme Court decision?"

"He was a colored boy, and he was murdered. Killed by white men."

"But I still don't see—"

"Taylor, killing this boy, that's the response. That's your story. I think you should send someone down here right away."

"I see. I understand what you're saying." He paused for a long time, and Clayton knew that Taylor was smoking and thinking.

"What about you, Clayton? Can't you cover it for us?"

"I live here, Taylor."

"Exactly. You know the people. You know the emotions, the nuances."

"I can't do it. You've got to send someone down here. And no one can ever know that I called you."

"Let me think this over, Clayton. I'll get back to you."

13

By Saturday afternoon the colored section of Hopewell was shrouded in fear, anger, and confusion. Every colored person in town had learned that Armstrong Todd was killed by the Coxes because he spoke French to Lily Cox. They also understood that he'd been murdered because of the Supreme Court's ruling against segregated schools.

They had known other lynchings, and the current crisis, like a roiling whirlpool, stirred the memories they thought they'd put to rest. "Remember when they killed them two brothers down in Woodville," Granny Jones said. "Them boys wasn't but twelve and ten years old, and they throwed them in jail, just 'cause they was running out of the woods where they found some white man's dead body. They brought in an electric chair from Jackson, put it on top of a car, and commenced to riding it around where the colored people lived. Then they fried them chaps till you couldn't hardly recognize they faces. And then, you know what? The next year the man's own son shot hisself in the head. Now you tell me what you think happened." Granny shook her head solemnly.

An old woman named Mattie cleared her throat. "They burned that Thomas boy up, wasn't three years ago. Said he attacked one of them white girls live right near the bayou. Lying trash!"

After the initial horror of the crime had registered; after the dark stain in the center of Odessa's front yard

had been washed away by the old woman next door,
who mumbled and sang "Rock of Ages" as she poured
a bucket of cold, soapy water and vinegar on the spot;
after grief, like a new neighbor, settled in the bones of
all those who lived on the garbage side of town and
their fresh sadness began to meld into the permanence
of their old hurts and ancient disappointments—then
something even more painful bore down upon them,
sweeping over the Quarters like a dirt-clogged wind:
there was a viper in their midst, slithering heartbeat
close. For when the moaning and shouting had diminished, it struck them that Armstrong Todd was dead because of Jake McKenzie.

"And I hear him in that back room telling Cox,
'Armstrong talking French to your wife,' " Darnell, the
dead boy's pool partner and friend, said late Saturday
night as he sat rubbing his eyes in Odessa's front room,
surrounded by others, while Delotha sobbed in the bedroom.

Darnell addressed the silent dark faces; he knew all
the people, and they listened to him attentively. "And
then Cox, he come shooting out that room, his face all
red and everything, and he didn't know if it was me or
Armstrong what did the talking, so he start asking me,
'Nigger, you talk crazy to my wife?' And I say, 'I ain't
said nothing to your wife.' " The young raconteur as-
sumed an arrogant and courageous tone that his listen-
ers recognized as the pure posturing they all did in
recounting tales of their run-ins with white folks. "Then
Jake, he pointed Armstrong out to Cox. He say, 'Hey,
you. You with the freckles. I'm talking to you.' That's
just what he did. He pointed Armstrong out to that
white man."

Mattie shook her head and mumbled, "Just like Judas
done Jesus."

One of the pool hall regulars, a man the color of a tar
road, slammed his fist into his palm repeatedly, each

blow harder than the last. "Somebody oughta kill that nigger," he said.

"Knowed all along he was evil," Mattie said. "Too ugly to be anything but wrong. He ain't never come to church, and he don't never speak. Can't even keep a woman. Run 'em off with all his drinking and meanness. And he don't take care of his own children."

"Black Jake. Ugly as a snake," a woman muttered. "Wonder what make a man so mean?"

Jake's crime was all the more heinous because the inhabitants of the Quarters weren't unfamiliar with betrayal, even the racial variety of that most grievous sin. The colored in Hopewell knew the Uncle Toms among them, but their betrayals were meager; their only motivation, a piteous self-interest, was understandable, even pardonable. Didn't they overlook the high-yellow Robillards' passing for white? And when Hattie brought her madam's two scrawny, washed-out youngins to church, showing them off like they were something rare and wonderful and better than their own children, they only smiled. They even tolerated Marguerite. No one snubbed her on the rare occasions when she came to Sunday services, decked out like the harlot she was, in gaudy finery paid for her by her white man. But what Jake had done was far worse than passing or whoring or even loving white babies better than your own. What he had done was incomprehensible. A boy was dead, handed over to white men like garbage wrapped in newspaper. And Jake wasn't sorry. Not one bit.

In his shack, Jake drank the mason jar full of moonshine that he'd bought earlier that day. As the liquor began to take effect, he thought about Armstrong's mocking words, and despite the strong arms of the whiskey pulling him down, he could feel his anger roused again. One thing he couldn't stand was niggers trying to be white! Jake fell back on his bed and pounded the center of his chest until a resonant belch emerged. Who did that boy think he was, trying to act all big just because he was from Chicago? He knew how to fix anybody who made him feel bad. He laughed aloud at his own slyness, the cagey way he had said to John Earl and the old man, "Mr. Cox sure did handle that trouble we had up at the pool hall. Sure did do that."

Early Saturday evening, Jake was leaning across the counter of the pool hall, playing his harmonica and singing a dolorous song about love and betrayal. He hadn't spoken to anyone since he'd left the Coxes the night before. No one had come into the hall all morning and afternoon, and now it was suppertime. Jake figured that people would return on Monday. By then they'd have forgotten the argument, and they'd drift back to the only recreation they knew.

He was pleased to have the solitude and liked filling the empty room with his rough voice and harmonica. He tapped his feet as he played, shaking his head from side to side. The music flowed out in smooth, easy passages that were as enticing and voluptuous as naked women eager to be loved. The music transfused him, as if everything old and weighty was being sucked out of his body and replaced with carefree feelings. Sometimes when he was playing, it almost felt like fucking to him, just a steady stream of pleasure that exploded at some high point in the song. While he was surrounded by his voice and notes, he got to imagining himself inside the harmonica, coming out into the world as pure music. And the Jake who made up songs didn't live in Hopewell, Mississippi. Nosuh! This Jake was citified and sophisticated. He was strolling down State Street (wasn't that the name of it?) and tipping his hat to all the ladies, who looked at him with instant recognition, who called to him, "Hey, good-looking!" "Hey, handsome!" because he was a famous singer and everybody knew him.

He was playing a love song, standing in the middle

of the pool table, when the door opened and revealed
Reverend Tolbert, who preached to colored Baptists at
Mount Zion every first and third Sunday; the minister
was accompanied by two somber-looking men, who
kept their eyes lowered. Jake snatched the harmonica
from his mouth and jumped down to the floor.

Reverend Tolbert looked around the room. He was a
short, fat man with calm, sad eyes. He cleared his
throat. "Evening, Jake."

"Reverend," Jake said. He nodded his head curtly at
the other two men.

"We come to ask you about the boy. To get to the
bottom of all this talk," Reverend Tolbert said.

Jake felt a swift ripple near his heart. "What boy?"

"The boy what got kilt. Armstrong Todd. Odessa
Daniels's grandson."

"Kilt?"

"Them Coxes got aholt to him. Shot him."

For a moment Jake couldn't catch his breath.

"Word is going around that you told Floyd Cox the
boy said something bad to his wife. We just wanted to
have a full understanding, to know the truth of the matter." The minister turned to Jake, who looked away.

Jake felt wild birds fluttering inside him, screaming
to get loose. He still had his harmonica in his hand, and
now he gripped it so tight that a jagged edge of the
metal cut into his palm. Looking at the dark, sweat-
stained faces of the three men, Jake realized that he
hated them all. "I didn't know that boy," he said. Then
he walked away from them.

He went behind the counter, still keeping his back to
the men. He could feel their eyes on him. What were
they staring at him for? If the boy was dead, it wasn't
his fault! Yella bastard shoulda kept his mouth shut, is
what he shoulda done.

Jake could hear the minister speaking behind him in
a slow, monotonous voice. When he turned around, he
saw that the three men were praying. He rushed toward

them, the harmonica raised like a fist. "I don't need none a y'all's prayers. What your prayers gon' do for me, huh? If you pray so damn good, you best pray for your ownself. Pray you eats more than grits and gravy this evening. Y'all ain't gon' play no pool, get the hell out of here."

The men stared at him silently. Then one of the deacons said, "Any colored man who'd turn on his own kind, knowing what we up against, is lower than a snake's belly."

Reverend Tolbert held up his hand, and the man became quiet. He looked at Jake. "We gon' pray for your soul, Jake. Anyhow."

"A nigger's prayers ain't shit," Jake screamed as they walked out the door.

14

By six o'clock Monday morning, Lily was on the back porch, scrubbing clothes over a washboard in a tin tub filled with hot, sudsy water, trying to finish her work before the gathering sun scorched everything around. She had on a dress that was so old it had grown slack in the front where it was supposed to be neat and fitted, and the color, once bright pinks and yellows, had been washed so many times that it had faded to a bland off-white. Lily's feet were bare, and already dirt had seeped into the crevices of her soles. It had rained Sunday night, and when she looked out over the backyard, Lily could see gumbo mud where the grass was sparse.

She'd been up since five, hoping to have a couple of hours for the clothes before Floydjunior awakened, but she'd been washing for a few minutes when she heard her son's first good-morning wails. Lifting him out of the crib, Lily held the baby out from her by his middle. His diaper was so loaded that it had dropped from his waist to below his belly button. "You sure do stink something terrible, Floydjunior," she said grimly, searching around the crib for a clean diaper. There were none. Lily lifted the baby's mattress and peeked underneath it. No diapers. She put Floydjunior back in the crib, where he instantly began crying, and looked on the floor. Nothing. From the bed, she could hear Floyd clearing his throat. Lily grabbed Floydjunior, hissing, "Hush up, boy!" while she took off the diaper he was wearing and dumped the contents in the chamber pot in the bedroom. Then, with a sigh, she pinned the same soiled cloth back on the baby. Carrying him on her hip, she went into the kitchen, rummaged through the free-standing pine box, with its three rough-hewn plank shelves, that served as a cabinet, and found a can of Pet milk, which she mixed with water and poured into a baby bottle. She stuck it in Floydjunior's mouth and he began sucking greedily. She carried him back into the parlor and laid her son in the crib, hoping he'd go back to sleep, but the moment she took her hands off him, he started squalling. She heard Floyd shout from the bedroom, "For God's sake, Lily, can't you keep him quiet? I'm trying to get me some sleep."

"Sorry, Floyd," she called, although she couldn't help feeling resentful.

She seized Floydjunior by his arms, ignoring his thin yelps of protest. Placing the boy on her hip, she toted him out the back door and plopped him down near the pile of dirty clothes on the porch. Several hens clucked and scampered near the steps, and Floydjunior squealed with delight. "Now you stay right there while I get these clothes," Lily said, frowning. As soon as she turned around, Floydjunior toddled down the stairs and made a run for the chickens in the muddy yard. Before Lily had a chance to grab him, he had fallen face forward, and when she lifted him up he was covered with thick ooze from head to toe.

I told Floyd that we needed a playpen, Lily thought angrily as she pushed Floydjunior under the pump in the backyard. The water was cool, and as it hit the baby's warm skin he attempted to jerk away from his mother, who held him securely around the waist. The tip of the pump grazed the top of his head, and the boy shrieked. *That Floyd,* Lily thought, as she rubbed the bruised spot and tried to calm her son with soothing words she didn't feel. *That Floyd don't never do what he's supposed to do. Why, if I was a man . . .* But Lily stopped herself from drifting along with those musings; such thoughts frightened her.

Now Floydjunior was sitting beside her, his empty bottle thrown carelessly on the porch; he was drumming on the wooden floor with an old spoon. Lily ignored the shitty smell that clung to him still. From time to time he would get quiet, and when Lily turned around she'd invariably yell, "No! No!" and pull the spoon out of his mouth, until finally she got so tired she snatched it away from him, whereupon he began to wail. "Dirty!" she said, putting her son's plaything in her pocket, but the boy only yelled louder as he watched his toy disappear. Why didn't he ever shut up? she thought. She'd washed only half of the clothes. She could hear Floyd getting dressed in their bedroom and knew that he'd want breakfast soon. "Here," she said, hurriedly wiping the spoon on her apron and shoving it into her son's hands. "You stay right there." Rushing into the kitchen, she let the back door slam behind her.

Floyd was sitting at the table, wearing only a pair of cotton briefs, smoking a cigarette and looking out the window. "How many eggs you want?" Lily asked.

"Gimme three. Scrambled. I got a taste for corn bread this morning."

There was a sudden constriction in Lily's head, as though someone had tied a rag around her skull and begun pulling it tight. Standing over the sink, Lily silently acknowledged the commencement of her daily morning headache.

After breakfast she cleared the table and washed the dishes with the water she'd heated on the stove. When the last dish was put away, Floyd came up behind her and began rubbing the back of her neck. Lily wanted to cry. "Floydjunior," she said.

"He's all right. He's on the porch, playing. Come here."

"But he might go in the road."

"We ain't gon' take long," he whispered. His hand

was on her thigh, touching her in a way that made her want to scream.

The washing wasn't finished until after three o'clock, and by that time the muscles across Lily's upper back felt raw and damaged, as though someone had deliberately been pounding and squeezing them. Floydjunior refused to take a nap when she put him down at noon. Instead he stood in the crib and shook the bars and roared his howls of displeasure like a tiny, frustrated lion, until she picked him up and sat with him in the chair by the bedroom window. She looked with dismay at the mountain of Floyd's clothes on the bed, still to be washed. When her husband was away on his trips, she had only her clothes and the baby's things to wash, and it was always such a shock, the amount of extra work when he was around. She didn't even really cook when her husband was on the road. The baby ate oatmeal for supper and something mashed from a can that she would heat up. Floydjunior didn't seem to cry as much when the two of them were alone. When Floyd wasn't around, she would sit in the dark in the parlor, or on the porch, listening to radio music, tapping her feet, dancing if she felt like it. She never danced when her husband was at home.

By late afternoon Lily was too tired to feel anything other than gratitude that Floydjunior had finally gone to sleep, that she had a few moments to sit and smoke before she had to get up and fry hamburgers and potatoes, squeeze lemons for lemonade, mix flour, lard, milk, and salt for biscuits, and steam some corn on the cob. Lighting her first cigarette of the day, she was so exhausted she believed she might not have the energy to inhale and exhale the smoke. The craving swept over her suddenly, as strong and burning as lust. She wanted to hear the sharecroppers singing. She hurled her cigarette into the mud, then stared forlornly at the empty Pinochet fields. Why couldn't they always be there, she wondered, singing the background music for her life?

The sun was still high and bright, and there was no breeze, and for a moment, even as the desire within her subsided, Lily realized that she hadn't thought about the boy, not once, that whole long day. For a minute, with the brightness of the sun in her eyes, the heat of a long day bearing down upon her, it was as though there had never been a colored boy speaking French to her in a pool hall. And that was when she saw the car turning into her yard, stopping just short of the first mud puddle. A familiar-looking car with a star on the side. "Floyd!" she called. "Floyd!"

By the time Sheriff Barnes got to the porch, Floyd was standing beside her, looking scared, but in a way that only she could recognize. The fear was contagious. Lily's shoulders began twitching, and she started biting down hard on the inside of her lip and scraping off the last bit of roses from her fingertips.

"Afternoon," the sheriff said. "Mighty hot, ain't it?" He smiled and revealed small, uneven teeth that were stained by tobacco.

"Yes, sir," Floyd said. "It's hot, all right."

"You mind if we step inside?"

Years later, when Lily had willed so many memories to fade, she would recall the way Sheriff Barnes walked into their house without wiping his feet. She would remember the mud tracks that led from the front yard up the steps, across her porch, and into her tiny parlor, footprints all the way to the one comfortable chair that she and Floyd had.

Lily could taste blood in her mouth from where she bit her lips.

The sheriff placed his hat on his lap, and his fingers thrummed the crown as though it were a little drum. Lily saw that his nails were cut neatly and were perfectly clean and even.

"Lily," Floyd said, "go get the sheriff a glass of water."

She was relieved that she was being dismissed, but

before she could leave, the sheriff said, "Don't trouble yourself, ma'am. I'd like to talk with you too."

When he said this, Lily looked at Floyd, who seemed nervous sitting across from the sheriff in a hard wooden chair. "Well, set down, then," he said to Lily, who immediately took the other hard chair, the only other one in the room.

"There's been some talk about that dead boy. Word is going around town that you and your daddy and brother know what went on. And you more than them. I thought you might want to tell me about it." The sheriff settled back into the chair, as though he was prepared to stay awhile. "What about it, Floyd?"

"I don't know nothing about no nigger," Floyd said too loudly.

The sheriff tilted his head a little and looked Floyd full in the face. His voice was almost paternal. "People seen you at the gran-mammy's house. Just tell me about it."

"Well, I say," said Floyd, jumping to his feet and shouting. "I say, what the hell is the world coming to when a white man comes into another white man's house accusing him of killing a nigger?"

The sheriff looked up, his eyes alert, his emotions controlled. "Now, didn't nobody accuse you of nothing, Floyd. I'm merely asking you what you know."

"A man's got a right," Floyd said sullenly. He sat back down in the chair. "A man's got a right to protect his wife." He spread his ten fingers like a comb and raked them through his hair.

"Well, yes, he does, and that's a fact," said the sheriff, leaning forward a little in the chair. "Was that boy bothering your wife, Floyd?" When Floyd didn't answer, he turned to Lily. "Was that boy bothering you, ma'am?"

"Oh," Lily said, startled that the sheriff had turned his attention to her.

The sheriff repeated the question.

Lily opened her mouth, then shut it; she looked at Floyd.

"I don't want my wife's name dragged through the mud," Floyd said.

"Nobody aims to do that, ma'am," Barnes said, looking at Lily. "I just want to know what happened. Did that boy try to bother you?"

Lily felt the weight of the sheriff's eyes on her and tried to think of something to say, something that would make everything all right again, something that wouldn't make Floyd angry. She shook her head.

"He didn't bother you?" the sheriff asked.

Lily looked at Floyd as if in a daze, before realizing that the sheriff had misconstrued her gesture. "Oh, no. I mean, yes, he did bother me," she said quickly. She took a deep breath. "I'm ashamed to say what he done."

Floyd stood up again. "That boy talked dirty to my wife." He looked at Lily as he spoke.

"Is that so, ma'am?"

She nodded.

"I went to the boy and I give him a good talking to," Floyd said, his voice loud and savage. "A good talking to. But I never laid a finger on that nigger, and that's the truth. If he's dead, must be somebody else killed him, 'cause it sure wasn't me."

This speech seemed to have sapped the strength from Floyd; he sat down wearily in his chair and fished in his pocket for a cigarette, but his pack was empty.

"Guess I'm out," he said.

The sheriff handed him a pack of Camels. "Can you smoke these?" he asked.

"Yeah. Thanks."

Floyd took several deep drags off the cigarette, then flicked the ashes into a glass ashtray that said "Mississippi State Fair" on the bottom. When he spoke, his voice was quiet and subdued, as if his last outburst had tranquilized him. "My wife is carrying my name. What kind of man would I be if I just let any ignorant nigger that wants to talk to her just any ole kind of way? A man's got a right to protect his property, his children, and his wife. Ain't that right? Ain't that what America is all about?"

"Well, man's got a right to protect his wife," said Sheriff Barnes, rising from the chair. "And so you're saying that you didn't kill that boy?"

"Never touched him," Floyd said. Lily was silent.

The sheriff smiled and nodded toward Lily. "Sorry to have disturbed you, ma'am."

"Oh, that's all right."

Lily remained in her chair as Floyd walked the sheriff to the door. Barnes held his hat until he was on the porch; then he put it on. From the window, Lily saw that the sheriff's hat made him look stronger and more imposing; Floyd seemed to shrink standing beside him, although her husband no longer appeared to be nervous or afraid. Now she could hear the two men laughing lightly. As she watched, Sheriff Barnes patted Floyd on his back before walking to his car.

Sometimes she didn't understand men, not even her own husband. She thought about what Floyd had said—that a man had a right to protect his property, his kids, and his wife—and the order of the words struck her. She thought that the way he said it made it seem that she and Floydjunior belonged to him same as if he'd bought and paid for them. *I won't think about that,* she told herself. The sheriff had come and gone, and Floyd hadn't been arrested. It was just as he and Louetta had said; there wasn't going to be any trouble.

15

As he watched Sheriff Barnes's car disappear, Floyd felt vindicated, almost cleansed. Before he left, the sheriff had told him a joke about a nigger and a bear and slapped him on his back, almost as though he was his son. Floyd didn't know why he believed the backslapping to be a particularly paternal gesture; his father had never touched him in that way. His father had never touched him at all, that Floyd could remember. All his touches were for John Earl. John Earl, who was taller and stronger. John Earl, who could shoot straighter and drink harder and was always brave. But of course, things had changed now.

Barnes didn't say it, but Floyd was sure that the sheriff would have done the same if the boy had talked nasty to his wife. There wasn't going to be any trouble.

When Floyd approached the pool hall on Tuesday, the place appeared quiet and empty. The rickety door, usually kept wide open during hot days, was closed tight. When he tried to open it, he discovered it was locked. He thought that perhaps Jake was ill, but then he knocked on the door and waited.

There was silence, and then a muffled "Who that?"

"It's Mr. Floyd Cox, Jake. Let me in."

The door was immediately flung wide open, although Floyd didn't see anyone in front of him. After a moment Jake appeared from behind the door.

90

"What the hell you doing, locking yourself in here?" Floyd asked.

"Afternoon, Mr. Floyd," Jake said.

"I asked you a damn question."

"Yassuh, I hear you."

Floyd surveyed the room swiftly. Nothing seemed out of order. Then he noticed a shotgun lying across the counter, next to the jar of pickles. The gun was usually kept behind the counter, out of view.

"What you got the gun out for?" Floyd asked.

"Well, uh, some of these peoples around here is mad at me on account of that, uh, dead boy. They think, uh . . ." Jake stumbled, not knowing how to present the delicate matter of Armstrong's murder to his presumed killer. He kept his eyes on the floor.

Floyd felt a growing tension across his shoulders. For a reason he was unable to explain, he couldn't bring himself to look at Jake. Jake was the only colored person he'd seen since Friday night, and the glowing darkness of his skin was an unspoken accusation. Floyd's hands trembled; he balled one into a fist and slapped it hard into the palm of the other hand. "Anybody bother you, you come see me," he said, shaking off his tension. He didn't have to feel guilty or judged, especially by some nigger who worked for him.

"Yassuh, Mr. Floyd," Jake said, brightening, raising his head a little but still not meeting Floyd's eyes.

"Anything going on around here?"

"Nothing much. Ain't nobody been in here. They mad."

Now Floyd looked at Jake. He needed a focus as the idea of angry niggers grabbed hold of him and penetrated. The niggers were staying away because they were mad. What did that mean? "So I ain't made no money since last week?"

"No, suh. Not a dime."

Floyd turned and walked toward the door.

"You want me to close up, Mr. Cox?" Jake asked. Inadvertently, the men locked eyes for a moment. They both looked away at the same time.

"No. Keep it open. They coming back."

Floyd's brother's house was quiet, the supper dishes already washed, by the time Floyd got there. When John Earl opened the door, Floyd took one look at his flushed face and bloodshot eyes and knew that his brother had been drinking for a while. He was surprised; he didn't usually indulge during the week. In spite of his intoxication, John Earl seemed nervous and alert.

"I was about to come to your house, Floyd," he said. "I got something I want to tell you."

John Earl poured Floyd a glass of white lightning from a mayonnaise jar and handed it to him. "Did you know there's reporters here in Hopewell?"

"Reporters? What do you mean, reporters?" Floyd asked.

"Newspaper reporters. From New York."

Floyd gave his brother a blank look. He gulped down a big swallow of liquor and paid silent homage to the fire it struck in his chest. It was good whiskey. Strong. He'd have to watch himself, or he'd be drunk as a fish. What did New York newspaper reporters have to do with him?

"They're here asking questions about what happened to Armstrong Todd."

Floyd still looked unfocused and confused.

"That boy you killed."

Floyd set his glass down much harder than he intended to, and the whiskey spilled onto the table.

"What are they trying to do?" he finally asked.

"They're trying to tell the whole United States what you done."

For the first time Floyd could remember, he saw fear in his brother's eyes.

"What'll it be today, Mr. Pin'chet?" Florine asked, pouring Clayton a cup of coffee. Her words were tight and

measured instead of loose and easy-flowing, the way
Florine usually was with him. He breathed in the strong
odor of coffee and chicken-fried steak as he waited for
the waitress to hand him the cup, but she didn't, and
when he looked up, Florine was staring at the booth at
the far end of the café. Her eyes were narrow, and her
mouth twisted up as though she were sipping vinegar. Finally she set the cup down in front of him. He nodded
his thanks and sipped the coffee, ignoring the menu
Florine offered him; she knew Clayton always ordered
the special. "I'll take the chicken-fried steak," he said.

The whispering began when Florine walked away
from his table, or so it seemed to Clayton. Usually the
café was noisy and vibrant at this time of day, and the
patrons, who all knew each other, exchanged greetings
and loud laughter. The Busy Bee was like one uproarious picnic during lunch, but today the air around him
was eerily charged with a susurrant tension he couldn't
name.

Clayton turned toward where Florine and the other
customers were staring and aiming their whispered
comments. Two unremarkable-looking men were sitting
in the very last booth in the café. He could see only the
back of one man's shoulders, neck, and head, but the
other man, who appeared to be tall and wiry, was facing
Clayton. That he didn't recognize the man facing him
wasn't unusual. A lot of businessmen used 49E on their
way to Memphis. But something about their manner
made Clayton realize that the two weren't traveling
salesmen and that they weren't southern. From where
he was sitting, their skin seemed very fair, almost pale
in contrast to most of the people in the restaurant, who
were ruddy if not tan. Clayton was about to resume
drinking his coffee, when the glint of a shiny object
resting on the table between the two men caught his
eye. He saw a large, heavy-duty camera with a flash attachment, the kind of camera that newsmen used. It

came to him then that Taylor McIntyre had sent the men.

While Clayton and everyone else was watching, the reporters got up and walked to the cash register. They were talking softly and seemed unaware of the uproar they were causing. As they stood at the counter, Clayton saw a young man he knew moving out of his booth, looking menacingly in the strangers' direction. The young man slipped between the northerners. Eyeing them with wary disgust, he addressed them in a loud, clear voice. "Ain't nobody coming down here changing our way of life. Y'all might have won the war, but there's some things we're just not gon' stand for in Mississippi."

The men said nothing for a moment. They just stood quietly, their brows drawn together in consternation. "Son," the tall one said finally, "we're not here to change anything. We just came to get a story. We're just doing our jobs." He handed Florine a five-dollar bill and waited for his change. She put it on the counter and turned her back to him. The silence in the café was as piercing as the crack of a whip.

"Why don't you go back up north and tend to your own problems, and leave us tend to ours," the boy said. He opened his mouth to say more, but he was interrupted.

"You gent'mens come again," Willow said loudly, smiling and flashing her four front teeth, which were gold and embossed with symbols from a stack of cards: a heart, a diamond, a spade, a club. She had slipped next to Florine behind the counter as soon as she'd seen the boy make his move.

"Thank you, miss. We will," said the shorter man.

Florine and several of the female customers gasped audibly when the reporter addressed Willow as "miss." As for Willow, she just smiled all the more broadly. She pointed to the camera. "What you gon' do with that?"

The short man chuckled a little. "Take some pictures," he said. "Want your picture taken?"

"I sure does," Willow said. She stepped back away from Florine and grinned, while the photographer took several shots.

"Is I gon' be in the newspaper?"

"Maybe."

"You gon' send me one, mister?"

"Sure."

"Send it to Willow Scott, Busy Bee Café, Hopewell, Mississippi. I'll get it. And thank you, gent'mens."

"Thank you, Miss Scott."

Around him Clayton could hear the comments, coming fast, now that the interlopers had gone.

"Goddamn Yankees. Ought to run 'em out of town."

"Outside agitators, coming down here starting trouble."

"Let them come down to Mississippi and take care of these niggers if they think we treat 'em so bad."

It was what Clayton expected to hear. It was what he'd always heard. Why, then, did the words always take him by surprise?

"Did you see them? Did you see them, Mr. Pin'chet? How do you like them Yankees coming down here stirring things up?" Florine hissed, slamming down Clayton's lunch so hard his steak bounced in the air in front of him. Clayton watched as her chest heaved in and out, every breath an angry explosion that reddened her face and further strained her soiled uniform. "And taking Willow's picture to put in the newspaper. Don't think she won't put on airs about that; she gets away with too much as it is. Why would anybody want to write something in the newspaper about a nigger anyway?" She paused, waiting for his response.

He wanted to give her one, to say to Florine that he believed that Negroes were human beings and deserved better than being murdered by trash like the Coxes. He wanted to stand on the top of the table and hurl his plate of steaming chicken-fried steak across the counter and tell all the customers in the café, as they picked the globs of mashed potatoes from their eyes and hair, that he, Clayton Pinochet, had called in the Yankees and was glad they were here with their notepads and pencils, their cameras and flash bulbs, and hoped that more would come, because it was time that the entire country learned about the barbaric cannibalism that was eating them all alive. A scream was burning through his throat like whiskey.

Of course, as usual, he remained silent. He could make a telephone call in the dark; he couldn't make a public statement. Strong words could lead to repercussions. There were some battles he just couldn't fight, at least not yet. One day he would speak out. One day he would save black people, lead them out of their misery. But not today. Instead he simply bent his head down over his plate. "Looks good," he told Florine. She walked away before he had taken a single bite.

16

There was no separate line for colored and white to buy tickets at the train station. The custom was for Negroes simply to wait until all the white people had been helped first. Delotha had steeled herself to be patient and calm, no matter how long things took. "Lord, don't let none of these crackers say nothing to me this morning," she told Odessa as they walked to town.

For her part, Odessa prayed for the same thing, albeit silently. She knew that her daughter had a temper. Once when she was a teenager, Delotha had called a white saleslady a bitch when she refused to let her try on clothes; she'd received a beating from the sheriff. Another time, when the white insurance man who sold Odessa her burial policy walked into the bedroom, where she was undressing, Delotha smashed a jar of Dixie Peach against his head. Only Odessa's pleas that her daughter had acted instinctively and not maliciously persuaded the man not to call the sheriff. In her daughter's present fragile state, all whites were enemies, and there was no telling what might happen if one of them provoked her.

There was no one in line when Delotha and Odessa arrived at the small depot, so they went straight to the attendant, a bald-headed, stuttering man whose widely flaring nostrils and pendulous bottom lip gave hint of a darker heritage than he acknowledged.

"Mister, I want to have my son's dead body put on

the same train to Chicago that I'm going to be riding on
tomorrow night," Delotha said.

The attendant smiled sympathetically, first at Delotha
and then at Odessa, who quickly looked away. He
clucked his tongue like an old hen. "I'm s-s-so sorry to
hear that. Was that the onliest child you had?"

Delotha nodded warily; she wasn't prepared for kindness.

"Lord have m-m-mercy. Well, He do know b-b-best.
We think we know, but don't nobody know but the
Lord. Was he sick?"

"No, sir," Delotha said.

"What! An accident?" The sympathy in his eyes re-
ceded and was replaced by a look of deep suspicion.

Odessa shifted her feet and switched her pocketbook
from her left hand to her right.

"Yes. An accident," Delotha said.

The man began frowning. When he bent down, the
top of his head shone like a lit-up globe. He slammed
down a form in front of Delotha and asked, "Can you
read?" She nodded. "You f-f-fill this out for m-m-me?"

Delotha completed the form. She wrote her name and
address. Under "Contents," she wrote: "Body of Armstrong Todd," and left blank the line that asked for
value. She handed the paper back to the man, who
scanned it quickly. Delotha watched him and knew the
precise moment when his suspicions that she was the
mother of the dead colored boy the whole town had
been talking about were confirmed.

The attendant, looking away from her when he spoke,
said quietly, "I ain't never shipped a d-d-dead nigra before. I ain't sure where I can p-p-put a colored body on
my train."

Delotha dug her nails into the palm of her hand so
hard she could see the imprints when she pulled away
her fingers.

No one spoke for several minutes, and then the clerk
raised his head to signal that he had figured everything

out. "There's a little b-b-bit of space in the livestock car, and I can put the c-c-casket in there. Nobody ought to mind that," he said. He was smiling. The top of his head glowed like a new moon.

"Livestock car?" Delotha said. Her voice was whispery and thin. She could hear her own heart beating as she waited for the man to explain, to tell her he was joking, that her son's body wouldn't be left with animals.

"I believe we're hauling some p-p-pigs on the train tomorrow."

"Isn't there some other place you could put him?" Delotha's voice was stronger this time, a loud, clear, angry voice full of unuttered curses.

"Now listen here, g-g-gal, you don't like the accommodations, you can arrange some others. That's gonna be thirteen forty-six. You need to p-p-pay it now."

He stared at the fifty-dollar bill that Delotha handed him and said, "Where you get ahold of that?"

Delotha could feel her mother's hands on the small of her back, pressing against her in tiny circular motions. "Mister," she said. Her voice was low and hard as glass. She swallowed, conscious of the word that was hanging in the air before her. She gulped again, shutting her eyes, concentrating on her mother's fingers, the tiny circles on her spine. "I don't have nothing smaller," she said finally.

The clerk took the money and ducked below the counter while the two women waited. When he stood up, he slapped the change on the counter. A quarter rolled to the floor; Odessa bent down and picked it up.

"The undertaker will bring the casket around tomorrow in the morning. If you just show him where to put it, he'll load it," Delotha said. Her mother's hand was still on her back.

"You know," the man said, fingering the fifty-dollar bill, "it's a sh-sh-shame. . . ."

"Come on, Mama," she said, trying to walk away

quickly, to escape the tiny eyes, the thick, dirty fingers, the killing words aimed at her heart.

"Sh-sh-shame you didn't teach that boy of yourn to watch his mouth. He might be riding with you and the rest of the colored people instead of going back to Chicago in a b-b-box."

Even as she and Odessa walked out the door, she heard him. "Y'all go on up to that Chicago and you forget your p-p-place."

The two women walked home in silence, and when they reached Odessa's house they sat down on the rickety porch chairs. Delotha pulled a Salem out of the pocket of her dress and lit it. The smoke curled up and burned her eyes; her fingers brushed at the tears until there were so many, coming so fast, that she took her useless hand away. If only she had it to do over again, she would have gotten Armstrong last summer. Now he had been taken away from her, by men she'd never see punished. She raised her hands and closed her eyes and began screaming.

Odessa got up and went into the house, then came back with a damp rag and began wiping her daughter's face. "Hush. Hush now," she whispered.

Delotha took the cloth away and let it fall into her lap. She began sobbing even louder than before. "Why did my son have to die?"

"Hush, honey. Don't cry. Don't cry."

But she couldn't stop crying or remembering the way Armstrong had wailed the day she sent him to Mississippi, the way he had pleaded in his letters that he wanted to come home. "God is punishing me, Mama," Delotha said in a moan. "He's punishing me for being a bad mother."

"No," Odessa said sharply. "This ain't your fault. You just wanted Armstrong to be somewhere where he could be looked after. That's why you sent him down here. If Wydell had been any kind of help to you ..."

When she heard her son's father's name, Delotha's

sobs choked off in her throat, and she felt a hatred so molten that the heat made her sway. "There ain't no justice for a colored woman, is it, Mama?"

Odessa sighed. "You go lie down. Rest your nerves."

Delotha was stretched across Odessa's bed, her eyes wide open and unfocused, when she heard the knock at the front door. It was a strange sound; most neighbors entered without such formalities, shouting their greetings as they walked in. She looked at her mother, who was sitting on the bed, then sat up so fast and hard the thin wooden backboard vibrated. She jerked herself to her feet and reached under her mother's bed.

" 'Lotha," her mother said with alarm.

Delotha felt around on the floor until her fingers clutched what she was looking for. She pulled the rifle out and placed it on her lap. The cold weight of the gun on her thighs was comforting, almost friendly.

"You put that thing away, girl," Odessa said.

There was riot in Delotha's eyes. "If it's them, Mama, if they done come back here, I'm gon' take them to hell even if I have to go with them."

"You put that thing down, hear me!" Odessa shouted. "You want to get yourself killed?"

"I don't care."

"Well, I do. I done lost a grandson, and I—I—" Odessa clapped her hand over her mouth. She shut her eyes tightly and rocked on the balls of her feet for a few moments before she opened her eyes. "Give me that gun." Delotha handed her mother the weapon. "I'll handle this."

When Odessa peered out the screen door, she didn't see anyone. Taking a deep breath, she stepped outside. Two white men (pale for this time of the year, she thought), one tall and wiry, the other thick and kind of short, were sitting on the rickety chairs on her porch, talking quietly. The short one carried a camera. They stood up when they saw her.

"Mrs. Daniels?" said the tall one.

Odessa stepped back when she heard the white man address her as Mrs. Her impulse was to run inside the house and grab the gun she'd taken from Delotha, but before she could open the door, the tall one was speaking again. His voice was rough, and his words came quickly, as though they had to race to be heard.

"We're reporters from the *New York Bulletin*. Do you mind answering a few questions about your grandson's death?"

Odessa stared at the men in front of her. Not at their faces; looking at white people's faces made her nervous, so she studied their necks and shoulders, their arms. Why would some New York newspaper care about Armstrong? Suppose Mr. Pinochet found out that she talked to them about how Armstrong got killed? He'd put her off his place in two minutes, and then where would she go?

"Mrs. Daniels?" She turned to the short, heavyset man. He was smiling a little, or at least his face seemed pleasant. "Mrs. Daniels, we heard what happened to your grandson. It was a terrible thing. We know things are unstable down here between whites and colored, and, well, ma'am, if we can write about what happened, it might be a chance to see justice done. The *Bulletin* is a powerful newspaper. A lot of people read it. The President of the United States reads it. If the right people learn about what happened, maybe they can put some pressure on the system so that the men who killed your grandson can be put in prison."

The brown eyes that looked into hers were warm and kind, but the sincerity she saw in them was as frightening to Odessa as looking down the barrel of a loaded gun. All she had wanted was for Delotha to take Armstrong back to Chicago and bury him, and for both their hearts to mend. She didn't know she could even hope for more than that. Now here was a white man telling her she had a right to justice, that maybe the people who'd killed Armstrong would be punished. But the men who were standing on her front porch didn't live in Hopewell. "I don't know nothing," she said softly. She didn't look at them. "Please go."

"Listen," the short one said. "Don't be afraid."

"You just don't know, mister."

The two men eyed each other; the tall one shrugged his shoulders and jerked his head in a quick motion that said they should leave. "We're sorry we bothered you," said the short man, with a kind smile. "Here's our telephone number, in case you change your mind." He handed her a slip of paper.

"I ain't got no phone, mister," Odessa said.

The men were turning to walk down the steps, when the screen door opened and Delotha stepped onto the porch. She'd been listening at the door and was struck by the word "justice"; she thought that finding that for Armstrong would be the last thing she could do for him.

Pulling her fingers through her wild, uncombed hair and snatching her frayed housecoat closed, Delotha felt old as she walked toward the men, old and weak, as though she couldn't get her bearings. But at the same time, she knew that she was waking up, reclaiming her vitality, her will, and all the power that Armstrong's death had drained from her. She looked the men straight in their eyes. "He was my son," she said, turning to Odessa. "She'll talk to you. We'll both talk to you."

17

Ida finished braiding the last of Sweetbabe's four thick plaits. Her father may have left his mark on her, she thought, fingering her son's crinkly plaits, but nobody would ever call her son a half-white bastard or a high-yellow nigger. And nobody would tell him his mother was a white man's whore. She wished her hair were nappy like his and that they shared the same rich pecan color; tears welled up in her eyes. As soon as she was able, she and her son would board the IC and head for Chicago. Life would be sweeter there. She gave Sweetbabe's head a little pat. "Go play," she said.

All around her she could hear her younger brothers and sisters. The two older girls were in the house, cleaning up the dinner dishes, and the boys were playing catch in the backyard. Sweetbabe wriggled out of his mother's arms, slid off her lap, and bounded a few steps across the front porch to where his grandfather sat. In the distance, Ida could see storm clouds growing. She stood up and poked her head in the kitchen door. "Fern and Lizzie Mae, is y'all chaps cleaning or clowning?"

"Ma'am?"

"Y'all heard me," she said, closing the door.

The two adolescents giggled. They were thin, brown girls, barely in their teens. There were fewer than ten years between Ida and her sisters, but they revered her like a mother, although sometimes she felt more like their girlfriend.

"We cleaning, Ida," Fern said.

"Come here, boy," William called to his grandson. His eyes sparkled with pleasure as he watched Sweetbabe amble toward him. "Your mama got you looking like a little girl. Give Granddaddy some sugar."

Sweetbabe planted a wet, sloppy kiss on his grandfather's jaw and then squealed with delight as he was crushed between the older man's arms.

"You gon' spoil that boy, Daddy," Ida said, smiling as she watched the two of them. "But I'm glad he got you, since his father ain't around."

William stared into the yard. "You don't hear from that boy no more?"

"No, sir."

"A man who don't take care of his children, he ain't much of a man in my book."

"I done learned that lesson. I guess my father wasn't much of a man, either." Ida watched as William looked straight ahead. "Daddy, who is my father?"

William stood up. "You need to get that boy a haircut," he grumbled. "Got him looking just like a little girl. He's too big for braids."

"He's just a baby," Ida said with a sigh. She was always trying to catch her father off guard, to get him to tell her what she needed to know.

"Boy's been walking five months. Next thing he'll be talking. What you gon' do then, put bow ribbons on him?" William gently set the little boy on the floor and watched him. "You a man, ain't you, son? You want to look like a little man. Get treated like a man, ain't that right?" Ida watched her father stare in her son's face, saw his gaze become unfocused and sad. " 'Dessa gonna miss that boy. He was good company." William started chuckling. "You remember when he first came? And he was sitting up on her porch and asked could he use the bathroom. And I told him it was out back."

Ida started giggling, remembering the look of incredulity on the boy's face. "He liked to had a conniption fit right on the spot. What'd he say? 'You mean you pee outside?' " she said, imitating Armstrong's northern accent.

William slapped his knee. "You couldn't get mad at him. He was just so funny. Ole Freckleface."

"Daddy. Tell me who my father was."

He gave her a quick look, and to Ida's surprise there was pain on his face. "Ain't I been a father to you?"

"Yes, and I love you, Daddy. I just want to know who the other blood half of me is. That's all."

"Well, I done told you; I don't know. Now you let it rest. Leave it alone."

In fact, Ida had little time to think about her white father. Her mind, conscious and unconscious, was filled with thoughts of Armstrong. For the first few nights after the murder, she had difficulty sleeping; when she finally dozed off, she often awoke with a start, as if someone had jabbed her in the ribs. Her dreams were such wild, violent hallucinations that she found no peace in her rest. She would hear screaming and begin running toward the sound. The faster she ran, the louder the shrieks would become, as if she were getting closer, but when she looked down at her feet she realized that she was barely moving. And then the real horror. She saw a little colored boy standing in the middle of a circle of white men. Ida couldn't quite make out his face, but she could see his brown arms and neck, and she could hear his cries of anguish as the men beat him. She raced toward him, only now the screams had ended and she could hear the voice calling "Mama. Mama." And she knew it was Sweetbabe who was in the circle's center, her only child covered with blood and bruises. And she ran faster and faster, but now she wasn't moving at all. And the voice calling "Mama. Mama" grew fainter and fainter until there wasn't any sound at all.

She woke up feeling both relief and pain: Sweetbabe

was alive, but Armstrong was dead because she had trusted a white woman with his life.

Her sisters were too young to be confidantes, and she didn't feel close to any of the women her age in the Quarters. Most of them were married, and some didn't trust a high-yellow woman with good hair around their men.

To her utter amazement, Ida longed for Lily when she awoke with a scream in her throat. At first she wouldn't allow herself to think of her lying friend, but snatches of old conversations invaded her consciousness. She recalled discovering that they both cried the day before their periods came on; and they both were nauseous during the early months when they were carrying their sons. She and Lily both thought that Evening in Paris smelled so good they wanted to sip it from a straw straight from the bottle. They had wept together.

But none of that mattered, Ida told herself sternly. Lily had gotten Armstrong killed. She was no different from any other treacherous white woman. "I hate white people!" She spit the words out into the dark air in her bedroom. The only response was her sister's heavy breathing. Lying in her bed, she was engulfed by smoldering anger and a slow, numbing sadness creeping inside her that was the same as mourning Armstrong, and she began to realize that part of her nightmare was losing Lily.

18

Even to a smoker like Clayton, the air in Mayor Renfro's office was thick with tobacco fumes. As he entered, he nodded to the men gathered there, men who'd known him since he was born. Seeing them, he began to shed the aura of invincibility that had been clinging to him since he called Taylor McIntyre.

His father had told him that his presence at the political meeting was mandatory. "We're deciding the future of this great state, and that's your future too, son." They called themselves the Honorable Men of Hopewell. There were none who frightened Clayton more.

As was the custom, the mayor hadn't been invited to the meeting but would be apprised at a later time of any public policy decisions stemming from it, if it was deemed politic to do so. Mayor Renfro was merely one in a series of figurehead politicians; the real power of the region was gathered in this smoke-filled room. Not that anyone would recognize by looking at them that these men wielded influence. All were simply dressed, one or two in dark suits, the others in work clothes, for most of them still monitored their field hands during planting and harvesting season. The primacy they enjoyed had been historically bestowed upon them; it was their legacy. Their great-grandfathers had made the family fortunes with blacks and cotton, and both had continued to enrich them. And not by chance.

The Honorable Men of Hopewell had blood on their hands. Since the days of the New Deal they had manip-

ulated relief benefits so that poor whites were often de-
nied payments and pushed out of the county in order to
keep in blacks who would work for starvation wages.
Over the years, Clayton had watched the Delta's power
brokers manipulate higher property taxes for the colored
and lower ones for themselves, so that essentially the
poor blacks wound up paying for both the white schools
that their children couldn't attend and the dilapidated
colored schools that were in session only after the cotton crop was harvested. Years before, these men had
shut down several fledgling enterprises owned by colored when the competition threatened the economic
health of white businesses. The would-be entrepreneurs
were sent fleeing for their lives, and most ended up in
Chicago. The decision not to sell life insurance to colored people had been made in this same room. And
much worse had been sanctioned on the second floor of
the municipal building by the Honorable Men assembled there. Much worse. And now they were going to
decide the fates of the men who'd murdered Armstrong
Todd.

The meeting started at six o'clock, and by the time
the last man had arrived, the two colored waiters sent
from the catering arm of the Busy Bee Café had set the
long table in the center of the room and were piling
plates with fried chicken, candied yams, collard greens
swimming in hog maws, and buttermilk biscuits. They
smiled and nodded as they served the food and poured
iced tea, greeting men they'd known all their lives.
"You gentlemens enjoy your supper," the older of the
two waiters said when everyone had a full plate in front
of him.

The Honorable Men ate heartily, chatting amiably
with each other, the conversations turning as they al-
ways did in such gatherings to crops and bloodlines.
Clayton heard Henry Settles saying to another member,
"Well, sir, the Settleses came down to Mississippi from
Virginia right after the Revolutionary War. On my

mother's side we can trace our roots to the Lees of Virginia." Clayton tried not to laugh. In the Delta, folks always bragged about their ancestry; he'd long ago suspected that none was as pure or aristocratic as they claimed to be.

After the coffee was served, Stonewall Pinochet rapped on his water glass with a spoon. "Cletus, Abe, you boys can come back later," he said, nodding toward the waiters, who bowed their heads as they left. "All right. All right. Let's come to some order here." Stonewall was usually at the helm of these meetings, or pulling the strings behind the scenes, not only because he owned more land than anyone else but because he had a way of wresting power from even the most formidable of his adversaries.

Clayton winced as his father stood up and held a copy of the *New York Bulletin* high enough for everyone to see. He looked at the angry expressions of the Honorable Men in that room and imagined how he'd be viewed if they knew that he, Clayton Pinochet, Jr., was responsible for that headline. He could picture his father, his face apoplectic with rage, his breath coming in heaving waves. He would probably hit me, Clayton thought, and he couldn't help smiling. His father hadn't hit him in a very long time; they hadn't stood within arm's reach of each other in years.

"Those of y'all with enough sense to be wearing your glasses will recognize this newspaper article depicting our fair town as a place where barbarians are bred who murder colored children," said Stonewall. "And this ain't the only article, neither." He bent down and picked up newspapers from Philadelphia, Chicago, Los Angeles, San Francisco, and Detroit. "Now, gentlemen, I don't have to tell you that this is a new day. And as our esteemed governor has told us privately, as well as publicly, Mississippi can't stand as an island. We can't be perceived as a group of savages. Wealthy northern industrialists don't invest in areas that are populated by savages. It's men like us who have shaped this region, and by God, we've got to take the bull by the horns on this whole affair. Gentlemen, we got us some rednecks that need to go to jail."

For a moment there was absolute silence, a stillness so complete that Clayton could hear himself thinking: *Thank God. Thank God.*

The uproar was sudden and clamorous. The idea that whites, even poor white trash, be punished for crimes against colored people was unheard of among the esteemed planters in that room. Several coffee cups crashed into their saucers, and the long wooden table was full of tiny puddles. Once they recovered from their shock, the men shouted vociferous objections, calling Pinochet a damn fool for even thinking such "treason." Stonewall looked at this gathering of his peers with silent equanimity until the din had diminished. "I'm ready to continue," he said evenly, waving his hand with a flourish.

"If you're suggesting that these two boys hang for killing a nigger, you're outta your mind, Stonewall. No jury in Mississippi is gonna sentence them," said one of the men with a wavering voice.

"You're liable to start a riot amongst these crackers if you even try to arrest them," said another.

"Gentlemen. Gentlemen," Stonewall said. "You're jumping the gun. All I said is that those boys need to be in jail. And they do. But I didn't say nothing about them staying there. I'm talking about appearances."

"Maybe we're better off letting those Yankees think we are savages. That way they won't try to send our little girls to school with a bunch of black apes," said Henry Settles. The waiter, who was pouring him a second cup of coffee, spilled a bit as he spoke.

"Henry, there's ways to deal with that. We got to think about the economic future of this state, as well as our own futures. We got a town full of reporters from New York City to Los Angeles to London, all intent on making Mississippi look bad. Everything we do from here on in has got to be done according to the letter of the law. Those crackers have got to be arrested."

"But how far are we gon' take this thing, Stonewall?" Henry asked. "I mean, if we arrest them Coxes, are we gon' let them get bailed out? Is it going to trial? Will they be convicted? I mean, man, you're tampering with dynamite here."

"We ain't never had a national—no, by God—an international spotlight beaming down on us, Henry. We got to take action," Stonewall said. "We set a reasonable bail. And yes, they go to trial. I'm talking about acting now so that we can continue with our way of life. Do you want the FBI coming down here?"

"Old Dwight ain't got the balls to do that," one of the men quipped. The room exploded in uneasy laughter.

"Yeah, nobody thought Old Dwight would appoint Earl Warren to the Supreme Court. And now they're saying we gotta integrate our schools. Gentlemen, we can't let anyone have dominion over our future but us," said Stonewall.

He is winning them over, Clayton thought. He could tell by the diminished intensity of the opposition. His father's facility with leadership had always amazed him; he was repeatedly stunned by the way Stonewall could cajole and coax people when he was feeling charming, or bully them when he was not. In the end, things would go exactly the way the old man wanted them to go.

"All right, we arrest them. Then what?" asked one of the men.

"We arrest three. We let two go. From everything I've heard, it was that younger boy that actually killed the nigra. Besides, we don't need but one symbol for justice, and I'm sure a sympathetic jury of his peers won't deal too harshly with him," Stonewall said.

Clayton watched as everyone in the room chuckled;

when he saw the others looking at him, he produced a smile.

"There's just one other related matter, and then we can call it a mighty fine night." Stonewall leaned over the table, and the other men drew in closer. "Now, the boy's mama is here from Chicago, and the word I'm getting is that she intends on taking the body back there for burial. Gentlemen, we got to keep Mississippi business in Mississippi. We can't allow that woman to take the body outta Hopewell. No telling what all might happen if she gets to Chicago with it. She might take a notion to call the newspapers up there; she might call the damn NAACP or some hotshot liberal politician trying to make hisself a reputation. That body's got to stay right here."

"How are we gon' get the mother to change her mind?" Henry Settles asked.

Pinochet chuckled. "I'm sure she'll listen to reason." He took a deep breath. "Gentlemen, are we in agreement?" The men in the room nodded.

The men stayed for another hour or so, drinking and soaking in the conviviality that flowed so freely now that the business had been resolved. Clayton wanted to leave immediately, to see if he could shake the feeling of revulsion that clung to him. He wanted to walk in the night air to clear his head, then run to Marguerite so that he could lose himself in her body, find his lost innocence between her thighs; but his father caught his eyes and imparted the silent message for him to stay put.

After everyone else left, Clayton's father turned to him. "Did you have anything to do with that story getting in the *New York Bulletin*?" His eyes probed Clayton's face for any hint of betrayal.

"No, sir," Clayton said, staring back at his father, who held his son's gaze for a few moments.

"I want you to do something for me and for Mississippi."

"What is it, Father?"

"I want you to talk to that boy's mama. I know he used to sweep up for you. You knew him. Get her to bury the boy here."

Clayton's laugh was short and hollow. "How do you expect me to do that? I don't even know her."

"You knew the boy. Tell her you were sorry to hear about her son. Then convince her that Hopewell is the place where he ought to be buried. Tell her we'll take care of all expenses. And give her this." His father placed a hundred-dollar bill in Clayton's hand. "For her inconvenience."

Clayton looked down at the money he was holding, and wanted to fling the bill to the floor and storm out in righteous indignation. He took a step away from his father. "Why are you asking me to do this? You know how I feel," he said.

"It doesn't matter to me how you feel. You've always been soft when it comes to niggers, Clayton. You tell that woman to bury her boy here, in Yabalusha County, because if you don't, Clayton, somebody else is gon' hafta tell her, and they might not be as soft on niggers as you are. Matter of fact, I guarantee you they won't be."

"Why did you bring me back here?"

His father looked at him with surprise. "Why, Clayton? Because everything I have is going to be yours one day, and there are things you have to learn so that you can take over. The Pinochet tradition must continue unchanged."

"I don't think I can learn them, Father."

"Of course you will, son. Of course you will."

19

When the sheriff came the second time, it was midday. From the porch, Floyd counted two men in the car, Barnes and a fellow who from a distance looked young and thin and who, when he emerged from the car, had legs so bowed they looked like he'd been born riding a mule.

Only when the two of them were walking across the front yard, their faces solemn and implacable, the young one with eyes that kept closing and shifting as though he were anticipating sudden movements, did Floyd notice the profiles of two men sitting in the back of the car.

They came up on the porch with easy steps, almost tiptoeing. But all the while Floyd could see their eyes, which were not cold, just resigned. From the eyes he sensed a warning, and by the time the men were on the top step, Floyd knew that the unimaginable was about to happen.

"Lily!" Floyd called. He heard the flurry of her skirt and knew she'd been right by the window, barely breathing.

She came through the door fast and said "Oh" as soon as she saw the two men, who still hadn't spoken a single word. She looked at the two of them with fear and then stared at Floyd as if he'd reneged on a promise. She wiped her hands on her apron over and over again; Floyd knew she did it to stop her hands from trembling.

"Guess you know why we come, Floyd," Barnes said finally. "If it was up to me, I wouldn't be here, but, well, I got no choice. All those out-of-town reporters done stirred things up, got everything all out of proportion. Anyway, it's political."

"Political?" Lily repeated. Her eyes were wild with confusion and dread. Floyd felt her shaky hand on his arm. Their eyes met.

"I'm being arrested, Lily," Floyd said.

She stepped back away from him, and her hand dropped to her side as though touching him burned her fingers. "Arrested for what?" she said dully.

"For killing that nigger," said the young one.

The words sounded so harsh, Floyd thought. He'd never been in jail before for anything, not even for being drunk. Up until that moment he'd never even associated the word "murder" with what he'd done to the colored boy. Murder was in the movies; it was what white people did to each other, crazy white people. It wasn't what white people did to niggers. He'd righted a wrong, that's what he'd done.

"What are you talking about?" Floyd asked.

"Maybe there's something you'd like to bring with you," said Barnes. "A harmonica?"

"Where are you taking him?" Lily asked, so frightened that her hands were bobbing at her sides.

"Ma'am, he's got to go to jail. You might can bail him out," Barnes said, looking questioningly at the leaning clapboard house behind him.

Lily would remember later that everything happened quickly after each of the sheriffs wrapped a hand around Floyd's arms. One minute she was walking Floyd to the police car, moving slowly like a horror-movie zombie, thinking she was dreaming and listening out for the baby all at the same time. And the next, Barnes was opening the car door and she looked in, and there were John Earl and Lester, sitting in the back, their faces like something carved in stone. Lily noticed

that when Floyd saw them he held his head up a little
and pushed his chest out before he squeezed in with
them, and John Earl and Lester separated to make room
for him in the middle, where the hump was located.
Then the car was gone, retreating down the misty highway. Lily stood in the grass staring until she finally felt
the soft drizzle that had begun falling. She thought if
she remained there long enough, Floyd would reappear
and her world would turn right side up again.

She raised her head when she heard the noise of the
truck, its motor loud and troubled. Louetta parked right
in front of Lily, pulling up so close that mud spattered
against the tops of her bare feet, her calves, the hem of
her dress. Inside the window of the cab, Lily saw
Mamie sitting next to Louetta, and the old woman's
face was as expressionless as a piece of biscuit dough.
But her sister-in-law had enough emotion for the two of
them. The door flung out like a sudden kick. "Them
bastards been here yet?" Louetta asked.

Lily nodded slowly, her comprehension coming in
waves. "They took Floyd," she said.

"Go get Floydjunior and come on!" Louetta shouted.

Lily tried to make her thoughts stay calm. Floyd had
vanished into the misty night, and now here was
Louetta, her fat face florid, her voice commanding.
Louetta reminded her of a man, she thought.

"Go where?" Lily asked.

"To the jail, of course," Louetta snapped. "Go get
Floydjunior and get in this truck. We gotta see about
bail and all."

"Bail?" The mention of money frightened Lily. She
wasn't used to thinking of it, other than when she asked
Floyd for some. If he wasn't here, where would she get
any? She was glued to the earth she stood on. Lily
looked helplessly at Louetta and began to cry.

"Lord have mercy, go get that baby and come on
here, now," Louetta said, her voice part wail and part
shout.

Lily felt the speed rising from her toes, the balls of her feet. The heat had spread to her soles before she realized that she was running. She raced into the house, scooped a startled Floydjunior out of his crib, and fled out the door.

"Come sit with your grammaw," Mamie said in a flat tone when Lily and the baby squeezed inside. Lily handed Floydjunior to Mamie, who settled the baby on her lap. He immediately began to squall, and Lily looked helplessly as Mamie jiggled him and finally smacked his fat little thigh, hissing, "You hush up now."

The jail was housed on the ground floor of the Hopewell Municipal Building, the only two-story structure on General Beauregard Street and the only one made of brick. It was right under the mayor's office. Inside, there were six cells, two for whites and four for colored. The two compartments for whites were painted pale blue and had windows and a commode in the corner. The rooms set aside for colored were unpainted and windowless, with only chamber pots to serve the prisoners' needs. Those airless holes were usually full on Friday and Saturday nights, when Barnes made his rounds to the juke joints that dotted the countryside and hauled in the drunks.

At the front door to the sheriff's office, the men waited while the sheriff went through his jangling circle of keys, found the correct one, and unlocked the door. The air inside the dim room reeked of sweaty men and stale cigarette smoke. There was a water fountain in the corner of the room, and Floyd walked quickly toward it. "Not that one. Over there," shouted the deputy, with alarm and disgust in his voice. "That un's for niggers." The bowlegged assistant pointed to a larger water cooler in the opposite corner, with the sign "For Whites Only" in neat black letters on the wall above.

When the cell door clanged open, Floyd's heart jumped. A man had been lying on his side on one of the two flat, hard bunks, but when he saw Floyd he jumped up quickly and backed against the wall. He was old and grizzled, and his eyes were bloodshot and wary, like those of an animal caught in the glare of headlights.

Floyd nodded curtly at the man and mumbled hello. It occurred to him then that he had no idea how long he would remain in the cell. He sat down on an empty bunk, his head in his hands.

"Whatcha in for, mister?" The man's voice sounded forced, as though it hadn't been used for conversation in a long time.

Floyd looked up into eyes that were unblinking and feral. "A nigger died," he said slowly. "Me and my daddy and my brother. They got all of us in here."

"That a fact?" the man said. "Say, you wouldn't happen to have a smoke on you, would you?"

Floyd patted down his shirt pocket, but it was empty. He shook his head wearily.

"Got any chewing tobacco? Gum?"

Floyd shook his head again. He wanted a smoke himself. John Earl and his father probably had cigarettes; Barnes had put them together.

His cellmate had moved closer to Floyd in anticipation of getting a cigarette. Now he was so near that Floyd could smell the day-old whiskey and vomit on his breath, the urine that had dried on his pants. The old man's red eyes were glistening like a rat's. "Me, I got no quarrel with colored. All men is brethren. 'At's what the Good Book say. Why'd you and your folk kill that boy?"

"Leave me alone," Floyd said. His voice was low, and he squeezed the sides of his head with his hands.

"For the fun of it? 'Cause he sassed you? Was you jealous of him? Did you want his woman? They got good-looking women."

"I ain't got to tell you nothing," Floyd said.

"Probably wasn't even your idea. You don't strike me as a man what comes up with ideas."

Floyd lunged forward and grabbed the old man by his shoulders. "Shut up! You shut the hell up, you goddamn nigger-lover!"

The man looked straight past Floyd's angry face. "I love everybody." He gazed at Floyd, his smile beatific, his eyes serene.

Floyd flopped over on his side, so the man could see only his back. "You get the hell away from me," Floyd growled. Moments later, he heard the man shuffle back to his cot.

Floyd lay on his side for a few minutes, listening to the sheriff and his deputy talk in the adjoining office. The words "peckerwood" and "trash" wafted through the air, and he felt a gripping in his bowels. He banged on the wall with his fists, and the sound was much louder than he had expected it to be. He got up and went to his cell door. By sticking his head through the space between two bars, he could see his brother doing the same. "That you, John Earl?"

"What you want?"

"When are we getting out of here?" Floyd's voice sounded thin and whiny. He instantly regretted having called John Earl, especially knowing that his father was listening to the entire conversation.

"As soon as Louetta, Lily, and Mama come bail us out."

"How much is the bail?"

"I don't know. Twenty-five dollars, maybe. I ain't sure."

"Twenty-five dollars!" Where would he get that kind of money? Floyd could feel panic welling up. He hated feeling frightened. He didn't want his brother and father to know that he was scared.

"You know what I think?" Floyd said, aware his voice was uncomfortably loud. "I think this is some kind of a damn joke, is what I think. Arresting us on account of a nigger."

"Sure it is," John Earl said. "They'll let us outta here, and that'll be the end of it."

Floyd sensed uncertainty in his brother. He waited for his father to say something, and finally called out, "Daddy, how you doing in there?"

"How the hell you think I'm doing?" Lester snapped.

Floyd could hear John Earl and his father talking in low voices. It was always the two of them. All his life he'd been standing on the outside of their circle. He kicked the wall that separated them and then fell down on his cot.

His mind drifted back to the first time his daddy had taken him hunting, when he was nine years old. Tramping through the woods, he felt sick and nervous, terrified that his father and brother would discover what he'd never told anyone: He was afraid of blood and guns. They came to a clearing and waited quietly, the smell of grass and leaves filling his nostrils. The air was damp and cold, and he remembered shivering, because his coat was so thin and much too small. He thought about the two crayons his teacher had given him and imagined the picture he would draw when he got home. One of the crayons was blue. He'd draw something with sky in it. Then he felt a tug on his coat sleeve, and when he looked up, John Earl, fourteen at the time, was smiling and aiming the rifle toward a young buck. The shot was like a bomb detonating. So loud. So fierce. And then the two others were running. Floyd hung back, and his father pulled him forward to see the deer, still alive, bleeding and twitching, a terrible, hysterical lowing coming from its half-opened mouth. He tried to think of the sky he'd draw, but he became dizzy and nauseated and pulled away from his father, but not hard enough. As his brother lifted his rifle and shot again, Floyd threw up. Later, when Lester slung the carcass over the borrowed mule, he said to his younger son, "I didn't know I was taking a girl hunting."

Floyd raised his head and stared between the bars.

There was nothing to see but a steel door. The old man looked in his direction; Floyd glared, and the man turned his head and started singing in a sweet, tremulous tenor. Floyd recognized the song as one that ole Hank always sang, the one he was singing on the radio after Floyd shot the boy. He thought of how his shoulders touched his father's, of how their voices blended and the cigarette smoke curled above their heads. His fist slammed into the mattress. What a fool he was for thinking that a song could last forever.

Louetta did all the talking. When the three women entered the sheriff's office, the deputy told them that Barnes was out to lunch, and so they sat on the hard wooden chairs and waited. Lily had put on shoes when she'd gone back to the house to get Floydjunior, but she hadn't had time to wash the mud off her legs and dress, and as she sat waiting in the office she was conscious of how she looked. She didn't want to be mistaken for trash.

Finally the front door opened and the sheriff came in, still sipping the last drops of a bottle of RC. "Afternoon, ladies," he said, taking off his hat. "I imagine I know why y'all are here. It's about the Coxes, ain't it?"

"Yessir," said Louetta. "What are they charged with?"

"Well, ma'am, they're being held on suspicion of—"

Louetta interrupted him. "Last Friday night, my husband, Mr. John Earl Cox, was at home with me."

"And mine was with me," croaked Mamie.

The two women looked at Lily simultaneously. She was overcome with sudden nervousness and couldn't speak. Louetta said, pointing to Lily, "She's too upset to talk, but her husband was at home with her too." Lily nodded without raising her eyes.

"Ladies, I reckon you'll get your chance to tell your side of the story in court," said the sheriff.

"Court!" Louetta cried.

"Yes, ma'am."

The women were silent for a moment. Lily looked at her sister-in-law, who seemed momentarily dejected.

"My boys ain't never been in no jail," Mamie said. "Can't we bail them out?"

"Well, now, ma'am, the bail ain't been set. Of course," he said, leaning in close to Louetta. "I might can work something out for you. A bargain rate."

Louetta reached up, grabbed the sheriff's hand, and shook it. "We'd like to see our husbands," she said.

"Well, I suppose that would be all right, but you have to go in one at a time," the sheriff said.

"I'll go first," said Louetta.

Floyd saw Louetta and then later his mother when they walked by his cell to get to the one that John Earl and his father were in. He didn't expect Louetta to have too much to say to him, but he thought his mother would visit with him longer than she did. She barely said hello to him before she ran to the back, where she spoke mostly to his brother. He felt lonelier knowing that she was a few feet away than when he was completely by himself. Lily would probably be coming next, he thought. He wanted a cigarette, something to keep his mind off his fear. If Lily knew how frightened he was, she wouldn't respect him.

The deputy led Lily in after the other women left. Floyd kissed her through the bars. He could tell by her resistance in her lips and the tense way she held her body that she didn't want to be touched, and making her kiss him made him feel powerful. The old man had the decency to look away.

"I'm going to need some money for bail," Lily said.

Floyd tried to sound nonchalant. "How much money?"

"The sheriff says thirty-five dollars." She whispered the amount as though saying it aloud was a terrifying experience.

Floyd kissed her again, longer and deeper, a kiss that

cut off her breath. He slipped his hands through the bars and grabbed her waist, and squeezed and pressed her against the bars until he heard her gasp. "Lily, Lily," he whispered when he took his lips off her mouth. "I done it for you. For your protection."

When Lily finally stepped back, away from Floyd, her face was flushed. She appeared unsteady, almost as if she'd been drinking. She said, "Thank you, Floyd."

"I'll be damned if I give this county a penny of my money. I believe I'll just set here and eat up their food."

"Oh, Floyd."

"You go on now."

Floyd watched her walk the short distance to the metal door, turn the handle, and mouth the word "Goodbye" before she closed the door.

He stared at the spot where she'd been just moments before. His breath came very heavy and fast, and he wiped the sweat off his forehead. Floyd stood facing the door for a moment and then walked to his cot and flopped onto it, remembering then that he hadn't asked her about Floydjunior.

Floyd was almost asleep when he heard the shuffle of feet nearing him. The stench of urine and day-old whiskey and vomit washed over him. He opened his eyes. The old man's face was close to his; he was missing some teeth. His voice was raspy, but his words were clear. "Son, you can't enter the kingdom. You got unclean hands."

20

Several barefoot children ran into the road when Clayton entered the Quarters. He knew that a car was a relative rarity in the neighborhood, especially one as shiny and chrome-rich as his Cadillac. As he parked the car he saw Odessa on her front porch. She stood up and folded her arms tightly across her chest, as though she were protecting herself. The clouds above him were dark and stormy as he walked across the yard; it would probably rain again before evening.

Armstrong's mother must be in the house, he told himself. He didn't want to see her, not yet.

When his feet were on the bottom porch step, he felt a tightening in his chest. He didn't want to walk up the steps; he didn't want to do what he'd come to do.

"How do, Mr. Pinochet," Odessa said.

"I'm fine, Odessa. How are you?"

"Oh, I've been better. Take a seat," she said, nodding to the chairs. They both sat down.

"I came by to say how sorry I am about Armstrong. He was a mighty fine boy."

"That's nice of you, Mr. Pinochet."

He tried to make his voice casual and light. "When are y'all planning on having the services?"

"Well, his mama's taking him back to Chicago tonight, and I guess it'll be three or four days before she gets him buried up there. She done notified the church and all, but she wants to send out notices."

Clayton hesitated. "I was wondering if I might speak to her, to both of you together."

"Yessir," Odessa said slowly, and he could tell that she suspected something. "I'll go get her. She packing." She walked to the door slowly, looking over her shoulder at him several times before disappearing inside the house.

Clayton wanted to flee. How could he say the things he'd come to say? His father had given him no choice. He thought about the lovely Picasso he had only recently hung on the wall of his house in the Confederacy. There was the possibility of a trip to Rome in the spring, when the city was its loveliest. He would just say what he'd come to say. He would tell her what a fine boy her son was, that he was sorry, but it was best for all concerned that the funeral take place in Hopewell. And then he would give her the money.

He looked up when he heard the screen door open. Odessa was leading a brown-skinned woman who looked just like Armstrong. She seemed forlorn and unmoored, as though without her mother to guide her she would have walked off in any direction.

"This here his mama," Odessa said. "Delotha, this Mr. Pinochet."

Clayton hesitated. "I—I just stopped by to say how sorry . . ."

The woman began sobbing and fell against his chest. Her weight, the tears dripping from her eyes, startled him, but only for a moment; then Odessa pulled her away.

"She ain't herself, Mr. Pinochet," Odessa explained. "She ain't up to no company."

In all his imaginings, he had never envisioned her crying. He knew her son had died, but he'd never expected that her pain might be anything he could recognize, almost as though he believed that Negroes had their own special kind of grieving ritual, another language, something other than tears they used to express their sadness.

Without thinking, he pulled the money out of his pocket and pressed it into her hand. "You take this," he said. The two women looked at the money and then at each other. "Sit down. We've got to talk." Odessa and Delotha stared at him and at each other. "This is important," he said firmly. They sat down.

"Where is your son's body now?" he asked Delotha.

"At the undertaker's. He's supposed to take it down to the station so they can put it on the train tonight when I go back to Chicago." Delotha looked at Odessa as if to figure out why Clayton was asking her such questions, but her mother's eyes revealed nothing.

Clayton drew his chair in front of the two women, so that he was facing them. "They're not going to take your son back to Chicago on the train," he said. He watched Delotha as she stole another look at Odessa.

"We made the arrangements yesterday," Odessa said. " 'Lotha done paid the money. They—they putting the casket with the animals. It ain't near white peoples."

"You don't understand. Certain people, very important people, want your son buried here in Hopewell. They think if there's a funeral in Chicago, it might make the newspapers up there and create more bad publicity for this area. Do you understand me?"

The women nodded. Delotha wiped her eyes and looked Clayton full in the face. "I'm not burying my son here." She held out the hundred dollars.

"Keep the money," he said, rising.

But Delotha pushed the money into his hand. "I gotta life insurance policy on Armstrong. They sell them to us in Chicago. I don't need your money, Mr. Pinochet."

She needed his help, though; that was clear enough. If only he could help her. If only he could help them all. Clayton folded up the money and put it back into his pocket. "You can't tell anyone I've been here," he said. The two women looked at him in silence. To Delotha he

said, "They're not going to let you on the train with
Armstrong's body. I'm sorry."

Delotha watched Clayton disappear down the road in
his car. She wiped away the last of her tears and felt her
eyes drying up; she was through with crying. Nobody
was going to tell her where to bury her child. They
might have killed him, but his body belonged to her.
She was his mother, even if she hadn't been the best
one. She stood up suddenly and felt more strength in
her body than she had since she'd come back home.
"William still got that flatbed truck, Mama?" she asked
Odessa. Her mother nodded. "Run over there and ask
him will he carry me to the funeral parlor right now and
if he'll take me to Memphis. I'm going to finish packing."

"Oh, 'Lotha," Odessa said, beginning to cry.

"Mama, we ain't got time for your crying. These
crackers ain't telling me where to bury my child."

Delotha tore into her mother's room and began
throwing her clothes in the worn suitcase she'd brought
from Chicago. By the time she had dressed and combed
her hair, she could hear Odessa and William on the
porch.

William's eyes turned hard as rocks when Delotha
explained what Clayton had said, but when she asked
if he would take her to pick up the coffin and then
drive her to Memphis to catch a train, he looked away
from her. When he turned back to Delotha, she could
see that he was frightened. "What difference do it make
where you bury him? Ain't gon' bring him back," he
said.

"You gonna help me or not?"

"Delotha," Odessa said softly, but her daughter's res-
olute eyes didn't move from William's face.

He answered slowly, "Delotha, you see how these
crackers is. And that's just the trash, what ain't got
nothing to lose. Now you telling me that Mr. Pinochet
and all the rest of them plantation owners don't want

you taking Armstrong outta here. What you think they
gon' do to me, they find out I helped you? You tell her,
'Dessa."

"Honey," Odessa said, "you know how things is
down here."

"Are you gonna help me, William?" Delotha repeated.

" 'Lotha, you don't live here no more, but I got me
a house full of kids with no mama," William said.

Odessa's neck jerked, and her words came out
harsher than they would have if she'd taken time to
think. "They coulda had a mama." She looked into his
eyes. "We all scared, William. You tell me a time when
we ain't been scared."

William McCullum was surprised when William and
Delotha came to pick up the casket, but after Delotha
explained that she simply wanted to save him a trip to
the train station, he seemed grateful. William and the
funeral director loaded the coffin onto the back of the
truck, where Delotha's suitcase was already sitting.
They covered the casket with a blanket.

The trip to Memphis took five hours, and after another hour they finally found the railroad station.
Delotha bought her ticket, while William arranged for
the casket to be shipped with the freight.

When he met her in the waiting room, William gave
her the receipt, along with several candy bars and some
apples. "You was moving so fast, 'Dessa didn't have
time to fry you up no chicken, did she? I know your
mama didn't want to put you on a train without no
greasy bag to carry. That ain't natural." They laughed
together for a moment. "Well, I reckon I better make it
on back down the road."

"Thank you, William. For everything," Delotha said.
"Sure wish you'd been the marrying kind. You'd have
made me a real good stepdaddy."

"Watch your mouth, now," William said. He hugged her good-bye.

At times the rhythmic motion of the Illinois Central train lulled Delotha to sleep, but her rest was as broken as bits of jagged glass. Once when she woke up, her face was wet with tears. Another time, she opened her eyes and saw people looking at her. The woman across from her leaned over and whispered, "You was having a nightmare, miss." The conductor came through moments later. The tall, lanky white man nodded at her as he passed by, but she looked at the large man's dough-colored face and felt convulsed with rage. She hated white people. Hated them.

By the time the conductor called out Twelfth Street in Chicago, Delotha felt exhausted and drained, as though she had run all the way from Mississippi. She made her way up the aisle and thought about the reporters from the *New York Bulletin*. Could she really receive justice for Armstrong? All around her, colored people, most of them migrants from Mississippi, their only possessions crammed into dilapidated suitcases and brown paper bags, rushed past her, in a hurry to taste the freedom of the Windy City. Looking out the window, she could see people waiting for their relatives to disembark. Already some of them were embracing, as brothers and sisters, cousins and uncles, welcomed kin whose eyes popped open as they beheld the opulence of the train station and the prosperous air of their city cousins. For a moment, Delotha's blood pounded with the euphoria that had surged through her body when she came to Chicago for the first time. *Everything was ahead of me then,* she thought sadly. As she reached inside her pocket and pulled out the claim check for her son's body, the momentary joy seeped out of her. She stepped off the train, and the breeze that blew over her was frosted with the first chill of a midwestern fall.

21

The last thing Wydell Todd remembered before he passed out and slid down the stool in the Down Home Bar and Grill was the red sequined dress that Big Mama Jordan was wearing, her strong voice belting out "No Good Man Blues." Not so much the dress, but everything it didn't cover; not so much the song, but the way the words cut into him. When he came to, the bar was closed and he was sitting in the alley in back of the club, in pants that were soaked with urine. With considerable effort, he raised himself to a squat, and then, balancing his body against the wall, he reached into his back pocket and pulled out a pint of bourbon that he had bought earlier that evening. There wasn't much left, but the burning sensation of the whiskey when it went down his throat woke him enough so that he was able to stand up completely. He put his hand on the wall to steady himself and took a tentative first step down the alley. He teetered, then slid down, falling on his back and passing out again.

When he woke up in his own bed three days later, Wydell had no idea how he'd gotten there. He looked down at the filthy jacket he was still wearing; blood was splattered all over it, and checking his pocket, he discovered that his wallet was missing. He had a vague memory of men and fighting, of a knife, of running and then riding, but when he tried to see a complete picture, all he could make out was a hazy outline.

There was a pounding inside his skull, as though ten

men were taking turns hitting him with a sledgehammer. He tried to get out of bed and stumbled to the window. Lifting the shade, he peeked outside; it was daytime. The clock on his nightstand said eleven.

"Mr. Todd. Mr. Todd." Mrs. Stewart, the old woman who rented a room to him, banged on his door. "I got to talk with you."

He unlatched the door and cracked it just a little. "Let me in, Mr. Todd," the landlady said in a loud voice.

He could tell how bad he looked by the shock he saw in Mrs. Stewart's dark eyes, by her sharp intake of breath, the way her thin, wrinkled fingers kept patting her gray hair and adjusting her glasses, how she kept backing away from him as she spoke. "Now look here, Mr. Todd. I told you when I let you have this room that I have a respectable house. The way you came stumbling in here the other night is something I can't tolerate no more. My other tenants are complaining." She wrinkled her nose. "And I want the rent."

Wydell nodded at Mrs. Stewart and went to get his wallet before he remembered that it was gone. "I got robbed," he said. He looked at his landlady; her dark face was filled with disgust and anger. "I get it to you first thing Monday morning after the bank opens."

"Today is Monday!"

Wydell stepped back, still feeling wobbly. "Ain't it Sunday?"

"Lord have mercy." She shook her head and sucked her teeth loudly. "You so drunk you don't even know what day it is."

Monday, he thought. He was late for work. Wydell sat down on the edge of his bed and rubbed his head. Usually he could manage to limit his binges to the confines of a weekend, but lately they had been spilling into the week. Only two months before, he had awakened on Tuesday morning, to find out that he had been unconscious all of Monday. His boss had warned him then about his absences. He wondered if he even had a job.

As Mrs. Stewart was leaving, Wydell glanced down the hall. The door to the bathroom was open, which meant that none of the other tenants was using it. He would wash up and get dressed. A bath would bring him back to life. He'd go to work and explain that he'd been sick. No, the boss wouldn't buy that. He'd have to think of something else. Maybe he'd tell him that somebody in his family had died.

He poured himself a glass of tap water and took three aspirins as soon as he got to the bathroom. Then he let the hot bathwater soothe and revive him. By the time he got back to his room and put on clean clothes, the aspirin had started to take effect. All he needed now was a cup of coffee, and he'd be good as new. He began to feel hungry. Maybe he would grab a bite at the diner on the corner and then go in to work. Then he remembered: he didn't have carfare, let alone money for breakfast. For a moment he felt despair, the kind of grinding desolation that usually propelled him on Friday evenings to the liquor store. Nothing ever went right for him.

He sat down on his bed and bowed his head until his chin was almost pressing against his chest. Mrs. Stewart was saying she was going to put him out. If he didn't get to work with some kind of alibi, he wouldn't even have a job. He felt his headache creeping back. He had to have money.

He stumbled to the rickety dresser and began snatching out clothes, letting them fall on the floor. Maybe he had stashed away a couple of dollars somewhere. In his frenzied search, he pulled all the pants he owned off their hangers, then, when he discovered there was no money in the pockets, left them in a heap on the floor.

He thought about Bertha, his old girlfriend, then remembered that she had quit him only the week before, calling him a drunken fool as she slammed her door in

his face. She wouldn't loan him a dime. And after all
the money he'd spent on her! Any man depending on a
colored woman to save his life might as well drown his
damn self.

As soon as Wydell thought those words, he admitted
to himself that he'd known an exception. Delotha had
tried to help him. Little girl stuck right by him when he
lost two jobs.

Drunk! That's what Delotha called him when she finally put him out. "No-good drunk, just like your no-
good daddy," she yelled. And even in the kind of stupor
he'd been in at the time, he could feel the searing pain
in his chest, as if his heart was on fire, that always
came when he thought about his father. Armstrong had
been screaming in the background. And drunk as he
was, Wydell could see that he was putting that same
pain in his son's crying eyes.

He didn't have time to sit around moaning over
'Lotha. He had to have some money before Mrs. Stewart set him out on the street.

Lionel! His cousin would help him get over. He pictured his stern, sensible face, the circles beneath his
eyes, and his hard, callused hands. Maybe Lionel
wouldn't give him enough to pay his rent—even though
he had it—but he'd at least give him bus fare and
enough for some food. After all, hadn't he let Lionel
and his wife come live with him and Delotha when he
first came up to the city? He shuddered as he remembered the four of them and little Armstrong squeezed
into one room. Of course, he'd have to listen to a lec-
ture. Lionel was always up in his face about quitting
drinking and finding the Lord. If he just let him hold a
few dollars, Lionel could talk all he wanted to, and
maybe he'd listen. The boy owed him, though. Didn't
he get Lionel a job pressing clothes at the same uniform
factory where he worked? Of course, pressing clothes
wasn't good enough for Lionel. Oh, no. Well, the nigger
didn't need to put on airs just because he had his own

shoe-repair business. An old shoe shop wasn't so much, although the way Delotha was always throwing it up to him, anybody would have thought it was some white folks' business. That shop wasn't anything but Lionel and his wife, Amelia, and a couple of machines. Niggers didn't know how to run anything, no way. Wasn't but a matter of time before Lionel would be right back there with him and the rest of them. Well, he'd just get a couple of dollars from him before he crashed.

Lionel's shoe shop was on Forty-seventh Street, nearly twenty blocks away. The wind was blowing just enough to feel nippy as Wydell trudged along. Walking was hard at first, and he felt every one of his cuts and bruises as he moved, but after a while his gait picked up and he began to enjoy the sun on his face. He was going to do better, and that was a fact. Lay off the drinking. As soon as he got straight, he'd go see Armstrong.

The sign on the door read: "Todd's Shoe Repair." Wydell turned the knob, but the door wouldn't open. Damn! Wydell looked at his watch; it was only ten-thirty, too early for lunch. Maybe Lionel was sick. But his cousin would have to be on death's doorstep before he'd take off work. Perhaps he had to run out and do a quick errand. But if that was the case, where was Amelia? The couple ran the shop together. Lionel just wouldn't close it in the middle of the day for no reason. Not as much as they loved money.

"Damn!" he said, striking the door with his fist. He was about to walk down the street, when he heard the shop bell tinkle. Wydell turned around, and Lionel and Amelia were coming out of the store, both wearing black. They stared at Wydell with expressions that simultaneously changed from incredulity to blatant contempt.

"Y'all looking at me like you smell me coming," Wydell said, grinning. "How are y'all doing?" He tried to make his voice light and pleasant. He laughed a little.

Had to make ole Lionel feel good if he was gon' talk him out of some money.

"We didn't expect to see you," Lionel said. His tone was solemn. He seemed to hesitate, than glanced at his wife, who didn't say anything. As if taking encouragement from her silence, Lionel blurted out, "Why aren't you at the church?"

Church, always church with Lionel, thought Wydell. He wasn't even inside his place, and here he was talking about church. Didn't even ask him for anything yet! But he needed the money. He had to get to work, and now he was so hungry he could count the wrinkles in his belly. He smiled. "Be glad to go to church with you sometime, Lionel. You know me, I want to keep in tight with the Lord. Heh, heh. Why you got the place all locked up? Where y'all on your way to in all that black? Somebody die or something? Hope it ain't nobody I know."

Why were they staring at him as if they had caught him with his hand in the cash register? Maybe Lionel had already figured out why he was there. Well, maybe he hadn't paid Lionel back from the other time he'd borrowed money, but that didn't give him no right to look down on him. After all, if it hadn't been for him letting Lionel live with him, Lionel wouldn't have nothing! Not the shoe shop, not that piece of a house he owned off Cottage Grove. Probably wouldn't even have that big-butt yellow wife of his, or them knock-kneed boys he seemed to think were the new messiahs. He had him a boy too.

"It's somebody you shoulda known," Lionel said so quietly, so solemnly, that Wydell felt fear, as jagged as a cat's claws, scraping inside him. "Wydell, where you been?"

It was on the tip of Wydell's tongue to say, "I been around," and to follow that with a grin, but there was something so disapproving in his cousin's face, yet at the same time so sad, that Wydell was afraid to speak.

Lionel said, "Don't you care about nothing no more?" He paused for a moment, and Wydell steeled himself for the onslaught of one of his cousin's high-and-mighty speeches about the evil of alcohol and the power of the Lord. "Man, we on our way to your son's funeral."

Wydell's head jerked like a balloon bobbing on a string; he looked at Lionel and then at Amelia. His son's funeral? What were they talking about? He'd just seen Armstrong only ... Wydell struggled to remember how long it had been. Surely only months. Only months, and now here was his cousin talking trash, pure trash. Wydell's mouth felt as dry as ashes. He wouldn't pay any attention to Lionel. "Listen, Lionel, can you let me hold five bucks till payday. I got kinda short on account of—"

"Man, did you hear what I just said? Armstrong is dead. He's dead, Wydell. And we're on our way to his funeral."

Wydell could see his cousin's lips moving, but why wasn't any sound coming out? If Lionel wouldn't loan him any money, then he might as well leave. Maybe he'd drive him to work, and then he could borrow a couple of bucks from one of the fellows on the job. He said to Lionel, "Say ...," but then he forgot what he wanted to ask him. He felt woozy all of a sudden, like when he first stood up that morning. He swayed a little and leaned into Lionel, who held him away with strong arms. His cousin's words, like a delayed echo, played over and over inside his mind. "I didn't know. I didn't know. Tell me what to do, Lionel," Wydell finally said.

"Come on with us," Lionel said. His tone was gruff. He began walking toward a dark green Chevrolet parked in front of his shop. He gave Wydell a little shove.

Wydell froze. "I can't go there, man. I—I ain't dressed. Delotha will be there. She hates me, man. She's always bad-mouthing me, Lionel. I can't go."

He felt his cousin's strong arm yanking him. Lionel's face was a mixture of anger, disgust, and sadness. "You didn't do right by the boy while he was alive. Can't you even do right when he's dead?"

Do right! Lionel was forever talking about doing right. Wydell's legs were wobbling, but he knew he was moving toward the car. He heard the door open and shut, felt the lurch of the automobile as it started off. Sitting behind Amelia and Lionel, he felt scared and confused. His mouth was so dry. Like sand. His boy was dead.

God, he needed a drink.

"The first thing Delotha done when she got here was call the newspapers, the white ones as well as the colored," Lionel said. "And she called the NAACP. That Delotha, she ain't nobody to mess with when she gets mad. I don't know how you could have missed hearing about this, Wydell. It's been in all the papers, even the radio."

As they approached St. Lawrence Avenue, Wydell could see a long line of people that snaked from the church's front door all the way down the street and then wrapped around the corner. There seemed to be hundreds of people waiting.

"Lord have mercy," said Amelia. "Look at all these folks."

Wydell, Lionel, and Amelia had to park nearly four blocks from the church. Wydell walked between Lionel and Amelia and didn't look at any of the people: not the old ladies who were crying, not the thin young men who were cursing. He stared straight ahead as the usher let them in.

Lionel whispered to Wydell that they should go up front and sit in the section for the family. "You go on," Wydell said to his cousin and Amelia. "I'll sit in the back." Lionel looked at him, then shook his head. "Don't tell her I'm here," Wydell said. "It'll only make things worse."

Wydell got at the end of the line making its way to the casket and waited with the strangers who'd come to look at his son's body. When he found himself before the casket, he forced himself to look; the boy's face was bruised, but still he seemed just to be sleeping, as though all Wydell had to do was shake his shoulder and he'd wake up and give him another chance. Wydell's knees began to wobble, and he started sobbing, holding on to the railing that set off the pulpit. He stood almost crouching in front of the casket for so long that the woman behind him tapped his shoulder. He jumped at her touch, then he took a last look and walked back to his seat.

The services were long and emotional. When the funeral was almost over, the minister led Delotha to the pulpit. She thanked everyone for coming and then she began crying, and the preacher and another man escorted her back to her seat.

Wydell stood up when Delotha started sobbing. It was an involuntary motion. She looked so small from where he was sitting, just a tiny woman crying for her son. Their son. His stomach was lurching and quivering; he felt hot and nauseated. He had to have some air; he couldn't breathe. The woman sitting next to him stared at him curiously, and he realized that he was crying again. He wiped his eyes and stood up. "Did you know that boy?" she asked him. Her face was calm, sympathetic—a mother's face.

Wydell pushed by her without responding. He was afraid of the answer.

22

As his father and brother stood outside Floyd's cell, neither one would look him in the eyes. The sight of the two of them confused and shocked Floyd. Why weren't they in their cell? John Earl did all the talking. He explained that the charges had been dismissed against them, not for any of their doing, of course, but because a witness had come forward to say that Floyd was the one who actually killed the nigger. John Earl was shifting his weight from foot to foot while he talked, and his father was looking anywhere but at Floyd.

"Listen," John Earl said quickly, his tone loose and jovial, though his eyes still avoided Floyd's. "This whole thing is gon' blow over. If you was a Pinochet or a Settles or any one of them rich bastids, you wouldn't even be in here. You won't have to serve not one day."

"I done served more than one day now," Floyd said, his eyes, like his father's and brother's, resting on the wall.

"Don't worry," John Earl said. The door to the sheriff's office opened, and the deputy motioned for them to leave. "Look, we gotta go now, but we'll come see you. And don't worry about Lily and Floydjunior. We'll look after them."

By the time the trial began, in late November, in Vanderbilt, the county seat, the entire Delta seemed to be in a state of shock. To most of the whites, the fact that a trial was being held at all was like a natural disaster whirling in their midst, uprooting trees and knocking out power. And the Negroes were careful to suppress any hint of jubilation they felt over the fact that Floyd Cox was in jail for murdering one of them.

The story, which since the initial fanfare had been relegated to the back pages of metropolitan newspapers in New York, Kansas, and Los Angeles, now once again appeared on the first, second, or third page of the dailies. "Well," Odessa told Ida as they sat inside William's truck and rode to Vanderbilt, "at least it ain't like Armstrong died and didn't nobody know anything about him." She put her hands on the younger woman's arm and was comforted by the warmth of her flesh.

Thanksgiving was only a week away, and the five blocks that made up downtown Vanderbilt were decorated with red, gold, and brown leaves, which had been strung up across the streets by members of the local Kiwanis in preparation for the annual Cotton Harvest Festival. As Floyd was led to his seat by the bailiff, a stooped old man who'd sharecropped until his sight began to fail, he looked out the window and stared at the giant paper leaves spinning in the breeze.

The court had been built after the Civil War, and the only modern accoutrements were the indoor bathrooms for whites and the three huge ceiling fans, which were blowing at high speed even in November. Floyd sat next to his lawyer, Waldo Anderson, who peered at his client through thick glasses with tortoiseshell frames and spoke in a high, whispery voice that made Floyd squirm as far away from him as possible. Unbeknownst to Floyd, Waldo's service had been paid for by the Honorable Men of Hopewell, who retained him for their own complex business dealings.

From his seat Floyd could look over and see Lily and Floydjunior, as well as his father and his mother, John Earl and Louetta, and their kids, all of whom were sitting in the row behind Stonewall Pinochet. From time to time Floyd would glance over at Lily, whose mouth

and eyes seemed pinched and drawn up, as though she
had just finished crying or was about to begin.

He was surprised at how crowded the courtroom was.
He'd been cooped up in jail for almost six weeks, and
even though the sheriff let him read the local newspapers and he knew of the attention his trial was receiv-
ing, he was astonished to look around and see that
every seat was taken; in some cases, two people shared
a chair. The courtroom was divided about evenly between the whites in the front rows and the blacks, who
crowded the rear. In the very front rows were seated the
wealthy plantation owners and the people who lived in
the Confederacy, and Floyd was pleased that the rich
people thought he was worth coming out to see.

He'd never seen so many colored people in his life as
there were in the back of the courtroom. Many of the
pool hall regulars were there, and none of them were
smiling. Jake was standing alone in the very last row.
He saw Odessa sitting at a table that was positioned off
to the side of the judge's bench. There were several colored men sitting there, all wearing suits and ties; some
had small notepads and pencils in front of them, and
one or two had cameras. The sight of these men perplexed Floyd until he turned to the other side of the
room and saw another table, with even more men, only
these were white, and they had the same notepads and
cameras in front of them as the colored men. "Who are
those guys, Mr. Anderson?" Floyd asked Waldo, pointing toward the white men.

"That's the press. You know, newspaper reporters.
Maybe even somebody from television."

"And who're they?" He pointed to the table of colored men.

Waldo chuckled. "You never heard of the nigra
press?" He winked at his client.

"You mean they got they own newspapers?" Floyd
was stunned. Before Waldo could respond, the mob of
white reporters, followed by the colored ones, rushed

toward Floyd, and for a moment he was frightened, not knowing their intent. He was dazed by the barrage of questions they shouted out. Had he killed the boy? Why had he killed the boy? What did he think of the Supreme Court decision on school integration? Floyd felt dizzy with so many men around, pressing in on him. He narrowed his eyes and clamped his lips down even more tightly, managing to look so fierce and unapproachable that some of the reporters retreated. Before he could answer one question, the bailiff ordered the journalists back to their respective tables.

No sooner had the room regained a semblance of order than Floyd was surprised to see everyone rising. He followed Waldo's example and stood up, looking around expectantly. The judge, an enormously fat man with roseate jowls so heavy that his entire face drooped from the weight, literally heaved himself into the room. He appeared overheated and agitated as he climbed the two steps to the bench and then settled himself there. As he surveyed the crowd, he took a deep breath and fanned himself violently with a piece of paper.

Waldo leaned over and whispered to Floyd, nodding toward the bench. "That's Judge Chisolm, a card-carrying member of the Klan, just like his daddy and granddaddy." Floyd sat silent as a jury of twelve white men, all clad in overalls, was quickly selected.

"Ever see anything so pretty in all your life?" his lawyer asked him.

The prosecuting attorney, Phineas Newsome, a nervous wisp of a man with thinning blond hair and an air of resignation, called the first witness. Darnell, visibly shaking, swore under oath that Floyd Cox was "plenty mad" when Jake told him that Armstrong Todd was talking French to his wife. He also swore that Lily Cox had come into the pool hall alone.

When Waldo was called to cross-examine Darnell, he took his time getting up from his chair. He was a tall man with sharp, pointed features. He stood so close to

Darnell that the boy could see the tiny blue veins in his long, thin nose. "Now then," he said, his voice low, "you say that Miss Lily Cox entered the pool hall of her own volition that day and stood there listening to Armstrong Todd as he spoke French. And that she smiled while he was talking. Is that what you say, boy?"

"Yessir," Darnell said.

"Why do you think a white lady would enter a business establishment with nothing but nigra men inside?"

Phineas Newsome did not object.

Darnell hesitated. "She was laughing. I guess maybe she thought he was funny."

There was an uproar when Darnell finished speaking, as the whites reacted to the boy's assertion that one of their prettiest women had been fascinated enough by a black boy to want to stand around and listen to him speak a language she didn't understand. Judge Chisolm turned red, more from his own sense of outrage at the testimony than from the ensuing tumult among those in the courtroom. Conscious of the reporters, he modulated his tone as he rapped hard against the oak bench with his gavel. "I'll empty this courtroom unless everyone present comports himself with some decorum. Mr. Anderson, you got any further questions for this boy?"

"No, sir, I don't."

Before the prosecutor could instruct his witness to step down, the judge bellowed out, "Mr. Newsome, get that boy off the stand."

Darnell left the witness box and walked straight out of the courtroom to a waiting car. There were two suitcases in the trunk, and the driver had orders to take him straight to Little Rock. There he was to board a train to Los Angeles, where he had relatives. His mother had put an empty mayonnaise jar in the back seat of the car and had told the driver, "Don't y'all stop to pee or nothing before you get to Little Rock."

Mr. Newsome, with a great deal of coughing and sputtering, called Odessa to the stand. She walked halt-

ingly, as though her legs were hurting her, and Judge
Chisolm, fanning himself and turning redder by the
minute, called out, "Step lively, gal. We don't have all
day."

"Tell us what happened on the evening of September
sixteenth, Odessa," Phineas Newsome said when she
was finally seated in front of him. "Tell us what you
saw." He avoided all eye contact and looked at his
watch.

Both blacks and whites leaned forward, waiting to
hear whether Odessa would be brave or foolhardy
enough to tell what she'd seen. Odessa looked over the
crowd in the courtroom until she spotted Ida, who nodded and smiled at her. Keeping her eyes on the light-
skinned girl's face, Odessa began to speak. "Armstrong
come home later than usual that day. He packed his
clothes, because he was supposed to be leaving the next
morning for school in Flower City. We had our supper.
I had cooked up some butter beans and rice. Some corn
bread. And so we ate that. Then I cleaned up, and pres-
ently I told Armstrong that I was going next door. I
asked him if he wanted to come with me, but he said
no.

"I musta been gone 'bout an hour, and when I come
back I seen him lying in the middle of the yard. I run
to him and he was bleeding. Armstrong told me, he say,
'Grandma, some white mens hurt me.' And I says, I
says, 'Honey, who hurt you so bad?' And he say,
'Grandma, Floyd Cox shot me.' That's all he said. And
when I looked up, I seen an ole black truck going down
the road."

"Who was in that truck?" Phineas asked.

There was absolute silence around her.

Odessa stood up. "It was Lester Cox, John Earl Cox,
and Floyd Cox," she said.

"No further questions," said Phineas Newsome.

Waldo Anderson peered at Odessa from behind his

thick glasses. "Odessa, what time was it when you got back from visiting your neighbor?"

"Going on nine o'clock."

"Nine o'clock. At nine o'clock it's dark, good and dark. How could you see that the men in the truck were Floyd, Lester, and John Earl Cox?"

"Maybe it was a little earlier. I seen them men."

"Your grandson had a smart mouth, Odessa. Big, yellow braggety boy from Chicago, he had to have made him some enemies. Who didn't like your grandson?"

"He didn't have no enemies that I know of."

"How could a dying boy say everything you said he did? Is your memory serving you correctly, Odessa?"

"Yessir."

"You're not lying to this court, are you, gal?"

Odessa lifted her head, looked at Waldo and then at the entire room. "I ain't the one doing the lying," she said.

"No more questions, Your Honor."

When the judge announced a lunch recess, Lily was taken aback. She had never been in a court before, and she expected the proceedings to continue until everyone had been heard, that the whole court case wouldn't last any longer than a party. She had adjusted to the rhythm of the questioning and answering, and she liked sitting and listening to the people talking about the death of Armstrong Todd; she liked the way her name sounded, coming out of the mouths of Phineas Newsome and Waldo Anderson. The only other time in her life her name was on people's lips was when she was Magnolia Queen, and that had been long ago. She felt like a movie star, listening to so many people speak her name, and she made her face look melancholy and introspective, the way Elizabeth Taylor's did in the movie star magazine she'd seen a few months before. But with the judge's abrupt announcement, people started leaving and she had to refocus her thoughts. What should she do during recess? She had brought food for the baby but none for herself, and she didn't have any money. She looked cautiously at Mamie, who was sitting next to her, but Floyd's mother seemed weary and as perplexed as she. Lester and John Earl appeared to be just as confused and uncertain as Mamie, and even Louetta, sweaty and breathless from the heat, didn't know what to do.

Floydjunior, meanwhile, was toddling over to the table where the Negro reporters were seated. Odessa was sitting with the men, fanning herself with a sheet of paper torn from a reporter's notepad. Her face was like a shell-shocked battlefield; her eyes were like open wounds. The little boy approached Odessa's chair, and without saying a word, he began rubbing her leg. She looked down and saw the baby, who grinned at her. At the same time, Lily realized that Floydjunior was gone. She gasped when she discovered him. Seeing so many colored men in suits when it wasn't Sunday made Lily feel strange. She'd seen colored men on their way to church in frayed coats and patched-up pants, wearing the same rough brogans they wore in the fields during the week, but the men in front of her weren't dressed in tattered clothing. They seemed prosperous and, as they busied themselves with their writing and picture taking, important. Her own dress, once a bright yellow but now faded, felt shabby. Lily was overcome with awe and envy before she realized what she was feeling. And so she stared longer than she should have, watching in fascination as Odessa turned away from Floydjunior. Even then she didn't move, not until she heard Mamie's sharp words. "Go get your baby away from them stinking niggers."

During the afternoon session, Waldo Anderson called several character witnesses to the stand, neighbors who testified that Floyd was a hardworking family man who didn't have a mean bone in his body. The preacher, whom Lily and Floyd hadn't seen in months, declared that Floyd was a "good Christian man whose guide was the Good Book." When Phineas Newsome asked one of his neighbors if the defendant got along with colored people, the man answered, "Well, Floyd was about like everybody else around here. He liked colored people in their place."

An attendant held the door open as John Earl swaggered up the aisle of the courtroom and then took the stand. Like Lester, whose testimony had preceded his older son's, John Earl swore that he, his brother, and his father had gone to the boy's house to "get him told" about "getting outta his place" with white women. "When we got there, the boy was setting on the porch, and me and my daddy stayed in the car and Floyd went up to talk to him. He only stayed with that boy about five minutes. Then he come back in the car, and we took off. When we left, that boy was sitting up on his porch and they wasn't a scratch on him. And that's the God's truth."

Lily's shoulders were stiff and aching as she listened to her brother-in-law. Why wasn't it enough to say that her husband had killed because he loved and wanted to protect her? She wanted everyone to know that.

When Waldo called Lily to the stand, her knees almost buckled as she was getting up.

"Now, Mrs. Cox," Waldo began, smiling at Lily in a patient, almost benevolent manner, "would you describe what happened on the day of September sixteenth?"

The lawyer had been over this question with her at least a hundred times, but Lily suddenly felt shaky. *They know I'm lying*, she thought, as she looked at the people. "My husband and I had gone to town in the truck to get some things from the drugstore, and on the way back we stopped off at the pool hall. Floyd went in, but I stayed outside, because he didn't like for me to go in there."

"So you stayed in the truck?"

"No, sir. It was hot, so I got out of the truck, just to

cool off a little bit. And as I was standing there, this colored boy, well, he come out and he give me such a look that I got scared. And I started to run back to the truck, but he wouldn't let me pass."

There was whispering in the courtroom, and Lily hesitated. She lowered her eyes. "And then what happened?" Waldo asked.

Lily fanned her neck with her fingers. She couldn't speak, with her heart beating so fast. She heard coughing, and her eyes moved toward the sound until she was staring into Odessa's unflinching eyes.

"And then what happened, Mrs. Cox?" Waldo repeated.

Even from across the room, Lily felt the heat of those eyes.

"Mrs. Cox?"

Lily looked at Waldo and spoke quickly. "He—he started saying nasty things to me. Horrible things." The beating of her heart was like gunshots exploding as she closed her eyes and imagined each one of the horrible, nasty things that the boy had said to her, until they became real. Somewhere in that vision was her uncle Charlie and his probing finger, as murderous as any weapon. Lily started crying, but by that time the noise from the courtroom—the outrage coming from the whites and the susurrant denials from the blacks— drowned out any sound she made.

Waldo dismissed Lily, because she was so "upset," and Phineas declined to cross-examine her. Lily sat in the stand, weeping softly, until the judge said gently, "You may step down, Mrs. Cox."

Waldo's last witness was Floyd himself. He had to repeat most of his answers because he was mumbling so low that nobody could hear him. He echoed his father's and brother's story about merely "giving the boy a piece of his mind" and swore that he never touched Armstrong Todd. "But he seemed kind of jumpy when I was talking to him," Floyd said. "I asked him what he was afraid of, and he said he'd had an argument with some nigger at the pool hall and that the guy had said he was going to get him.'"

The judge slammed down his gavel as the people in the back began muttering. "You nigras keep quiet, or out y'all go!"

Floyd sat in the stand, his mean eyes riveted on Odessa's face. Watching him, remembering the times she'd been under that same hard gaze, Lily began trembling.

The two lawyers gave brief, emotionless summations. Waldo Anderson stood before the jury and said, "Do your duty as Anglo-Saxon Americans." As for the prosecutor, Phineas Newsome coughed and sputtered for three minutes before finally saying, "Grant justice to the family of Armstrong Todd." He did not make eye contact with the twelve men he was admonishing, and they didn't look at him, either.

The jury brought in a not-guilty verdict in less than thirty minutes.

Lily carried Floydjunior in her arms and tried to get to Floyd, who was surrounded by reporters and photographers. As she pushed her way into the throng, Lily heard the questions. "How does it feel?" "Is it what you expected?" Then she heard: "Here's his wife and kid. Let's get a family picture." Someone grabbed her arms, and she was pulled next to Floyd, who didn't look at her, until one of the photographers said, "How about a kiss?" Floyd bent down, and Lily could smell his breath and his sweat, and then he was kissing her. She could feel his tongue pressed against her teeth, and the heat from his chest bearing down against her nipples, hear the words pelting against her mind like bullets: I got a man who'll kill for me.

She opened her eyes and saw the back of a woman with skin the color of the inside of a peach, the two braids like heavy ropes hanging down her back. She was balancing a little boy on her hip. Lily wanted to call out to her, but she had to swallow Ida's name with Floyd's spit.

23

Lily overheard the woman in front of her say, "Do you realize that never again will people be crippled and maimed by this dreadful disease. It's like a miracle." She shifted Floydjunior from one hip to the other, then gently rocked when he began to whimper. They'd been waiting outside Dr. Mitchell's office for nearly an hour, and the boy was getting cranky. An article had appeared in the *Hopewell Telegram* that the vaccine to prevent polio would be dispensed at the doctor's office at no cost, to anyone who wanted it. Lily arrived late and stood at the end of the line for white people, which led to Dr. Mitchell's front door. Now she craned her neck to see who was ahead of her and sighed, realizing it would be nearly another hour before her turn came. As soon as Lily saw the Negroes forming a silent queue outside the physician's back door, she pulled up the collar on her jacket and lifted Floydjunior in front of her to shield her face.

Since the trial, the Negroes had assiduously avoided whites, and now, being so close to so many, they were visibly tense. They had good reason to feel afraid. Floyd's acquittal and the press's subsequent departure gave the whites of the Delta license to act out the hostility that had been held in check by the glare of national attention. A week after the trial, a young black girl was whipped for "sassing" a white storekeeper. Two weeks later, only one week before Christmas, Sheriff Barnes took a colored man to the chain gang for three years for stealing three Moon Pies. The sheriff stopped at his own house and had the man remove his old shingle roof and put on a new one before transporting him to the state prison. The prisoner slept in the sheriff's backyard for nearly a week, his hands cuffed, his legs shackled. After the roof was finished, the prisoner erected a picket fence around the yard, to Mrs. Barnes's specifications.

A month had barely passed before another colored boy, this one seventeen years old, was shot down by a white man who was suspected of having fathered three of the lightest-colored children in the Quarters. The whole incident was hushed up pretty quickly by the Honorable Men of Hopewell; at least they kept the killing out of the local and national papers, which took some doing now that Yankees were hungry for news that would put southerners in an unfavorable light. Although it never made its way to print, the story was passed around town by whites and blacks alike.

At the Busy Bee, Jesse, Clyde, and Gilroy grumbled about "sassy nigras" as they sipped hot coffee to ward off the December chill. Gilroy said, "All that unrest in Montgomery has these niggers stepping outta they place. If they think Rosa Parks and some scrawny colored minister gonna come down here stirring up trouble, they been tasting too much moonshine."

None of the men who slurped coffee at the café could deny that right next door, so to speak, trouble was not only stirring, but bubbling and brewing. "Boycott!" Clyde said. "Them niggers will be walking till doomsday before they set down next to white folks." When articles in the Jackson paper informed them that after two months, the bus boycott in Montgomery was gaining momentum, they could only sputter angrily, "They better not try no shit like that here!"

But Hopewell's colored population did not have insurrection on their minds. They spoke not a word about integration, higher wages, or justice. Still, the newspaper reporters and television cameras were not quickly forgotten. The realization that people all over the country had witnessed their oppression encouraged new dreams. In subtle ways the death of Armstrong Todd began to change them. While the storekeeper was beating the colored girl with his own belt, the child, who was nearly twelve, was heard saying, "But I was waiting a long time," in a tone that implied her insubordination was justified. The owner of the market gave her three extra licks for her impudence. After the girl was whipped in the grocery store, in full view of her parents, her brother asked his father, "Why you let that white man do that to her, Daddy?" He was a child, not more than eight. The father's only answer was a lowering of his eyes. Nor did other Negro parents have a response for the persistent questions put to them by their children. More than one family packed up and boarded the IC because of this new, untamable spirit in their young.

The Moon Pie Thief turned out to have a rather hefty wife, who showed up at Sheriff Barnes's office one afternoon, inquiring about her husband. When he refused to reveal his whereabouts, she informed him in a loud, strident voice, "You ain't got no right just locking him up like that. These ain't no slavery times." She slammed the door as she left, shouting, "I'm calling me up some newspapers."

Even whites were shaken by the trembling earth beneath their feet. Little towheaded kids, children old enough to know better, asked their mothers, "Mama, is niggers as good as us?" More than one colored housekeeper scratched her head in astonishment when her madam suddenly inquired, her fingertips resting lightly on her maid's shoulder, "Do you think I treat you fair?" In the days after Armstrong's death, colored children ran home clutching shiny dimes that white men pressed into their palms for no reason whatsoever (although several did rub the little boys' heads first). Several of the well-to-do ladies from the Confederacy allowed themselves to consider that Armstrong Todd's death was awful and perhaps uncalled for, although they didn't utter these sentiments aloud, and certainly not to their husbands. They were both moved by the depth of their own sensitivity and frightened by its implications.

By the time Lily got inside the doctor's office, Floydjunior was asleep on her shoulder. Lily shook the boy gently. "Floydjunior, you gotta take a shot," she said, placing him on a chair next to Dr. Mitchell's nurse.

The boy took one look at the hypodermic and shinnied down the chair, then bolted out the door. Lily pushed her way through the throng, calling, "Floydjunior! Floydjunior!"

When her son saw her, he ran again. Lily caught him by his shirt collar. Floydjunior howled and wriggled away and started running again, but he took only a few steps before he bumped into another little boy, and both children fell down. Lily grabbed Floydjunior and then heard "Sweetbabe."

Lily froze, recognizing the voice and suddenly realizing that she was surrounded by silent colored people. If she turned around she'd be face to face with Ida. She didn't want to see the hatred in Ida's eyes. At the same time, she wanted to embrace her friend, to reclaim her. "Come on, Floydjunior," she said, grabbing her son's hand and lowering her eyes. She pulled him into the doctor's office and held him on her lap with both arms around him, while the nurse administered the shot. After her son finished crying, Lily said to the nurse, "Well, at least we don't have to worry about getting crippled no more."

After the first of the year, a new appliance store opened in Greenwood, offering everything from refrigerators to toasters, all with "easy payments." Weiner's, the Jewish-owned department store in Hopewell, began selling television sets "with low monthly payments" not long after the trial. Lily watched TV whenever she went into the department store, which wasn't frequently. If the owner had the sets on, sometimes she'd look at *I Love Lucy*, slipping into the world of the Ricardos, momentarily forgetting who she was. When the show was over, she'd walk out in a daze, mambo music playing in her head. She wanted to have red, red lips and a bow mouth, to be silly and forever rescued from any predicament. It felt good to escape from reality, from people staring at her in a cold, distant way, as though they didn't want to get too close. She wished Floyd would buy her a television.

Their money had started running out the day Armstrong Todd was killed. That was when the colored people stopped coming to the pool hall after work and the juke joint on weekends. After the trial Jake came in each day and swept the place out and then sat at the counter playing his harmonica, waiting for people to show up. A whole month passed, and no colored person set foot in the place.

Lily was visiting Louetta one morning, drinking coffee in her kitchen and looking out the window at their children playing, when her sister-in-law handed her a box of food: grits, peanut butter, Pet milk, and a lot of canned goods. "What's this for?" Lily asked.

Louetta smiled, and her fat cheeks bunched up in two crimson puffs. "I just thought this might help y'all out a little."

Lily put a finger with a bare nail in her mouth and began chewing. "Help us out?"

Louetta looked at her with such earnest dismay that later Lily berated herself for doubting her sister-in-law's sincerity. "Doesn't that Floyd tell you anything?" She set down her coffee cup. "Honey, y'all are outta the pool hall and juke joint business."

"What do you mean?"

Louetta leaned across the table, her eyes bright as polished stones. She looked as though she had a delicious bit of gossip to share, but then her face became somber and she covered Lily's hands with hers. "Honey, y'all don't have no more customers."

Lily stood up. "I hafta go," she said. "Floydjunior," she called through the window.

"Now sit down. Don't get upset. Stay here."

Lily didn't say anything. She walked out of the kitchen door and called Floydjunior until he ran to her. As she trudged out of the yard, Louetta called out, "You didn't hear it from me."

Lily didn't tell Floyd anything. Like him, she pretended, hoping that things would get better, until she couldn't pretend anymore, because there was no soap powder at the house, no toothpaste. And then no milk.

"What are they trying to do?" Floyd finally asked aloud one night when he and Lily were lying in bed, their backs barely touching.

"They're trying to starve us out," Lily said, her voice flat and thin. "They hate us." She barely had spoken the words before she began to cry.

They lay in the dark, Lily's sobbing the only noise. She didn't know whether she was crying because colored people hated her or because she felt helpless and afraid that they would become trash, that she'd turn into one of the gray-faced, toothless old white women who lived so close to the Quarters that they could smell what the niggers were having for dinner. In all her life she'd never conceived of Negroes as having any kind of power that could affect her. Now she was overwhelmed by the realization that the niggers not only could but were going to destroy her family without so much as raising their voices. Lily began to hate colored people with a simmering bitterness she had never known she possessed.

"Do you think," Lily suggested timidly one night in March, wiping at her eyes, which seemed to water perpetually, "do you think that maybe you ought to sell the place?" It was the first time she'd ever said anything about business or making money, but the words had formed in her mouth and rushed out before she could even think about them.

Floyd responded with customary silence, and for the next several weeks Lily waited impatiently for him to bring up the subject, but he never mentioned it. Weeks later, when she finally repeated her suggestion, she was far less tentative. "Are you trying to tell me what to do now?" Floyd said. His eyes were mean and narrow.

Lily quivered inside. "Maybe . . ." She wanted to say that maybe they could make enough money to live off until he thought of a way out, but Floyd's eyes stopped her. There was no sugar, she thought, but she didn't bring that up, either.

Weeks later, Floyd officially closed the pool hall and put a For Sale sign on the door. There were no takers, but he did manage to sell the pool table and cues for forty-five dollars.

Just looking at the dollar bills lying on the chest of drawers made Lily want things she thought she'd forgotten about: lipstick, shampoo, stockings, perfume, candy, movie magazines. She'd had none of these luxuries in so long that she'd almost stopped believing in the possibility of her ever having them again. She didn't dare hope for what she really wanted: a television.

Lily stood in front of her mailbox, trying to decide whether or not she should open it. Floyd was sitting on the porch, smoking and watching her. For months, that had seemed to be all he ever did. The quick walk to the edge of the yard to get the mail was a respite from Floyd's vigilant gaze. She rarely went out of the yard anymore. Maybe once in a while she'd go with Floyd to visit his family, and of course she had to buy food, but mostly she stayed inside. She didn't like the way people stared at her or turned their heads to avoid having to speak when she approached. Men's eyes walked all over her body as though they were familiar with it. And the women, well, they might as well have spit on her.

The Negroes glared whenever she passed them alone. It was as if they dared her to tell her man. They were laughing at her.

She hated them.

The letters had begun arriving even before the trial was concluded. Lily screamed when she read the first one. "Motherfucker, we are coming down there and lynch your white ass," it said. The second letter was addressed to Lily. It contained a picture of Armstrong Todd after he'd been shot. The boy looked as if he was asleep.

Now she shuffled and then stacked the letters in her hand. Some were for Floyd Cox, some for her, others for the two of them. They came from faraway places like New York and Chicago and Philadelphia, even Memphis. A few came from the Delta.

Lily trudged back to the porch and handed all the letters to Floyd. "You read them," she said. She wanted to go in the house and lie down before Floydjunior woke up from his nap. Mostly she didn't want to be with Floyd when he opened the mail.

As she cleaned up the kitchen after supper, Lily brooded about the money stashed in Floyd's pocket. If she had just a few dollars, she'd feel better. She went out back, grabbed some wood from the pile, and put it inside the stove in the kitchen. She balled up an old newspaper and shoved it on top and then tossed a lit match inside. Then she went outside to pump water for her bath.

While she was in the kitchen washing herself in an aluminum tub, Lily stared at her feet, which were small and bare, her toes unpolished. She held out her hands and studied her bare, uneven nails, remembering the time not so long ago when her toes and fingertips were bright red, as bright as lollipops, and how once she dreamed of taking those toes and fingernails to Memphis. As she shampooed her hair she thought about the small blue bottle of perfume in her bedroom; there were only a few drops left.

She slid into bed smelling clean and fresh, her hair still damp. Floyd's body was very still beside her; she pushed into him with her breasts. Despite everything, she was still beautiful, and Floyd would always take care of her; that was the most important thing. "Floyd," Lily said softly, "we need some milk for Floydjunior. He ain't had none in two days and ..." She knew as soon as the words were out that she had spoken too soon, that she should have waited until later. Lately it was always so frightening to ask Floyd for things. Sometimes, when she wanted him to buy food for the baby or to please give her thirty cents for cigarettes, she would find herself biting down on her lip, afraid to speak. Before, she knew how to make him want to give things to her, but now as she brushed up against him in their bed, he pushed her away. And it was her fault, for not waiting for the right moment.

"You blaming me for that?" Floyd said. He leaned over the bed and reached for his shirt where he'd dropped it on the floor. He fished around in his pocket until he found a cigarette, and then he lit it.

"No, honey," Lily said. She knew that she didn't have the right tone; her voice wasn't soft enough. Sometimes when she thought about what might happen to her and Floydjunior if Floyd wasn't able to take care of them, if things didn't start getting right again, it made her so weak and nervous she would walk out back and run pump water over her head.

"Do you want me to go over to Louetta's tomorrow and ask her if they got some milk?" Lily didn't mean for the words to sound so irritable.

Floyd leapt to his feet with such swift fury that the mattress beneath him bounced wildly. "Dammit. You saying I can't feed my own kid?"

Lily trembled. She had gone about this all wrong. Backward.

"Floyd . . ." Lily said. She put her hand on his arm; he snatched it away.

"We don't need no handouts."

"I'm not saying—"

"Then what are you saying? Huh?"

His palm came across her cheek, burning like a flame. She felt the heat, and then she saw a quick, blinding light as he hit her again. Blood gushed from her lip. She covered her face with her hands. Floyd began punching her in the stomach. She screamed, "Stop! Please stop!" and wondered if she resembled her mother, hunched over and cowering. She backed off the other side of the bed. Her mind was spinning, as it did the time Floyd gave her a great big jelly jar full of white lightning. He just stared at her vacantly. Instead of rage, there was defeat in his eyes, and she didn't know which one was harder to see.

24

Ida kept her eyes on Sweetbabe as he scampered beside her; she tried hard not to look at Odessa's yard as she passed, but she couldn't stop herself. Even though almost a year had passed since Odessa moved to Detroit, where one of her sisters lived, tears came to Ida's eyes whenever she even so much as glanced at the empty house.

This early evening she was walking at a brisk pace, carrying five fried-chicken suppers to old Miss Rozelle, who ran a rooming house. Ida was a good cook and had begun to earn extra money selling dinners. She carried the food in a sack with one hand and tried to hold Sweetbabe's hand with her other, but he kept snatching it away and racing ahead of her. When she called his name, he looked over his shoulder, grinned, and kept running. They were nearing a bend, and sometimes even on this sleepy, dusty road, cars would come speeding around the curve. Ida ran up to her son and grabbed him firmly by his fingers. "You hold my hand, boy. Stop trying to be so mannish." She knew that she was supposed to whip his behind—it was the way all the colored mothers dealt with even minimal defiance in their children—but she couldn't bring herself to cut a switch or even swat him with her hand. She liked Sweetbabe's runaway spirit, and something told her that her son was a child to be reasoned with and not whipped. Besides, she had noticed that the white mothers—not the rednecks and trash but the women

162

from the Confederacy, who had colored maids to clean and tend the babies—never hit their children.

She dropped off the dinners at Miss Rozelle's, and when the old woman put $3.75 in her hand, Ida became so excited she almost forgot to thank her. Every penny was being saved so that she and Sweetbabe could move to Chicago. She had decided that she wasn't going to wait any longer. Lizzie Mae was nearly fifteen; she could help with the younger ones. Besides, if she got a good job in Chicago, she could send money home. She had nearly seventy-five dollars saved; when she got two hundred dollars, which she figured she'd have by the end of the year, she and Sweetbabe were leaving. What happened to Armstrong would never be her son's fate.

Ida and Sweetbabe passed the edge of the colored settlement and kept going. Before she realized how far she'd walked, she could see the railroad station. Though she admitted that she missed sitting on the bench and watching the trains—she hadn't done that in a year— she couldn't bring herself to confess that she missed Lily. Now, thinking of Lily, she started shaking with rage; the woman hadn't even looked her in the eyes at Dr. Mitchell's office. She'd heard talk in the Quarters that even the white people didn't want anything to do with Lily. Served the heifer right, Ida thought. She tried to push out of her mind the times they talked and dreamed together, the night the white girl cried out the story about her uncle. Such memories only made her pity Lily, and she wanted to hate her. "Let's go home, Sweetbabe," she said.

But the lights from the station, the only lights around them, attracted the small boy, and he pulled away from his mother and ran toward the depot.

"Sweetbabe!" Ida stamped her foot. Then she laughed, watching the boy's legs move so fast, seeing him look over his shoulder to see if his mama was coming after him. "Boy, you so silly," she called, still laughing.

The dog came out of nowhere, like a sudden summer storm. A scraggly, mean-looking mutt, part boxer and just about that size, swaying as if he was being blown across the road. He jumped on Sweetbabe and bit him three times before Ida had time to scream. The dog ran off when he saw her racing toward him with blood in her eyes.

"JesusJesusJesus." Ida took a deep breath. "Hush, baby," she said, her hands snatching away Sweetbabe's clothes, touching every part of his body to see where he was hurt. He cried and tried to pull away, but Ida held him with stubborn, iron fingers and found the three tiny punctures, not even bleeding, just three small pricks that held her entire life inside. *Please don't let my baby have rabies,* she prayed. She picked up Sweetbabe, then sat down in the road and cradled him in her arms. She was too scared and frantic to think, so she rocked back and forth until she could feel the panic ebbing away. She had to get Sweetbabe to a doctor.

Ida stood and peered down the road. She thought of running back home but remembered that her father had gone to a Mason meeting, taking the truck. The only other person she knew with a car was at least two miles past her house. She squinted toward the train station, and sitting under the only streetlight for miles around was an ancient mule and wagon. Behind it, in the shadows, was a blue Cadillac.

When the train stopped at Hopewell, Clayton was surprised at how tired he felt, far more exhausted than if he had driven down to Hattiesburg. He'd been to a wedding and done a bit of courting, public wooing that would put him in good stead with his father, who was no longer subtle about his desire that his only son find a bride. How had his father put it? "Now, boy, you don't have to get rid of that gal you got stashed away, but by God, I want some grandchildren." He should have driven, he knew that now, but he'd allowed himself to become so overwhelmed by the enticement of more than three hours of leisurely, uninterrupted reading time that he never considered the lurking horror that awaited him on board: time to think. For more than a year, he'd plotted his entire life so that there was absolutely no space for wondering, for rehashing, for idle and dangerous musings. Clayton thought Faulkner would occupy the entire ride, but *Intruder in the Dust* had been more engrossing than he'd expected, and when he finished it, just as the train pulled into Jackson, and lost his seatmate simultaneously, there was nothing else to do but drift into deep contemplation.

At first he thought of Ellen, the Hattiesburg debutante who'd invited him to her cousin's wedding. She was pretty enough and rich enough to demand his contemplation. Ellen came from a good family and had nice breasts, big and firm; the thought of them should have caused him to swell and stiffen, but it didn't. He'd barely paid attention to Ellen's breasts when, only hours after the wedding, he found them in his mouth, thrust there with only a halfhearted invitation on his part. Nothing at all really had his attention these days.

He looked at the empty seats around him, searching for a newspaper, a magazine, something discarded and readable, but there was nothing. He looked out the window at the rows and rows of cotton. It was while the train sped by the cotton that visions of Armstrong Todd entered his mind. Placing his hands on either side of his head, Clayton pushed against his skull, as though he were cracking a walnut. He shut his eyes tight, but Armstrong was waiting for him in the dark and was there again when he opened his eyes.

When Delotha left town with her son's body, his father had summoned him to the library. Clayton stood before him, in front of the immense walnut desk. "You know that woman left town and took the body with her," his father said.

Clayton hadn't smiled, but he failed to mask the pleasure in his eyes.

"Did you help that gal?"

"No, sir, I didn't."

"But you wanted to, didn't you?"

"Father, I did what you told me to do. Haven't I always done that?"

His father stood up. Clayton was always amazed at how huge his father seemed, how imposing. He put both hands down on the desk in front of him. His hands were big, his fingers long and thick. "There's something wrong with the way you think. Always has been. If I find out—and I will find out—if I find out that you had anything to do with that gal leaving town . . ."

"I did what you told me to do."

"You don't understand what's important," his father said. He sighed and sat down at the desk, eyeing the books that lined the shelves.

"I understand what's important, Father. I just don't act on it."

The truth of those words was uppermost in Clayton's mind as the train gave a lurch and pulled into Hopewell, where he was the only passenger to get off.

He had just put his suitcase in the back seat and was opening the front door, when he heard her voice. "Mr. Pinochet, please, for God's sake, take me to a doctor. A dog just bit my baby. Please, Lord Jesus. Please."

"You're William's daughter, aren't you?"

She barely nodded, and said softly, "Ida."

Clayton stared at the woman's face and was hypnotized by the wildness in her eyes. She looked stricken and crazy and desperate, and her cry for help wasn't a plea at all; it was an order.

"Get in."

The Cadillac took off, and they had gone for half a mile before Clayton realized that the woman and the little boy were sitting next to him. On the front seat.

"I'm going to take you to Dr. Richards," Clayton said.

"Dr. Richards don't treat colored people, sir. Take me to Dr. Mitchell. You know where he stay?"

"Yes."

In the dimness, Clayton stole glances at the woman, at her pale skin and eyes, her thick braids and the way she clutched her child, as though her life depended upon holding him tight.

"How many times did he bite him?" Clayton asked.

"Three. Two on his leg and one on his arm. I thank God for you, Mr. Pinochet."

The boy was whimpering softly as his mother rocked him and the car sped along the dark highway.

"He won't die, will he, Mr. Pinochet?"

Clayton looked at the woman; there were tears in her eyes. He felt her hand clutching his arm and leaned over and patted her shoulder. "Don't worry. He'll be all right. I'll help you."

The porch light at Dr. Mitchell's house came on when Clayton knocked at the door. He could hear movement inside and then a deep, almost gruff "Who is it?"

After Clayton responded, the door opened and Dr. Mitchell, a spare, unsmiling man wearing glasses, peered at them silently for a moment, before raising a finger toward Ida, who was crying and trembling. "You. Go around the back door."

Dr. Mitchell led them to the smaller of the two examining rooms. There was a scale and a table with stiff white cloth spread across it; the air was filled with alcohol fumes. He put the boy on the examining table and inspected his wounds.

"I count three bites, Mother. You count any more?"

"No, sir. Just three." Ida began to moan and rock back and forth on the balls of her feet.

"All right. All right. Stay calm now, Mother."

"Is he gon' die, Dr. Mitchell?" She wrapped her long,

thin arms around her body and clutched her middle as though holding herself upright, willing herself to stand. "I can't lose him. I can't lose my son."

The room felt hot to Clayton, unbearably hot and airless. He moved closer to the window in the back of the room and raised it. For a moment he wished that he'd never seen the pale-yellow woman and her small boy. The last thing he wanted to witness was how much colored women loved their sons. Her words made him think too much about everything he wanted to forget. Watching the woman cry made him feel a deep sorrow and an even deeper shame, a sudden, frenzied fear that he didn't expect.

Clayton was surprised to be standing next to the doctor, who was hovering over the boy. "How's he doing, Doctor?"

Dr. Mitchell glanced up at Clayton. He tilted his head back a little. "She work for you?" he asked.

Because he was taken by surprise, Clayton said, "Yes," and then sat down on one of the hard-back chairs.

"You ever seen the dog before, Mother?"

"No, sir. Is he gon' be all right?"

"If he's got rabies, he's going to die. That's the fact, Mother."

Clayton watched the woman's face turn pale and grayish. She was standing, and her entire body began fluttering, and then suddenly she just slumped, caved in as though someone had punched her in the stomach. "Here now," Clayton said, lifting her by her elbows and pulling up a chair for her. "You just sit down. Rest yourself." He turned to Dr. Mitchell, who was washing the boy's wounds with soap and water and hydrogen peroxide. "Isn't there anything you can ..."

"I would tell you to take him over to Chilton County Hospital, but they don't take colored. I'm going to give the boy a shot for infection, and I'll give her some ointment for the bites. If the dog wasn't rabid, the child will heal up. Best thing she can do is keep an eye on him. If he's got rabies, God help her, she'll know within a week. Poor little thing."

When they returned to the car, Ida and Sweetbabe sat in the back. Clayton saw her in the rearview mirror, holding her son against her shoulder, her head buried in his neck.

She started crying again when he dropped her off, soft, thin sobs that seemed to rack her entire body. She managed to thank him for his help and was about to climb the wooden steps that led to a clapboard house, when he called out to her. "I'll pray for the boy." He never prayed. He didn't know why he said he would, but he knew that he had made a solemn promise that he wouldn't break.

Beneath Ida's sad eyes he saw a smile. "Thank you, Mr. Pinochet," she said, then disappeared into the house.

Clayton came back a week later, early on a Saturday afternoon. Along the road, people who were sitting out on their porches, digesting dinner stood up and craned their necks when the blue Cadillac drove into Ida's yard; they leaned forward when Clayton got out. Ida came to the door and shooed her brothers and sisters back in the house. "Oh," she said, when she saw who it was.

"I just came by to see if your boy was all right," Clayton said shyly. He was conscious of all the stares coming from the neighbors and surprised by Ida's beauty, fully visible in the waning daylight.

"Yessir. He's all better. Look like he didn't have no rabies after all, thanks be to God. Sweetbabe!" She called loudly, and her son scampered out the front door. "See. Fat and healthy. His name is William. We call him Sweetbabe." She laughed and scooped the boy up in her arms and kissed him on the neck.

"Well, that's fine. Just fine. I'll be going."

"Thank you for your concern, Mr. Pinochet. Say thank you, Sweetbabe," she admonished the little boy, who mumbled "Thank you" like a little parrot.

Clayton nodded, shyness taking over, and he stepped down from the porch. He looked to the left and right; the neighbors coughed and averted their eyes. "Well, I'm glad he's better."

He felt lighthearted when he drove away. He turned on the radio and whistled "Hound Dog" along with Elvis Presley. His good mood took him through the rest of the early evening, and later that night, when Marguerite opened the door to the neat brick bungalow, it occurred to Clayton that it was the first time in a long time that he hadn't come to her burdened with sadness.

Marguerite handed him a glass filled with bourbon and ice. She had been singing when he came in the house, and as he drank she hummed soft, hopeful notes until the air around them vibrated with the unseen spirit that inhabited her song. "What are you singing?" he asked her.

"An old song. My mama and them used to always sing it."

She watched him drink, and when he was finished she came over to him and put her arms around his neck. Clayton patted her arms, then removed them. He took a long look at her face. "Do you ... are there ... ?"

"What? What you want? You want to eat?" Marguerite asked anxiously.

"I was just wondering if you had any board games or cards. Checkers. Anything like that? What do you like to play?"

She stared at him. "You ain't never asked me about no games before." Then she went into the dining room, and when she came back she was holding a box of checkers and a board. "I bet I can beat you," she said.

They played for hours, first at the dining room table

and then in the bedroom, where they put the board in the middle of the bed and sat cross-legged, laughing at each other's foolish moves, each crowing about his skill, sitting in silent concentration. "You seem so happy tonight. Usually you sad. Real quiet," Marguerite said.

"I'm not sad now." Clayton gently placed the game on the floor and reached for Marguerite.

Marguerite sat up. She was wearing nothing under her thin robe, and when Clayton undid her sash, her jelly-bean-shaped nipples jutted out. Clayton bent down and put one of her nipples into his mouth and stroked the other one with his thumb until Marguerite began to breathe faster, as if she'd been running. Pulling her body beneath him, he slid inside her, was still for a moment, and then, with his fingers, he spread out her hair around her head like a fan.

His white hand was clamped over hers; looking at the contrast of their skins excited him. He began to move inside her.

When they had finished, he asked her, "How old are you?"

She looked surprised and then a little frightened. "Twenty-four. Why you ask me that?"

"I just wondered, that's all. Next time I come by, I'll bring you a Scrabble game. You know how to play that?"

Marguerite shook her head.

"It's a word game. Whoever makes the best words wins."

"I'm not too good at spelling."

"They don't have to be big words," he said, laughing.

Marguerite hesitated. "I'm not too good even with little ones," she said softly.

"Spell 'cat.' "

"*C-a-t,*" she said proudly.

"Spell 'mouse.' "

"*M* . . ." She turned her head and started to climb out of bed.

Clayton pulled her back. The skin on her shoulder was warm. "I'll teach you," he said.

25

Floyd could tell that Lily wanted a cigarette by the way her eyes followed the Winston dangling between his lips. He had two others, but he didn't offer her one. Lily was sitting at the table next to Floydjunior, who was feeding himself oatmeal and jelly bread. "Is it any coffee?" Floyd asked Lily, who shook her head and didn't take her eyes off his lips. He tucked his shirt in his pants and buckled his belt while he stalked around the kitchen, looking for coffee. Floydjunior reached out for him and called, "Daddy," but Floyd ignored his son.

"You want some breakfast, Floyd?" Lily asked, getting up. "I thought I'd ask you what you wanted, because there ain't much here. We out of eggs and bacon. There ain't no grits, but there's some oatmeal and some—"

"I ain't hungry." He had to be absolutely starving to bring himself to eat the government surplus that Lily had taken it upon herself to bring into his house. Nasty powdered milk, peanut butter in a silver can, stiffer than a dead coon. That's what the United States of America called giving a veteran a helping hand, he thought. Just looking at the plain wrapped boxes was enough to make him want to slam his fist into a wall. He told Lily he didn't want no handouts, that he could earn his own way, but all she cared about was Floydjunior having milk. She didn't care about how he felt.

Out of the corner of his eye, Floyd watched his wife gazing at their son, and he felt a sharp cramp in his stomach. "I'll be back later," he yelled as he closed the kitchen door behind him. He was halfway across the front yard when he heard Lily behind him on the porch.

"Floyd," she called.

He turned around.

"Are they gonna pay you today?"

"Yeah," he said, and started walking again.

He had a job digging a series of ditches on one of the large plantations. The farm manager who hired him had looked at Floyd skeptically and said, "Now, you understand that you're gon' be working with niggers."

"Yessir," Floyd had said. The man had shrugged his shoulders and told him to come back the next morning at seven o'clock. The pay was two dollars for the day, fifty cents higher than what the colored were earning.

He took a back road to the job site, which was about a mile away, to avoid passing the pool hall and seeing the faded For Sale sign, which had been up for more than a year. A few months earlier, he was on his way home carrying three freshly killed rabbits in a burlap bag—he'd bought them from one of his neighbors—and he passed the place and, without thinking, opened the door and walked in. The pool table was gone, and the room seemed large to him. He remembered when the place was full of laughing Negroes, spending money and having a good time. "This here was the only spot they could come and have fun," he said aloud. "If it wasn't for me, they wouldn't had nothing." He was silent for a moment; then he yelled, "I ain't never mistreated nobody." He stood there a long time, breathing in the faint sour odors of pickles and mildew, until he became aware of the sound of raindrops. But when he looked around, he discovered that it wasn't rain that was falling but the blood from the dead rabbits, dripping through the gunny-sack onto the dirty floor.

"I put you in a spot by yourself," the foreman said, handing him a shovel. Floyd walked over to the place the man had pointed out and began digging.

After half an hour, his arms felt as though they were about to fall off. He'd done construction but nothing as hard as this work. He looked around him; the niggers were digging in an almost synchronized rhythm. From time to time one of them would say something, and the others would laugh. Floyd strained to hear what the men were saying.

By noon his entire body was sore. He sat down under a tree and ate his lunch of government cheese between two slices of white bread. Lily had fixed him a jug of iced tea, but there wasn't enough sugar in it. He lifted his head when he smelled the chicken, and glancing over to where the colored men sat in a clump, he could see that several of them had fried-chicken sandwiches and huge slabs of cake. Then he saw their eyes, full of rage and hatred, just staring at him. They want to kill me, he realized. For a moment, he couldn't move or even breathe.

By the end of the day, when the boss placed the two dollars in Floyd's hand, his palms were almost too sore to hold the money. "This ain't no fit work for a white man," the foreman said. Floyd didn't comment. "Say, if you'd like a little taste, I got a friend not far from here that brews some mighty good hooch. Just go down this road and take the first bend to the right and keep going straight about a hundred yards. A colored fellow will come out, and you tell him I sent you." Floyd nodded, carefully putting the two dollars in his pocket.

He followed the curve of the road to a clearing and stood there for a few minutes. When he saw Jake, he was surprised.

He looked older, thinner, and even uglier than before. The colored man's head began bobbing like a cork in water. "How you been getting on, Mr. Floyd?" Jake asked, grinning and nodding his head.

After a day of feeling shut out and lonely, Floyd was warmed by the sight of his old employee. "Oh, I'm doing all right. How 'bout you?"

"Can't complain. Don't nobody want to hear it." Jake and Floyd laughed together. "So, Mr. Floyd, what can I do for you?"

"How much is a pint?"

"Thirty-five cents, suh."

Floyd handed Jake the money.

"You wait right here, Mr. Floyd."

Jake returned in less than five minutes and handed Floyd a small bottle wrapped up in newspaper. Floyd took off the paper, unscrewed the top, and began gulping down the liquor, not even pausing when it burned his throat.

"Careful now, Mr. Floyd. You gon' wake up tomorrow morning with your head split wide open," Jake said, chuckling, but Floyd kept drinking until he'd emptied a third of the bottle. He turned to go, but then he stopped and spun around to face the tall, dark man in front of him, who started grinning as soon as he saw Floyd's eyes. "I want to ask you something, Jake."

"Yassuh."

"I always treated you right, didn't I?" Floyd asked, wiping his mouth with the back of his hand.

"Oh, yassuh." Jake stepped backward. His eyes darted back and forth. "You one of the most fairest mens I know."

It was dark by the time Floyd got home. He finished the last swallow of whiskey on his front porch, and then he fell over one of the chairs. When he looked up, Lily was standing in the doorway, staring down at him. Floydjunior was next to her. "What happened?" Lily asked, but he could tell by the way her lips were pressed together, the way her eyes avoided his, that she knew he'd been drinking.

"You don't want to look at me?" Floyd said.

"I kept supper—"

"You kept me some supper, did you? What do we

have for supper—something courtesy of the United
States government?"

"I'm taking Floydjunior inside," Lily said. Her voice
sounded frail, as though the words and the person
speaking them could be broken into tiny pieces and
scattered all over.

"You ain't going nowhere," Floyd said. He lunged in
front of the door. "You don't need me to get your food
no more, is that it?"

"Floyd . . ." Lily said. He liked the way she called his
name. He liked her begging him. Why shouldn't she
beg him? If it hadn't been for her, he'd still have his
business. He wouldn't have to be digging ditches with
niggers for two dollars a day. If she'd listened to him
and stayed out of the place like he told her to, they
wouldn't be eating surplus government food like they
was. . . .

"I ain't trash," he screamed.

Floydjunior started crying. Lily rushed toward Floyd,
both hands balled up into small fists, held elbow-high.
"You scaring him! You scaring him!"

His neck and back were unbelievably stiff as he
lurched toward Lily, as though his body had been
yanked and twisted out of alignment. He'd never felt
such soreness in his arms as when he grabbed her; it
was as if someone had taken a hammer to his muscles.
The palms of his hands were lumpy with blisters; he
could feel them oozing as he slapped her. He was hurting so bad he almost didn't feel his wife shaking as he
punched her. He hit her again to make her stop shaking,
and again to shut her up. And she did, making a helpless, gulping noise like a person accidentally swallow-
ing an ice cube. Her palm covered up Floydjunior's
mouth so that only the thinnest whimper emerged. They
were so quiet he thought that both of them might not be
breathing, except they were watching him with eyes as
wide and frightened as Armstrong's had been.

* * *

Floyd wasn't surprised when John Earl told him that he and his family were moving to Birmingham. After the trial, his hauling jobs dried up. For no reason that his brother could understand, his customers stopped calling him, and when he contacted them they made excuses. After six months passed he couldn't keep up the payments on the house, and when the truck broke down he couldn't afford to fix it, so he sold it for half of what it was worth. For the last few months, he and Louetta and their two girls had been living with Lester and Mamie.

The night before John Earl and his family left for Alabama, Mamie cooked a farewell dinner. "Lord, we want to thank you for putting food on our table this evening. We're grateful for your blessed bounty, Lord," Lester prayed. "And we just want to ask that you be with John Earl and his precious family as they travel to Birmingham to start a new life. And Lord . . ." Lester's voice broke. He stood up and walked over to John Earl and placed both hands on his shoulders. "This is my son," he said, his lips trembling. "My son."

Floyd bent his head down low over his plate and began eating very fast.

"It'll be all right, Daddy," John Earl said. "Why, me and Louetta and the girls will do just fine in Birmingham. Don't worry about us."

"You'll have to ride the bus with the niggers."

There was absolute silence at the table; even the children were quiet.

"Well, maybe you can be somebody in Birmingham," Mamie said. She held her hand over her heart; her fingers were wrinkled, the cuticles ragged with bits of food under her fingernails. "You stay here, they'll treat you like trash. Just like they done my poor Dolly," Mamie said. She began wiping at her eyes with the corner of her apron and shaking her head. "Them Pinochets and Settleses and all them other fancy folks, they won't let you rise above where you started from, not around here they won't. If you can't trace your people back to General Lee, well, then, you're nothing, is what you are. I tell you, them rich folks'll side with a nigger before they side with us."

"We're scattering all over the place," Lester said. "The wind's just blowing us every which way, all because . . . all because . . ." His eyes darted between Lily and Floyd.

Floyd turned, to see his father staring at him. "That's right, blame me," Floyd said, his breath coming in short, blustery spurts, patches of red sprouting on his cheeks. He pushed his plate away and stood up. "I told you I handled that boy. I told you. But no, no, it wasn't good enough for you. You said I had to teach that boy a lesson. So that's what we set out to do. The three of us. We all was in on it, Daddy. All of us. But who sits in jail for weeks, huh? Who gets charged? Who goes to trial? You talk about the family scattering. Well, you ask me, it's done been scattered a long time."

"What was we supposed to do, Floyd, sit in jail just to keep you company?" John Earl asked. "They dropped the charges against us."

"You was supposed to be my brother. And you was supposed to be my father," Floyd said, staring at Lester. He snatched his hand away from Lily, who was trying to grab it. He wanted to say that they were supposed to love him. He could taste those words in his mouth. "All my life, nothing I've ever done has been good enough." He was almost whining now, his voice high and trembly, his eyes searching his father's expressionless face. "Now you're blaming me. I done what you wanted me to do."

Floyd glanced at his father's stern, silent face. He didn't look at his wife. He didn't see the shock, the pain, and the budding rage that were plainly visible as she heard the words "I done what you wanted me to do." And by the time he did look, her eyes and mouth were tranquil, her feelings hidden in a place that would take him years to find.

26

Delotha was surprised when, after the funeral, she began to get letters; she was stunned the first time cash fell out of one of them. About half of the letters were from white people, asking her forgiveness. Folded into most of these were five- and ten-dollar bills, sometimes checks for even greater amounts. One letter read: "One of these days the colored and the white will learn to live like brothers and sisters." The letter was signed, "Yours in Christ, Miss Minnie Mobley," and was postmarked from Denmark, South Carolina.

There was a letter from Hopewell with five hundred-dollar bills inside. "I hope this money will help you get started on a new life," the letter said. Delotha looked at the money over and over again, scarcely believing that she was holding such a huge sum in her hands. The letter was unsigned, but she knew it was from Clayton Pinochet. She felt that, just as she believed that he wanted to help her the morning he came to Odessa's.

She got letters and sympathy cards from colored people too, and some of these contained money, although not as much as the white people gave her. The colored people sent one or two dollars, and sometimes they enclosed fifty-cent pieces and quarters. Even dimes.

In all, she received nearly three thousand dollars. She gave Odessa five hundred dollars to help her get settled in Detroit. The rest she put in the bank and forgot about.

There was hate mail also. One letter read: "You black

bitch. If you taught that nigger boy of yours how to act
around white folks, he wouldn't be dead. Served him
right." Another said: "You better keep your black ass
right there in Chicago. If you come back to Mississippi,
we'll kill you too."

She put the letters on top of her dresser in two haphazard stacks.

Nearly a year after Armstrong's funeral, she leaned
over the long table at the Fine Rest Mattress factory on
the city's west side and examined the ticking for holes
and other flaws. She had worked there for nearly seven
years, and the cottony smell of the place was familiar to
her. The women around her talked softly; when she
looked up, they turned away. They knew what had happened to her son and had sent a floral bouquet to the funeral, with a pale blue sash that had the words "With
Sympathy" embossed on the fabric. At first when
Delotha returned to work, they felt sorry for her, but after months passed and she still barely spoke, they began
to think she was odd.

Flexing her fingers, she glanced at the clock. She was
tired, her shoulders achy. Break time was an hour away,
and she had nearly two hours before lunch. The supervisor, a fat Polish woman, nodded when Delotha told
her she was going to the washroom. Inside the small cu-
bicle, she smoked two Salems, one behind the other.
Then she vomited. She rinsed her mouth with water
from her cupped hand before going back to the table.

At the blowing of the noon whistle, she felt the sensation of pressure, and when she looked up, a woman
was tapping on her shoulder. Shirley, who worked next
to her, was standing in front of her. Delotha saw her
mouth move up and down like that of a ventriloquist's
dummy, but she couldn't hear any sound coming out.
When the woman's lips became still, Delotha shook her
head and fled past her. She went outside to an alley behind the factory and began eating the lunch she'd

brought. She could feel the bologna sandwich in her mouth but couldn't taste anything. She dumped the food back into the paper bag and threw it in the trash can; then she smoked under the hot August sun until it was time to go back inside. There was a slight wind blowing, and she could smell meat, raw and slightly decaying, coming from the stockyards, which were a few blocks to the west. When she first came from Mississippi, the odor used to sicken her, but she barely noticed it anymore.

When the bell rang, Delotha opened the door. Nathaniel came in and handed her a bottle of Scotch and two fried-chicken dinners from a church supper sale. He took a long look at her apartment, which, Delotha realized, he'd started doing recently. There were ashtrays full of cigarette butts in all the rooms and a stack of unread newspapers by the door. Dirty plates were piled up in the kitchen sink, and the trash can was overflowing. The door to her room was wide open; her bed was unmade, and a jumble of clothes lay on the floor. Delotha watched Nathaniel—neat and dapper in dark blue pants, a white shirt, and a plaid sports coat—as he looked around. His hair was cut down low, and his mustache was trimmed as neatly as a preacher's. She didn't care; whatever he thought, whatever he said didn't make any difference to her.

He poured them both a drink, and she lit a cigarette. "Why you gotta smoke so much, baby?" he asked. She didn't reply, just sipped the Scotch and kept smoking. Nathaniel started eating his supper, which was still warm, but Delotha told him that she wasn't hungry, she'd eat later, and he frowned at that. She didn't care about his anger, about pleasing him or not pleasing him.

After they finished their drinks, she went into the bedroom, which reeked of Evening in Paris. Days before, she had broken a bottle and hadn't bothered wiping up the spill. She picked up the clothes on the floor

and tossed them on a chair, then smoothed the sheets
down while Nathaniel watched. She took off her clothes
as though she were sleepwalking, before he even kissed
her, and when she saw him staring at her, she said,
"Come on. What are you waiting for?"

When he entered her, she began crying.

"Jesus Christ!" he said, pulling out, holding his rigid
penis in his hand, stroking it consolingly. This had happened before. He stood up and began putting on his
clothes. She stayed in the bed, weeping quietly. "I can't
do nothing for you, baby," he said, and closed the front
door behind him.

Nathaniel called her once or twice after that and sent
her a card on her birthday, but then she didn't hear from
him again. She didn't miss him, or the friends she'd had
at work, or the people from church (she never went
anymore), or going to the movies on Saturday nights
(she stopped going), or her sisters and brothers, or even
Odessa. She didn't miss any of them.

She began dreaming of baby boys, a yard full of sons
who all looked like Armstrong, all calling her name.
The same dream two or three times a week.

The tiny explosions began right before Christmas.
One night when she was pressing her hair, the straightening comb singed her edges and she slammed it across
the floor. She picked the comb up and beat it against
the linoleum until the wooden handle broke off in her
trembling hand and there was a burned spot on the
floor.

Her sister came one Saturday morning in February
and looked around with bold, judgmental eyes. "'Lotha,
why you don't clean up?" she asked. Outside, snow was
falling and the wind was howling like a starving wild
animal.

Afterward Delotha remembered standing up, and she
remembered shouting, "Get out! Get out! Get out!" An
hour later, she was shocked to find herself seated at the

kitchen table, a cup of tea in front of her, her sister's hand moving over her back as softly as a prayer.

She couldn't stop shaking.

The Monday after Mother's Day, she boarded her evening bus on Western Boulevard and worked her way down the crowded aisle, heading toward the only empty seat she saw. But when she got to it, a man was settling himself there, opening a newspaper, his thick white fingers carefully turning the pages. There was a terrible beating in her chest, almost, but not quite, pain. Leaning down over the man, Delotha became conscious, not of the torrent of curses she was yelling, but of the man's startled gray eyes, the confusion and fear in them. She didn't recall the bus driver's asking her to leave, his pushing her off the bus; she recollected only standing in the street, watching the bus recede. She remembered the people walking by, the shock on their faces, the way they trudged on, then looked back at her over their shoulders, watching her, listening to her scream long after the bus had disappeared. "You white mother-fucker. I'm not sitting in the back."

Two days later, she went to AAA Pawn Shop, which was only a block from the el, on Forty-seventh Street. Dirty snow was piled up near the curb, and the people, thoroughly chilled despite their layers of clothing, moved down the street so quickly that they seemed to be propelled by the fierce wind blowing off the lake. When she stepped inside the shop, a bell rang. She was so relieved to be warm that she didn't speak for a minute. "I want to buy a gun," she told the owner.

There was a mole on the old man's chin, and he was standing close enough to her so that she saw the long hairs inside his nose. He smelled stale, like day-old bread and sour milk. "What kind of gun?" he asked.

"A thirty-eight."

He brought her a tray full of revolvers. "This is a nice one," he said, holding a gun out to her.

Delotha held the pistol in her hand. It was hard and cold, and when she closed her eyes she could hear the terrible report of bullets.

"What you going to shoot, lady?" the man asked her. He was smiling.

She didn't answer.

Delotha bought the train ticket late the next day, and that evening she boarded the Illinois Central heading south. The loaded gun was in her purse, next to six packs of Salem cigarettes. She figured that by the time she ran out of cigarettes she'd be back home.

At Memphis the train sat in the station for nearly half an hour. Delotha remained seated, smoking and looking out the window as people got on and off. She kept reviewing her plan, which was simple: to kill Floyd and Lily Cox. Take her own justice. Just take it the way they always did. Just knock on the door and *Blam! Blam!* And another one for their child. *Blam!*

As she gazed at the platform, a woman and a boy of about thirteen walked by and then entered her car. They both had faces as round and dark as Moon Pies and glossy hair that curled. They took a seat across from her. Delotha tried not to look at them. She fished around in her pocketbook until her fingers touched the hard, cold steel, and that reassured her, calmed her fluttering heart. *Blam! Blam! Blam!* But she couldn't keep her eyes off them; she wanted to see them smiling at each other. And then the woman, the mother, reached into her bag and pulled out a brush and attempted to fix the boy's hair, only he pulled away, laughing, both of them laughing, and the boy said, "Stop, Mama."

Where was the moaning coming from? Who was sobbing? People were turning around, craning their necks, looking over their shoulders.

The pain was a wild, hairy beast, sinking its teeth into her; it seemed to swallow her whole. Delotha stumbled out of the train, crying so hard she could barely see. She wandered around the station until she found a seat, and she waited for the next train back to Chicago.

After she returned from Memphis, she cried all the time and prayed for the courage to avenge her child's death.

She heard a papery splatter one Sunday morning while she was sitting in bed smoking, and when she looked up, a pile of letters had fallen to the floor. She hesitated for a moment, then went into the kitchen and returned with three empty shopping bags. She stuffed all the letters inside and shoved them in the back of her closet, where it was dark and cool. When she was crouched down on the closet floor, she felt something hard behind the bags. She reached back and pulled out a framed picture of herself and Wydell. Their faces were so young that at first she didn't recognize them. He was wearing a short-sleeve shirt, and she had on a dress with tiny flowers on the bodice. His hand was across her shoulder, and one of her hands reached up to grasp his fingers. They were smiling at each other. The tiniest pinpricks of pleasure began warming her belly and breasts as she stared at the photograph. With a moan, she raked her fingers across her stomach and bosom, as if to erase the desire that had surfaced. Then she slammed the picture to the floor. You and your promises, she wanted to scream. If you'd done what you was supposed to do, I wouldn't have sent Armstrong away.

It wasn't until she walked out of the closet and saw the trail of blood that she realized that her thumb was cut. She rinsed it off and put a Band-Aid on it, then got back in bed and lay there without moving for a moment, before reaching across her pillow and groping for the cigarettes that were on her nightstand. She closed her eyes as she inhaled, and when she opened them they were full of tears.

After she finished smoking, Delotha fell asleep and dreamed of little boys. Little brown boys who looked like Armstrong. All different sizes. They were in a yard with a high wall, and she was taking care of them. Wydell was in the yard with her, and she realized that all the boys who looked like Armstrong also looked like Wydell. She felt her husband's lips on hers. He touched her breasts.

She woke up with a slick wetness between her legs, dripping down her thighs. She put her fingers inside her and twirled them around and around and rubbed her other hand back and forth across her nipples, until she felt a quickening sensation in her groin, then the hard pleasure of contractions rippling through her. "Wydell. Wydell," she said softly, over and over again. She was still saying his name, calling it gently, like a lover, when the fire in her body went out. She heard herself for the first time. Wydell? Her fist exploded into her pillow.

Wydell. The Coxes. She couldn't think of one without thinking of the other.

On her lunch breaks, while she smoked Salem after Salem, she made a new plan: She would kill Wydell first, then murder the Coxes. She would go to Floyd and Lily's house and climb in their window while they slept. Shoot him in bed while his own wife watched. Kill him first and then shoot her. Shoot her for telling the lie that killed her son. Or she would get a bomb. Throw it through an open window. Run to the road and watch gleefully as their house burst open like a ripe seedpod.

But for Wydell she chose a butcher knife. The cut: a long, low, jagged one across the throat. She would wait until he was drunk one night. Find him in some South Side bar, some dive that couldn't even afford a broken-down blues singer. Delotha would warn the patrons to clear out (just seeing the gun in her hands would make everybody scatter); then she'd fire a single bullet in Wydell's chest. That would stun him. Then she'd slit his throat and watch him die.

She began looking for Wydell. She phoned his old place of work but was told he had left long ago. One Saturday morning she got dressed and put a knife in her purse and went to where Wydell lived when she'd seen him last. The woman who opened the door had stains on her housedress and loose, unfettered breasts that hung soft and low on her belly. She looked at Delotha curiously. "Wydell left here two, three years ago," she told her. Her eyes softened, and so did her voice. "Baby, he somebody you want to let stay gone."

She searched for him in South Side bars on Friday and Saturday nights, but no one had seen him. The bartender at the Down Home told her that Wydell hadn't been there in months. "Good-looking woman like you ain't got to be chasing down no man," he said to her.

She went to Lionel's shop one Saturday morning. Lionel came from around the counter when he saw her, and he gave her a long, tight hug. "Where you been, girl?" he asked.

"I ain't been nowhere, Lionel."

Amelia attended to the few customers, and Lionel took Delotha into the room behind the shop. They sat on two hard-back chairs. Delotha lit a cigarette. "Lionel, you seen Wydell?"

Lionel looked at the wall. "Not in a while. Why you ask?"

"I want to make sure he knows about Armstrong."

"I'm sure he does."

"Why you think that?"

"It was in all the papers, colored and white. Ain't no way he could not know." He looked at Delotha. "Why you keeping away from everybody? I talked to your sister last week. You don't call nobody. You don't visit. Can't nobody visit you, 'cause you don't answer the door. That ain't no way to be."

Delotha sighed. "I don't know how to be around people no more, Lionel."

"Aww, honey. Sure you do. Everybody know how you feeling."

Delotha stood up. "Do you know where Wydell is working now?"

Lionel fiddled with his watch. "Delotha, what you wanna find Wydell for? Last I heard, he was drinking hisself half to death. Wherever he is, just let him stay there. Say, what you doing tomorrow? Come go to church with me and Amelia and the kids. Then you come to our house for supper."

"Lionel, I—"

"You be ready at ten o'clock."

The church was on the South Side, near the ballpark. The minister and most of the congregation were from around Greenwood, and a few faces looked familiar to Delotha. Lionel had to sit in the front row with the deacons, and Amelia was singing with the choir, so Delotha sat with Henry and James, their two sons, who were six and eight years old and who fidgeted relentlessly throughout the service. Delotha gave them each a piece of Juicy Fruit gum, and they were still for as long as the sweetness lasted and then started rocking back and forth on the pew like little metronomes.

People knew who she was; she could tell by their smiles, whispers, and stares. She didn't stand when a woman in a flowered dress called for visitors, even when Henry whispered, "Cousin 'Lotha, stand up." The choir sang, "Oh, Mary, Don't You Weep," and after the song was over, her stomach and head felt calm and settled.

The preacher had a slow way of talking. He waved his long, dark fingers a lot for emphasis and looked into the eyes of the people sitting in his congregation. He talked about Job and suffering, about not giving up on God. Letting the father take care of things. "Wellwellwell, you oughta just trust Jesus sometime. Ain't that right?" And the congregation responded with amens and nods. Toward the end, he launched into a kind of sing-

song rhythm, and Delotha could hear the people around
her saying amen. Some of the people around her started
hollering and waving their arms. Several women let
their bodies shake and quiver, while they just moaned.
Delotha was surrounded by wailing and amens and
"JesusJesusJesus," and before she knew it she was on
her feet too, hollering and waving her arms. The church
was like a merry-go-round, the way it was spinning.
She was too dizzy and too far away to reach anyone.
Suddenly there was cool air on her face, and when she
looked up, two nurses in white were standing over her
with fans, pushing her down in her seat with strong
arms and telling her, in voices that seemed to know, that
everything would be all right.

The reporter from the *Chicago Courier* came the following week, a camera swinging from his shoulder. He
looked younger than she'd expected, far younger than
his deep voice sounded on the telephone when he explained that he wanted to do a story about the aftermath
of Armstrong Todd's death. He couldn't have been
more than twenty-three, a tall, lanky yellow boy with
not a trace of hair on his face. They sat in Delotha's living room. It was the first time she'd had company in
her home in a long while, and she was uneasy. She
asked him if he would like anything to eat or drink, but
he refused.

   He pulled a notepad and a pencil from his jacket
pocket, then looked at her. "How has it been for you
since your son died?" he asked.

   She had expected little questions, tiny baby questions.

   When the reporter left, the ashtray on her coffee table
was full of cigarette butts, and her pack was empty. She
sat on the sofa until it got dark outside, and then she
went to bed. A week later, when she read the article,
she didn't even remember wearing the dress that she
had on in the picture. She didn't recall saying any of the

words that the newspaper said were hers, although the part that read "I can't forgive, I just can't" sounded familiar.

27

The thought came to Wydell while he was sitting at the bar: What if he had been there, waiting at Odessa's, when those crackers came? Armstrong would have called, "Daddy! Daddy!" He knew where Odessa kept the shotgun. Those Coxes would have hightailed it if they saw a gun, even if they had three of their own. They never liked odds that weren't completely in their favor. When he aimed the rifle and said, "Y'all just leave my son alone," they would have cleared out. He sighed and signaled the bartender. He needed another drink.

At eight o'clock there were only a few people at Scott's Bar, a new place Wydell had found. The men around him were talking about Floyd Patterson's title bout, which had been fought earlier in the week. Wydell wasn't interested in the fight or the conversation; he ordered three whiskeys, one right after the other, and listened to La Vern Baker's loud rendition of "Jim Dandy."

"Oh, I almost forgot to tell you," the bartender said, pouring his third drink. He wore his hair in a gleaming, towering process and resembled an older Jackie Wilson. "A woman come in here looking for you. Good-looking woman," he added.

Wydell had the glass in his hand, and he gulped down the contents before he raised his eyes. Bertha, his old girlfriend, wasn't much to look at. "When?" he asked.

"Couple weeks ago."

"What'd she want?"

The bartender chuckled. "She wanted you, man. Don't ask me why. She didn't leave her name. How you know a fine-looking woman like that, Wydell?"

"That musta been my wife," he said.

The bartender studied Wydell for a moment, as though he were used to seeing him in rags and suddenly he appeared before him in a suit and tie. He frowned. "I ain't even tell you what she look like."

"She look like a beautiful woman with smooth brown skin, hair to her shoulders. Good hair. We come out of Mississippi together."

"She sure was built."

Anger rose in Wydell so swiftly he wasn't aware of it, until he saw ice cubes scattering and slipping on the counter, his glass rocking and spinning in a thin puddle of bourbon.

"I didn't mean nothing by it, man. No insult intended. Y'all got kids?" The bartender was standing in front of him, the whiskey bottle in his hand.

Wydell nodded as he sipped from his refilled glass. Staring at the bartender, he thought he looked cockeyed, as if one of his eyes was just dancing around in the socket, back and forth, every which way. Kids. Kids. The word seemed to have an echo.

"Yeah. No. We had a boy. He died."

"Sorry to hear that, man. Real sorry."

The bartender was smiling, showing nice, even white teeth. The flecks of gray in his greasy hair made him appear older than Wydell. He had a wise, kind face, eyes that said he might listen to him explain how nothing ever worked out for him. Nothing. No one had felt sorry for him in such a long time. "Listen. Listen." Wydell grabbed the bartender's wrist. "Listen. The white people killed my boy." It was the first time he'd spoken those words aloud to anyone. He was afraid of the words, scared that somehow people would see through them and realize that the blame belonged to him.

"What white people?" The bartender's eyes flickered with faint recognition.

"In Mississippi," Wydell whispered.

"Was that your son, man?"

"Yeah. That was my boy. Armstrong."

"Armstrong Todd."

Wydell's head jerked a little, and he rubbed the back of his neck. "Yeah." Hearing his son's name after so many months of trying not to think about him was like pouring salt into an oozing sore.

He could smell the pomade on the bartender's patent-leather hair. "Man, that cracker should die for what he did, man. That was your son? Jesus, man." The bartender balled up his fist and jabbed at the air, his outrage fresh and real. Wydell was too astonished to speak. He was so anxious to forget his son's death that it never occurred to him that other people wanted to remember. "But the paper said he lived in Mississippi. I thought you and your wife lived here."

The words came as though they were traveling through a tunnel. "We wasn't together," Wydell said slowly.

"The mama went back to Mississippi?"

"No. She ain't never going back there. The boy, he was staying with his grandma. Her mother."

The bartender opened his mouth and then closed it without speaking. Then he said, slowly, "Well, I guess she had her reasons. Sending him down there. Anyway, it sure was a damn shame, what happened."

Wydell lifted up his glass for another refill. Ice tinkled down the sides, and the brown liquor swirled to the bottom. Wydell could hear the questions the bartender didn't ask. What was his boy doing in Mississippi? Why was he living there? Wydell had never thought of those questions. What difference did it make? His boy was gone.

But the questions nagged him, wouldn't disappear, and suddenly he grabbed hold of them as if they were a lifeline. Why couldn't 'Lotha raise the child herself, instead of shipping him off to Odessa? Women were supposed to raise their kids, to protect them. She was always telling him that he wasn't nothing; well, what about her? He kicked the bar in front of him. "A mule got a better chance at living than a nigger in Mississippi. And that's the truth."

Several of the people at the bar were staring at him, and for a moment he was scared in a way he didn't understand until he realized that he'd spoken aloud. A man stood in front of him. "I read about what happened to your son, man. That was a damn shame. Seem like the colored man don't have a chance in this world, do he?" He shoved his hand toward Wydell, who grasped it in his own.

The rest of the faces in the bar offered him sympathy. And why shouldn't they feel sorry for him? He deserved all the pity the room had to offer. His son was dead.

Wydell got out of his seat and straightened his jacket, then carefully walked over to a nearby table, where three women were seated. He saw red hair, red lips, and held out his hand. Wydell liked watching the colored lights in the plastic chandelier almost as much as he liked feeling the swell of flesh just above the woman's soft hips as they slow-dragged around the room. "Sure was sorry to hear about your son," she whispered in his ear. "White folks is so mean." He didn't have to reply, just nod a little.

When the record ended he went back to the bar. He smiled as he watched the bartender pour him more whiskey—on the house—and listened to Sam Cooke. More people came up to him to tell him they were sorry about Armstrong, to shoot the breeze a little. He liked being around so many people who were laughing and having a good time. His fingers started tapping against the bar. And Delotha was looking for him. Fine Delotha, with the candy-apple ass and jelly-doughnut thighs. He laughed aloud at their old joke and didn't care that the people at the bar were looking at him. They were still smiling. They were still on his side, even if he wasn't nobody. Even if he was all kinds of wrong, and jive, a mother was supposed to protect her child. He knew why Delotha was trying to find him. He didn't have to worry about her hating him. She wanted to apologize for not taking better care of his son.

Wydell began spending most Friday and Saturday nights at Scott's, drinking until he felt settled and in control, until he chased the face of his child out of his head. But sometimes, even when he was so drunk he could barely stand, Armstrong wouldn't go away.

Wydell had gone back to work the day after the funeral, had walked there with stiff knees and a groggy head, the bruises on his face still hurting. He arrived early at Erlinger Knitting Mills. The glass double doors on the brick building were unlocked; he climbed the stairs to the second floor.

Danny, the foreman, an angry-looking Italian with a punched-in nose and protruding teeth, was sitting in his office, drinking a cup of coffee and stuffing a Danish into his mouth. Hearing Wydell's knock, he nodded for him to come in.

Wydell began speaking before Danny had swallowed his food, because something in the foreman's dark eyes told him that he should talk fast. "I'm sorry I been away. There was a death in my family." He spoke cautiously, the words coming from behind his teeth. *Just don't ask me no questions,* he thought. *Don't ask me who died or none of that.* But Danny only shook his head. He stood up.

"Where do ya come up with that crap, Todd? You ought to burn in hell, lying like that. JeeeesusChrist. Ya been on a drunk." He had a heavy, rough voice that sounded like chains going over ice and gravel. "Listen, I'm warning ya. You're the best; you can outwork any five men I got, but this is the last goddamn time. Ya hear me?" He pushed his face so close that Wydell could smell a full blast of last night's garlic and tomatoes mixed in with the morning coffee. Wydell felt pure terror under his boss's hard stare. He stepped back until his shoulders slammed into the wall. Wanting to flee from Danny's fierce eyes, he hated himself for feeling so cowardly.

"You gotta cut down on the booze, man."

"Yeah, Danny. I'm gonna do that." He despised himself for whining in front of a white man; he'd been doing that all his life.

" 'Cause I'm telling ya, this is the last goddamn time."

"Thank you, Danny."

Wydell didn't drink for three days straight; he went to work and stayed there as long as he possibly could, came straight home, ate supper, and went to bed. He didn't want enough space in his life to allow room for thinking. Thinking choked him like a killer's hands tight around his throat. Thinking was his son's baby face hovering just above him. Thinking was Armstrong's voice whispering in his ear. He wanted to keep his son's ghost at bay. He would go back to his old routine and drink only on weekends.

During that first week, he took all the overtime Danny gave him. Pressing was the only job colored men could get at the knitting mill, besides janitor. Wydell had learned not to think of what he couldn't do, although sometimes when he walked past the throngs of white men coming from the other side of the building, where the machine operators were, there was a plucking inside his head, like fingers pulling on nerve endings.

As he pressed clothes, Wydell remembered how, when he was a boy, his father would walk out of Pinochet's fields with the expression of a whipped dog.

It didn't take much, not much at all, for his father to grab him by his elbow, yank him behind the house, and make him strip down. He would stand in front of the big man, naked and shivering, and his father would walk toward him, holding the whip high in his hands, saying, "Didn't I tell you? Didn't I tell you?" Didn't I tell you to put lime in the outhouse; to weed the garden; to put more paper in your shoes and not go barefoot in the rain? To not throw in your daddy's face everything you learned at that fool schoolhouse, "'cause it ain't gon' do you no good no way."

He had gone to Delotha after the worst beating. She had been his girl for as long as he could remember, so he went to her with his back crisscrossed with scars and blood, defeat in his eyes. She had kissed his eyes, wiped away the blood, and said, "We leaving here." She was only fourteen years old, but she was as tough as any grown woman. Up until that moment, he'd never believed in the possibility of escape, even though he heard the whistle of the Illinois Central every night. "Anyway," she whispered later as she washed his back, "we gon' have us a baby."

He thought about Delotha when he was working. Not the screaming banshee she became, but the old Delotha from Mississippi, the girl who waded in the creek with him and outran him in footraces, the girl who showed him her pea-size breasts when she was only ten, the girl who threw her dress over her head and spread her legs out wide for him behind the last row of cotton a few years later, biting down on the fleecy white balls surrounding them to muffle her cries at orgasms.

He had lost Delotha. He had lost everything. Wydell began to avoid anyone or anything that would remind him of Armstrong or Delotha. He didn't visit anyone, and no one came to see him. When the questions from the people at Scott's Bar began to be too probing, he stopped going and instead picked up a bottle from the liquor store on Friday evenings. He would sit in his bed with the lights off and the radio on, smelling tomatoes and garlic from the pizza stand on the street below, and drink until he fell asleep. More than once he woke up as wet in his pants as a thirteen-year-old boy, his dick limp and soothed, Delotha's name in his mouth as alive and hungry as another tongue.

He was on his way to the liquor store one evening, and there was Armstrong, his little boy's face hovering over him. "Daddy! Daddy!" Wydell started running.

He escaped that time, but he couldn't control Armstrong's visiting him, calling him, making him think. Once, when Wydell was eating lunch at work, Armstrong called him, and he looked and there was the baby face, big eyes filled with tears. And Wydell started to leave, but the baby face followed him. "Go away," he said. But Armstrong stayed there for a long time, even though he kept telling him to go. And then, when he looked up, there was Danny staring at him, his mouth open, his ugly buckteeth sitting up in his head.

Three weeks after Eisenhower was reelected, Wydell found a copy of the *Chicago Courier* in the lunchroom at the mill. He opened the paper and saw Delotha's face. When he finished reading the article, he was too sad to move.

He hadn't been at the presser ten minutes when he heard Armstrong again. "Daddy! Daddy!" The voice came from within the hissing steam.

"Go 'way, boy," he whispered. "Go on, now." The man working next to Wydell looked at him, then quickly averted his eyes.

"Daddy! Daddy!"

"Leave me alone!"

"Daaaaddddy!"

He started running, knocking over clothing bins, bumping into racks of ironed garments. Workers stepped back and watched. "Go 'way!" Wydell screamed. "Leave me alone." He could feel the baby breath on his shoulder. Armstrong smelled like milk and talcum powder. He pushed chairs out of his way and shoved tables aside, scattering clothing all over the floor. Everyone had stopped working now, and they were all staring at him.

"He won't leave me alone."

One of the white men went to get Danny, who suddenly loomed over Wydell, the sharp edges of his broken teeth flashing. "Awright. Awright awreddy. Enough is enough. I told you about the drinking. You're through!"

Wydell was crouched in the corner, sobbing, his hands crisscrossed in front of his face. "Take him away," he cried.

"What the hell are you talking about?" Danny said.

"Hey, Danny," said one of the other workers, a thin man with a shock of hair like spliced wires. "He ain't been drinking."

Danny stared at the trembling, screaming man in front of him. He wiped his hand across his mouth. "Okay. Okay. You," he said to the man with the wiry hair. "You keep an eye on him. I'm gonna go call somebody."

28

Delotha let the telephone ring eight times before she answered it. There was no one she was expecting, no one she wanted to hear from.

Just from the way the man said her name, she could tell that he was white. Listening to his voice, she began rocking on the balls of her feet. He probably had never set foot outside Illinois; the twangy way he chewed up his words and spit them out at her told her that much. Accent so thick and corn-fed she could barely make out what he was saying, and she wouldn't even have tried, except that he said "Wydell Todd"; then she started paying attention.

"Say that again. Would you please repeat that?"

The man coughed right in her ear. "Ma'am, I'm trying to tell you that we have Wydell Todd in custody here, and—"

"Custody? Wydell in jail?" She was reaching for her purse, fishing around for the Salems and matches.

There was a laugh, brief and clear as open skies. "Ma'am, I'm calling from Cook County Hospital. We have a Wydell Todd. Is that your husband?"

When he said the word "husband" she stiffened. She hadn't thought of Wydell in that way for a long time. "Yes," she said.

"Well, ma'am. He was brought in yesterday; we're legally bound to notify the next of kin, and then it's up to you whether you want to sign him in or out."

"I don't understand. Are you saying he's sick?"

"Ma'am, he's in the mental ward."

Delotha watched as the ashes from the cigarette fell on the floor. She wasn't close to an ashtray.

"Ma'am?"

"Yes."

"Can you come down here?"

The corridor in the psychiatric wing was painted gray, and there were little black hands, with fat extended index fingers, pointing the way to the various wards, to the bathrooms, the nurses' station. The strong scent of disinfectant wafted through the air, burning Delotha's nostrils. Everywhere she looked, she saw white people dressed in white. Looking at them made her angry, almost hysterical. Delotha studied the hands for a moment and then followed the one that led to the information desk. A woman with hair as gray as a thundercloud looked up when she cleared her throat. "Yes?" she said.

"I'm Mrs. Todd. I got a telephone call about Wydell Todd. You have him here." She didn't want to talk to the white woman any longer than she had to.

The woman pursed her thin coral lips and began scanning the sheets of paper attached to a steel clipboard. "Just a moment," she said. She made a telephone call. Delotha heard her say, "I assume it's his wife," and then the woman hung up the phone. "Sit over there," she said, pointing to the reception area.

Delotha reached in her purse for a cigarette and felt the sharp knife pressed against the pack of Salems. She had barely finished her cigarette before a tall white man with thinning brown hair was standing in front of her, carrying a chart in one hand. "Mrs. Todd?" he asked. When Delotha nodded, he sat down next to her on the vinyl-covered sofa, so close that their knees touched lightly. She moved her legs. "I'm Dr. Blumberg. I just wanted to chat with you briefly before you see your husband. What have you been told?"

"Only that he's here. I don't even know how y'all got

my name and number. Wydell and me ain't been together for a couple of years."

"I see. Well, there are any number of ways we could
have found your name. He may have listed it with his
employer. It was probably on his military record. Any
number of ways." Dr. Blumberg pulled out the chart
and studied it briefly. "It seems your husband's boss
called the police after he began tearing up the place.
When the police determined that he hadn't been drinking, they brought him here. Apparently he was halluci-
nating while he was on the job, imagining that someone
was after him, that kind of thing. He seems to have
calmed down since he's been here, but of course we put
him on medication. Which isn't to say that once he's released there wouldn't be a recurrence of that kind of behavior. There are simply no guarantees. You need to
think about that before you consider signing him out.
But you also need to know that we've been evaluating
him, and in my professional opinion I believe his violent outburst was triggered by an emotional buildup that
reached its climax during an intense and protracted de-
pression." He looked at Delotha, who was lighting another cigarette.

"Listen," she said, "is Wydell crazy? Is that what you
saying?"

The doctor laughed. "I don't think so. No, he's not
crazy. He just got very upset after being really sad for
a long time, and he started acting violently. I think it
was a temporary reaction. Do you understand?"

"Yes. But you saying that I get to decide whether he
stays in here or comes out?"

"According to the law, yes. That is correct. Would
you like to see him now?"

Puffing rapidly on the cigarette, Delotha tingled with
excitement, anger, and fear. "All right," she said, standing up.

They walked down a long corridor until they came to

metal double doors. Dr. Blumberg pushed them open, saying, "Mr. Todd. Your wife is here to see you."

There were two long rows of beds, occupied by listless-looking men. Wydell was sitting in the bed closest to the doors, his eyes wandering passively around the room. He looked up when Delotha came in, and she could see the initial shock in his eyes change as his face became suffused with slow, radiating happiness. There was no mistaking it. And then something else, easily identifiable. Delotha felt his eyes wander from her face to her breasts and hips. Her body tingled everyplace his eyes touched. "Hello, Delotha," he said, and just that greeting was like his fingers all over her. The doctor pulled a chain that hung down near the bed, and a curtain enclosed them. "I want to see him alone," Delotha said firmly.

Dr. Blumberg nodded. "I'll be back in ten minutes," he said as he left.

"I been looking for you, Wydell. I went to the Down Home and . . ." Anger began spurting through her, like a faucet turned on full force. She wanted to snatch the joy from his face.

"I know you hate me," he said. "I'm at your mercy now."

Delotha moved toward him until she was standing right beside the bed. Water was rolling from under her arms, down her sides, her back. Her teeth were clenched tightly when she spoke, and her fingers were balled up tight as a skein of yarn. Her pocketbook snapped open, and she grasped the blunt handle of the knife in her hand. She bent her head down, until her nose was almost touching Wydell's and she could smell his dry breath. "I don't know who I hate more, you or the white people." She slowly raised the knife.

"Ain't that every colored woman's dilemma?" Wydell asked quietly.

Delotha's laughter sounded rusty, the tenor of it so rough it seemed to scar her larynx as it made its way out of her throat. She hadn't laughed in so long, and she couldn't stop. The knife clattered to the floor as she put her hand on Wydell's shoulder to steady herself. She felt him stirring beneath her palm. Without thinking, she pulled his covers down because the room was so warm. His arms were hidden, bound up in the swirl of white fabric that locked him in. Delotha said, "Lord have mercy. What in the world . . ."

She wished she hadn't spoken. What did she care how they treated Wydell, if they wrapped him up in a gunnysack? What did she care how pitiful he looked, with his hangdog expression and mournful eyes, sadder than all those times in Mississippi when she wiped blood off his back? Without being conscious of what she was doing, she loosened the ties that bound his sleeves and helped him out of the straitjacket.

Delotha sat down and pulled her chair close to the bed. "Armstrong is dead," she said. "You know about that?"

"Yes."

"Floyd Cox shot him. . . ."

"I know." He made a sound, soft and primordial. When Delotha looked up, there were tears in his eyes.

"Why you crying now, Wydell?" she said. "You let all that time go by, and you never even came to see him. You know how many nights that boy cried for you?"

"I didn't have no money."

The tears were falling from Wydell's eyes. Delotha had never seen him like that, not even after his father used to beat him. He looked small and weak, sitting up in a hospital bed. "He wasn't crying for money," she said.

"Why you send him down there? Why you didn't keep him with you?" The sudden meanness in Wydell's voice overwhelmed his tears. "What kind of mother would send her own kid to that hellhole?"

"What kind of mother?" Delotha lunged toward Wydell, her fingers curved to grip his throat.

He grabbed her by the wrists and held her away from him. She was surprised at how strong he was. "You better calm down, girl. That white man come back here and put both our asses in straitjackets. Then who gon' sign us out?"

Again the rusty laughter. Right there in Wydell's arms, she was giggling and gasping for breath, her head so close to his chest that she could hear his heartbeat. His thin white hospital gown suddenly turned wet from her tears. "Delotha," Wydell was saying, "I'm sorry. I'm sorry I said that. I ain't got no right. . . . I know you hate me. I deserve it."

"When I went home and saw Armstrong lying there dead, I went crazy. Why they have to do that? Why?" She began sobbing, her breasts heaving, her fingers splayed out across Wydell's chest, which was full and powerful and familiar. His arms roped around her. They cried together for a long time before she realized that she had been lulled by Wydell's warmth, by their communion of tears. Being in his arms was like a second funeral, full of mourning and sweet release.

"I can do better, Delotha." He spoke softly, but the words slammed into her like a wild storm.

As she looked into the familiar eyes, what she felt was not desire, not love, but a deep yearning. He was half of what had been taken from her. And she was the other half.

29

Wydell wouldn't let Delotha sign him out of the hospital that first day. He insisted upon remaining there for four months, long enough to purge from his body the memory of alcohol and banish the phantoms of his dead son from his mind.

Delotha visited him daily. She took Wydell a little radio, and sometimes they listened to dance music or White Sox games as they sat in the dayroom. Lionel and Amelia declared that they were courting and said that Delotha probably fell back in love with Wydell while he was in the hospital. Delotha kept silent; she wasn't sure if she loved Wydell. All she knew was that he was half of Armstrong and she was the other half; that genetic link was foremost in her mind.

Being with him again, she felt at peace, almost as if she'd gone home after being away for years. She could talk with him for hours about Armstrong, and he would listen to her without fidgeting with impatience or changing the subject. "Do you remember that little truck he used to drag around all day long? He'd have it at the table when he ate, and he took it to bed," Delotha said once as she was about to leave the hospital. Wydell closed his eyes and rocked in his chair, and when he opened his eyes they were both crying, holding each other.

Other times they talked about white people, in low, intense voices. "I don't even think they're human,"

Delotha said. "They ain't never gon' be happy until they put colored people back in slavery."

"They so scared of colored men. That's why they killed Armstrong—scared he was good as them," Wydell said.

They no longer blamed themselves for anything.

Once in a while, they just had a good time laughing as they sat in the dayroom playing cards or checkers, reading the newspaper and eating fried chicken and potato salad. Delotha found tranquillity as the old Wydell, the boy she'd known so long ago in Mississippi, gradually reemerged. She even stopped smoking. The craving for cigarettes faded like a fever.

The longing for her son didn't disappear. When Delotha left the hospital, she mourned in her small apartment, overcome by loneliness and grief, so disconsolate she couldn't speak or even cry. What she wanted more than anything was a chance to begin again, to have a brand-new Armstrong filling her womb.

Her mother, who thought she was a fool for getting back with Wydell, declared she was an even bigger one to consider having children with him again. "You know sooner or later he gon' mess up," Odessa warned her. "Niggers always mess up."

"You'll see, Mama. Everything will work out," Delotha told her.

When Wydell was dismissed from the hospital, he and Delotha went to his old landlady and retrieved the belongings she had stored for him, and then took a bus to Delotha's apartment. She had begun cleaning the place regularly, the way she had before Armstrong was killed. Wydell stood in the doorway, his eyes darting around the room, taking in the gleaming orderliness. He lowered his head and whispered. "I always knew you'd do good."

They drank coffee together in the kitchen, and Wydell held his cup carefully, as though he was afraid he might crush it between his fingers. After they finished, Wydell asked if he could wash up, and she led him to the bathroom. He stared at the pink walls and the clean pink rug on the floor and seemed startled when she handed him a towel and a washcloth. "I'll be in the bedroom," she said.

He was cool and sweet-smelling when he lay down next to her. They hadn't been in bed together in more than six years, and for the first few moments neither one of them moved. Looking at each other, they laughed nervously. Then Wydell leaned over and whispered in Delotha's ear, "Johnson missed you, baby."

It was what she wanted to hear.

"He got to show me how much," Delotha said as she carefully inched her fingers toward his groin.

Wydell's hands were light on her shoulders; he rubbed her until she began to tingle. She had forgotten how his touch made her feel as if she was drowning in sweetness. Delotha wrapped her arms around his waist, her heated thighs encircled his hips, and she pulled him closer to her. He would fill her again, she thought, put another Armstrong inside her, and this time she would do better. This time she'd take care of her son and not let anyone hurt him. She slithered up against Wydell's chest and tightened her arms around him. "Put it in," she whispered.

Then Wydell turned her face toward his, and in the dim bedroom light she could see that he held something in his hand. "I want to wear this," he said. She watched in horror as he rolled the rubber onto his erect penis. "I don't want no kids. Let it just be us," he said, grabbing her wrists, "just us."

"But I want a baby," she said. "Your baby."

He looked at her with a wild sadness in his eyes. "We can't bring Armstrong back."

"I didn't mean that."

"That *is* what you mean. You just don't know it."

"No. I want a new baby. We're still young."

"No," he said sadly. "We ain't."

* * *

The first year they were together, Wydell wore a rubber whenever they made love. At first Delotha would whine and cry and say that she could feel the thing, that it irritated her, but Wydell wouldn't listen. She thought of putting a tiny pinprick in the prophylactics, but Wydell hid them.

She began bringing children into their home: a neighbor's baby, a friend's toddler. "Ain't he cute, Wydell?" Delotha would say, jiggling the child on her lap.

But although Wydell might grin at the baby or even slip his finger into its tiny fist, he remained adamant about their not having a child.

She knew that he was afraid of being a father, that having children was more frightening to Wydell than being locked up in a liquor store, but her desire was greater than his fear. At night she dreamed of Armstrong when he was a baby, his tiny mouth on her breast, how she held and rocked him to sleep. When she woke up, her arms felt empty and useless.

She thought of a plan.

"Wydell, you and me need to go into business together," she said one Saturday morning when they were drinking coffee in the kitchen. "Open up something, like Lionel done." He hadn't worked since Danny fired him. She saw his shoulders stiffen, but she continued. "Now, what makes sense is this: I can do hair, but I don't have a license. You ain't never used your GI Bill. Why don't you take up barbering, and I'll get my license for cosmetology. Then you and I can open up a beauty salon and barbershop." She spoke the words the way she saw her dream: a neat, orderly reality. But one look at Wydell's expression and she realized that her simple idea of hard work and prosperity was as real to him as being able to make gold out of shit. In that split second she saw that he didn't believe in himself and that he never had. If he was ever to have faith and self-confidence, she would have to give it to him. It came to her then that she could forge a trade-off: she would mold Wydell Todd into a successful, sober man, and in return she would demand that he give her a child.

She knew how to please him.

In the morning she woke him with kisses and soft probing fingers. When he opened his eyes, her breast was near his mouth and her thighs were wrapped around Johnson. As soon as she came home from the factory, before she took out the chicken or the hamburger she'd cooked the previous night, she led him into the bedroom, stripped his clothes off, and made love to him across the made-up bed. At night she tossed her bra and panties to the floor as she danced for him, her fine, tight ass bumping from side to side, beckoning him to enter her.

"Baby," he told her, "you driving me crazy."

"I love you, Wydell," she said. And it was true. She'd fallen in love with him as she had when they were kids in Hopewell, with no one to hold on to but each other. She believed in him again, the way she had when they were children. "You're gonna be somebody, Wydell."

And so Delotha accelerated her plan into phase two. She wrote away for an application to barbering college and filled it out for Wydell. When he was admitted to the school, she rode the bus with him for the first several weeks. At night she zealously helped him study, and later she quizzed him in preparation for his state examination. "Baby, you can do it," she said. When he failed the first time, she coaxed and cajoled him for several hours until he agreed to take it again. And when the notice came saying he had failed the second time, she tossed the letter to the floor and climbed on his lap, undressing them both, kissing and licking him until he promised he'd take it again. "You're a smart man, Wydell, and I'm not letting you give up," she told him. The third time, he passed, and their celebration was two days of serious lovemaking that left them drained and hungry for more. Delotha never asked if he liked barbering or even if he was interested in it. What she saw when she visited him at school was that he was good at cutting hair and brought to the task the same qualities he'd exhibited in Pinochet's cotton fields: thoroughness and decisive energy. She no longer worried that at any moment he would run to a bar or liquor store and topple her finely wrought plans. Month after month went by, and he never touched a drop of liquor.

"I'm so proud of you, baby," she told him.

"I'm proud of myself," he said in a voice filled with wonder. And then: "Thank you for sticking by me."

After both she and Wydell received their state licenses, they took jobs so that they could learn the business. When a year had passed, Delotha told Wydell that they should begin looking for a place to open up their own shop; she ignored the trepidation in Wydell's eyes. She found a suitable building on Forty-seventh Street and informed Wydell that they were buying the place and would live on the second floor. He looked at her in amazement. "How are we supposed to do that?"

When Delotha told him about the money that people had mailed to her, Wydell said, "You the kind of woman who always has something up your sleeve."

They called the place Wydell and Delotha's House of Good Looks, and from the beginning there was an air of bustling prosperity. People seemed to come to them as eagerly as if the couple stood at the door and drew them in with a hypnotic flute. True, they were competent and offered good service for a fair price. But there was something else that aided Delotha's relentless march toward the good life: the memory of Armstrong Todd. Most of their clients remembered the brutal murder and their own subsequent rage and helplessness. If they couldn't punish the white trash who killed the boy, they could at least patronize the mother and father's business.

Wydell changed. He seemed taller and stronger;

whenever Delotha looked at him, he was smiling. By the time the state troopers were escorting the Little Rock Nine to Central High, Wydell had hired another barber.

"You done it, Wydell," Delotha said. "You're smart and you work hard. We wouldn't have nothing if it wasn't for you. And pretty soon, we'll have us a house, a house big enough to raise a child in." She smiled at him.

That night in bed, as they were about to make love, Delotha took the rubber that Wydell was holding in his hand and threw it on the floor.

"Now, Delotha . . ." Wydell began.

Her body was trembling. "Wydell, you can be a good father if you set your mind to it. Look at all you done accomplished." When his face remained stoic and unchanged, she added, "You make more money than a lot of white men." She began to cry, softly at first and then in a gradual crescendo that seemed destined never to abate.

Wydell was quiet for a long time before he spoke. " 'Lotha, I ain't no fool. I know if it wasn't for you, we wouldn't have nothing. I can see that you been building me up. You gave me back my manhood, and I love you for that. What you asking me to do now—to be somebody's father—I don't know how to do. You know how I was raised. What I'm saying is, the only father I ever had is not the kind I want to be." He looked at her, his eyes brimming with tears, filled with the deepest sadness she'd ever seen.

Delotha moved toward him, her thighs arching out to welcome him. "I'll teach you, Wydell," she said.

Their daughter, Brenda, was born nine months later; Delotha swallowed her disappointment that she wasn't a boy. There was time to try again.

After Delotha came home from the hospital with their baby, she watched Wydell gazing at her for hours. Slowly he became enchanted with her little fingers and tiny toes, with her curling hair and the soft suckling noises that she made with her bottle. "Go ahead and touch her," Delotha said, and she smiled as Wydell stroked the baby's tiny hand.

A few days later, she brought the baby into the living room, where Wydell was sitting, and placed her in his lap. She showed him how to let his daughter's head rest against his shoulder and how to rock her. Then she said, "Tell her you love her, Wydell. Say, 'Daddy loves you.'"

Wydell whispered the words into the baby's ear and kissed her cheek.

One day, without Delotha's asking him to, he picked up the baby, holding her head carefully, as he'd seen her mother do. He sat on the edge of their bed and rocked her in his arms very gently. "I love you, baby," he said to the little girl. "Daddy loves you." He looked up when Delotha came near, and she saw tears in his eyes. "I'm not gon' mess up this time," he said.

30

Watching Elvis Presley, with his spiky black crew cut and army uniform, wave to the crowd on the evening news, Marguerite thought to herself that he could be colored, all that dark hair and those big thick lips. There were plenty of Negroes just as light as Elvis Presley. Her friend Ida was just about his color. The boy who was killed three years before wasn't much darker. Elvis, with his little twitchy behind, sure wanted to sound colored. She wished there were a war, so he could get blown to bits. There were boys in her own church who could sing ten times better than Elvis Presley, but they'd never get to be on television. They wouldn't get to be nothing.

She gazed at the art on the walls surrounding her. Sometimes she hated the pictures that Clayton was constantly hanging up. Picasso, Renoir . . . She could remember some of the artists' names, but all she really knew was that the pictures cost a lot of money. He told her that he had to be surrounded with beauty so he wouldn't see the ugliness in the world, but she wondered why he didn't buy everybody in the Quarters a new house if he didn't like seeing ugly things.

Clayton had started buying art after Armstrong was killed. She knew that the boy had worked for Clayton and that he had been as sad as any of the colored folks when he died, but unlike them, Clayton hadn't cried. After they freed Floyd Cox, he hardly talked for a few days and left their bed only to eat and go to the bathroom. Then when he did get up and leave the house, he came home and started throwing pictures up on the wall, as if all those flowers and old-fashioned white people that made the house so lovely could make the world outside their door beautiful.

He bought himself another Cadillac too, a white one, and a cream-colored Chevrolet for her. She liked her new car, but she'd hardly ever driven the old one. After the trial, Clayton had gone to Memphis and come back with two shopping bags full of dresses and shoes for her. As if she had someplace to wear them. Sometimes she thought it was a sickness, the way he bought things.

Marguerite turned off the television as soon as Clayton walked in the door, bringing a little of the cool autumn weather. His face looked flushed and happy as he spread the books out on the kitchen table and then held up each one to show her. "I got these primers from one of my little cousins," he said, smiling proudly. He pulled his chair around so that he was sitting next to Marguerite, who began flipping through a book; her terror deepened with every page she turned. The smell of freshly brewed coffee pervaded the room, and from time to time Clayton and Marguerite sipped from their cups.

"I can't read hardly nothing out of this," Marguerite said softly. Why did she ever think that she could learn to read? She was too old. She'd managed for months to evade Clayton's persistent quest to teach her, but now he was insisting that she begin in earnest. Closing the book, Marguerite stood up, pulling at the waist of her pedal pushers, smoothing the checkered fabric around the swell of her hips. She adjusted the buttons of her blouse and let her hands rest on the top of her breasts, looking at Clayton the whole time.

He cleared his throat and opened the book that Marguerite had closed. "I don't expect you to be able to read anything. That's why I got you these books. To teach you. Now quit fanning around and sit down."

She seemed shocked by his sudden severity, but she silently obeyed him. When Marguerite was once again beside him, he asked her, "Do you know your alphabet?"

She nodded and began to recite it for Clayton, smiling as she called out the letters in a singsong.

"Very good," he said when she had finished. "You're going to be reading in no time." He turned to the first lesson in the book and studied it intensely for a moment. "Every letter has a sound. When you put all the sounds together, that's reading. Today we'll go over the sounds. You have to memorize them. Now repeat after me. *A* says 'ah.' "

Clayton took Marguerite through the alphabet like a drill sergeant leading his troops to battle. He yelled when she got something wrong, and he kissed her when she pronounced the sounds correctly. At first she passively let Clayton give her the knowledge, but after a while, when she had read several words correctly, she grew exuberantly aggressive, shouting out the answers to questions that Clayton hadn't finished asking. They worked until nearly nine o'clock, and at the end of the lesson Clayton read her *The Little Engine That Could.* When he finished, Marguerite washed the coffee cups and then brought out a bottle of bourbon and two glasses. She placed the glasses on the table and poured each of them a drink.

"You like teaching me to read, don't you?" Marguerite asked, her hand resting lightly on his.

"Why do you say that?"

"Because I ain't never seen you excited before."

"You haven't?"

Marguerite laughed, and Clayton joined in. "Not that kind of excited," she said. "You know what I mean. Why you doing this?"

"Everyone should know how to read," he said, taking a sip of the bourbon. "If you can't read, you can't make decisions. You can't be anything in this society."

"I can't be nothing around here whether I read or not."

There was a tiny flare of anger in her face, like a match burning in total darkness. When she noticed Clayton looking at her, more in fascination than in shock, she quickly smiled. A few moments passed, and when he searched Marguerite's smooth brown face, her expression was tranquil and seductive once again. She reached for his hand across the table and said, "I love you for helping me."

In January, Clayton's father summoned him to the family hunting lodge for the annual week-long party in the woods just northeast of Greenwood. Stonewall Pinochet deliberately chose back roads as he and Clayton drove to the site. "Takes a little scenery to get in the spirit of things," he said jovially. Even on a stark winter day, the countryside was beautiful. They passed through little towns as picturesque as a watercolor and drove by creeks and streams that meandered for miles. "My God, this is pretty country," Clayton said again and again, as he steered the Cadillac down narrow highways and dirt roads. They had loaded the trunk with their clothes and rifles, and every once in a while, when the car would come to a sudden halt, he could hear the guns clattering in the back.

They got to the hunting lodge by midmorning, and by late afternoon all the guests had arrived. Small by upper-crust Delta standards, the lodge was a plain wooden one-story building, with a porch that ran the length of the house in front and led into a hallway and a large parlor, and another porch that swept out from the kitchen and bordered the backyard. The house had sleeping and bath accommodations for ten guests, as well as the kitchen, a formal dining room, the parlor, and a library. Nearly a football field away, there were several cabins for servants, and behind these the stable and a kennel, which were maintained year-round. A cook and a maid were always on the premises during the season, and Pinochet and one or two of the guests each brought along a colored man to fetch and clean the quail and pheasant that they shot. Stonewall and his friends hunted on and off from the time the cotton harvest came in, during December, until late March, when planting season rolled around again. But the first week of January was special, a time when the Honorable Men of Hopewell assembled, assessed, and arranged. For most of the years of his life, Clayton had been part of the great festival of blood and gore, as he called it: the real carnage being not so much the limp carcasses of dead birds that would later adorn their table but the murderous decisions that were made.

Clayton loathed hunting and despised being forced to pretend that his thinking was aligned with that of the self-proclaimed leaders of Hopewell. One day he'd tell his father no. No, he wouldn't go to the lodge. No, he wasn't interested in running the town or aspiring to political office. No, he didn't hate the colored and he didn't see the need of keeping them down. He could taste the rebellion, a strong, bitter taste in his mouth. But for now, he swallowed it.

Early that next morning, after a breakfast of scrambled eggs, grits, bacon, and homemade crackling bread, the men went out to the stable and chose horses, which the colored men saddled for them; they rode out, with the dogs sprinting ahead of them. The horses trotted for a mile or so, until the dogs' steady barking alerted the riders to the proximity of the prey. They were standing in a dense thicket at the base of a huge old pine tree, whose heavy branches seemed to stretch out in all directions for miles, when Stonewall fired the first shot. Clayton watched one of the beagles retrieve the quail his father had felled. The dog barely had the bird in his mouth for a second before Elijah, the colored man his father had brought with him from Hopewell, took the victim and dropped it into a canvas bag. The dog's mouth was rimmed with blood, and he was yelping for more. All around him, the air was alive with the reports of bullets as more and more of the quail came rushing out of the huge pines.

"Why don't you shoot, son?" his father said, looking at him for the first time.

"I'll leave them all for you, Father," Clayton replied.

That night the cook prepared roast quail, new potatoes, and string beans. The hunters ate huge portions, letting the juice dribble down their chins, slurping and chewing with gusto. There were no women present to chastise them for their lack of table manners, and that was the way they liked it.

The maid brought bourbon and coffee to the library, where the smoke from cigars, pipes, and cigarettes was like a thick fog. Clayton wanted to leave, to stand on the back porch in the crisp air and smoke his cigarette alone, but he knew that to do so would displease his father. Clayton didn't want to make his father unhappy; he was planning to ask him for money.

As if on cue, his father said, "Gentlemen, I've got an idea. Hell of a good one, if I do say so myself."

The men assembled laughed, and the idle small talk that they'd been engaging in ceased. They moved their chairs forward and leaned in toward Stonewall, their eyes bright and eager.

"You know the old ways are coming to a close," Pinochet said. "Why, I remember the time when the fields were full of nigras singing and picking cotton. Now it's mostly machines. The Delta's always meant cotton, gentlemen. Well, cotton's hard on the land; we all know that. It's a poor rat that's got but one hole. It's time for a change, my friends. The Delta needs new industry if the people are going to be able to make a living. Otherwise all those nigras who used to be in the fields, the ones that haven't caught the train to Chicago or Detroit, well, they're going to be emptying out the state coffers because of all the money that's being used to pay them welfare checks."

"Stonewall, the Delta's farming country," said Henry Settles. "Always has been. You go importing some heavy industry down here, well, it just ain't gon' work. For one thing, the people ain't trained. For another, machinery will cost a huge amount of money."

"Henry, I'm talking about farming."

"Well . . ."

"Catfish farming."

Stonewall beamed as the faces of his guests registered surprise and confusion. Clayton knew his father enjoyed shocking people almost as much as he liked being able to sway and manipulate them.

"Farming catfish? I didn't know they growed from seeds," one of the guests said. The others laughed.

Pinochet bent his head forward so that he could look every one of the men in the eye without so much as turning his head. "Listen. You breed them just like you breed hogs. Just because they're in the water don't make no difference. If you all will remember, we used to breed the nigras."

The discussion lasted until way into the night, as the men debated the pros and cons of bringing a fishing industry to the Delta. Clayton was about to leave on several occasions, but each time his father caught his eye and he sat back down. He didn't say anything, didn't contribute to the debate in any way, not even in enthusiasm; he just sat by idly, sipping his bourbon and smoking. But he heard enough to know that the new industry his father was heralding offered nothing to the legions of poor whites and blacks who had become idle because of the mechanization of cotton farming. The profit margin of catfish farming would be maintained by the abundance of cheap labor in the area.

By the time the discussion ended, it was after midnight and more than a few bottles of bourbon had been consumed. Clayton was making his exit with the rest of the guests, when his father grabbed him by his arm.

"What do you think about my idea?"

His father's eyes were red, and his cheeks were as rosy as if they'd been frozen in a permanent blush. Clayton searched his face to see if he was drunk and decided that he wasn't. "Sounds like a great business opportunity," he said cautiously.

"I want you to be part of it, son."

Clayton shook his head ruefully. "I'm no farmer, catfish or otherwise."

His father waved his hand impatiently. "Oh, come on. Are you intending to play newspaperman all of your life? My God, Clayton, you're thirty-six years old. You need to start making a commitment to something. What about Ellen Houston?"

"What about her?"

"Are you going to marry her?"

"No."

"Well, who the hell are you going to marry, and when?" His father's eyes seemed redder and certainly angrier than when Clayton had looked at them a minute earlier. "You know what your problem is? You let a little nigra pussy get you sidetracked."

Clayton started walking out of the room. Stonewall followed him, his footsteps slightly unsteady. "You better not be in love with that bitch," he said. "I got a right to have grandchildren. White grandchildren. And by God, I'm going to have them."

Clayton's eyes still burned from the smoke-clogged room. He opened the heavy oak door and walked onto the front porch. The air was dry and chilly, but not cold. As he leaned against the railing of the front porch, everything was quiet. Then, from a great distance, he heard the muted echo of a train whistle blowing in the night. He was glad that somebody was getting out. Shutting his eyes, he imagined the last time he was with Marguerite, the tangle of their thighs, the springy abundance of her hair, the way she straddled him to take her pleasure on top, then let him pull her under him so he could take his. And he thought of Etta, of sitting in her wide lap, his head against her deep bosom, and listening to her sing, her voice at once mournful and palliative, but always lulling enough to put him to sleep. Why was it, he wondered, that so often when he thought of one woman he thought of the other?

Ida flipped over the last tamale in the iron skillet with a spatula that had seen better days, then, satisfied that it was brown enough, dumped the contents of the frying pan onto the last clean paper plate. She'd been up since five-thirty that Saturday morning, cooking dinners for her steady customers, and now she was surrounded by twenty paper plates in her crowded kitchen, with potato salad, tomato slices, and a thick tamale on each of them. She counted the plates carefully. Twenty plates. Fifteen dollars. She couldn't help smiling; in two weeks she and Sweetbabe would be leaving for Chicago.

"What you doing, Mama?"

Ida turned around at the sound of her son's sleepy voice. Sweetbabe stood in front of her, clad in a pajama top and undershorts. He was tall for a four-year-old, with legs as thin as a newborn colt's. Glancing at his legs, ashy in the morning light, she could no longer see the dog-bite puncture marks. His feet were bare.

"Boy, why you didn't put something on? You'll catch cold," she fussed.

Sweetbabe rushed toward her, his head burrowing into her belly. His arms tugged at her waist; she hugged him back. "Who's Mama's loving boy?" she asked. When he mumbled his answer deep in her apron, she laughed. "You hungry?"

He pulled away from her, nodding silently, still wiping sleep from his eyes.

She fried some bacon and eggs and heated up two biscuits from the previous night's supper and listened approvingly while her son mumbled the grace she had taught him. "Mama," he said, his mouth full of food, "is we moving to Chicago?"

"Yep."

"When?"

"In two weeks."

"And we gon' live there forever?"

"We'll come back to visit sometime. You can spend the summers."

"Mama, I don't want to go."

"Sweetbabe, you gon' like it. They got all kinds of things to do there. And they got good schools so you can grow up to be an educated man."

"I can be an educated man right here," the boy insisted, his mouth set in a stubborn frown.

"No, baby, you can't," Ida said softly. "Now you eat."

Her father hadn't liked the idea of their leaving any more than Sweetbabe liked it, although gradually he was won over. The last time they'd spoken about the impending move, he said grudgingly, "I guess maybe you're looking to find a husband in Chicago, 'cause they sure got some no-'count men 'round here."

Ida had to suppress a bitter laugh. She'd experienced a few of Hopewell's trifling colored men, enough to know that she wanted something better for herself and for her son. She had been stunned when Sweetbabe's father, a boy she'd known practically all her life, ran away to Detroit when he learned that she was pregnant. Until her child was nearly two years old, the trauma of her lover's betrayal numbed any desire for romance. Had she covered herself in black and sprinkled ashes over her head, she couldn't have grieved more. "You had a baby. You didn't die," Odessa told her more than once. But her pain seemed to be a kind of death to Ida.

And then, right around the time Sweetbabe started going to the bathroom on his own, desire began surging through her, as uncontrollable as a virus. She met men on Saturday nights at juke joints in different towns that bordered Hopewell. They were sharecroppers, mostly cotton pickers; some were bootleggers. A series of quick, clandestine affairs, carried out more often than not in the back seat of a borrowed car, was the means of her reentry into the world of romance. Ida put her hands over the men's mouths when they started promising her things, closed her ears when they started lying. *Don't expect nothing from any of them,* she told herself; that way she wouldn't be disappointed. Her father was wrong. She wasn't looking for a husband in Chicago. She was looking for what she'd come to believe only she could provide for herself and Sweetbabe: a better life.

Ida turned away from her son and walked to the kitchen door. "Fern! Lizzie Mae!" she called. She heard the soft patter of feet coming down the narrow hallway, and then the two thin, brown-skinned girls stood before her.

"Ma'am?" they said in unison.

"Y'all get dressed. I need you to make some deliveries for me. There's the list over there. Sweetbabe is just about finished eating; you can take him with you. He can carry some. Can't you, little man?"

When she was alone in the kitchen again, she sighed at the prospect of the grueling labor that still lay ahead of her. There were ten fried-chicken dinners to cook, and nearly as many people wanted spare ribs. Ida cleared off the wooden counter and starting cutting up chickens.

By five o'clock the dinners had been prepared and delivered, and the dollars from the day's work were resting in the bottom of Ida's drawer with the rest of the money she'd earned. As soon as she put the money away, Ida slipped on a pair of old tennis shoes and a sweater and bounded out the door.

The sky above her on the dirt road wasn't quite dark, and the February air was mild and crisp. Ida started run-

ning, long, easy strides, but gradually the wooden
shacks and shotgun houses began to be one long blur as
she picked up speed. She had always loved running, and
when she was in school she usually beat even the fastest
boys in races. One time she had spent the night at the
home of the colored schoolteacher. The woman had hot
and cold water and an indoor bathroom, the first Ida
had ever seen; she insisted that Ida take a bath. When
Ida was covered with the soapy warm water, her body
felt brand-new. Running was like that for her.

She stayed out until she thought her legs were going
to fall off and she was so hot and breathless she could
barely move. Ida was almost limping by the time she
reached her house. The front window shade was up, and
inside she could see several of the neighbors gathered in
the parlor with her sisters and brothers, almost like a
party.

When Ida opened the door they all looked up at her,
but nobody said a word. Her breath was returning as
she looked around the room, staring at each person.
Sweetbabe wasn't with them. She balled up her fists
and held them stiffly at her sides. "Where's Sweetbabe?" The question came out shrill, almost hysterical.
She looked at Lizzie Mae and Fern. They were crying.

Fern spoke quickly, wiping her eyes. "He's all right.
He went next door to play."

"It's Daddy, Ida. Daddy got hurt. Bad," said Lizzie
Mae. "He was putting a roof on a house over by the
Confederacy, and he fell off the ladder. They think he
done broke his back."

As it turned out, William's back wasn't broken, but
his hip was fractured in several places. Dr. Mitchell
kept him in traction at the Yabalusha County Hospital
for more than a month, then sent him home in a wheelchair, with a hospital bill of almost $250, and told him
that he needed to think about a new way of making a
living. His days as a builder were over. "Just as soon as
I'm able to get around, I want you and Sweetbabe to

catch that train to Chicago," William told Ida. "I don't want you staying here on my account."

"Just get well, Daddy," Ida said.

Ida put all thoughts of Chicago out of her head and turned her attention to the immediate and pressing issue of earning a living for her family. The hospital bill stalked her mind like a monster. At night she couldn't sleep, and during the day her temples pounded; sometimes the pain was so intense it was like being struck blind, over and over again. One rainy March night, as she sat in the kitchen, the bills arranged around the table like so many pieces of a jigsaw puzzle, she looked up and Lizze Mae and Fern stood before her.

"We can quit school and get jobs," Fern said.

Ida was so intent on the numbers on the slips of paper before her that the voice of her sister startled her. She looked toward the girls and stared for several seconds before she actually saw them.

"What?" She spoke slowly, like a drunk not sure of her words. "What'd you say?"

"She said we can quit school and get us some jobs," Lizzie Mae repeated.

Ida shook her head. All the numbers had made her dizzy. "They ain't no jobs around here, or haven't y'all noticed. Why do you think everybody be wanting to leave? They don't even hardly have cotton-picking jobs no more."

Her sisters said nothing, but their expressions bore the pain and frustration of not being able to help. "Y'all just go to bed. Everything will work out," she added, but not very forcefully.

Ida went to all her Saturday and Sunday dinner customers and tried to sell them dinners every day, but there wasn't enough money in the colored community to support such an enterprise, and whites in the area who could afford her food had their own cooks. Miss Rozelle told her, "Chile, you need to get on the county.

At least that way you know you ain't gon' starve to death."

Ida reflected on the hopeless faces of some of the people on relief and realized that there were different kinds of starvation. She was young and strong; she'd rather work.

At night she ran until every part of her hurt, and then she ran beyond the pain. When she took off her tennis shoes, she always expected to see blood gushing from her feet.

One Monday afternoon, the postman handed her a letter with her father's name on it. After a second she opened it. The letter was official and said that if William's hospital bill wasn't paid by a certain date, they would lose their home and land. Ida folded the letter and slipped it back into the envelope and put it on the kitchen table. Then she put on her nicest dress, blue cotton with an A-line skirt, and her best shoes. She placed the black hat on her head and began walking to town.

The strong breeze raised Ida's skirt as she knocked on the back door of the Busy Bee Café. No one answered for a long time, and then the door swung open and Ida looked into the stern face of Willow Scott, whose braid was lifted off the back of her neck by the surge of wind that rushed through the door. "What you want, baby?" Willow said. She said "baby" as if she could have been talking to a child or her man.

"Miss Willow," Ida said, her words running together almost as fast as her heart was beating. "Miss Willow, do they need another cook here?"

Before she could answer, Florine came bustling to the back door. "What's that about a cook?" she asked.

Ida looked from Florine's tired fat face to Willow's thin one.

Ida said quickly, "I was just wondering if maybe y'all needed another cook."

"Don't need but one cook," Florine said, and walked away.

"She ain't nobody to be telling you nothing," Willow said without trying to lower her voice. Then, in a gentler tone, she asked, "How's your daddy doing?"

"The same."

"You still going to Chicago?"

"I can't go now. When he gets better, me and Sweetbabe will go. Be good to be someplace where he can get an education and where I don't hafta hear people calling my mother names."

Willow grabbed her arm. "Your mama was a good woman. You remember that."

"You all were friends, weren't you?"

"Your mama and me was tight partners," Willow said, smiling.

Ida searched the smooth brown face. People had told her that Willow was a strange woman, that she knew voodoo and magic and wasn't afraid of anything or anybody. That she didn't lie. "Miss Willow, do you know who my father is?"

Willow put her hand on Ida's face. "Girl, I don't even know who my own daddy is. Don't much care, neither. I know he's an Indian man. Choctaw." Someone called, "Willow!" from inside the restaurant.

"Whoever mine is, I hate him," Ida said.

Willow shook her head. "Don't do that, child. In life, the trick is just to do what's necessary to keep on living. Hating him is like trying to run with a sack of rocks in your drawers. It'll slow you down; might even get you killed. He ain't done right by you, but you remember this here: Life will give you what you deserve, even when people don't. You don't believe that, you just keep on living."

"Willow!" the same voice called again.

"You rest your mind," Willow said, then disappeared inside the restaurant.

As she was walking away, Ida saw the white Cadillac parked in front of the diner. Turning around, she peered into the big glass picture window and saw Clayton eating by himself and poring over a newspaper. She quelled the urge to tap on the window and wave.

She was halfway home when she heard the car behind her and felt a gush of air as the Cadillac passed by. Then the car came to a slow stop.

"Ida, I'm going your way," Clayton said, smiling.

She got into the back seat.

They didn't speak at all during the ride. Clayton rolled down the window and lit a cigarette. When they reached her house, Ida thanked him and was about to get out, when words clumsy as a turned-over glass of buttermilk began spilling from her lips. "I need a job, Mr. Pinochet. I know Armstrong used to work for you, and I thought maybe there might be something I could do. My daddy got hurt, and I have to make some money. If I . . ."

His cheeks looked as if someone had rubbed lipstick across them. "I'm sorry," he said. "I don't have a job. I just can't help you."

He seemed so sad when he spoke that Ida had to fight the urge to put her arms around his shoulders, to tell him that everything would be all right. Later, after she had had time to think, she told herself that her interpretation of Clayton Pinochet's mood must have been wrong. What in the world would a rich white man have to feel sad about?

31

Dora, the midwife, handed Lily the new baby after she washed her and wiped her nostrils with a clean rag. "A girl, Miss Lily," the old black woman said. "Has your milk done come in yet? The little gal's hungry, ain't you, honey? What's her name?"

Lily felt the glow of her own smile radiating inside her. She had had two miscarriages since the trial and was beginning to fear that her body, like her life, would always betray her. Holding her daughter, she felt renewed. The baby was heavy, she thought, bigger than Floydjunior had been. "Doreen," Lily said softly, pulling open the top of her gown and pushing her nipple into the baby's mouth. She kissed the crown of the baby's head, tasted the damp blond curls. A girl! She knew that Floyd didn't want another baby; he'd gotten angry when she told him she was pregnant, but oh, he would be happy when he saw how beautiful she was. Her mama always told her: Sons will leave you, but daughters stay. She thought about the men who'd passed through her own life: her daddy, with his heavy, mean hands; her two brothers, who'd gone off to Detroit after the war and hadn't been heard from since; Uncle Charlie, fingering her private parts and whispering nasty secrets in her ear. Floyd. Mama was right. Men took from you, one way or another.

Outside, an unexpected February storm had iced all the roads and made getting around on foot or by car nearly impossible. Lily could hear tiny drops falling inside the kitchen and her bedroom. The baby sucked so vigorously that Lily gasped and held her breath until she got used to the pulling sensation on her nipples. Then she began to relax. "Don't be so greedy, Doreen," she whispered. As she nursed, she watched the rain falling in the corner of the bedroom, a steady drip sliding down the wall, which was permanently soggy from water damage. If they didn't get another roof put on the house soon, the one they had was going to cave in. Floydjunior was asleep in the living room, and for a moment she panicked, thinking that he was getting wet. She shifted her weight a little in the bed, and her nipple fell out of the baby's mouth. The wail, thin but piercing, rattled her, and she could barely manage to pull the baby to her other breast, wincing again as the newborn's mouth clamped down hard around her unchristened nipple.

The midwife looked out the window. Her plain black-rimmed glasses slipped down on her wide, flat nose as she shook her head. She was a short, narrow woman; her waist ran into her hips without any indentation. "Sure is some ugly weather," she said. "I hope one of my boys comes for me. I sure don't want to be walking home in that mess." She looked around the room and then stepped to the bedroom door and craned her neck, listening to the drops falling in the other rooms. "Honey, you gon' drown in this here house. Is y'all got some buckets or something?"

"In the kitchen. Under the sink." Lily was relieved that she hadn't had to ask her.

Dora's heavy steps echoed throughout the house. Lily leaned forward, listening to whether the midwife had found the pots, then lay back when she heard the rattling under the sink and then the sound of the containers being set beneath the leaks, the steady plop, plop, plop.

"These gon' fill up mighty quick, the way it's coming down," Dora said, putting a pan under the drip near the window. "When's your husband coming back?"

"I don't know," Lily answered dully. Floyd had been gone for nearly a week on a construction job in Louisiana. Before that he'd been out of work for the entire winter.

The day before he left, Floyd chopped a load of wood and dumped it on the back porch, not even in a pile. Just let it spread out thick all over the place, so that she and Floydjunior could hardly walk through. He borrowed a car and drove to the Jitney Jungle, a new grocery store halfway between Greenwood and Hopewell, and brought home two bags full of food, mostly canned goods, Spam and pork and beans. After he set the groceries on the table he said, "When he was running for president that Kennedy talked a mighty good game about prosperity being for all Americans, but he's a politician just like the rest of 'em. Don't none of 'em mean to help a workingman, and that's the goddamn truth."

Lily only half listened; she was too busy putting away the food and wondering if it was enough to last. They still had a few jars of the vegetables she had canned in the summer. As long as she had bread, she could always make herself and Floydjunior a peanut butter and jelly sandwich.

Floyd told her that he didn't know when he was coming home.

"Well, we'll probably have us a new baby when you get back," she said. She tried to make her voice light and gay, to hide the fear that she felt at being left alone so near her time.

Floyd just grunted, and she thought: *That's right. Blame me.*

Mamie came to the house right before Floyd left. "My men didn't spend not one night in jail until you come along, Miss Magnolia Queen," her mother-in-law told her, speaking as casually as if she were reporting the weather.

She sipped iced tea made with Lily's own hands and

sat down at her kitchen table. "Some women will drive a decent man to do things that will cause a lot of heartache. I reckon John Earl, Louetta, and them would still be living right here in Hopewell if it wasn't for that trouble you caused," the old woman told her, right in front of Floyd. "Of course, they's doing fine. New house with a bathroom. Everything."

Floyd sprang from his chair and stalked out.

Lily had sent Floydjunior to get the granny, who'd delivered her baby after her water broke. She knew he had to wade through gumbo mud and had worried about him catching a cold, especially since the soles of his shoes were as thin as a drinking man's promises, but she hadn't had anybody else to send.

"That's gon' be fifteen dollars for bringing that youngin," the midwife said.

The baby had stopped nursing, and when Lily peeked at her she was falling asleep. She lifted Doreen to her shoulder and softly patted her back until she heard a thin burp. She kept patting and rubbing her daughter's soft back and shifting her eyes, so she didn't have to look at Dora, whose usually pleasant mouth was now tight. Lily whispered, "Is it all right if I pay you after my husband gets back? I ain't got no money right now."

A horn blared right outside the house, and Dora pulled up the shade at the bedroom window and looked out, then gathered her purse and the large plastic bag that contained her towels, the alcohol, and cotton swabbing. She looked at Lily doubtfully. "I know about that trouble you caused. I be trying to act like a Christian. I just hope y'all don't cheat ole Dora."

She wanted to ask the woman to stay with her, but she was too scared. "Can you come back in the morning?" she managed to whisper.

The midwife said, "I can't make you no promises."

When Lily heard the front door close she began crying. The rags between her legs were wet with blood and sticking to her thighs. Suppose the blood didn't stop?

She could bleed to death in a house where the rain came in.

The midwife didn't return the next morning. Lily tried to stand up, but everything started whirling around, so she stayed in bed all that day and kept Floydjunior home from school. She called her son to her. "Now you're gon' have to be mama's little man, since Daddy's not here. I want you to go get some wood from the back porch and put some in the stove to keep the fire going. And then I want you to empty them buckets and pans and set them right back down where they was."

Floydjunior gave her bed a swift hard kick.

"Floydjunior, you mean ole thing, you stop that," Lily yelled.

Standing in front of his mother's bed with his two fists balled up, he looked like a little old man. "Go do like I told you," Lily said.

The baby began to cry; Lily fumbled around with her top, trying to get her nipple into the baby's mouth but not wanting Floydjunior to see. Then the baby dropped her breast, and for a moment it was dangling in full view of her son. The boy stared at her in a mean, frightening way. Lily slipped the nipple back into the baby's mouth and shielded the exposed side of her breast with her hand.

"Why ain't he here to tend to the fire and empty the water buckets? Why do I have to do what he's supposed to be here doing?" The boy's green eyes flickered with anger.

"Floydjunior, you hush up and go do what I told you to do right now, before I get out of this bed and give you a good switching."

"You can't get up. You're still sick from having a baby."

Lily swung her feet over the side of the bed and attempted to stand, but she was overcome by a wave of dizziness.

"All right," Floydjunior said, his voice tight. "I'll do it, but it ain't fair." He gave the bedstead one final, fierce kick.

Floydjunior made them peanut butter and jelly sandwiches two days in a row. He didn't bathe or brush his teeth, just fell into bed dressed in the same dirty clothes he played in all day long. The rags between Lily's legs were soaked and smelled rotten, and the tops of her thighs were itchy with dried blood, when finally the rain stopped. She made Floydjunior go fetch Mamie, who came hours later, driven by a neighbor who had a car.

"Why, she looks like Dolly," Mamie said when she saw the baby. She started crying and handed her back to Lily. "You don't know," she said. "You just don't know."

"These is terrible times we's living in," Mamie said later when she calmed herself. "In North Ca'lina them niggers is trying to eat at the Woolworth's with white folks. Sit-in, they call it. Lordy, Lordy. What is this world coming to? And they say that Kennedy is on their side. He's gon' try to make them as good as us."

Mamie stayed for two days, bursting into tears whenever she went near the baby and lashing out against the integration that she declared would be the ruination of everyone. In between crying jags she cooked and made Floydjunior bathe, but she didn't wash the dishes or any of their dirty clothes.

"I wish I could do for you," Mamie said, "but this arthritis has got me down. And then every time I look at that child's face . . ."

Right after Mamie went home, Lily saw Jacqueline Kennedy for the first time on the television that Floyd had bought at Weiner's. She was sitting on the sofa, nursing Doreen, and when she saw her, Lily thought that Jacqueline Kennedy—who wore a short dress, as she guessed most of the stylish women in Washington, D.C., and New York and Memphis did—was pretty enough to be a movie star; Lily was awed by her whispery, proper voice. She talked as though she was used to servants bringing her breakfast in bed and pulling down her covers for her at night. After a while, Lily couldn't listen to Mrs. Kennedy's well-modulated tones any longer, and she turned off the television.

They were paying for the TV set on time, and already they'd received several letters from Weiner's, chiding them about their overdue account. Floyd balled up the letters and threw them into the trash.

After Mamie left, Lily looked in the pantry; there wasn't enough food to last them until Friday. There were some eggs, a few slices of bread, half a can of government peanut butter, a little bit of sausage, and some butter beans. They didn't have milk or cereal, not even cheese, and no vegetables. Well, she thought, if they ran out, she'd have to send Floydjunior over to Mamie's. She didn't have any choice. Floyd hadn't given her any money.

On Thursday night Lily and Floydjunior ate one egg apiece and half a slice of bread with peanut butter on it. When they were finished, her son told her that he was still hungry. "There ain't no more food," Lily said.

"But I'm hungry," the boy said.

"Tomorrow you can go get some food from Grandma Mamie."

"But you're supposed to feed me, not Grandma. You and Daddy!"

The boy's face, his blazing eyes, stayed in her mind late that night as she tried to trace the path that had led to a dinner of one egg and a piece of bread smeared with government peanut butter.

In the morning she sent Floydjunior down to Mamie's, and he returned with a small sack of grits and four cans of pork and beans. "She said this was all she could spare until she got to the store," Floydjunior said, his little face grim and angry. He dropped the food on the bed, where Lily was feeding the baby. "What are we gonna do when this is gone?" he asked suddenly.

"By that time Daddy'll be here," Lily said softly.

"No he won't," Floydjunior yelled, slamming his fist against the edge of the bed. Before Lily could respond, he ran out of the room.

Four days later, Lily sent Floydjunior to the midwife's house. "You tell her your mama said could she spare a little food, because your daddy ain't come back yet."

"I don't want to eat nigger food!"

"It's better than no food," Lily said grimly, giving him a hard push. When she heard the front door slam close, she began crying again. *I don't even have no white people to go to,* she thought, remembering bitterly how angry Floyd used to get when her friend Corinne came around. Now she had no one.

Dora sent her a mason jar of peach preserves, half a loaf of white bread, some government powdered milk, which Floydjunior refused to drink, and the message that she wanted her money. There was enough food for three meals. In the middle of the second one, Lily began crying again.

In all, she went to Mamie and the midwife seven times before the minister from Starlight Baptist, her church, came knocking on the door. Floydjunior led him into the bedroom, which smelled like blood and baby pee. Lily was sitting in the bed, the covers down around her ankles, nursing the baby. She heard a sharp intake of breath and then a quick, deep cough. "Oh," she said, looking up to see a tall young man, whose face was turning red, while his wide-open gray eyes stayed on her exposed breast.

Lily pulled the cover up around the baby's head. "Yessir?" she said.

"Miss Lily?" He wasn't from the Delta, she could tell from his voice, which had more of a lilt to it, like singing. As he spoke, he pulled his fingers through his short brown hair. His fingernails were clean and evenly cut. "I'm Reverend Alston from Starlight Baptist."

"Yessir." She couldn't speak above a whisper.

"We got word from your mother-in-law that you just had a baby and might be needing some help. She sure is a pretty little thing. I thought I'd come by and just see what it is you needed."

His voice was like an arm around her shoulders. "I . . ."

Reverend Alston sat down on the bed and put his hand on her face. "Miss Lily, you just go on and cry."

Her head dropped against his shoulder. "It's been so hard," she said. "And it's all my fault."

"I hardly see where having a baby and trying to feed your kids is your fault. Where's your husband?" he asked gently.

"Louisiana. He's working there."

"When is he coming back?"

"I don't know. He's been gone three weeks, and I ain't heard from him." She began crying again. "I don't know what to do. I can't feed my boy."

Reverend Alston patted her back. "Now, Miss Lily, the church can certainly help you out for the present time. And you need to know that in the event your husband has deserted you, you can get assistance from the government."

"What do you mean?" Lily wiped her eyes and drew the back of her hand across her nose.

Reverend Alston cleared his throat. "Well, Miss Lily, have you ever heard of welfare?"

"But that's for coloreds."

"Well, no, white folks use it too sometimes. But let's not even think about that right now. I'm sure your husband is trying to get back home to his pretty wife and baby and fine son." He smiled at her, and for the first time in a long while Lily felt safe.

Reverend Alston returned later in the day with several boxes of food, which he brought into her kitchen and put away. "I just can't thank you enough," Lily said when he was about to leave.

"This is from the church, and we're just glad to help. Please call us if you need anything. Just send word by your mother-in-law. And we'll keep you in our prayers."

"Yessir. Thank you."

The baby was nearly a month old on the day a weary Lily heard an old truck drive up into the yard and then men's voices, thick and heavy as work boots. By the time she got up, the truck was backing out of the yard and Floyd was in the bedroom. She smelled him before she saw him, smelled the hard work and the meanness that circled the days he hadn't washed, just as clearly as she did the embedded grime and perspiration. When Floyd came toward her she looked up, not knowing whether to smile or scream, wondering why she wanted to do both.

"Hey," she said softly, calling to Floyd, her own voice a surprise to her. The baby was sleeping on her lap. *He will love her*, she thought so hard she knew she was praying. *If he just smiles, if he just looks happy for a minute* . . .

Floyd pulled off his shirt and pants and let them fall on the floor. He walked over to Lily and looked at the baby in her arms. "What you got there?"

"Doreen." *Be happy*, she thought.

Lily watched him pull the blanket back and look at the baby's chubby legs; he picked up one of her tiny feet in his hand, then gazed at her toes. His restless eyes traveled the length of the smooth, round body. He touched her fingers and shoulders, and all the while he wasn't smiling, all the while his eyes were fixed in a hard stare, examining the new flesh as if he was searching for some blatant flaw. Bending down, his mouth almost touching the soft skin, he pursed his lips and blew a little air on the baby's face until she opened her eyes. His face didn't soften even then; he just stared some more, studying every inch of her with a frightening intensity. Lily wished that he had never come back, that she could get along without him. She didn't want his hateful gaze all over their child. She covered the baby with the blanket and shielded her from his eyes. "She'll get cold," Lily said.

"Where she get that hair from? Blond."

She started rocking the child in a slow, soothing rhythm, her hand patting the baby's back. Floyd took another step toward her, and she narrowed her eyes, almost closed them. His smell was clogging her nostrils, and his breaths felt like rocks landing on her body. She started humming a tuneless song with no beginning and no end, and for the life of her she couldn't remember where she'd first heard it. She turned away from Floyd, because she didn't want to see what was there in his eyes, what had been there for five years now: If she would go into a room full of nigger men, what else would she do? What else had she done? "She got my mama's hair," she said when the song ended.

Floyd was closer to her now, pressed against her so that she could taste the stink of him. He said, "Your mama's hair."

"That's right." She held her breath. She didn't want to smell him or taste him.

He walked away from her, with his head turned, so he could still see her. Standing by the bed, he pulled off the rest of his clothes and then kicked them into a corner. "Heat me up some water, will you?"

32

In the morning Floyd sat on the edge of the bed, counting his money, while Lily nursed the baby. He could see her eyes on the dollar bills sprinkled softly on the dingy spread. Nearly a month of working, and here was good money to show for it, he thought, sighing. One hundred seventy-five dollars. That would last them a little while. Maybe his luck was changing. The foreman said he'd get in touch with him soon for another job. If only he could keep working steady, they could get out of the slump they were in. Probably just as well he closed the pool hall; a lot of the niggers had left town.

"Floyd," Lily said softly, "we need food bad."

He turned to look at her. Her hand was against her breast, guiding the nipple into the baby's mouth. The mouth that, to his eyes, didn't resemble his in the least.

"I bought y'all plenty a food before I left."

"That didn't last but a week and a half."

He stiffened a little. "What'd y'all do after that?"

"Your mother gave us food and"—she hesitated for a moment—"she sent the people from the church around. Reverend Alston, that's the new pastor, he brought us some things. But now it's just about gone. He said if we needed anything I should just send word through Mamie."

"You didn't run begging to them church folks, did you?"

"I just had a baby, Floyd. I couldn't go running nowhere."

Floyd stood up, inhaling deeply. He started walking toward the door.

"Where you going?" There was alarm in Lily's voice, and Floyd liked hearing it.

"To borrow a car so we can go get some groceries."

Forty dollars. Lily held the money Floyd had given her balled up in one fist. She hadn't touched money for months. She remembered that once when she was a girl and her mother baked five potato pies and sold them for thirty-five cents apiece, she kept taking the money out of her pocket and smiling at it, as if it was something alive and breathing; and now here she was, smiling at the money Floyd had given her, grinning because Floydjunior and even the baby were in the car and she was alone in the store with money in her hand.

Piling staples on the counter—potatoes, flour, sugar, coffee, rice, bread—her eyes got wider each time she saw something else that she wanted. Spam. Tuna fish. Pork and beans. Jell-O. Lemon Jell-O. She bought Octagon soap powder and Bon Ami cleanser. Was there enough money for apples? For bananas? She wanted real milk, not the powdered kind.

"You sure do look happy, Miz Cox," said the clerk at the counter, a round, rosy man.

And that was another thing. People were speaking to her and Floyd again, going out of their way to say hello and comment on the weather. The sudden civility frightened her until she began to realize that they were being forgiven, partly because time had passed, but mostly because of the "unrest" that was spilling over from Little Rock and Montgomery. As long as the niggers were following that scrawny, uppity preacher in Alabama, no white person could be left out of the fold. Especially those who proved they'd take a stand. "Yes," she said. "Oh, yes."

The total was $35.14. Her hand closed over the four one-dollar bills, the three quarters, one dime, one penny.

The clerk was busy putting her groceries into bags. Lily peered out the window. She could see Floyd sitting in the car, looking bored. When the clerk handed her the change, she peeked out the window again. Floyd's head was turned. She didn't want her hands to be empty ever again. She stuck two of the dollar bills inside her bra and kept the rest in a tight fist as she followed the boy carrying her bags.

The foreman for the job Floyd had in Louisiana didn't write or send word the first week, and one afternoon early in the middle of the second week, Floyd called him on the public telephone at Burke's Drugstore. The man's voice sounded sleepy when he answered. Yawning, he told Floyd, "It's kind of dry right now, Cox. Might be a couple of months before anything comes up."

Floyd lit a Winston and started walking along Jefferson Davis Boulevard, pulling up the collar of his thin wool jacket. There weren't many people out; too cold and damp. Most of the men were probably off in the woods, hunting. He walked up and down the block, looking into store windows in a desultory manner. A couple of men who were standing outside the Busy Bee Café spoke to him, and for a minute he thought he might go inside and sit down and drink a cup of coffee in peace and quiet without a screaming baby in the background. His hand was on the door when he realized that what he really wanted was something stronger to warm him up.

Jake was standing in the clearing, marching back and forth, stamping his feet and singing, when Floyd came up to him. Niggers seemed always to be singing, he thought. "Hey there, Jake," he said. Frosted air stood between them.

Jake smiled. "How you been getting on, Mr. Floyd?"

"Fair to middling."

"I been doing about that myself. Wife and family doing all right?"

"Everybody's fine. Say, I wonder could I get a pint off you?" He held out a dollar.

Jake reached in his pocket and pulled out a thick wad of bills, held together with a rubber band. Then he reached deeper into his pocket and handed Floyd two quarters. "I'll be right back."

Spring came, and the foreman from Louisiana still hadn't sent word. Floyd began calling up all the bosses he'd worked for in the last few years, and all of them said the same thing: no work. More and more often, he wandered down Jefferson Davis Boulevard, looking in the store windows and then going by the still to buy a pint from Jake.

One night when he came in, Lily said, "We could go to Birmingham, like Louetta and John Earl done. Didn't they look fine the last time they come home. Floyd, they have a car and a telephone, a bathroom and—"

"Ain't what I give you good enough?"

When she didn't answer him, he slapped her across the face twice, so fast she was inclined to believe it never happened.

In June, Floyd joined a work crew that was clearing out five acres of woods for a new road. He was one of two white men working with about twenty colored. The second day on the job, the foreman came to him. "The niggers know about that boy you kilt," the man said. He gave him six dollars for the two days he worked. Floyd walked back home and sat on his front porch, drinking the last of a pint he'd bought from Jake.

Lily came out later and stood in front of him. He could feel her looking at him. "They let me go," he said.

"Why?" He could hear tears in her voice.

"Damn niggers didn't want to work with me, that's why."

All he had left was $37.53, and how far would that go? He slammed his fist into the doorjamb.

The next morning he left the house early and walked to the Confederacy, where the lawns were clipped and accented with rosebushes and clumps of zinnias and hydrangeas. He went around to the back door of the first house he saw. When he knocked, a scrawny black girl, still in her teens, came to the door. "Ask your missus to come here," he said.

"What you want with Miz Jameson?" the girl asked. She had a dishrag in one hand, and the other was placed on her hip.

"I want to see if she has any odd jobs she needs doing."

"Humph." The girl shut the door squarely in his face. Moments later, a middle-aged white woman appeared.

"Morning, ma'am. I was wondering if you needed any work done. I'm between jobs, and I got me a family."

"Well." The woman stared at him a long time, studying his face. Finally she said, "Well, I got some wood that needs stacking, and my garden needs weeding. How much will you charge me to do that?"

"Well, I don't know. What do you think is fair?"

"Tell you what. I'll give you five dollars. Will that do?"

Floyd wanted to ask to see the wood and the garden, but he was afraid that if he made such a request, the offer would evaporate. "That's fine, ma'am."

The skinny black girl led him around to the back of the house. The garden was about half an acre, and the pile of wood could have filled a quarter of the garden. He was looking at a full day's labor.

Floyd worked straight through the day, and sometimes he could hear Mrs. Jameson giving orders to the colored girl, telling her, in a pinched, superior voice, to wash the dishes and iron the clothes. And at times she would come outside and in that same self-important tone command him to do her bidding. He remembered when he had the pool hall and gave the orders.

When he finished it was almost dark, and his arms felt as though they were on fire. Mrs. Jameson handed him his money and said, "Come back tomorrow morning around nine o'clock. You can scrub the floors and wash the windows." She didn't ask him. They were standing on the back porch, and he kept his eyes on the floor. "Yes, ma'am," he said.

Walking home, he kicked every rock that was in his path. Going to the back door like a goddamn nigger and then working like one too. Well, no more, by God. No more. If he'd been able to keep the pool hall, why, he wouldn't have to go begging for a job. By God, he wouldn't beg for one now. Damn if he'd go back to that bitch's house in the morning.

He had to wait ten minutes before Jake appeared in the clearing. He smoked three cigarettes and slapped at the mosquitoes that circled his head, until he heard footsteps, twigs breaking, grass rustling.

He drank the first pint standing there, jawboning with Jake. "I'll take another one," he said, handing Jake the empty bottle.

"Mr. Floyd, Mr. Floyd, you better take it easy," Jake said, laughing.

Floyd watched as Jake pulled out his money roll. The size of the wad startled him. There must have been two or three hundred dollars in Jake's hand. Maybe more. He rubbed his hand across his mouth and then licked his lips. With three hundred dollars he could start over, maybe go someplace else and open up a little business. A poolroom. A juke joint. Someplace where the niggers didn't know him.

He saw a rock the size of a cantaloupe not ten steps away from him. A rock that size could knock somebody out. He could take it and bring it down over Jake's head, not hard, just hard enough to stun him, grab the money, and run. There was nobody around. Why should he have to work like a nigger? It wasn't fair. He had had a business, and now it was all gone.

"Here you go, Mr. Floyd," Jake said, handing him another bottle. "You have a good evening, now, suh. You all right? You don't look too good."

Floyd's knees were wobbling, and his face had turned pale.

"I'm all right." He stared at the rock. Then Floyd looked at big, black, greasy Jake, who towered over him. What if Jake hit him? Floyd looked at the rock again, then walked down the narrow path to the road.

Lily and Floydjunior were eating supper when he stumbled in. She got up as soon as she saw him, and was looking over her shoulder as she went to the stove and started dishing up another plate. His son stared at Floyd quickly, then bowed his head when Floyd looked their way. "I have your dinner right here, honey," she said.

"I ain't hungry," Floyd said. When he looked at Lily she stepped back. "What are you looking at?"

"I . . . I . . ." She held her breath.

Floyd moved toward her. "Why don't you ask me what I been doing all day? Ask me."

"Where'd you go, Floyd?"

"Over to the Confederacy. I been working like a nigger all day. I stacked wood and I weeded a garden. And I got me five dollars to prove it." He patted down his pockets and pulled out four crumpled one-dollar bills. "I had me five dollars."

She began to bob back and forth, like a rubber doll blowing in a stiff breeze. "Things will get better, Floyd. We just have to—" The baby began crying from the bedroom, a soft whining sound.

He whispered the question. "Why did you go in there that day? Why didn't you mind me?" He put his hand on her upper arm. Her flesh was soft where he squeezed. He wanted to hurt her. He heard a sudden shuffling, and when he looked at the table, the boy was gone.

"I have to go get the baby." Lily's voice was patient, with an expectant lilt to it, but fearful. "I have to feed her."

He wasn't letting her go. Not to feed a yellow-haired baby that didn't even look like him. "Why'd you go in there? Answer me that?" He thought about his father and John Earl, the two of them standing outside his cell, unable to look him in the eyes.

"Floyd, the baby . . ."

The slap left a bright trail of strawberries across her cheek. "Why'd you go in there and ruin everything? Huh?" he said, shaking her by the shoulders until her head seemed to be dancing on top of her neck. He punched her in the face, and she fell on the floor, moaning; he kicked her in the stomach three times, and when she tried to crawl past him, he kicked her again.

When he came in, Lily was sitting in the bed, nursing the baby and smoking a cigarette. Doreen's eyes were closing. "I'm sorry, honey," Floyd said, rubbing his hand across her thigh. "Did you hurt yourself?"

She leaned away from him and held the baby closer; Doreen's eyes opened wide. "Just let me feed her," Lily said. Her lip was bruised, and her eyes were swollen and turning dark. When he pulled the sheet down, her raised nightgown revealed black and blue blotches on her thighs.

"My God," he said, stepping away from the bed. "My God."

He watched as Lily fed the baby. "I'm turning us into trash, Lily."

"We ain't trash, Floyd."

Later, after she put the baby back in the used bassinet that one of the church ladies had sent over, Lily checked on Floydjunior, who had fallen asleep on the couch in the living room with his clothes on. She turned off the light without waking him. Then she went back into the bedroom. Floyd was snoring and trembling in his sleep. Watching him, she was convulsed with fear and overwhelmed by the sickening memory of being held prisoner on her uncle Charlie's lap. She gazed at herself in the cracked mirror above her ancient dresser, and she wanted to scream. She looked like her mother, battered and beaten down, her looks and her spirit pummeled out of her. *I have to get away from him,* Lily thought. She slipped out of her dress and threw it over the rickety chair in the corner of the room, then leaned across her husband's still body and put her hand in his pocket. She pulled out the four dollar bills. She took one and put the rest back. As she held the money in her hand, the idea came to her, as slow and drifting as an unformed song. She lifted the mattress back slowly and pulled out a ragged scarf, untied the knot and tossed the new dollar in with the others, then wrapped up the scarf and pushed it under the bed. And now there was music inside her, filling her mind with familiar voices and soothing visions. She could almost sing the words, but instead she whispered them. "I'll take my own self to Memphis."

33

Floyd kept his head bowed low as he walked to Mrs. Jameson's house. Whenever he raised it, to see what was in front of him, pain sharp as an ax blade nearly split his skull in two. By the time he reached the big white house, he had to stagger up the back porch stairs to the kitchen.

When the skinny colored maid opened the door, the odor of baking biscuits wafted out. The girl took one look at Floyd's ashen, unshaven face, his bloodshot eyes and completely disheveled appearance, and asked, "What's wrong with you, mister?" shrinking back from him as if he were a lunatic with a communicable disease.

He stumbled inside and sat down on the first chair he saw. "Nothing. Can I get a cup of coffee?" Everywhere he looked, little wavy lines vibrated back and forth.

The maid peered at him for a long while, then shook her head and mumbled to herself while she fixed him some coffee. He drank two cups fast, and when he stood up, he didn't have the sensation of floating anymore. "Your missus said she needed floors scrubbed and windows washed," he said.

"She your missus too." The girl smirked. "I'll show you."

The house was large and sunny, with lots of windows, and Floyd cleaned every one of them with the ammonia and water the girl gave him. "Miz Jameson know I don't wash no windows," the girl said as she showed him where the ladder was. He started outside. He climbed to the second floor and did the bedroom windows, while the sharp ammonia seemed to burn holes in his nose. Every once in a while, he sensed someone's presence and looked around to see Mrs. Jameson quietly observing his work. Or sometimes it would be the girl. Watching him.

At noon the maid gave him lunch. Red beans, rice, and biscuits. She set his plate on a little wooden stool on the back porch. When he looked through the window, he saw her eating at the kitchen table, a chicken breast in her hand.

The master bedroom was bigger than his entire house. There was a bed with four high posts, a dresser, and a vanity, all of the same gleaming mahogany. The comforter and the curtains were of matching velvet, a little worn but still lovely, and there were contrasting throw pillows across the bed. Of all the rooms in the house—and there were many beautiful rooms—this one made him angriest. All this, he thought, walking toward the dresser. They got all this.

He looked behind him, past the bedroom door and into the hallway. There was no one there. Then he opened a drawer quietly, and the odor of violet sachet filled his nostrils. He fumbled through silk stockings and sheer underwear; lacy things clung to his fingers. He felt the money, sandwiched between two handkerchiefs. Floyd glanced quickly toward the door; then he was taking the bills out and stuffing them in his pocket. Closing the drawer. He stepped away from the vanity and began wiping the dust off the windows with a soft, dry cloth. His swipes were nervous at first, but gradually he became calm and even happy. His luck was starting to change.

Mrs. Jameson tipped him fifty cents, dropping the two quarters in his palm, then rubbing her plump fingers together quickly and wiping them on her dress. She told Floyd he had done a "wonderful job." She asked

for his telephone number in case she needed him to help
out again. "My girl's daddy usually does all my odd
jobs, but he's done taken sick lately. I get so used to
them doing everything, I forget about my own people."

"I ain't got no phone, ma'am," he said, casting his
eyes downward.

Floyd counted the money as he was walking home.
One hundred seventy-three dollars. He leaned against a
tree. He'd misjudged the thin pile of bills. When he first
glimpsed the money, he thought there might be twenty
or thirty dollars, enough for him but not so much to
Mrs. Jameson. Not anything she'd even worry about, no
more than to ask the girl if she knew anything about it.
But one hundred seventy-three dollars. That was an
amount she would miss.

He began running, looking over his shoulder as he
passed trees and houses, as the tension rose up in him
and sweat streamed from his dark curls. When he was
closer to his house he slowed down. She didn't know
how to find him, Floyd reasoned, walking quickly, trying to get away from the area as fast as possible. People
like her, they never knew how to find people like him.

Lily had supper on the table. She was holding the
baby in her lap and eating her dinner. Floydjunior was
chewing noisily and smacking his lips and laughing.
They got quiet when Floyd came in. "What! Are you
keeping secrets?" he said. He laughed. Floydjunior
stared at his father.

Lily stood up, shifted the baby to her hip. "Sit down,
honey," she said softly.

Floyd washed his hands at the sink and then took the
empty seat next to Floydjunior. He leaned over and ruf-
fled the boy's hair with his hand. The boy smiled, suddenly excited.

"You want tea, Floyd?" Lily asked.

"Gimme water." He began eating from the plate Lily
placed in front of him. "This is mighty tasty, Lily. Real

good," he said. Lily almost spilled the glass of water she was pouring.

"Thank you, honey."

After dinner, while Lily was washing up the dishes, Floyd sat on the porch and held the baby on his lap. He bounced her up and down and tickled her under her fat little chin. He realized for the first time that Doreen looked like his sister. "You know, this baby's the spitting image of Dolly," he called to Lily.

The screen door opened and Lily came outside, still wiping her hands on her apron. She stood next to Floyd. "That's what your mama said."

"Little Dolly," he said, tossing the baby into the air.

He called Lily darling that night in bed, while his hand was traveling around the curve of her hips, while his tongue was lathering her nipples. Darling, he called her, his fingers inside her. "We're gon' move away from here. Start all over again. It'll be better, you'll see." Then he was on top, her belly soft below him. Her hands were on his shoulders, pulling him in closer. Darling! Darling! And he was able to hold off this time; he waited until he felt her burst inside, and then he released, sobbing, joyful. She was still clinging to him. Crying a little, soft, happy tears.

The next morning, even before he smelled the coffee, he heard the car in the yard. Heard the fluttering of the chickens' and guineas' wings as the birds scattered away from the wheels. When he peered under the shade, he saw the star on the car door, but by the time he had his pants on, Sheriff Barnes was already coming across the front yard.

He told himself not to run, to stay calm, but memories started chasing him, five-year-old recollections, buried until now: the steel bars closing him in, the clanking sound of the lock on the cell. Bright, vivid images, rolling before him like a picture show. And then, clear as day, his cellmate. The old man—his rheumy eyes, the stench of alcohol and vomit and urine—

leaning over him while he was lying on his bunk in the cell, telling him he had unclean hands.

Sheriff Barnes caught Floyd before he was halfway across the backyard. His bowlegged deputy held the gun on him while the sheriff clamped the handcuffs over his wrists. "Seem like Mrs. Jameson's maid knowed you, Floyd. She remembered you from when that boy was kilt."

They found the money in the bedroom, where he'd left it. Lily cried when she saw the crumpled bills. "What's going to happen now?" she wailed as they loaded Floyd into the car.

As they were driving away, the sheriff, without turning around, said to Floyd. "You'll be in a cell by yourself; you're the only white man I got right now. But listen to this: I picked up four niggers today, trying to register to vote. Can you imagine that?"

Floyd said he couldn't.

Lily stood up when Judge Chisolm gave out the sentence. When she heard the words "two years hard labor," everything that had been vague and mutable about what Floyd had done, about the possibility of punishment, became real and hard and fixed. (Later Sheriff Barnes informed him that with good behavior, he might be out in less than a year. Of course, that year included painting the sheriff's house inside and out, working alongside the four black would-be voters, whose cheeks were bruised and lips swollen from the "talking-to" the sheriff and his assistant had given them.) Up to the last minute she had expected exoneration, or at least no punishment. Like before. The last time they were in this courtroom, everything had ended with flash bulbs and kisses, with forgiveness and jubilation. The last time, their lives had been handed back to them.

But not this time.

From where she was standing, Lily watched the back of her husband's shoulders as they slumped, and saw the way his head jerked to one side. Floyd swallowed hard again and again and began rocking on his heels. He turned to face her just once, but then yanked his head around. Moments later, the assistant deputy escorted Floyd back to the jail. When he left the room, Lily sank down in her seat and began crying. How on earth could she take care of herself and the children without Floyd?

On the morning Floyd was to leave for prison, Lily walked with her children to Mamie and Lester's house. As they trudged down the road, she explained to Floydjunior that his father was going away to work and that he'd be away for a long time.

"He ain't," Floydjunior said when she finished talking, his angry eyes peering into hers.

"Why, Floydjunior," she said, shocked and frightened by his outburst.

"The kids in school told me he's going to jail for stealing," he shouted. "You don't have to tell me a lie. And I know something else, too." He was standing directly in front of her with his fists balled up at his sides.

Whatever it was, she knew she didn't want to hear it. Was, in fact, afraid of it. "What?" she said finally.

"He killed a nigger for you. That's what." He was smiling, with tight lips that were full of malice.

Standing in the middle of the road, her son's words echoing around her, Lily was aware for the first time that the death of Armstrong Todd was not behind her. She felt his memory growing inside her like a new life.

Mamie took a few moments to open the door. Lily could hear her shuffling around inside, and then finally she appeared, looking older than her sixty years, as worn out and dried up as a woman of eighty. They sat in the front room for a moment and watched *I Love Lucy* on a small Philco black-and-white television set. No one said anything for about ten minutes, and then Lily rose and said she would go next door to get her ride to town with Mr. Drummond. She kissed the children.

Mamie picked up the baby and walked Lily to the door. "John Earl has never shamed this family," she whispered. "Never."

Sheriff Barnes said he was making an exception, letting Lily in when it wasn't really visiting hours. Then he smiled at her, looking at her breasts at the same time, and said, "Go on in now."

Floyd was sprawled out across the cot, his face turned toward the wall, when the deputy opened the cell. "Hey, Floyd," he called. "Somebody here to see you."

Floyd shifted his body slowly, as if he was trying to avoid putting pressure on a wounded part of him. His deep, expressionless eyes did not change when he saw her. Lily almost thought his eyes were closed, the way he was just staring straight ahead and not focusing on her. The words seemed to sprout in her mind like seeds: This time is worse than before. But she didn't understand in what way it was worse until she realized that this time Floyd looked beaten. She sat down on the cot. "Floyd, honey," she began, but she couldn't think of anything else to say.

Neither one of them spoke for about five minutes, and in that time anger began palpitating like a heartbeat inside her. Why had he been so stupid, taking that woman's money? Didn't he even stop to think that she might call the sheriff?

Did he ever think at all?

She thought of the days of hunger right after Doreen was born, and shuddered. What was she going to do? Didn't he ever think about his own kids? Didn't he think about her? She was the one who was going to suffer.

Just like before.

Now he was speaking, mumbling in a low, almost incoherent voice. Lily bent her head to his lips. "Stick by me, Lily. Please be waiting for me when I get out."

Her tears came fast and loud. Her body convulsed in jagged spasms. She closed her eyes and saw Sheriff Barnes's mud tracks across her clean floor. Who would ever have suspected where those footprints would lead? She had maybe fifty dollars tied up in the scarf under her mattress. How far would that get her? She was a fool for ever thinking that she could save enough money to escape on her own. Lily recalled how firm Ida's resolve seemed when she said she was going to Chicago. She wasn't like Ida; she wasn't that strong. She grabbed Floyd's arms and dug her nails in hard. She wanted to shake the living daylights out of him. She said, "All I know how to do is wait for you."

34

Marguerite sat in bed, balancing a copy of the *Jackson News Leader* on her thighs; a pillow cushioned her back and neck against the wooden headboard. She read aloud in a smooth, melodic drone as Clayton, who lay next to her, listened. ". . . The casket bearing the body of the late President was then taken . . ." When she finished the article, she folded up the paper and flung it on the floor. She grabbed a heavy black comb from the nightstand and began parting and combing her thick hair so vigorously that he could hear the crackle of electricity. Clayton watched silently as Marguerite's fingers clenched the comb and her bottom lip began to tremble. "I hate that he had to die," she said. "He was trying to get us some rights. That's why they killed him." She turned to Clayton suddenly. "Did you vote for him?"

Clayton didn't answer for a moment, and Marguerite stared at him unflinchingly. Learning to read had changed her, he realized. He'd never thought of her as intelligent before. He'd never really focused on her mind. But the last few years, as he watched her lips struggle to say the sounds and saw the light go on in her eyes as she began to recognize more and more words, he saw what was inside her, and it was like looking at her naked for the first time.

"I'm very proud of you," he'd told her when she began reading without his assistance. She was the only person in his life he felt that way about, and through her he was even proud of himself. But along with his new-

260

found pride, there was fear, fear that she now had access to a world he no longer controlled. "Yes, I voted for him," he said quietly. "But you mustn't believe that Negroes don't have powerful friends who want to help you."

Marguerite shook her head slowly. She bunched her full lips in a sideward grimace.

"Contrary to what you might think, Marguerite, it's not only the President who can make a difference. There's Congress and the Senate, the Supreme Court. . . ."

"You and me can't drink a glass of water in public together," she said.

Clayton hesitated. "I'll bring you back something when I go to Memphis next week," he said.

She nodded without looking at him.

"We don't have to drink water in public, do we?" he said evenly. "We can drink our water right here. That's why I bought you a house. Our home is beautiful, Marguerite. Let's not allow the world's ugliness to invade what we've created." He put his hand on her arm and was grateful that she didn't pull away, as she sometimes did.

"I want things to be different," she said.

Later that evening, Marguerite drew her pillow from the headboard and placed it on the bed, then let her head sink down in it, her braids encircling her skull like a halo. She sighed. Then she sat upright, propping herself on her elbow, and looked at Clayton's sleeping body next to her. She wanted to wake him up and tell him, "This is a pretty house you gave me. I'm grateful to you. But if this is the only place I can drink a glass of water with you, then it ain't no house, Clayton. It's a prison."

The bedroom walls were covered with paintings, so many flowers and pastoral scenes and soft white faces dancing around her that sometimes she wanted to vomit. And when she turned around, Clayton was bringing in more pictures, buying her more clothes. Her closets were so full she could barely close the doors. Last year he had bought her a mink coat, which she wore only in their bedroom.

A rabbit-ear white man from Texas. What's he gon' do for us? She wondered if Clayton wanted black people to go to school with whites and work the same jobs and be able to vote. He was forever talking about how blacks were treated so badly, but what did he do to help them? She wondered if he was there when the civil rights workers held a sit-in at the Busy Bee Café the week before. What would Clayton do if some black person tried to sit next to him at a restaurant? What would he do if she were that person? For nearly ten years, all she had ever been concerned about was that Clayton took care of her. He'd rescued her from winters that whistled through the cracks of her tar-paper shack like a freight train. He'd delivered her from hunger. He'd brought her to a place where she was safe and warm and well fed, but that wasn't enough any longer. She'd never asked him if he thought she was as good as he was, but suddenly that was all she wanted to know.

Carefully she lifted the sleeping arm that held her too tightly around her waist and set it down next to his own body. Then she reached under the bed for the manila envelope. A pencil and several application forms were inside. Earn your high school diploma, the papers said. She paused to read the instructions, then wrote her name and address. While she was writing, she felt Clayton's hand groping for her even as he slept. She shifted her body and moved out of his reach.

Ida closed her bedroom door and leaned against it, momentarily relieved to breathe air that was free of cigarette smoke and the fumes of bootleg whiskey. Even in her room she couldn't escape the loud strains of James Brown—"Please! Please! Please!"—whose rough shouts seemed to cut through her stereo like a jagged blade. She pulled away from the door and went to her closet, reached in the back, and drew out three bottles of white lightning. Outside her room was the raucous laughter of a houseful of people feeling no pain. She clenched her eyes and imagined her entire house empty and peaceful.

In Hopewell and its environs, Ida's was the place to be on Friday and Saturday nights. To get in cost a dollar, the whiskey was fifty cents a drink, and fried-chicken, catfish, and tamale dinners were another dollar. People from as far away as Yazoo City came to her door some nights, looking for a good time. And at Ida's, that's exactly what they got.

The idea to turn her house into a weekend pay party came from her cousin Louis when he was home from Chicago for a visit. The same year the Illinois Central stopped operating, Ida heard a knock on her door one day, and when she opened it, there he was. Tall and as narrow as a piece of wire, he had on a flaming red suit and bright yellow patent-leather shoes with little crooked heels that leaned so dangerously to one side that it appeared they would fall off at any minute. And he wore a hat, canary yellow, with a high crown and a twirling red feather that tilted toward the sky like some bird about to take flight. Under the hat was the slickest, shiniest head of conked hair that Ida had ever seen. Louis had always been what the older folks in Hopewell called "worldly."

"In Chicago we give rent parties," Louis told her, after she fed him breakfast. "We party all day and all night. Girl, you need to throw you a rent party."

Louis took her to a bootlegger he knew who had a still on the outskirts of town, and Ida bought two bottles of his finest white lightning. Her cousin found a stereo and some record albums for her to borrow. "How y'all stay in this backwater place without no music?" he asked disdainfully. Two days before the party, he spread the word among all the people he knew in Hopewell and nearby towns that there would be a pay party at

Ida's home. "Now you need to send them children off somewhere," he told her. "They stay here, they liable to get miseducated."

She made fifty-three dollars that first night, and even after Louis took twenty percent, she was looking at money it would have taken her more than two months to earn as a maid. She told herself she wouldn't be running a juke joint for long. As soon as her father was well enough to go back to work, she and Sweetbabe were heading up to Chicago.

There was a knock on her bedroom door and then her father's voice, low and furtive. "Ida. Ida. Sheriff Barnes out here asking for you."

"He the most paid-off cracker in Mississippi," Louis said when he told her that the sheriff would want a cut. She hadn't had three parties before Barnes knocked on her door, his eyes on her hips, his hand held out.

She opened the dresser drawer and fumbled around until she felt her wallet. She pulled out twenty-five dollars and put the money in the pocket of her dress. After she shut the drawer, she opened her bedroom door, then locked it with a key.

The sheriff was around the back of the house, standing a little ways from the porch, in the shadows. "Hey there, Ida," he said when he saw her coming toward him. "Looks like a nice little crowd tonight." He grinned and let his eyes travel all over her body. The sheriff made her feel dirty, the way he looked at her.

She nodded to him and handed him the money.

"Well, thank you kindly," he said. He moved closer to her with a sudden, sinuous movement that affected her like fingernails scraping a blackboard. "Did I ever tell you," he whispered, his breath hot and sour, "did I ever tell you how much I like me some yella peaches?" He put his hand on her arm.

She could hear him laughing as she snatched herself away.

The house was hot inside. Couples were groping and

twirling in a furious fast dance to the strains of Smokey Robinson and the Miracles. Looking at her customers, Ida realized that she was in for another long night. She hoped that nobody would start fighting.

Around two o'clock in the morning, when the party began to get quiet and the loud music had been replaced by a steady spate of slow-drag records, there was a knock on her front door.

She'd never seen the two black men standing before her. One of the men was the color of weak tea, and the other was as dark a chocolate as she had ever tasted. They were dressed almost identically, in khaki pants, plaid shirts, and tennis shoes. She was mesmerized by their hair, which stood out wildly, encircling their heads as though they'd both stuck their fingers in an electric socket at the same time. Ida remembered seeing another person with hair like theirs, the grandson of one of the women in the neighborhood, a boy who'd come home for the summer from Chicago. No one said anything for a moment, and the three of them just stared at one another until finally the chocolate-colored man said, "We heard we could get some drinks here."

"And something to eat," the other man added.

They weren't from the Delta or even the South; Ida knew that much from their voices. She figured that they were civil rights workers, which should have scared her but didn't. She stood in front of them, her eyes riveted to their hair.

"May we come in?" the chocolate one asked softly. His accent sounded hard and busy to Ida, like high heels on concrete, the way she imagined Chicago, but his eyes were soft and so frankly interested that she felt embarrassed and looked away. She had been blocking their entrance with her body, and now she stood to one side to allow them room to enter. "It costs a dollar to get in," Ida said.

The rest of the people stopped slow-dragging and stood in the middle of the floor as though they'd been caught in a game of Red Light/Green Light, their bodies slumped over each other and motionless. The music ended, and no one bothered to put on another record. "Sit anywhere," Ida told her new guests. "I got whiskey and I have fried-chicken, tamale, and rib dinners."

The two men ordered drinks and two tamale dinners. They ate and drank and didn't dance; neither did anyone else. Everyone was too busy staring at their towering hair.

The chocolate one was Dan. The other one was Eddie. They were both from New York and gave no reason for being in Hopewell. They became regulars.

One Saturday night, when Ida was in the kitchen fixing plates, she looked up and Dan was standing in the doorway, staring at her and smiling. "I can't get enough of your cooking," he said. She put her hand to her blouse and fingered the top button, afraid that it would pop open from the sheer power of his eyes. Later that same night, Ida overheard Dan asking one of the men if he would like to register to vote, that he and Eddie were working with a group of people who wanted to make sure that blacks in Mississippi started voting.

Ida pulled Dan aside as he was leaving, and spoke carefully, in a low voice. "Dan, people come to my place to have a good time. If they get scared to death while they're here, they won't come back."

"What are you talking about?"

"I'm talking about this: Colored people don't vote in Hopewell."

"They don't vote because they haven't been allowed to vote. That's going to change."

"What do you know about a town like Hopewell? Y'all come down here from New York like you gon' save somebody's life, but more than likely somebody will get killed."

"We're trying to change things. We know you're scared. We're scared too, but I'm more afraid of what will happen if we don't try."

"You can't come to this house talking to people about voting."

He stepped toward her, smiling as he moved. "Well, can I come and talk to you sometime? You're not married, are you?" He was grinning at her, his hands in his pockets, his wild, angry hair standing out from his head like a wiry halo.

"No. You're trouble." Her chest felt tight, as though a small rubber band was wrapped around it; she could hardly breathe.

"Yeah. I am."

She was still smiling when she watched him drive away in that strange, insectlike car of his.

He came back on Sunday evening, just as Fern and Lizzie Mae were putting away the dinner dishes. She was sitting on the front porch, watching Sweetbabe play with one of the neighbor's dogs, when she saw Dan coming across the front yard. He was on her porch before she had a chance to worry about how she looked. "I told you I'd be back," he said.

He stayed until almost midnight and returned with such consistency and regularity that Ida got used to his being there. Sometimes he would bring a half-gallon of ice cream and spoon up some for all the family. Once he brought two live hens to Ida and shielded his eyes as she chopped their heads off. When he was feeling homesick, he would sit on her porch and sing rhythm-and-blues songs: the Temptations, the Dells, Smokey Robinson and the Miracles. He knew all the parts.

"You a one-man show," Ida said, grinning.

"Live at the Apollo," he said, and then laughed at her puzzled look.

Fern and Lizzie Mae teased Sweetbabe and called Dan his new daddy. Ida didn't correct them.

They were sitting in the parlor alone one Wednesday night, when Dan leaned over and kissed her so softly she wasn't sure it had happened, except that suddenly she was kissing him back. His hands were warm under her blouse, his fingers hot as they unhooked her bra and pulled it down. He raised up her blouse and stared at her breasts until she felt her nipples stiffen from the intensity of his gaze. Then he pulled her blouse down and said, "Where can I make love to you?"

They didn't even bother to pull down the covers on her bed. She lay back and stretched out her arms to pull him down on top of her. "Wait," he said. "Sit up."

He smiled the whole time he undressed her, and he kissed every bare part of her. She was glistening from his tongue by the time he was lying naked beside her. When she felt his tongue between her legs, she tensed up. No one had ever put his mouth on her there before.

"What are you doing?"

"I want to taste you," he whispered.

"That's nasty," she said.

"Who told you that?" he said, laughing softly.

"White people be doing that."

"Do I look white? Baby, I don't want to make you do nothing you don't want to do. I just want to make you feel good," he said, rubbing her thigh until she felt herself going limp. "Let me just kiss it real quick. Let me kiss your pussy so fast you don't even know I been down there." She giggled. "That all right with you?"

She felt his lips on her pubic hair. "Now, you tell me when to stop, baby."

His lips were traveling from her hairy mound to her thighs. She lay back and put her hands on Dan's neck. "You tell me when to stop, Ida." Then she felt something soft and wet between her legs, moving up inside her. "It's all right," he said. "It's how we make love in Harlem." When the first wave of pleasure hit her, she collapsed into him, grabbing his shoulders, kissing his chest and the palms of his hands. After her body became peaceful, he started kissing her all over again. He moved his mouth swiftly from one breast to the other until she began shivering and arching, and then he slid into her. They made love until neither one of them could move. When they finally fell apart, he said softly, stroking her ass, kissing her breasts as he spoke, "You got the best cooking. You got the best pussy. Man would be a fool to leave a woman like you."

She put her hand over his mouth, but he pushed it away. "I know what I'm saying." He kissed her mouth, and his tongue tasted strange to her until she realized that she was on his tongue.

"Nobody ever done that to me before," she said softly. "Down here they think doing that is dirty."

"Do *you* think so?" He held her chin with his hands and guided it until she had to look at him.

She closed her eyes. When she opened them she was smiling.

"Maybe next time you'll do me."

She made a face.

"I'll put something on it to make it taste real good."

She gasped and covered her face with her hands so she couldn't see him. From behind her hands she asked, "Like what?"

"Honey. Barbecue sauce. Melted chocolate. Whatever you want."

"You so nasty," she whispered.

"Where'd you get this white-girl hair? You part white, ain't you?"

She nodded, lowering her eyes.

"William ain't your real father?"

"No. My real daddy is white, but that's all I know."

"Hey," he said, moving close to her, kissing her on the mouth. "Ain't nothing to be ashamed of." He hugged her.

She moved away. "Yes it is."

"Hey," he said, grabbing her and pulling her close. "It ain't your shame. And it ain't your mama's, either."

She started crying. "Thank you. That's the best thing anybody ever told me." They were quiet for a long time, and then Ida moved in closer to him and pulled him down so that his head was lying on her breast. His wiry hair was scratchy on her bare skin. So much hair. "Why'd you come down here?"

"To help black people get registered to vote."

"How did you decide to do that?"

"I got inspired after I went to the March on Washington."

"I was watching the March on Washington on television, but they blacked it out before I could hear Martin Luther King Junior speak."

Dan lifted his head and looked at Ida. "What do you mean, 'blacked it out'?"

"If there's something that the white people don't want us to see on television, they just take it off. Make the screen go black. That's how they do down here."

Dan nodded; his eyes looked past Ida. Before, she hadn't noticed the veins in his neck, but now they seemed to stick out. There was something about his expression that made her think he didn't know where she was. When she pressed her soft breasts into his back and rubbed her hands across his chest he didn't respond, and moments later he stood up. "I gotta go," he said, putting on his pants.

"Are you gon' come back?"

He bent down and brushed the top of her ass with his lips, licked the tips of her breasts, and then kissed her mouth. "Yeah."

Dan came back every night that summer, always bringing her a little present, as well as treats for the others and cigarettes for her father. "One day," he told her, "when things have changed, this won't be a bad place for black folks to be. We've always run to the big cities, but our future is in the South."

"My future's in Chicago," she felt like saying, but she didn't want him to stop talking about Mississippi, about the way it could be. Everything he said she could see, and what she saw made her dreams of life in Chicago grow pale.

"I could be happy here," he told her. She didn't say so, but she was dreaming of happiness too.

She heard the chugging sound of his Volkswagen—the only one she'd ever seen—one night. Dan ran across the yard and grabbed her up by her wrists, then swung her around and leaned her way back, kissing her until she was breathless. When he let go of her, he said, "I think I've got a man who'll register."

His eyes reflected a shimmering kind of delirious joy that she'd never seen before; it frightened and amazed her all at once. There was danger in his eyes, at least a warning, but before she could heed it, they were in her room, taking their clothes off, and the radiance in his eyes was for her.

He pushed her down on the bed. "Do you want to take your turn?" he asked. She looked up, and he was crouching over her, his knees on either side of her neck, lowering himself slowly.

He tasted almost sweet.

Afterward Dan whispered to her, "I'll be back tomorrow."

But he didn't come back the next day or the next or for too many days to count without pain sweeping through her like wildfire. Every night she wasn't with him, she cried and remembered his faint sugary taste in her mouth. She closed her eyes in the middle of the day over a sink of dirty dishes and recalled his smoothness on her tongue, remembered the stiffness between her teeth. She wondered how long she'd be able to taste him.

She blamed herself for his desertion. She was a whore for letting him lick her down there, a whore for taking him in her mouth. During the day she was listless, and at night she ran for miles in dazed circles, trying to make herself tired enough to fall asleep. The family got on her nerves, and she shooed Sweetbabe away when he wanted to read aloud to her, even though his teacher had told her he was slow and needed prac-

tice. At the party on Saturday night, she burned her tamales, the first time that ever happened.

When Ida brought the sheriff his money that night, he
wasn't waiting in the back, where she usually found
him. She stood near the back porch for a moment and
then walked around the house to the front, in time to
see Barnes peering through the window of the living
room, where her customers were dancing. "What you
looking at, Sheriff? You ain't never seen colored people
having a good time before?"

He whirled around at the sound of her voice, and
when he faced Ida, his hand was on his gun. Ida wobbled a little on her feet as she watched the sheriff's fingers. She didn't know what to do or say, and in her
confusion she kept her eyes on Barnes in a fixed, penetrating way that conveyed more power than she felt.
When she looked at his hands again, they were dangling
by his sides.

"Oh, I sure done seen that," he said.

She couldn't speak for a moment, not until after several deep breaths. "What *ain't* you seen?"

"I'm looking for two northern nigras who done come
down here trying to get the rest of y'all worked up
about voting. Ain't no need of that. Any nigra around
here can vote, so long as he can pay his poll tax and answer a few simple questions. That's the law, and I mean
to uphold it."

Ida handed him the twenty-five dollars. She concen-
trated on making her voice calm and unconcerned. "All
the people in my house is from right around here."

"Well, it'd be healthier to keep it that way." He gave
her a long appraising look, as though she were standing
undressed in front of him. "Peaches," he said, grinning.

Ida had been in bed for an hour, trying to sleep, when
she heard movement outside her window. In the moonlight she could see the shadow of a man. Even before
she heard the tapping, she was running to the front door.

"Dan, the sheriff is looking for you and Eddie," she said, after she closed the bedroom door.

"Eddie's gone. The organization sent him to the eastern part of the state. You gotta help me, baby."

"Where you been? I didn't hear—"

He waved his hand. "I was working about fifteen miles south of here. Trying to get folks registered. I almost had two guys who were willing—"

"Why you didn't come see me or call?"

"I was working, baby." His words were tight and hard as bullets. "I need your help." He squeezed her arm. "Let me talk to some of your customers. Try to get them registered. It's—"

"I told you before, I can't let you do that."

"Well, then you talk to them."

"And say what?"

"Tell them to register to vote. Tell them they can make a difference in their own lives."

"Do you know what you asking? You asking me to get some people killed, that's what. In case you ain't heard, this here is Klan country. Those good-timing folks feed my family. And if they get run off or killed, are you gon' do that?"

"You're a leader, Ida," he said, seizing both her wrists. "You have influence around here. People respect you. If you tell them to do something, they'll at least think about it."

"I'm not a leader, Dan."

"Ida, listen—"

She held her hand up; the fingers splayed out wide and then slowly curled up. "You better go."

She told the family that Dan had gone back to New York, and when they asked if he would ever return, she said no and offered no further explanation. Gradually their references to the Moon Pies and RC Colas Dan used to bring them, the funny things he said, dwindled and then ceased altogether.

Ida's grief was not so easily dissolved. She cried in

spells that summer when she least expected to: after a long run, in the middle of counting money, while she combed her hair. There were tears in the dinners she served and in the glasses of white lightning she sold. Days filled with weeping passed one after another, and weeks went by without her smiling. Sometimes she wore the same dress for two or three days in a row, and her hair often went uncombed. Then one day, long after Sweetbabe had stopped mentioning Dan, she heard her son's thin, angry voice declaring, "I'm going to kill Mr. Dan for making my mama so sad." She looked in the mirror in her bedroom, and her mouth fell open at the puffy eyes, uncombed hair, and bedraggled figure she saw.

She began running every night like a demon, and during the day she cooked until her fingers refused to move. She expanded her vegetable garden, and when the crop came in she canned everything she could. Her goal was simple: to forget his laugh; to not think of his touch or his taste or the taste of herself on his lips.

At the end of the summer Ida paid her father's hospital bill. Dr. Mitchell declared that his patient was as well as he would ever be and he'd have to get used to life in a wheelchair. William barely reacted to his pronouncement. Lizzie Mae and Fern eyed each other and then Ida with frankly selfish alarm. Recently they each had been promised a job in Chicago. Ida quietly accepted her father's fate, as well as her own inevitable future.

In the fall, four black men attempted to register to vote in Hopewell. The next day Mount Zion Baptist Church was bombed.

By the time the people from the Quarters got to the church, the moon was the only light. But that was all the illumination anyone needed to see Sheriff Barnes standing in front of the smoldering wreckage with his arms folded. Two of his deputies were beside him.

"Y'all might as well just turn around and go on home," he told the crowd. "There ain't nothing you can do here."

There was silence for a minute, and then someone called out, "Was it anybody hurt?"

"We'll find that out in the morning," the sheriff said.

The crowd groaned. One of the men said, "Whoever is in there could be dead by morning."

"Ain't nobody going in there tonight," the sheriff said. "Go on home now."

The air was filled with acrid smoke as Ida walked back to the Quarters with the rest of the people. She sat on her porch with her neighbors for a few moments, but she couldn't concentrate on what they were saying. She knew she should go to bed, but when she arrived at her house she was tense.

Ida began running, and for a moment, as the wind hit the sweat on her body, she felt cool and weightless. She momentarily forgot about the smoldering embers she'd just left, the odor of death and destruction all around her, how desperately she wanted to leave Hopewell. As she swooped like a comet past the last house in the Quarters, she became loose. There was a grove of oak trees at the end of the road, and she told herself she would turn back when she reached it. Then she saw a splash of khaki almost hidden among the trees and bushes. Just as her eye caught the patrol car on the side of the road, hands were pulling her into the foliage. "Peaches," she heard on the tongue that was wet and hot in her ear.

He pushed her to the ground and straddled her, then yanked her blouse up. She tried to scream, but he covered her mouth with his hand. When she bit him, he punched her jaw, and she felt as if she was going underwater.

Blam! She thought the noise was another bomb, even her own screams, until Sheriff Barnes slumped to the ground, his tongue slithering down the side of Ida's

face as he fell. Ida stared at him, at the blood seeping
from his back; stunned and horrified, she opened her
mouth to yell, but before she was able to do so, she
felt someone's palm against her lips. "Don't make no
noise. Don't say nothing. You hear me?" Ida nodded
silently, her eyes darting around her as the hand was
removed.

"Miss Willow!"

The bronze woman was already dragging the sheriff's
still body into a clump of bushes. "You don't know
nothing. You ain't seed nothing. Understand?"

Ida nodded, not looking at the body that lay at her
feet.

"Now you go home."

"But Miss Willow—"

"You go home," she said fiercely, her long black
braid licking the wind.

Ida began running.

"Bad grass don't die," was what people whispered in
the Quarters the next morning. Sheriff Barnes had been
found with a bullet in his back, just barely alive. Before
he passed out, he managed to whisper that Willow Scott
had shot him.

As for Willow, folks said that when deputies went to
arrest her, they found her rocking chair swaying back
and forth on her front porch, and inside her house was
a potful of savory filé gumbo warming on the stove.
The table was set for one, but the best cook in Yabalusha County had disappeared without a trace.

For the rest of the year, Ida worked as though she
was part mule, driving her father's truck to neighboring
towns on Saturday mornings and selling dinners and
pies and cakes, before coming home and cooking for
her Hopewell clientele and then hosting the weekend
parties. Whenever William asked her why she was
working so hard, she declared that she wanted a new
house with indoor plumbing, and a separate building for

her business. And money for Sweetbabe's college education. If she was doomed to remain in Hopewell, by God, her son was getting out.

35

Inside Wydell and Delotha's House of Good Looks, the dryers and electric clippers were silent and the hands at the shampoo bowls were suspended in the air as everyone listened to the news reporter on the black-and-white television set placed in the middle of the floor. "To repeat," said the newscaster, a thin blond man with glasses and a calm, sober expression on his face, "four students, alleged protesters of the war in Vietnam, have been shot by the National Guard today at Kent State University in Ohio. University officials . . ." As the reporter droned on, the customers shook their heads.

"White folks is so crazy. They got tired of killing black people, so they went over to Vietnam and started blowing up some yellow people. Now they killing their own children," Maudine said.

Delotha parted her customer's hair and began making row after row of tiny corkscrew curls with the hot irons. Her face was suffused with anger, as it always was when she thought about white people. Delotha winced both from the memory of dead children and from the persistent kicks of the unborn baby she was carrying.

"You all right?" Maudine asked, noticing her hairdresser's face.

"This baby is bowling in my belly," she said, and joined in as Maudine laughed. "And I thought I was going through the change!"

"My mother had a change-of-life baby. They usually boys, you know." Maudine leaned back a little in her chair and observed Delotha's belly. "And you carrying low too. I know that's a boy. Guess that would make Wydell happy."

Delotha didn't answer. When she had had another girl two years after her first daughter was born, she wailed with grief, as though her son had been seized from her again. She told herself that it wasn't that she didn't love her daughters; she did. But her immense hunger for a son was so overwhelming that her yearning for the unborn at times eclipsed what she felt for her living children. She failed at nursing either one of her daughters; her milk never came in for Brenda, and after two days of suckling Karen, her breasts became swollen and infected and she had to resort to the bottle.

She peeked in the back, to Wydell's part of the shop, which was filled with men waiting to get their hair cut. Wydell did a bigger volume of business than she did, and by now had hired four barbers. She watched for a minute as he finished trimming a little boy's hair, lifting the tight Afro with a pick and then patting it down to conform to the rounded shape of his young customer's head. Wydell wasn't looking her way, but she smiled at him anyway. She didn't want anyone to know how badly she wanted a boy, not even Wydell. Armstrong had never stopped haunting her, and she still grieved for her dead son, crying for him when her husband didn't see her. Even though she and Wydell had become prosperous, renting out the apartment above the shop and buying a three-story brick house not far from their business, there was something missing. For fifteen years, she'd wanted to retrieve the child she lost. And now, at forty-four, she had one last chance.

As Delotha curled Maudine's hair, she glanced from time to time at the large clock on the wall. At three-forty she padded to the door of the shop, opened it, and looked up and down Forty-seventh Street, before closing it and returning to her customer. She glanced at the row of women waiting to get their hair done and sighed.

The shop bells chimed, and Delotha raised her eyes, looking first at the clock on the wall and then at the two little brown girls in the doorway, one a bit taller and heavier than the other, their pressed hair braided and beribboned, their bright yellow book-bags banging against their thin legs. They raced into the shop, bumping into each other and panting like puppies. "If you left school as soon as the bell rang, instead of hanging around playing double-dutch, you wouldn't have to run," Delotha said. The girls glanced at each other sheepishly, biting down on their lips and pulling on their braids, trying to avoid their mother's eyes. "Look at me when I'm talking to you," she said sternly. "And say hello to Miss Maudine." Both girls drew a deep breath; they turned to face their mother and mumbled their greetings to her customer. Delotha's voice softened. "Y'all go get started on your homework. I left you some cookies on the table," she said. The two girls scooted past their mother's station, calling out greetings to the other hairdressers and the customers in the front of the shop, who leaned forward in their seats and greeted the girls with a flurry of waves and "Hey, babies." Delotha sighed as she watched them. The girls were a constant reminder of her past trauma and what it had taught her: She couldn't save them. They could be snatched away, stolen, brutalized, or killed at any time, and there was nothing she could do about it. Often when she tiptoed into their room at night to watch them sleep, she became angry, filled with a bone-chilling rage that rendered her body frigid and untouchable. Sometimes the only way she could bear to watch them walk away from her was to pretend that they weren't hers, as though she were an observer rather than their mother.

Delotha, satisfied that her children were safe and under her control, returned to her work. But out of the corner of her eye she saw Wydell turn off the electric clippers and lay them down. He whisked his blue work jacket carefully with a miniature broom before stepping away from his customer. He was barely in the aisle before Brenda and Karen were in his arms, squealing as loudly as they did in Washington Park. "How's my girls?" she heard him say, hugging his two daughters simultaneously. They chatted briefly and excitedly, telling him all the things they never seemed to want to tell her, before they opened the door to an adjoining room and disappeared.

It was funny, Delotha thought to herself, how Wydell turned out to be a better mother than she was. Only to herself did she admit that Wydell took care of their girls because she had neither the time—what with the administrative duties of the shop, as well as the customers— nor the inclination. Strange how one minute Wydell had been afraid of children and the next he'd begun doing everything for them. He was the one who cuddled them when they were babies and who played peek-a-boo. Wydell took them to the zoo and for walks. She knew that she pushed them away. And the more she did, the more Brenda and Karen turned to Wydell. But as God was her witness, if she had a boy, she'd do better.

"So when you dropping that baby?" Maudine asked.

Delotha chuckled softly. "The sooner the better," she said, handing her customer a mirror and giving the chair a push so that it would swivel around, allowing Maudine to see the back of her hair.

In bed that night, Delotha lay on her side, and Wydell's arm caressed her belly. With each of her pregnancies he delighted in feeling the baby's kicks. "This is gon' be the biggest one," Wydell said softly. He laughed as the outline of a tiny hand or foot poked out from Delotha's abdomen. Delotha started weeping, softly at first and then with gathering force. "Why you crying, baby?"

She didn't want to tell him that she was crying because she was afraid that she was carrying another girl.

* * *

The telephone calls had begun in early August. First the *New York Bulletin* and then other papers across the country. As the weeks passed, the entire country seemed to notice that the benchmark of fifteen years was approaching since Armstrong Todd's death. Only five years earlier, Rock of Ages Baptist Church, where Delotha, Wydell, and their children were members, had held a small service; the city's black newspaper had sent a reporter to the house, and a brief article had appeared. But now the event was heralded with more fanfare than Wydell and Delotha had expected. Newspapers called from all over the country. After a decade of riotous upheaval in black communities, the nation's editors were willing to be introspective, even if they refused to take a stand. Each week during the summer brought more interviews and photographers in need of a family shot. White men with cameras instructed the Todds not to smile, to look pensive, and for each parent to put a hand on a daughter's shoulder. Reporters asked Brenda and Karen if they would be afraid to go to Mississippi today. They pointed to the large picture of Armstrong that was placed in the center of the mantelpiece and asked Delotha earnestly, "Your son would be thirty years old today. If he were alive, do you think America would have fulfilled its promise to him?" Every white reporter asked: "What do black people want?"

Delotha answered most of the questions, managing to contain her rage at the idea of white people being inside their home. Wydell was quiet; the photographer didn't have to ask him not to smile.

On a hot day in September, Rock of Ages held its Fifteenth Anniversary Memorial Service to Commemorate the Memory of Armstrong Todd. The huge church was full as the white-gloved junior ushers, chosen instead of their elders because they symbolized the lost youth of Armstrong Todd, passed out programs. The choir sang, and the minister preached about loving your fellow man and quoted from Martin Luther King's "I have a dream" speech. Wydell, Delotha, their daughters, and Odessa sat in the first pew, next to Lionel and his wife and family, which now comprised five strong-looking boys.

Odessa, who had taken the Greyhound from Detroit to be present, leaned over the two girls and whispered to Delotha, "I just wisht he could see all this." Her bottom lip trembled a little, and she patted her daughter's hand. When her mother released her fingers, Delotha carefully placed them back over her belly.

The house was sweltering when they got back. Wydell turned on the fans, but they merely churned the heated air around. In bed, Delotha heaved herself over on her side and then slowly shifted again; when Wydell put his hand on her belly, she slapped it away.

"It's too hot for all that," she said. "It's too hot to even sleep." But in a moment she heard Wydell snoring next to her, and she began drifting off herself.

Delotha awoke to fierce pain. She grabbed Wydell's arm and shook it. "The baby's coming," she said.

Under the glare of Cook County General's fluorescent lights, Delotha bellowed and grunted. Propped up on her elbows, peering into the wide V-shaped arc her legs made, Delotha pushed. Biting her lip, her breaths torn off like pieces of rag, she grunted and sweated and screamed until she saw the crown of the baby's head emerge. The surge of hope that sparked through her like fireworks was even greater than her pain. She spoke directly to God: *Lord, give me a son, and I won't let nothing happen to him.* A rubber-gloved hand reached for the slick, slimy head, and now a body, tiny, squirming, slid out of her and the struggle ended. She heard crying, her own wails of relief, and then a frail echo. The doctor had to repeat himself, because Delotha's eyes were full of tears and she didn't seem to understand. "You have a son, Mrs. Todd," he told her. A son. And then the baby was in her arms.

His name was ready for him: Wydell Henry Todd, Jr.

She and Wydell had agreed. Delotha shifted her hips on the narrow delivery table. She examined the baby from his damp curls to the curve of his toes. She smiled at his little bow mouth, his tiny flat nose and glistening eyes. He was so much like her first boy. "Armstrong," she said softly, pressing her lips on the nape of his neck, the side of his face, next to his little ear. "Armstrong," she repeated, and her fierce voice rose. "No white person will ever hurt you."

36

When Lionel and his family came to the hospital three days later, he told Wydell that he should pass out cigars. "A man your age having a baby, and a boy at that, ain't no everyday occurrence, is it, Amelia?" he said, patting his belly, which had grown rotund after his fortieth birthday.

His wife threw back her head and laughed. "For you it is," she said, shifting their two-year-old son from one large hip to the other. She smiled congenially at her four other boys, who ranged in age from seven to twenty-three and were all assembled in front of the nursery on the maternity floor of Cook County General. As they looked through the huge pane of glass at the rows of babies inside, Wydell searched excitedly for his son among the assortment of infants lined up before him. "He's got a lotta hair," Wydell said nervously, his eyes jumping from one tiny face to the next. He didn't recognize his baby among the newborns. "Where is he?"

"Take it easy, Wydell," Lionel said. "They ain't lost your boy. Go ask the nurse where they put him."

Wydell nodded anxiously and then walked over to the nurses' station. When he faced the young blond woman, who was almost as pale as her uniform, he was too nervous to speak.

"May I help you?" she asked.

He forced out the words, then trembled while she looked at her chart. Why was it taking her so long? An

involuntary shudder racked his body. Something bad
had happened to the baby. The boy was dead. The white
doctor and nurses had killed him. A terrifying numb-
ness began to spread throughout his groin, traveling into
his chest.

"Your son is with your wife, Mr. Todd." The nurse
had a voice like Christmas: hopeful, serene, and cheer-
ful all at once. "She's feeding him. You can go see
them in her room, if you like. Is there anything wrong,
Mr. Todd?"

He could barely shake his head. The sudden relief
that rushed through his body unbalanced him, and when
he started back to where Lionel and his family were
waiting, he almost stumbled. "Delotha's feeding him,"
Wydell said. He started laughing for no reason at all.

Later, in the hospital room, while Lionel, Amelia,
their oldest boy, and Wydell crowded around Delotha,
his apprehension seemed to come and go as fast as good
weather in Chicago. He was able to smile when Lionel
said that the boy would probably have the Todd freckles. But when Delotha said, "Of course he will. All the
Todd men have freckles," he was filled with dread. Another boy, he thought. They kill the boys, the men.
Hang them by their necks and then torch their lifeless
bodies. Throw them on the chain gang for nine hundred
years. He wiped his mouth and let his hand settle on his
lips for a moment. The horror and fear he initially felt
when the doctor announced that he had a son crept
around his shoulders, the weight of it like ten iron bars.
He was good with girls; he could guide and protect
them. What would it take to save his son? He wanted to
reach out to Delotha, to touch her, to have her squeeze
his hand, but she was busy with the baby, nuzzling his
neck, caressing him in a way that took her attention
from everything else.

Before he left, Lionel pulled Wydell aside. "I'm
proud of you, Wydell. The Down Home used to be your
second home, but you put all that whiskey drinking and

foolishness behind you. I ain't known too many men who've turned their lives around." He patted Wydell's shoulder.

Delotha burst into tears as soon as Lionel and his family left. Wydell was sitting in a hard-back chair near her bed, and he stood up and reduced the volume on the hospital television, which was playing a rerun of *I Spy*. He sat with his back to Robert Culp and Bill Cosby and pulled his chair close to Delotha's bed until his knees jammed into her mattress. "Don't he look just like him?" she wailed. "It's like holding the same baby."

Wydell stole a quick look at his son, then reached over and patted Delotha's shoulder. She'd been through a lot, poor thing. "He ain't the same baby," he said, taking the child from his wife.

Wydell sat with the baby propped up in his lap. "This boy's heavy," he said. "Delotha, we're all done grieving." Knowing that Delotha needed him made him feel strong, and when he spoke his voice was firm. She looked at him, wiping her eyes, and he could tell that if he made her think he believed what he was saying, she would stop crying and be happy, at least for that moment. He wanted to give her that. Delotha nodded slowly. Wydell settled back in his chair and relaxed his back, which had gone a little stiff on him. "Now. You want to call this boy Junior, Wydell Henry, Henry, W.T.? What?"

"Black folks don't call people by initials anymore, Wydell," Delotha said, as a shadow of a smile crossed her lips.

"Whatcha talking 'bout, girl? What about B.B. King?" She giggled. "But B.B.'s a home boy."

"Well," said Wydell, holding the infant high above his head, "this here's a home boy too."

Brenda and Karen ran from the house as Wydell helped Delotha and the baby out of the car. Odessa stood in the doorway, beaming, stretching out her arms toward the baby. After everyone was inside the house, she started to cry. "What's the matter, Grandma?" Brenda asked. Odessa shook her head, then wiped her eyes. "Just happy," she said.

The girls were excited and clamored around the baby, following their mother's every move, which was unusual, because most of the time they anticipated her need for them to disappear and they obliged. But they had lived with the memory of their dead brother for their entire lives—his picture adorned the walls in the living room and their parents' bedroom—and could hardly contain their enthusiasm for the real man-child who was now in their lives. Brenda and Karen hovered around the baby, begging to hold him, until the infant began crying and an exasperated Delotha shooed them out of her room.

Wydell was astonished when Delotha pulled down the front of her gown and gave W.T. her breast. He had never considered the possibility that she would nurse, since she had given both girls Similac. As Wydell watched the baby suckling his wife, he was vaguely aware of an uneasy feeling, a pinprick of annoyance deep within him. Delotha was talking to the boy, murmuring into his ear. "Mama's baby. Mama's little man." And she was rubbing his warm back as she fed him.

"Delotha, I want—"

"Not now, Wydell."

"I won't stay out but a month at the most," Delotha told him several days later. It was only six o'clock on a Saturday morning, and no one was awake but the two of them. Delotha had cooked Wydell breakfast and was spooning eggs, bacon, home fries, and biscuits onto his plate. Saturday was the shop's busiest day, and there was no telling when he'd get a chance to eat. "When I go back, Mrs. Brown said she'll keep Armstrong for me," Delotha said.

"W.T.," Wydell said quickly. It wasn't the first time Delotha had called the baby by his dead brother's name.

"What did I say?" she asked, then shook her head, understanding her mistake.

Wydell thought about Mrs. Brown, an older woman who lived on their street and had baby-sat the girls before they went to school. Sometimes he thought the old woman was a little too quick with a switch, but she kept his daughters clean and well fed. "You take as much time as you need," Wydell said. "No need for you to hurry back. The shop is doing fine."

But as the days stretched into weeks, Wydell was amazed when Delotha seemed not to want to return to work. When the girls were born, Delotha had stayed home barely two weeks before she hurried back to the beauty parlor. One evening, as Wydell was sweeping up, he was surprised when he overheard Sharon, one of the newer beauticians, who rented a booth from his wife, commenting on the way Delotha had parceled out her customers among the three hairdressers.

When he came home that evening, Delotha was stretched out across the bed, playing with the baby, kissing him, tickling him as he kicked his tiny feet. "You think you'll be coming in anytime soon?" he asked her.

"I think I'll stay out a little longer," she said with a languid air.

"It's time to reorder supplies."

She didn't turn her head. "You do it, Wydell."

The baby started crying then, and when Wydell went to pick him up, Delotha almost snatched the boy out of his hands. "Armstrong wants me," she said sternly. Wydell didn't bother to correct her. She lifted the baby to her and began nursing him.

Wydell had a sudden urge to beat his fist against the wall. Every time he turned around she had one of her fat titties stuck up in the boy's mouth! Night and day she was all over that boy, and when Wydell came near, she was either hushing him up or shooing him away. He used to know something about babies, he thought.

He looked around the room. The bed was unmade, and there were diapers everywhere. And Delotha was getting fat. With the girls, the weight fell off her quickly, dissolved in the heat of her constant motion. But this time, every ounce she had gained during the pregnancy stayed on her, and she seemed to be putting on even more. When she bent down to pick up the baby, her stomach lapped over her navel. The flesh on her thighs and hips rippled as she waddled around the bedroom. Her soft milk-filled breasts had grown huge, the nipples stretched out like swollen kidney beans. In the shop, whenever there was a slack period he found himself looking out the picture window at the young girls with their hip-hugger bell-bottoms and teeter-totter platform shoes, their huge Afros and tight tie-dyed T-shirts and dangling earrings. Still, even with the extra weight, Delotha was the one he longed for, but she didn't seem interested in him. The baby was nearly three months old, yet whenever he tried to touch her she jerked away and told him she was tired. She didn't even laugh when he joked about Johnson's being lonesome.

One evening when all his customers had gone, he wandered to the front of the shop, where the women got their hair done. Maudine was there, waiting for one of the older hairdressers, who was with another customer. As soon as Wydell sat down next to her, the door to the shop opened and a tall, athletic-looking black teenager headed toward the barbershop. Holding on to his arm was a thin, sallow-faced white girl, wearing a T-shirt with a picture of Malcolm X on the front.

"Well, Lord Jesus!" Maudine snapped. "Would you look at that? Niggers is truly losing they minds. These Blackstone Rangers is going crazy, beating and killing folks. Kids is running around here smoking reefers all day long. Ain't never seen so many hopheads in my life. And if that ain't enough, now these black boys is crazy for white girls. Ten years ago they got killed for looking at 'em, and now—" She looked at Wydell's stricken face and fell silent.

"Times change," Wydell said. He cleared his throat. "I want to ask you something, Maudine." He saw a flicker of interest light up her eyes. "Ever since Delotha had the baby, she seems like, uh ... What I mean is ..." He stood up abruptly. "Never mind," he said. "Never mind."

37

Mr. Drummond's car radio was tuned to the station in Jackson when Lily got in. Nearly seventy, the old man was hard of hearing and had turned the volume of his radio all the way up. As Lily settled into her seat, the air around her was painful, each decibel like a piercing needle. She clapped her hands to her ears, then leaned over to admonish Doreen, her ten-year-old daughter, to sit back and keep quiet, although if the child had made any noise, Lily certainly couldn't have heard her. Before she turned around, Lily smoothed her daughter's red dress and patted her yellow curls. As she faced the front again, she heard the announcer say, his voice like a sonic boom, "Well, men, what do you think of women's liberation? Pretty soon the gals will be driving trucks and we'll be staying at home with the babies. What's this world coming to?"

"What'd he say?" Mr. Drummond yelled at Lily. He always hollered whenever he spoke to anyone.

"I wasn't paying no mind, Mr. Drummond. Something about women's liberation."

"What the hell is that?"

Lily shook her head. "I don't know." Women's liberation. She mouthed the words softly to herself, but they didn't mean anything to her. Women. Liberation. Separately, yes, but not together.

She looked out the window. The Yabalusha River slithered alongside the road like an inky black snake, accented by the daffodils and crocuses that had just recently sprouted. Lily let the dark, flowing ribbon hypnotize her and remembered when, long ago, she had dangled her bare feet in that same water. She looked along the bank and saw paper cups, several McDonald's bags, as well as bottles and soda cans that people had thrown out. ". . . The three convicts escaped at daybreak this morning and are believed to be in the vicinity of . . ."

"What did they say about convicts?" Mr. Drummond shouted. His voice was like a loudspeaker blaring into her ears. Lily was beginning to feel the prickles of a newborn headache, slowly growing at her temples.

"They ain't caught nobody yet," she said. Hearing the word "convicts," she had reached inside her purse and pulled out a cigarette from a pack of Winstons and lit it; before she had blown out the first drag, she had a picture of Floyd in her head, from the last time she'd seen him, up at the prison near Yazoo City, where he was serving a seven-year sentence for his third burglary conviction. The last time she saw him, he wasn't handsome anymore, and she wondered whether she looked pretty to him.

Seven years. Another burglary, just as botched as the other two had been. And this time the jail was integrated.

The radio announcer went on and on about the escaped convicts, and Lily listened intently, no longer rattled by the loudness of the broadcast. He wouldn't try running off, she thought, and held that idea in her mind. The last thing she wanted in her life was for Floyd to come back unexpectedly.

After a silent pause, the music of the Beatles filled the car. Not an old song, but it wasn't one of the latest, either. "Yesterday, all my troubles seemed so far away. . . ." Lily knew the words. She'd spent too many days and nights sitting on the back porch listening to the radio not to, so she sang along, but her heart wasn't really in it. She'd take a good Patsy Cline over all the new singers, groups or singles, any day of the week. Patsy was a woman who knew how to get a message across. But she was gone now.

Lily didn't bother asking Mr. Drummond to turn down the volume; she knew from experience that he'd pretend not to hear her. Besides, as loud as the radio was, the car was more peaceful than her own home, what with Mamie criticizing everything she did.

Lily and the kids had moved in with her mother-in-law after Lester died. The day of his funeral, rain had come down in torrents, and when they returned home Floydjunior shouted, "Mama, look!" Lily, her eyes following her son's pointing finger, gasped and started running. Like a fallen cake, the roof of her house had caved in.

They had nowhere else to go, and Mamie reluctantly took them in, which wasn't the same as welcoming them.

Mr. Drummond parked the Ford under a huge magnolia tree right in front of the Vanderbilt courthouse. Lily grabbed Doreen's hand. "I don't want to go in there with you," the child said.

"You hush up and come on."

"I hate that place," Doreen whined.

Lily and Doreen climbed the stairs to the second floor of the courthouse, where the Yabalusha County Department of Social Services was located, and pushed through the glass door to the waiting room. She grimaced when she saw the horde of black and white women and children crowded in the small room. There wasn't a vacant seat anywhere. Everyone had come to fill out recertification papers. Even under normal circumstances it was an arduous process, but today she could see that she'd be waiting for hours. The room was hot, and a condensed odor of unwashed underarms and wet diapers and stale panties clung to the air. She pressed her head against the wall and it felt damp, as though even the paint was sweating. With every other breath she could smell the pervasive musky funk. Nigger stink, that's what it is, Lily told herself. She glanced around, searching for a seat, and caught the eye of a morose-looking black woman who scowled at her and rolled her eyes with such apparent hostility that Lily looked away. *That's the way they been acting ever since integration,* she thought; *just as mean and hateful as they can be.* She always dropped her head when they looked at her; she'd been doing that for so long it was more or less an instinct. And here she was, trapped in the same room with them.

She wrote her name on the sign-in list and then stood in the back near the water fountain, trying to keep an eye out for a seat. She wouldn't drink water from a public fountain if her life depended on it. Not anymore she wouldn't. There was a No Smoking sign, but she lit a Winston anyway. Several of the other women were smoking. Across the room she saw a white girl with long blond hair walking toward a younger black boy, who was sitting on the floor playing with a ball; the girl was wearing a red dress, and she was smiling. Moments later, the two children were on the floor together, their heads almost touching, as they rolled the ball back and forth between them. Lily felt her neck snap as she looked behind her. Nobody was standing there. "Doreen," she called. "You come over here right now."

Doreen walked to her mother, her reluctance showing in the set of her head, the feigned nonchalance in her eyes. "I don't want you playing with them," Lily whispered.

"We was just having some fun, Mama." She looked around, her wrinkled nose sniffing the air. "And you didn't bring me no toys."

"You don't need no toys. Just stand by me and . . . and"—Lily struggled for words—"and just think nice thoughts to yourself."

"Nice thoughts like what, Mama?"

"Something nice," hissed Lily.

"It was fun playing ball. Can't I please go back over there?"

"I have told you before, you don't play with them."

"But he has toys."

It was on the tip of Lily's tongue to say that if it hadn't been for niggers they wouldn't be sitting up in nobody's welfare office. "Just do like I tell you. There, look. That lady just got up. Go sit down."

Lily had been waiting for almost two hours when she heard her name called. She walked into her social worker's office and was surprised to see that Mr. Murphy, who'd been waiting on her for nearly four years, had been replaced. The new man's name was Mr. Wingo, and as he flipped through a folder he asked her to have a seat beside his desk. He was bald and so fat that his tiny pig eyes were partially hidden inside folds of flesh. The white short-sleeve shirt he wore was wet under his arms. But he smelled fresh, nice and lemony.

He stared at Lily for a moment, and she shifted a little in her seat. "Now, Miz Cox," he said, leaning forward so that she could smell his minty chewing-gum breath. "Says here that you've been on the county"— she winced—"for about four years. We're here today to ask you some questions and ascertain whether or not your situation has changed. You follow me?"

Lily nodded.

"It says here that you have two children. Is that so?"

"Yessir."

"And you're still living at the home of Mrs. Mamie Cox." His eyebrows rose slightly.

"She's my mother-in-law."

Mr. Wingo's head bobbed up and down, and he made rapid check marks in the folder. "And your husband, Floyd Cox, where is he?"

"Up to Parchman."

"When is he due out?"

Lily's eyes darted around the room. "In about five years."

"It says here you were having problems with the boy, Floyd Junior. How are things with him now?"

Lily sighed. "Floydjunior, he's in Vietnam right now. So I have me a little peace, but before he left, it was just terrible. He just wouldn't do right, Mr. Wingo. That's all there is to it. He quit high school, and when he was there he was always getting into fights and making trouble. When he quit he'd sit around the house and drink beer and argue. But like I say, he's over there fighting. I just hope when he gets out, things will be different."

She began to weep softly; Mr. Wingo handed her a tissue, and the kindness of the gesture made her cry even harder. "I'm sure it's difficult having your husband in prison and crowding in with your mother-in-law. We have you on the list for public housing. It's such a long list, but maybe I can pull some strings." He had his hand on her shoulder; she could feel the moisture through her dress.

The sound of his zipper was as violent as a raised fist.

He was leaning over her, and his fingers were hard on her neck. She smiled automatically, then stopped when she realized that he was pushing her head down below his open belt buckle. Her thoughts came in a slow, fuzzy pattern. "Come on, darling," Mr. Wingo whispered. His hands guided her head, until her chin rested on top of his pig's belly and slowly slid downward. "Uncle Charlie, stop," she said weakly, but the grip on the back of her neck only got tighter.

"You want a house, don't you? All of you bitches want houses. You know you like this," he said.

For one frail moment, she thought: *I did something wrong to make him think I want this.* A small voice in the back of her mind whispered that maybe she could tell him nicely that he was mistaken, sweetly, so as not to hurt his feelings, so that he would still like her, but then the voice faded and she was on her knees, gagging and groping, unable to stop the terrible stinging in her nipples.

When she looked up, Mr. Wingo was standing straight, and she could hear his clothes rustling as he tucked in his shirt, pulled up his pants. Zipped them. She sat on the floor, bewildered, scarcely recognizing the hand he offered her, unaware that she was being pulled to her feet. "I didn't know whether or not you were on those birth control pills. Lotta girls are on them nowadays. That's why I . . ."

She nodded and caught herself as she swayed.

He was back at his desk, sitting down, looking at her folder. "Everything seems to be in order, Miz Cox." His pants and shirt looked tidy again, and his tone became brisk and businesslike.

She had a vague inclination to scream, but when she looked into Mr. Wingo's face, so professional and stern, she couldn't think of any reason to do that. He handed her a tissue and pointed to her mouth and she was embarrassed, with him watching her wipe away his semen, as though she had belched in public. She felt ridiculously safe and grateful when she finished. "Thank you," she whispered. She didn't know what to do with the tissue; she saw no wastepaper basket, so she balled it up and held it in her hand. She stood for a few moments, with the wet tissue tight inside her fist, not knowing whether she should leave or if Mr. Wingo wanted anything else, until he coughed and then stood back, holding the door for her. And she was embarrassed again; she judged her face to be scarlet as she rushed past him.

She bolted toward the water fountain, gargling and spitting into the basin until she was almost choking, then searched around the room so frantically that all the colors melted together. Blindly Lily grabbed Doreen's hand and ran, took the stairs two at a time and raced to the big magnolia tree, leaving the stench of urine and funky underarms far behind her. She was surprised at how calm her voice was, how controlled. "Mr. Drummond, I'm ready to go," she said. She was grateful for the loud radio, for screaming music that wouldn't let her think.

38

They were out of toothpaste, so Lily filled her mouth with Bon Ami cleanser and water and scraped her tongue and the roof of her mouth with her toothbrush, pulling it back and forth, back and forth, until the bristles were bloody. She turned on the tap in the bathtub. The pressure was so low outside the city that water barely trickled from the spigot, and in minutes the hot water had run out and what was dripping from the tap was ice-cold and rust-colored. Lily felt as though she was bathing in shit.

That night she dreamed she was a child again, sitting on the porch with her uncle Charlie. She was bouncing on his lap and they were playing a game, when suddenly his fat, swollen fingers were inside her. She woke up screaming repeatedly, "I told him to stop," until she heard Doreen, who slept next to her, yelling, "Mama! Mama!"

"I told him to stop!" Lily whispered.

Doreen put a small hand across her mother's forehead and patted her nervously. "I think you had a nightmare, Mama," she murmured. "Mama, let's not go back there no more."

"Back where?"

"To the welfare office."

"I have to go back, so I can get the money."

"No. You can get a job. Working is better. That's what my friend Barbara Jean's mama says. She's a nurse."

Lily stared at the ceiling with wide-awake and very focused eyes, desperately wanting to go back to sleep, to shut down the lid on her mind, make it airless and tight, so that the day's memories and others, more ancient, would suffocate and die. But they were just beginning to come alive.

There was no one she could tell. No one would believe her. Just like before.

The next morning she was too weak to get out of bed, and for three days she refused to leave the room, and when she finally did, there was intense bewilderment in her eyes, a startled gaze that looked as permanent as a scar. Lily moved as though she had been wounded; for weeks, she couldn't walk without holding on to things around her: the wall, chairs, the sofa. She started sentences and didn't finish them. Began cooking and left the pots to burn on the stove. Her mind opened up, as if a bolt that had kept it shut for years became unscrewed. She cried some of every day, in such protracted spells of weeping that by nighttime she was completely worn out. She sobbed so easily and so frequently that Mamie declared she was crazy as the day was long. "Just what's done got into you?" the old woman asked her, patting wisps of wiry gray hair. Lily had no answer.

She peered in the mirror, noticing for the first time the thin wrinkles below her eyes, the lines etched above her lips and on either side of them that didn't disappear after she smiled, which she hardly ever did. What was it her mother had told her: "All a woman has got is her looks, for just a thin sliver of time. You squander your beauty, you done lost your life." She had thrown away her beauty, the same as her mother. Pretty girls such as she had once been were going off now and getting jobs as secretaries in Jackson and Yazoo City; working at McDonald's and Kentucky Fried Chicken. On the television commercials, the McDonald's people looked so perky, seemed to be chirping like sprightly magpies.

"May I take your order, please?" The thought of them made Lily cry.

April came and went as Lily observed most days from her bedroom window; the absolute farthest she ventured in the outside world was the front porch, where she sat in a soiled bathrobe, her hands folded in her lap, listening to the dull hum of an International Harvester dusting the sprouting cotton with weed killer. Looking out on the fields and seeing only steel machines and occasionally one or two men made her feel empty and lonely and full of vague yearnings.

She told Doreen on one of the many days the child stayed home from school, "I miss something, and I don't know what it is."

All summer long she sat on the porch and looked out over the Pinochet fields across the road, the perfect rows of cotton. Then one day when the wind was high she heard the rustle of the cotton stalks waving across the land, and she knew what it was that had disappeared. "There used to be singing in them fields," she told Doreen.

"What kind of singing, Mama?" Ever since her mother had started acting peculiar, Doreen tried to stay close to her. She was sitting on the top step of the porch, weaving leaves of grass together. Her face lit up when she realized that her mother was about to tell her something that she never knew or even thought to ask about.

"The colored people used to sing all the time when they picked the cotton. My Lord, they could sing so beautiful. I wish I could shut my eyes and see them fields full of singing niggers. It's beautiful when they make background music for your life."

"But Mama, they're gone. Barbara Jean's mama said all the niggers run off to Chicago, 'cause there wasn't nowhere for them to work around here. Reckon do they sing up in Chicago?"

The thought that the music, her music, had been

transported, dispersed among the Yankees, silenced Lily. But only for a moment.

Her quiet weeping went on for some moments before Doreen said, "Mama. Barbara Jean said that my daddy killed a nigger for you. Did he, Mama?"

She stopped crying long enough to look Doreen in the eyes. "Not for me he didn't." She whispered, "That's the sad part."

One morning in early October, when there was just enough of a chill in the air to serve notice that summer was really gone, Lily sat on the front porch, balancing a plate on her lap. She sniffed her wrist and could detect nothing on her skin except the faint odor of Cashmere Bouquet, two days old and almost faded. She held in her mind the barest outline of the memory of Evening in Paris and the magic it once brought, but that thin recollection was powerful enough to send her to her bedroom, where she groped under the bed for her handbag. In her wallet were one five-dollar bill and four ones, with three pennies in the change purse. For a fleeting moment as she held the money between her fingers she remembered that she had two weeks to go until another check came, that they were low on eggs, and that she didn't have a Kotex in the house, but by that time she was moving too fast to care.

To get to the drugstore, Lily had to walk past the new McDonald's. She'd seen it only once before, and now, as then, she was struck by the elegance of the plateglass picture windows and the spotless interior. Everybody in town, at least all the teenagers, seemed to be inside, sipping Cokes and eating french fries. There were white ones and black ones inside, and they all looked happy. She counted the money in her purse once again. If she had enough on her way back, she would buy a soda. The idea thrilled her, and now she tingled as she almost ran across the street to the drugstore.

Inside Burke's Drugstore, the fluorescent lights made her blink; Lily shielded her eyes as she walked from

aisle to aisle, searching for the perfume section. So
much had changed. The merchandise had been re-
arranged. She looked for someone to help her, but nobody seemed to be around. Then she saw the cosmetics
section and rushed toward it, but when she scanned the
aisle, she didn't see the dark blue bottle she was looking for. She began to weep, even as she was trying to
find someone who worked in the store, someone to help
her. She thought she saw a woman's skirt pass quickly
across the aisle, and she ran after her, but when she
turned the corner, there was nobody. She decided to go
back to the cosmetics section, to search the rows of perfume again. Evening in Paris must be there. But she
didn't know whether to go left or right. She ran one
way and wound up in front of a row of deodorants, and
then she raced around the other way, colliding with an
array of brooms and mops; they clattered and toppled in
front of her. She bent down and stayed in a tight
crouch, weeping loudly, too weak to rise. Then there
were fingers gripping her shoulders, a soft "Miss . . .
miss." Too soft to interrupt her sudden screams. She
couldn't stop, not even when the fingers were no longer
gentle, when the nudging turned to strong, steady shaking that rattled her brain but did not return her to her
senses, because she didn't want to think. In the midst of
it all she thought: *I should have started screaming a
long time ago.*

Lily had never actually been inside a police car. She
sat in the back, and whenever Barnes's bowlegged deputy, who was now sheriff, turned around to look at her,
she lowered her head.

The chickens scattered when the car drove up in
Mamie's yard. There was another car in the yard, a dark
blue Impala that Lily didn't recognize. A woman, so
huge she looked as if she'd been pumped up like an air
balloon, was sitting on the front porch. Her hair was
brick red and her cheeks were blushed as pink as bubble
gum. For all her vibrant colors, the fat woman was as

stiff and solemn as a mountain. "You stay inside," the sheriff said. Lily didn't move.

She heard him talking to Mamie, and she slid down inside the car. She didn't want her mother-in-law looking at her while the sheriff told her what she had done; that made her feel like a trapped child. Mamie said loudly, "She been crazy as a bedbug for going on two or three months. Just loony tunes, if you ask me. Course, nobody ever does ask me a damn thing. They moved in on me, her and two youngins, nigh on five years ago. Not so much as a by-your-leave, and now she's done gone crazy on me."

Lily started weeping again and—since the idea of her being the old woman's burden was funny—laughing a little too.

Mamie muttered something that Lily couldn't hear, and then the sheriff opened the car door and helped her out. The car was squealing down the dirt road by the time she stepped on the porch.

Mamie was sitting there with a white bowl on her lap. She was scowling as she snapped the string beans on a small table in front of her. "If you're gonna act a fool in town, you ought to keep your ass at home," she said, furiously breaking the vegetables in half and throwing them into the large bowl. "Well, can't you speak to nobody?" she said.

It was then that Lily recognized Louetta under all the blubber. "Well, Louetta," she said softly, "I didn't hardly know you. You look . . ." She paused, trying to figure out something kind to say.

"She looks big as a goddamn pregnant elephant, that's what she looks," said Mamie.

"Well, you certainly seem healthy," Lily said, smiling.

Louetta could barely move her head to nod a little. Even her mouth, a vivid slash of orange, seemed lost in her gigantic face, until she opened it. Then Lily could see that all her top teeth were missing, knocked out or pulled, she couldn't tell which. "I done left John Earl," she said.

"What?" Lily said.

"She left my boy. That's what she done," Mamie said.

Lily stole a look at Louetta. Her tent of a dress barely covered her arms. Under the edge of the fabric she saw bruises. The hands that lay folded in the enormous lap were shaking. Louetta attempted to bend down and retrieve her purse but decided against it. "Lily, hand me my bag, will you?"

Lily passed the purse to her and watched as Louetta opened it and extracted a bottle of red-and-white capsules. "Can I get some water?" she asked. Lily went inside and came out moments later with a glass of water. "Thank you," Louetta said. "My nerves are bad."

"Why'd you leave John Earl?" Lily finally asked.

"No good reason. Not a reason in this world," Mamie said.

"Mamie, I had me some reasons. Lily, John Earl done got to be a drunk. He don't do nothing but set up in the house day after day drinking liquor. And when he's drunk he likes to beat up on me. After the girls got growed, I just couldn't take no more. I figured I'd come home and stay with my mama until I can come up with another plan."

Lily was astonished. "But I thought everything was going so well. Y'all wrote that you had the house, and what about your beauty parlor business? And I thought John Earl was doing so good on his job."

"It was going good for about two or three years. For the last ten, it's just been going. I was too ashamed to tell y'all the truth. That's why we didn't come to Lester's funeral. We didn't have no money, and John Earl was too drunk to come if we had had some."

"I ain't got to set here, listening to you berate my son," Mamie said, rising. She slammed the porch door behind her.

Louetta let out a long whistle, and when she pursed her lips, her cheeks quivered. "That woman ain't slacked up taking her mean pills."

They both laughed, stretching out the sound for as long as they could. When they finished, Lily began crying again. "How can you live without him?" she asked Louetta. "Ain't you scared?"

"I sure am. I ain't been without a man my whole life. I was raised to be some man's wife, and I tried to be a good one. Oh, I know I done let myself go and all, but Lily, I tried. I cooked. I cleaned. I had babies and raised them. I gave that man all the sex he ever wanted. But there was a meanness in him. I didn't see it so much here, but when we got to Birmingham, it come out. He pulled a gun on me and the kids. Told us he'd blow our goddamn brains out."

"What happened?"

"He fell out drunk, and when he woke up he forgot he was mad until the next time."

"But what about his job? How'd he keep his job, doing all that drinking?"

"Honey, John Earl ain't worked steady in years. I been carrying the family on what I make doing hair. So you can imagine how we been living. The girls turned wild. Wouldn't mind me. Didn't want to stay in school. Melanie run off two or three times. The last time I didn't even bother to go looking for her. I heard she had a baby. Belva moved to Houston with a girlfriend. She wrote me she had a job dancing somewhere, but that's been a while back."

"I didn't know Belva could dance," Lily said. As she spoke, she curled a lock of hair around her finger. When she looked at Louetta, her face seemed to have momentarily bleached out; except for the two strips of blush, her cheeks had turned alabaster white.

"Well," Louetta said slowly and very softly, "she calls it dancing."

"Floydjunior quit school. He might as well have

stayed home the last two years he was there. All he did
was get kicked out all the time for fighting and causing
trouble. He's over in Vietnam. I hope he makes it out.
Doreen does better. She don't give me no trouble."

"Is she in school with the niggers?"

Lily lowered her eyes. "I can't afford no private
school. That's for them rich folks."

Louetta shook her head from side to side. "Lord, who
ever thought this day would come," she said. Drumming her stubby fingers on the side of her chair for a
moment, she brightened. "I heard about Floyd. What'd
he do this time?"

"Burglary. Again."

"Poor Floyd. He ain't much of a thief, is he? But I'll
say this for him: He do keep trying. Them boys, the two
of 'em, John Earl and Floyd, they had so much"—
Louetta paused for a moment and closed her eyes—
"promise." She sighed. "You know what I mean?"

Lily nodded.

"It ain't like neither one of them was gon' set the
world on fire; that's not what I'm saying. But it just
seems like they was entitled to something. To a job. To
a decent house." Her thoughtful expression turned almost malevolent. "And I know when it all started going
downhill, Lily. I know why things ain't worked out for
neither one of us. See, this country started going to the
dogs when they commenced to integrating. Now you
got niggers with jobs, and white men can't find work. I
ask you, is that right? In Birmingham I used to see niggers dressed in suits. Suits! Going to work. The women
wearing high heels and dresses, going downtown to
their jobs. That's what's done happened to us, Lily. I
mean, why should the kids try hard in school when they
know damn well that when they get out, everything
that's worth having is going to them?" She pulled an
Almond Joy from her purse, one of several candy bars
that Lily saw, snatched off the paper, and bit down violently. "What'd that Eastland say? 'The only choice is

to resist.' Or something like that. Well, you ask me, we didn't resist hard enough. That's what I think. Who in the world ever expected niggers to get together? They was running around sitting in and lying in. We shoulda done the same, as well as burn a lot more crosses."

"That's about the only comfort I got left," Lily said. There was a dreaminess in her voice.

Louetta looked at her sharply. "What is?"

"Knowing that everything that's gone wrong is because of the niggers," Lily said. "Believing it in my heart. Everybody needs something to believe in." She started tapping her foot against the porch, and the more she tapped, the giddier she felt. "I been thinking about things I thought I forgot about. I've been crying a lot. Mamie says I'm crazy. I reckon that is being crazy, ain't it?"

"I don't know. I'm not one to cry. What I do is eat."

Louetta had kept her bag on her lap, and now she opened it and pulled out the bottle of pills. "You need to get your doctor to prescribe you some of these." She held a pill between her thumb and forefinger. "Valiums. They calm you down. I can't make it through the day without two or three. Girl, go get you some water and take one. See if you don't feel better."

Lily stared at the tiny capsule. "You sure this don't do nothing to you?"

"What it does is open up a little door inside your head. You step inside, and life looks nice and hazy, that's all."

Lily went into the house, got a glass of water, and swallowed the pill Louetta had given her. Within ten minutes the world slowed up considerably.

Louetta stayed at Mamie's house for five days, which were spent mainly on the front porch sharing a tranquilizer-induced calm with her sister-in-law. They didn't talk much after their initial conversation, but for the first time since she'd known her, Lily felt close to Louetta.

When Louetta left, she took the tranquillity with her, and the day after she was gone, Lily said she couldn't get out of bed. She started crying again and wouldn't even eat the Snickers and potato chips that Doreen offered her for breakfast. Just shook her head no and kept crying, so that it seemed all her insides would fall out. "Mama, please eat something. I have to go to school," Doreen whispered. Lily wouldn't answer and didn't acknowledge her daughter's goodbye kiss.

In the kitchen, Mamie's angry mutterings rattled the pots. There was silence, and then Lily heard the old woman's voice become engaged in a one-sided conversation, proper and ladylike.

Lily ducked her head under the cover and tried to make herself small. She didn't mean to be any trouble. If everyone would just leave her alone, she would do right. Concentrating as hard as she could, she tried to summon the energy she knew she needed to get out of bed, but even thinking of swinging her feet onto the floor made her confused and dizzy. I'll try again a little later, she told herself. From her bedroom window, the sounds of the International Harvester sweeping up rows and rows of Pinochet cotton were as loud and jarring as an airplane flying overhead. *They used to sing in them fields,* she thought, and now she couldn't think of one nice song to sing to herself. All the music and the words had gone right out of her head.

"Miss Lily." The man's voice startled her, even though it sounded kind. "Miss Lily, can you get out of bed? I'd like to talk to you."

The warning came from deep within her chest. She pulled the covers around her more tightly.

"Come on now, Miss Lily."

The man's hands were heavy on her shoulders, his fingers hot, insistent. Don't pull on me, she wanted to say very quietly. Please, don't pull on me. All she could manage was a tiny yelp.

"I'm taking you someplace nice," the man said, pulling the covers off her face. He stretched out his hand toward her.

Lily rolled over toward the wall, then jumped out of bed and stumbled toward the door, but Mamie was standing there, her thin, flabby arms folded across her chest. "Lily, there ain't nowhere for you to run," she said quietly. To the man she said, "Everything seemed to come down on her all at once. Poor thing."

"Where are y'all fixin' to take me?" Lily asked.

"Miss Lily, you're going someplace where you can have you a good time. Would you like that?" the man asked, his hand still extended. He was dressed in white, even his shoes.

Her heart started fluttering, and Lily touched her chest with her fingertips. What she thought of then was that fabulous golden city to the north. She would wear Evening in Paris all the time and paint her fingers and toes. The lost voices of the cotton fields would croon to her there. "Yes," she said, smiling a little as she took the hand. "Take me to Memphis."

39

"And so, Honorable Men of Hopewell," Stonewall Pinochet said, his glass raised high, his face exultant as he regarded his colleagues seated around him in the mayor's office, "we are toasting a most momentous occasion: the groundbreaking for the New Plantation Catfish Farm and Processing Plant!"

Clayton swirled the liquor around in his glass and then set it down on the table. It was hard to believe that engineers had begun digging up 75,000 acres at the point where the property of most of the men seated in the room converged. The land was in the process of being transformed into breeding ponds for catfish, and adjacent to the water, the largest fish-processing plant in the South was being erected. Pain was creeping up the sides of his head, as stealthily as a cat. He looked at his watch, timing his exit, knowing that he had to stay long enough so that he left his father convinced that, as his heir, he was sufficiently knowledgeable about and interested in his business affairs and political maneuverings.

The meeting broke up around eleven, and the two ancient black men collected the brandy snifters and smilingly accepted five- and ten-dollar tips as they helped the Honorable Men put on their coats and handed them their hats. As Clayton stood up, his father put his arm on his shoulder; he flinched. "Stay a moment, will you," he said. Clayton sat back down.

His father smiled exuberantly, as if he were on a

campaign trail. What never failed to amaze Clayton was Stonewall Pinochet's unfailing ability to see every relationship he had as a means to further his own cause. And his son was no exception. "Clayton, I'm excited. New Plantation is going to revolutionize this area. The old way of life is gone. What we're doing here is re-shaping the economic future for people in this region. Now, I've spearheaded this movement, but I'm not going to live to see all the fruits of my labor."

"Why, Father, I'm quite sure that you're going to live forever," Clayton said.

His father chuckled. "I'm a tough son of a bitch, but I'm not immortal. Clayton, you've never been interested in taking charge of the world around you. You're soft. I don't know whose fault that is. Your mother and I both indulged you. But that's neither here nor there. The point is this: Life is about continuation. The Pinochet name and tradition must go on." He leaned in, so that his nose was almost touching his son's. Clayton turned his head away. "New Plantation needs you. I want you to be part of the management team."

"I'm a newspaperman."

"That newspaper hasn't made a quarter since you started it."

"I didn't say I was successful," Clayton said with a harsh, dry laugh.

"That's because you don't think success." Stonewall tapped the side of his head with a thick finger. "Knowing who you are begins in the mind. You've always been the renegade. But no more. You write up a nice little editorial and tell your public goodbye. Monday morning, you're coming to work for me."

Even as his father spoke, Clayton could sense his rage diminishing, the helplessness enveloping him.

"Clayton, it won't be worth your while to fight me on this."

"I know," he said.

* * *

Clayton could hear the television when he opened the door to the brick house; he picked up the voice of the governor, droning on and on about the newly integrated schools. He sounded calm and precise, unlike the rabble-rousers of the past. The same speech had been playing on the radio all day; he'd heard it at least three times. After sixteen years of evading the issue, Mississippi had finally had to abide by the Supreme Court decision. On the morning news there had been stories showing the returning students, black and white together. At an elementary school, a black girl and a white girl held hands.

How old would Armstrong be now? Clayton wondered.

Standing in his doorway, he heard twin laughter, the one voice gay and vibrant, the other low and throaty. He paused, almost waiting to discover that he was in the wrong house, because the brick house was for the two of them, Clayton and Marguerite. No one else. He walked into the kitchen, and sitting in one of the chairs was a small, thin woman with dyed red hair. She was smoking a cigarette, and when she saw Clayton she dropped it. He tried to mask his shock, his inexplicable and growing anger, by smiling. "Clayton, this is my sister, Esther. Esther, this is Mr. Pinochet. Clayton," Marguerite said, with her lips tight and bunched together. He nodded his head, and the two women became silent, almost sullen. He left the room, and moments later he heard the front door open and then slam shut.

Marguerite stormed into the bedroom and said with an intensity that stunned him, "I have to be able to see people in this house. I will not be nobody's prisoner."

She stood in front of him, her eyebrows raised, her fists clenched, and he got up from the bed and put his arms around her and whispered, "Of course you can have company."

"I want you to put the house in my name," she said. Facing her, he tried to pinpoint the actual moment when their relationship had begun to change, when Marguerite became a woman who had her own opinions and demands.

He stepped away from her. "I'll never leave you, Marguerite. I'll always take care of you. I love you."

Her face was stern and unsmiling. "Something could happen to you, and your father would put me out of here in three seconds. If you love me, put the house in my name and give me the deed."

He went to his bank the next day and had the papers drawn up. And that night in bed, after he showed her the documents, she made him feel the way he had the first time he made love to her, and he thought peace had returned.

But the house wasn't enough. Every day she seemed to push him a little more, toward some frightening point he kept trying to veer away from.

When he found the high school equivalency degree from the correspondence course in the bottom of her drawer, he jumped away as if retreating from a loaded gun.

"I want something out of my life," she said when he showed it to her. "I don't want to be stupid anymore. Clayton, I want you to send me to college."

"To college. Why?"

"I want to be somebody besides . . . besides your whore."

"You're not a whore, Marguerite."

"Then what am I?"

"You're the woman I love." He steeled himself for what he knew would come next.

"Then why did you make me kill your babies?"

Clayton sighed. "Do we have to talk about this now?"

He was relieved when she started crying. Her tears were less accusatory, easier to take, than her rage. He reached for her and she pulled away, but he wouldn't let go of her arms. She struggled against him for a while,

almost fighting, and then she became limp and soft. He
put his arms around her, and she didn't try to stop him
when he kissed her neck. "I'm sorry. I'm sorry," he
said. "I'm sorry." Her weeping grew softer, and still she
didn't pull away. "I'm sorry, Marguerite. I love you. I'll
make it up to you." He waited a moment, then kissed
her for a long time, breaking away to stare into her eyes
and then kissing her again, until he felt her fingers
climbing like ivy up his back.

"Marry me, Clayton," she whispered. "Marry me and
we can leave here."

He let the idea of leaving Hopewell, of escaping from
New Plantation and his father, sink in. He could begin
again.

They packed for a week. His father was sanguine
when Clayton called and told him that closing up the
newspaper was taking longer than he thought. He told
Clayton, "Son, you're finally taking control of your
life," and agreed to give him $25,000 to pay off ex-
penses. Clayton drove to the most exclusive jewelry
store in Jackson and bought Marguerite a ring, a diamond encircled by smaller stones. He bought a new car,
a black Cadillac, and kept the rest of the money for living expenses once they reached Chicago, where they
decided to go because Marguerite had relatives there.

They left town early on a Friday morning right after
New Year's Day. Marguerite cried when he placed the
ring on her finger. She had made fried chicken and potato salad and filled a large thermos full of coffee, and
as they drove, the tantalizing aroma of the food and the
rich grainy odor of coffee filled the car and seemed a
good omen for their journey. Marguerite prattled constantly, and when she wasn't chatting, she sang along
with the radio or without it, and Clayton smiled at her
obvious happiness. Her mood was infectious, and they
hadn't been on the road for more than fifteen minutes
before Clayton began singing too, albeit a bit off key.

The black Cadillac had just passed Greenwood and

was about to turn on Route 55 when a police car flagged them down. "Lord have mercy," Marguerite said, a look of complete terror on her face. She started climbing over her seat to the back.

"What the hell are you doing?" Clayton asked. He grabbed the waist of her skirt and yanked her back down. "You stay put. I'll handle this."

Clayton swerved over to the side of the road, stopped the car, then reached into his wallet for his license. He rolled down the window and handed it to the middle-aged officer, who had hunched shoulders and a potbelly. A few minutes later, as the policeman handed Clayton his license and a ticket, he said, "Mister, I'd slow down if you and your maid want to make it to wherever you're going."

"I'll sure do that," Clayton said. He nodded and smiled as the officer left.

They were silent for a long while as they drove, and from time to time Clayton glanced at Marguerite when she was looking out the window. His maid, that's what the cop had called her. And he hadn't bothered to correct him. He hadn't said, "No, sir. This is my fiancée, soon to be my wife." What would people call her when they walked down the street together in Chicago? What would their neighbors say when they saw them going into the same house at night? Was there even a neighborhood that would accept them? Suppose he didn't find work? Would anyone hire a white journalist with a black wife? His forehead was wet when he wiped the back of his hand across it. "Hand me a cigarette," he said to Marguerite. She lit it and passed it to him.

The houses along the road began to grow closer together after they crossed the Tennessee border. "Are we getting close to Memphis?" Marguerite asked, sitting up tall in her seat and straining to look ahead of her up the road.

"Pretty close," Clayton said. Marguerite looked at him, a long, penetrating gaze.

"You've changed your mind, haven't you, Clayton?"

"What do you mean?" He wanted his voice to sound strong and assured. He wanted to feel that way too, but instead he was trembling at the thought of his future as the husband of a black woman.

"Clayton, when we get to Memphis, you take me to the train station."

"Marguerite . . ."

"You can't do it, Clayton. I knew it all along, but I just wanted to believe in us for a little while."

"Come back to Hopewell with me, Marguerite. I'll have another house built. A bigger house. We can have a baby. We—"

"You always do the easiest thing for you, so you can keep on living and not feel guilty. You're weak, but I'm not. I love you, but I have the strength to leave you, Clayton. And that's just what I'm going to do."

As the door to Clayton's office on Main Street slowly opened, it took Ida a few minutes to realize that the thin, graying man with the sagging face and hollow eyes staring at her was the same person who had saved her child's life years before and had helped her in little ways ever since. Of course, the entire black community knew that Marguerite had finally left Clayton Pinochet; the news had filtered out by way of her redheaded sister, who was only too happy to report to her closest friend, on solemn vows of secrecy, that Marguerite was living in Chicago in a nice apartment, had a car, and was enrolled in college and studying to become a teacher, all courtesy of Clayton Pinochet's generous monthly stipend. That one of the most infamous of their fallen women should make such a complete and victorious turnaround was, of course, too big a secret to keep and soon became grist for Hopewell's black gossip mill. In the eyes of the sisters of the black community, who had witnessed numerous clandestine affairs between white men and black women that ended disastrously for the women and their families, Marguerite was deserving of respect, even if she had been a white man's whore for more years than they could remember. Why, she'd come out better than a lot of white wives.

Unlike most of Hopewell's sisters, Ida had never judged Marguerite harshly. She always thought of the woman everyone gossiped about as the victim in her relationship with Clayton Pinochet, but now, as she stood facing Clayton, Ida felt overwhelming pity for him. The man was grieving, she thought. The idea of a rich white man crying over a black woman so absolutely stunned her that for a moment she wasn't able to speak. "Yes?" he said, staring at Ida as though trying to place her. Then: "Oh, Ida." He opened the door fully, and she came in.

"Mr. Pinochet, I come to ask you a favor," she said slowly. She shook her head as he motioned for her to sit down. Somehow, looking at Clayton's unhappy face, she found it difficult to bring up her own troubles.

"If I can help you, I will," he said calmly, and smiled a little.

"My boy Sweetbabe, William, started over to the white school last September."

Clayton looked disturbed. "I do hope he hasn't run into any"—he floundered, seeking the right word—"uh, trouble."

"Well, there's all kinds of trouble, but my son can take care of himself. Mr. Pinochet, I wonder if you can help Sweetbabe with his reading. See, he ain't never been no great shakes, and now, in this new school, well, it's a lot harder than the old one. I'm afraid he won't pass."

"Why not ask one of his teachers?"

"Sir, them teachers don't want to help him."

"Well, why not one of the old teachers, from the other school?"

Ida took a deep breath. "Mr. Pinochet, Marguerite told me how you taught her to read." She pronounced the name very gently and had to hold herself back to keep from patting his shoulder, but Clayton winced just the same. "She said you had a gift. I sure would appreciate it if you'd help my son."

Sweetbabe knocked on Clayton's office door nearly a week later. Tall and muscular, he wore glasses and seemed to be peering over them, as though he was attempting to bring the world into focus. He appeared at once bookish and athletic, and with his narrow shoulders and slender hips, Clayton thought he had the look of a long-distance runner. He had on dark blue pants and a dress shirt, tucked in neatly; his loafers gleamed. The boy's costume reminded Clayton of his prep school days in Virginia, when the students were lined up and checked to make sure they were abiding by the school dress code.

"Well, William, you sure have grown," Clayton said, and then stopped himself, realizing that he sounded foolish and was probably embarrassing the boy. "So your mother says you're having a little difficulty with reading."

"Yes, sir, I am. I brung my books."

Clayton flipped through a book of short stories and readings and opened to the middle. "Let me hear you read a little bit."

All the smoothness disappeared from the boy's voice. He stumbled, stuttered, and slurred, until Clayton told him to stop. "What grade are you in, William?"

"Tenth. I got left back once."

"Didn't the teachers at your old school know that you were having problems?"

"Yes, sir," Sweetbabe said softly. "It's just that now, at the new school, my problems look real big. I gotta learn how to read better, Mr. Pinochet."

"I see. I see. Well, William, I'm no expert teacher. . . ."

"Mr. Pinochet, if you'll just take some time with me,

I'll work real hard. It means a lot to my mama for me to have a good education. That's her dream. For me to go to college and get a good job in Chicago. If you'll just help me . . ."

Privately Clayton thought Sweetbabe had as much chance of going to college as a pig did, but he sensed a single-mindedness about the boy, an obduracy of spirit, that prevented him from dismissing the goal as entirely impossible. For a moment he pictured Marguerite, recalled the way her eyes lit up when she began reading. He had to admit that he liked seeing that light, being responsible for it. He pointed to a chair. Sweetbabe sat down. Clayton had talked his father into letting the newspaper remain in operation for a little while longer. It would be nice to have a young person in the office again. "I'll work as hard as you do," Clayton said.

Sweetbabe grinned. "Yes, sir."

Clayton's father called him a few days later and requested that he come for dinner that Saturday. "Dress, son. We're having guests."

Clayton dusted off his tuxedo and had his shoes polished. Since his mother's death, his father hardly ever socialized, and as he drove to his house, Clayton wondered what commercial or political debt his father owed that had prompted him to arrange a dinner party.

He arrived at seven, and the house was fairly shimmering with the opalescence of white roses and blinding lights. The maid poured him a glass of bourbon. "The guest is in the library," she said.

Strains of Frank Sinatra were playing as he entered the room. For a moment he didn't see anyone, and then he smelled cigarette smoke. At the far end of the room, nearly hidden by a bookcase, sat a beautiful, regal-looking woman with fine long legs crossed at a purposeful angle. She appeared to be about thirty, although she might have been a bit older.

When she saw him she smiled. "You must be Clayton," she said, walking toward him, extending her hand. She had a lovely body, he thought, as she neared him; quite a bit of it was showing, through tasteful splits and slits in her clothes. When she was right in front of him, she kissed him, and he tasted the tobacco and bourbon on her tongue. "Your father has a headache," she said, kissing his cheek. "I think we'll be dining alone." She pulled down the top of her dress and stood back, so that Clayton could see how ripe and fleshy her breasts were. He looked for only a moment.

He ran up the wide staircase and when he reached the landing opened the door to the first room on the right. His father was lying down in a massive bed with a huge, finely carved mahogany headboard; he was sipping an iced drink and watching television. His gray head bobbed up and he coughed when his son came in.

"I can find my own hookers, Father," Clayton said.

The old man struggled to sit up. "She's gone, that black gal. She left you. You're only fifty. That's young for a man. You must marry and father children. White children. You must. Life is about continuation and tradition. The Pinochet name must endure, the way it always has. It can't die; it can't change."

Clayton couldn't swallow; his throat seemed clogged and knotted; he felt fists punching him inside his stomach. He turned and began walking toward the door.

His father was still sputtering and mumbling, his words ripped apart by loud wheezing and choking sounds. He managed to spit out, "I just wanted to get you going again."

Clayton stopped just short of the door and turned around to face his father. He said quietly, "I won't let you control me anymore."

Clayton parked his car in front of the brick house. Even from outside, the place looked empty and forlorn. Loveless. Sitting alone, he remembered something Etta told him when he'd come to her as a child, crying because he feared the hard fists of a bully. She'd pulled him onto her wide lap and said, "If they know you scared, you's already licked." Why had he forgotten that for so many years? He had loved two black women: a mother he wasn't allowed to claim and a wife he was forbidden to honor. Facing the empty house, he cried for both of them. And for himself.

Ida couldn't keep a smile off her face as she and her father listened to Sweetbabe read the *Telegram*. Every time she tried to assume a solemn expression, her lips would commence twitching and she'd break out in a grin. She just couldn't help herself! After just a few months of Mr. Pinochet's tutoring, her baby read almost like a preacher. At the same time, in the midst of her happiness, she felt like crying. She couldn't help wondering, as Sweetbabe's smooth voice glided over the words, if her son would have been better off had she moved to Chicago long before. Instead she'd stayed in Hopewell, and Sweetbabe had inherited the same inadequate schools that she attended, at least until recently. Burning anger sizzled inside her. If he'd been in a good school, with new books instead of the torn-up hand-me-downs they gave the black schools, if he could have used the library in Greenwood and hadn't grown up with those hateful "Colored Only" signs, telling him he was less than human, he would have learned a lot sooner. The boy wasn't stupid; he just needed some help. Life ain't fair, she thought. She sighed and walked to the edge of the porch and looked down the road. Many of the houses she saw were empty; the inhabitants had moved to Chicago.

"You listening, Mama?" Sweetbabe asked.

Bless his heart, Ida thought. One thing about that boy: he didn't give up. "I sure am. You sounding good too, baby."

Ida closed her eyes and envisioned her son in a suit and tie as he stood in front of a Chicago classroom.

He'd talk proper, and the children would mind him, and he'd never have to worry about making a living. Crashing through her reverie was harsh reality: ever since her party business folded, she didn't have enough money to save for Sweetbabe's college education. A welfare check didn't stretch that far. Her son's voice, steady and smooth, began a new article, interrupting her reverie.

"Keep reading, Sweetbabe," Ida said. "I'm going inside to fix dinner. Daddy, don't Sweetbabe sound good?" she asked, raising her voice and looking at her father. The old man's eyes were closed, and his chin almost touched his chest. "Daddy! You 'sleep? Daddy!" She walked over to the wheelchair and gave her father a little shake. He didn't move. She shook him again, harder. "Daddy! Daddy! LordJesus! Sweetbabe, call the ambulance!"

Everyone in the Quarters, what was left of it, turned out for William Long's funeral. Lizzie Mae and Fern and the rest of his children returned from Chicago, and when the services were over, Ida thought it had seemed more like a family reunion than a burial. She cleaned William's room out the next day, the first really thorough cleaning it had had in years, since William never allowed anyone to touch any of his things. Everything smelled like peach-scented pipe tobacco, and when Ida closed her eyes she imagined her father still in the room, puffing on his pipe. She gathered up his suits and work clothes to send over to the church; then she emptied the drawers and sat down on the bed to look through pictures of her father and mother and the children when everyone was younger. She cried a little.

"Ain't no telling what he had under this bed," she said to herself as she put the pictures away. Bending down, she took a long swipe with the broom and hit against something hard; she guided it toward her.

A metal box emerged, old and rusty. Inside, there were papers, faded and almost yellow with age, and three pictures. A solemn colored woman and a white baby. Another of the same pair, only in this one the woman was smiling, and looking at the happiness in her face, Ida recognized her mother and realized that she was the white baby. In the third picture she was sitting on her mother's lap, and a man stood behind them with one arm around her mother's shoulder. A white man. She turned the picture over. The three faded words were like neon lights flashing before her: *Mama, Daddy, Baby.* "LordJesus."

Dan's words came back to her. "It ain't your shame. And it ain't your mama's, either."

She stared at the man's face. He looked like someone she knew. She went to the window and held the picture, old and faded, up to the light, but she couldn't say who the man was, only that he was familiar.

The box.

She carefully emptied the contents on the bed, then painstakingly examined every slip of yellowed paper. They were letters. Love letters. *Darling Susie, I miss you so. I will meet you tonight. You know where. Dearest Susie, I can't stop thinking about you. You get me so excited. I will see you tonight. My beautiful Susie, Don't worry. I will help you with the baby. Here is some money to help out. Sweet Susie, our baby is beautiful. Here is some money for food and clothes. Don't worry. I'll never leave you.* All unsigned.

No name. Her head began throbbing with pain. All those years of wondering and hoping, and now she'd never know who her father was. "Why can't I know?" she cried. "Don't I deserve that?" She threw the letters and photos on the floor, hurled herself across the bed, and began sobbing.

Nearly half an hour passed before Ida calmed down, then rose and began collecting the papers and pictures from the floor. Someone in the Quarters might recognize the man in the photo, she thought. Then she real-

ized sadly that all the old-timers had moved away or
were dead. With a deep sigh she picked up the last of
the three pictures, and was about to place it in the box
with the rest, when she noticed that it felt different from
the others. She examined it more closely and discovered
that what she held in her hand was really two pictures
stuck together. Carefully she separated the two photographs.

In the fourth picture the white man was holding the
baby. Ida peered at the photo, studied it from every angle. It was useless; she didn't know the man. Resigned
to the fact that the situation was hopeless, she turned
the photo over almost carelessly. Not until she held it
up to the light did she see the faded words: *Stonewall
holding Ida.*

Stonewall Pinochet. Clayton's father. Her father.

Not her shame.

Once ground was broken on the catfish ponds, the ex-
pectations of Hopewell's blacks soared with every
speck of dirt scooped out by the excavator. The old-
timers, who'd chopped and picked cotton in their youth,
were so thoroughly riddled with rheumatism and arthritis that they could barely manage to satisfy their curios-
ity by walking to the edge of their porches and staring
at the heavy equipment for a few moments before col-
lapsing into rickety rockers. But the younger people,
those who had failed to take either the Illinois Central
or, later, the Amtrak to Chicago and were now surviv-
ing on welfare checks and fatback, were excited. There
hadn't been prospects for employment in Hopewell
since the last of the manual laborers had been run off
cotton plantations by automatic pickers and chemical
weed killers. The Quarters was rife with rumors of jobs
and prosperity. When the news filtered throughout the
community that their salvation could swim and tasted
great fried, they were no less thrilled. Nor were they de-

terred when they heard that the labor was arduous and dirty. They'd do whatever was necessary, as they had always done. Months before the first pregnant catfish was dropped into its new home, the mood of black Hopewell was as close to celebration as it had been since the Emancipation Proclamation.

Once she recovered from the shock of discovering that the richest white man in the county was her father, and accepted the fact that her life wouldn't change one iota because of it, Ida was as overjoyed as any of her fellow unemployed residents of Hopewell at the news that the catfish-processing operation was scheduled to be in full operation by the end of the year. Her once bountiful savings had been eroded by William's funeral, and sales for her dinners were slow due to the fact that many in the community preferred eating out at the new McDonald's rather than take home her fried chicken and tamales. Whenever she passed the golden arches, she experienced a sharp cutting sensation in the middle of her chest. She needed no other reminder that she was running out of money. When Clayton brought Sweetbabe home one chilly evening, she approached the black Cadillac as it drove into her yard.

"Evening, Mr. Pinochet."

"Evening, Ida."

Ida smiled as Sweetbabe walked toward the house; she turned to the car as the front door slammed. "Mr. Pinochet, is you the one putting up the catfish factory?"

He looked at her in a sharp, almost angry way. "No. That's my father."

Ida almost felt like laughing, thinking of how shocked Clayton would be if she said, "You mean *my* daddy." Instead she said, "You know I been looking for work. I was wondering if you'd ask your daddy if I could get a job when the place opens."

"You wouldn't want to work there," Clayton said. "The pay isn't going to be good."

A stab of disappointment pricked her chest, but it was quickly replaced by pragmatism. "Any little bit would help right now."

"You don't understand," he told her. "It's going to be just as bad as—as sharecropping ever was."

She spoke slowly. "I understand what you saying, Mr. Pinochet. I do. And I thank you for telling me, but I need me a job."

"I'll do what I can," Clayton said, turning to go.

"Wait, Mr. Pinochet. I got something else I want to ask you."

Clayton looked at Ida; she stepped toward him, smiling shyly. "You saved my baby's life twice, Mr. Pinochet. You saved him from the dog bite and you taught him how to read. And you know I'm grateful. I hope you don't mind, but I told a few folks how much you helped Sweetbabe with his reading, and, well, some of their kids is having problems too." She looked at him, still smiling.

"Now wait a minute, Ida," he said. "You're not suggesting that I tutor some more children, are you? I'm not running a school."

"Well, why ain't you, Mr. Pinochet? That's just what you should be doing. A lot of good that newspaper will do if there ain't nobody around who can read it. These black kids around here are behind. They need the kind of help an educated man like you can give them. And"—Clayton could sense her choosing her words carefully—"if you fill your time with doing something purposeful, you won't have a minute to brood about what you're missing. You know, I always wanted to leave Hopewell, to go to Chicago. Well, that didn't work out, and so now I want to make it better where I am. If you tutor these kids, Mr. Pinochet, I'll help you."

He smiled. "What kind of help are you going to give me?"

"Mr. Pinochet, anything you ask me to do, I'll do.

And I'll make sure that you have a decent meal every day. Scrawny teachers don't last too long."

"Well, there is one thing you can do. You can call me Clayton."

40

Floyd had two miles to walk after the Trailways bus dropped him off at the tiny station that was part of Antoine's Country Store, just outside the city limits. It was dusk, and he could see through the big picture window that the place was neat and well stocked; there were bottles of gin in the cooler, and he thought back to the time when Mississippi was dry and had nothing to offer but moonshine. He remembered Jake as he watched several old black men standing around outside, not talking to each other or drinking sodas, just leaning against the wall of the store, as though they were part of a display. Jake was a good nigger, he told himself, wondering what had happened to him.

He slung a battered khaki duffel bag over his shoulder; it wasn't heavy, since it contained only a few clothes, his toiletries, and $189.75, money he had earned in jail.

The weather was cool for April, and Floyd pulled up the collar on his black wool jacket and stuck his hands in his pockets. He had walked nearly half a mile when he realized that he'd forgotten to buy cigarettes; for a minute he thought about going back to the store, but then he figured that somebody at the house would have some. Lily still smoked; being in the nuthouse hadn't cured her of that.

Even in the semidarkness he knew all the bends in the road by heart, knew that he was passing a strip of land owned by the Pinochets, land that was as familiar

330

to him as his own skin. Yet as he walked he sensed a change around him; the earth didn't smell new and rich, the way it usually did in the spring when it was freshly plowed. He smelled raw fish. Walking across the road, he peered into the shadows, then squatted down on the ground and stuck his hand between the posts. Water. Water where there once had been land.

"Hey, there. What're you doing?"

Floyd whirled around. In front of him stood a man in a uniform that looked gray in the dark. "Who's that?" Floyd asked.

"You ain't trying to go fishing, are you, mister?"

"Fishing? No, I ain't fishing. Look here, ain't this Pinochet land? What's all this water?"

"This is the New Plantation Catfish Farm and Processing Plant."

"When did all this get here?"

He could see the man's eyes squinting in the dim light. "You must not be from around these parts. This place has been here going on five years now."

"Well, I'll be damned. Where do they plant the cotton?"

"They still got some a little farther out."

As Floyd stood on the bottom step of Mamie's house, he could hear Gerald Ford's nasal twang droning on and on about the end of the Vietnam War, saying that the United States would be accepting Vietnamese refugees. Floyd cleared his throat, then spat on the ground. They'd lost the goddamn war because the army was full of trifling niggers, and now here they were getting ready to let some new, slanty-eyed niggers into America. *That's all we need,* he thought, *some slanty-eyed niggers stinking up the country. Shit. A white man don't have a place in America no more.*

He looked up when the door opened, and he saw his mother peering at him in the darkness, looking frightened until she recognized him. "Floyd. Floyd, honey. I thought I heard somebody out here. You're home," she said. She turned around and called into the house. "Floydjunior, Doreen, your father's home." Her voice changed to a hard bark. "Lily. Lily. Come here."

A few moments passed before Doreen came out and hugged him stiffly. Floydjunior appeared but kept his distance and tried not to look at him. Floyd tried to remember something, anything, about his children, but he didn't know their favorite colors, the foods they liked to eat, whether or not they were smart. And he didn't know what they thought about him. His eye began to twitch. "Do any of y'all have a cigarette on you?" he finally blurted out.

Floydjunior slowly reached into his shirt pocket and pulled out a pack of Marlboros. He shook the pack, then reached inside the opening and retrieved a cigarette. He lit it and inhaled deeply. "This is my last one," he said. As he walked into the house, he slammed the door behind him.

Lily came outside then. Her feet were bare, and she was wearing a housecoat. Deep circles ringed her eyes, and there was a sprinkling of gray in her hair. "Hello, Floyd," she said. Her voice was barely audible and sounded strange to him, as though it belonged to another person.

"How you been, Lily?"

"Fine. I been fine."

"You got a cigarette on you?"

The newness of freedom was as strange to Floyd as the first night he'd spent in jail. Everyone and everything made him think of time, mostly the lost years he couldn't reclaim. His mother was now an old, bent woman with fingers that couldn't hold a pot sometimes. Watching her halting moves, the gingerly way she settled into the sofa, was like seeing the hand of a clock speeding around in double time; to look at her scared him, as many things did. When he thought about going out to find work, his knees buckled and he couldn't catch his breath. He didn't want to go back to jail—the niggers were brutal and way too plentiful—but he didn't have any idea how he was going to make a living. When he considered his prospects, he felt as though he'd failed already, and the enormity of his defeat was like a mountain welded to his back.

He tried not to look at Lily. Every time he did, he wondered whom she'd been sleeping with while he was away. Even with the bags under her eyes and the gray hair, she wasn't bad-looking, older. And she still had a nice shape on her. The first few times when he was inside her in bed, he kept his eyes and ears open, waiting to hear her call him by some other name, to see if she did something to him he hadn't taught her. He sniffed her to see if she smelled like another man. To see if she smelled like a nigger.

Being in the same house as his children was frightening. The last time he'd lived with them for any time, Doreen had just been born, and now she was close to fifteen years old, listening to nigger music that blared from the radio. Diana Ross. Marvin Gaye. The Temptations.

Floydjunior hardly even spoke to him. "How was it in 'Nam?" he asked his son one night after supper, but the only answer he received was a quick glance with sullen eyes.

Coming back into their lives made him feel as though he had acquired new cellmates.

Still, sometimes when Floyd thought he was alone, he'd turn around and Doreen would be staring at him. She reminded him of Lily. Her hair was lighter, a dirty blond, but she had the same green eyes, the same sweet baby-girl ways. Like Lily, he thought, before all the confusion.

At dinner three days after Floyd came home, he reached for the last biscuit on the dinner table. And Floydjunior reached too. Their fingertips touched, and Floyd looked up into his son's malevolent eyes. "When

was the last time you bought us some food?" he asked
his father, in a voice that was cold as packed snow.

Lily pushed her chair back and rose, but not all the
way. Her body seemed crouched, suspended in air, as if
she didn't know whether to sit or stand; she looked as
though she was about to cry.

Mamie said, "Now y'all be nice to one another." She
sounded screechy and pitiful.

Doreen said, "Floydjunior, don't you start no mess,
hear?"

"Who the hell you think you're talking to, boy?"
Floyd asked. He was wearing a T-shirt, and now he
clenched his fist and the blue mermaid on his biceps
started dancing.

Floydjunior stood up and leaned over his father. A
lock of dark hair fell into his eyes, and he yanked it
back. "You ain't never done shit for us, and now you
want to come in here and eat up all the food. Fuck
that." He swept the side of his hand across the plate the
biscuit was on, so that it clattered and the biscuit went
flying across the table, bouncing into Mamie's chest
and then falling to the floor. "Why don't you get the
fuck out of here, you tattooed son of a bitch."

Lily's body swayed slightly.

"You put me out," Floyd said, standing up. A picture
came into his mind, clear as sunlight: his father, his
brother, and him in the smoke-filled cab of his father's
truck, Hank Williams's voice, full force and pure.

Floydjunior shoved his chair aside, sending it crashing into the kitchen door.

"Now y'all be nice. Be nice," Mamie pleaded.

Floyd was thinking that he would land one dead on
his chin, just knock the little bastard flat on his ass so
he'd think twice before he started any more shit with
him. He took a quick look over his shoulder, a prison
habit he hadn't tried to break. Somewhere in his mind
he told himself: *This is my son.*

"What you gon' do? Kill me like you killed that nigger for Mama?"

Bright pink splotches spread across Lily's face, as if someone had slapped her. Lily whispered, "He didn't kill no nigger for me." She sat down.

In a way, Floydjunior reminded him of Salinger, one of the menacing blacks in the joint, who liked to slam his food tray into Floyd's back when he stood behind him at mess, whispering in his ear, "You killed that black boy, didn't you? You better watch out, cracker. The brothers is gon' kick your ass good."

And they did, finally catching him alone in the yard one morning when there were no other white men around. They didn't even say anything; Salinger grabbed him, and then he felt the fists, tasted his own blood, heard the crack of his breaking teeth.

"I ain't killed nobody," Floyd said to his son, feeling the fight seep out of him.

It was what he always told the niggers.

Late at night Floyd could hear his son stumbling around on the porch, trying to open the door, at first cussing softly to himself as the key missed the lock. Then, as he failed again and again, the oaths became louder. Sitting on the sofa, watching television, Floyd knew his son was high, not in a whiskey kind of way, but from drugs. At first he thought the boy was only smoking reefer, but that was before he saw him nodding and scratching as if fleas were all over his body. And he remembered the old-timers at the joint, how their wives and girlfriends would smuggle the stuff in in cakes and pies, even in their pussies, needles and everything, which was really a waste of time, seeing as the guards didn't really give a shit. And then they would wait until late at night and cook the stuff right in their cells and then shoot up. Floydjunior was into something a lot harder than reefer.

Floyd followed his son the next night, stood behind some bushes just outside a noisy juke joint in night air that was redolent of roses and whiskey and smoky barbecue, and watched as Floydjunior handed some money to a thin, jumpy black man who wore sunglasses in the dark and kept one hand in his pocket all the time. The man disappeared inside the club and came back moments later. He handed something to Floydjunior, who slunk away without looking back.

Floyd beat his son home, and when he heard Floydjunior's key in the lock, he opened the door and the boy almost fell flat on his face. He grinned at Floyd, the first time he'd smiled at him. Then he stood up slowly and stumbled into the living room and flopped onto the sofa. He drew his knees up into his chest and encircled them with his arms and started rocking. To his father he looked like a weak, helpless baby. Floyd's rage welled up suddenly.

"You dope-fiend son of a bitch," Floyd yelled, grabbing him up in his chest and throwing him off the sofa. Floydjunior's body slammed against the floor, and he moaned.

Floyd reached down and shook him by his shoulders, so that his head wobbled back and forth, like a balloon on a string. "You ain't gon' be nothing. You ain't gon' be nothing," he yelled over and over.

Hearing footsteps behind him, Floyd spun around to see Lily's face, the sleepiness jolted out of it. Mamie and Doreen were behind her, their frightened eyes darting from Floyd's face to Floydjunior's. "What's the matter?" Mamie asked.

"This boy is a damn junkie," he sneered.

"A what?" Mamie asked.

"He's talking about that stuff Floydjunior puts in his arm, Grandma. The dope," Doreen said.

"Y'all know about what he's doing?" Floyd turned from Doreen to Floydjunior, who lay in a slobbering, moaning heap on the floor; and then he faced his mother, trying to get his bearings.

Mamie was fully awake now. Her eyes flashed, and

for a moment she seemed to be the Mamie of long ago. "What was we supposed to do about it, Floyd? You go off on a stealing spree and we was left to pick up the pieces, and there was right many pieces to pick up."

"There wasn't no men around," Lily said softly, a look of incredulity on her face as if she were hearing something unbelievable for the first time.

Floyd lowered his eyes and shifted from foot to foot. He could tell that his mother was choosing her words carefully. "Maybe you could find you a little something to do, Floyd." She stood before him, a small, hunched-over woman, her face pinched and wrinkled, with an expression that, when he found the strength to meet it, was immeasurably hard.

In the morning Floyd walked down the road, and the smell of fish blotted out every odor the air carried. He watched as the New Plantation workers, mostly black women, ran flat-footed to their jobs, the same way their mamas had run to the fields years before, their faces grim and set as they tried to make it inside before the whistle blew. He had decided that he would go to the office that very day and find out what kind of work they had to offer, but when he watched the women and imagined being inside the processing plant, a squat concrete building, gutting and cleaning fish all day long, he turned right around. He'd rather chop cotton than be cooped up in a room full of niggers.

At home Floyd found his son in the front room, watching *Sesame Street* with a sullen face, his bad teeth hidden behind tightly closed lips.

"You follow any of the teams?" Floyd asked his son.

Floydjunior grunted.

His son didn't respond to Floyd's heavy-handed efforts at conversation. He wouldn't discuss cars or hunting or whiskey or football. And the more his son refused to talk, the harder Floyd tried.

He wanted to redeem himself, to save the boy.

Floydjunior was watching the evening news when Floyd came in again and sat down on the sofa. He saw his son's shoulders stiffen, his mouth get tight, and the muscles in his jaws start working as he swallowed hard. Floyd looked at the screen. A black man in a suit and tie was smiling and answering questions posed by the white newsman. The black man owned a business, a contracting company, and he was talking about his success: his nine employees; his government contracts; his dreams of expansion.

The mermaid on Floyd's biceps started dancing.

Floydjunior was rocking hard on the sofa, a kind of steady, rhythmic rolling motion, as though he was ready to pounce. Suddenly he leapt to his feet. "Look at that. Just look at that." He was staring at Floyd, waiting for an answer. "Goddamn niggers," he snarled. "Goddamn niggers have everything. There ain't nothing left for us."

Floyd's loud, excited words merged with his son's last breath. "They giving them everything. Affirmative action. And where's the affirmative action for white men? That's what I want to know. Goddamn niggers." He moved closer to his son, and now they were standing next to each other. He could hear Floydjunior's rapid breathing, and then the boy was looking him dead in the eyes, not smiling or welcoming him. Just looking.

But that was a start. The quick, quiet comments came later, the slow smiles later still. But the weeks passed, and then they were laughing together, with pauses in between, when Floyd talked long and hard so that the mermaid danced as Floydjunior listened.

The night that Floydjunior didn't go to the juke joint, Floyd stayed with him. And the next night and the next, until the chills and vomiting passed. All of that wasn't so bad and didn't last more than those few days. Afterward he was just weak. Floyd told Lily, "He ain't like some I've seen, where the drugs get aholt and then won't let go."

In the fall Floyd and Floydjunior were hired on a crew to put up a 7-Eleven halfway between Hopewell and Jackson; they boarded with a widow, who charged them eighteen dollars a week for a room with two single beds, a chest of drawers, a radio, and three meals a day. The job lasted nearly three months, and during the entire time they were working, neither one of them touched anything; Floyd didn't even drink a beer. At night they sat up in their beds, listening to the radio and sometimes playing cards.

When the 7-Eleven job ended they went to work on a housing project in Jackson and stayed in another rooming house together. There was a television in the parlor, and after work they sat with three other men and smoked cigarettes while they watched *Bonanza* and *Gunsmoke*.

With half their earnings, they bought a ten-year-old Chevrolet Impala from a used-car salesman in Jackson, and when they drove up in Mamie's yard later that day, the old woman hugged her daughter-in-law in her excitement. Floyd handed Lily a twenty-dollar bill and put the rest of his pay in his sock drawer. When he came back outside he said, "Come on, y'all. Let's take a ride." Lily, Mamie, and Doreen piled into the car, and they drove to McDonald's to have french fries and sodas; Floyd and Floydjunior couldn't stop looking at each other, couldn't stop grinning.

That fall the two men repaired the front steps and replaced the rotten wood on the back porch.

Mamie said it was a miracle, the way Floydjunior's attitude had changed.

Floyd got a call from one of the managers of the housing project, asking if he would like to be part of a work crew that was building a hospital not too far from Jackson. The job would last for at least a year and included medical benefits.

He told Lily, "What I'll do is this: I'll send you most

of my pay, and you save it. I'll just keep me a little to live on. When we get enough, we'll move."

He liked the way her eyes started coming alive, and looking at him as if he were important.

"Can we go to Memphis?" she asked.

New energy seemed to flow from Lily. She grinned whenever he counted the money in the drawer. In bed she no longer lay beneath him like a stone. Sometimes she played with him.

The week before he was supposed to start work in Jackson, he took Lily to McDonald's for dinner. She wore white shoes and a pink dress that wasn't as faded as most of her others. When they left the restaurant, Floyd took her hand and said, "Let's walk a little while," and they went down near the river and then strolled to the Confederacy to look at how the rich people lived.

41

Lily opened her bedroom drawer and slipped the money inside a white envelope. Floyd sent her a one-hundred-dollar money order every week, along with a little note telling her how he was doing. In his first letter, Floyd wrote that he was working with niggers, but he never mentioned that again, and she figured that he must have other things on his mind now that he was making steady money.

Because it made her so happy to see the pile growing, Lily dumped the contents of the envelope out on the bed and began counting. Five hundred dollars. She frowned, then added up the money again. Five hundred dollars. She consulted the little notebook she kept under her bed. According to her ledger, there should have been six hundred. She reached beneath all her underwear and Floyd's socks, searching for the money, and then pulled the drawer out completely to see if the bills had somehow fallen into the crevice. She found nothing.

"Mamie, some of Floyd's money is missing that he sent me. One hundred dollars. You ain't seen it, have you?"

Mamie was lying on the sofa in the living room with a patchwork quilt wrapped around her legs, watching *The Price Is Right* on the television. Dirt was embedded in the creases of her neck. She smelled old and unwashed. Her only answer to Lily's question was a grunt.

"You hear me, Mamie?"

The old woman raised her head a little. "Yeah, I hear.
See there," she said. "You brung them youngins and
moved in on me without so much as a by-your-leave,
and now, now that I'm old and can't do for myself, you
and Floyd want to leave me all alone. Ain't that gratitude for you." She flung her head back down.

"I asked you have you seen my money, Mamie."

Mamie raised up again. "Your money, is it? When
you and them youngins was eating up my food and
drinking up my water and laying all over my furniture,
you didn't hear me claim nothing, did you? You know
why? Because I'm a Christian."

"Mamie, you answer me."

She pursed her lips so she looked like an ancient
Kewpie doll, and rolled her eyes just hard enough to
mock Lily. "You ain't pretty no more. You know that,
don'tcha? You ain't no Miss Magnolia Queen. You just
can't fan around here and get your way. The Delta's
done worn you out just like it did me."

"You answer me!"

"Ain't seen *your* money!" Mamie began wailing as
soon as she turned back to the television. "Just look at
that. Look what you made me do. I done missed all the
bidding."

Doreen was sitting on the back porch, her eyebrows
jammed together as though she were in deep contemplation. *That girl is always trying to figure something out,*
Lily thought. "Doreen, have you been in my drawer,
messing with your daddy's money?"

"No, ma'am," Doreen said without changing her expression.

"There's a hundred dollars that's missing."

"Floydjunior probably took it," Doreen said, looking
at her mother reluctantly.

"What?"

"He's on that stuff again, Mama."

Lily sat down next to Doreen because she didn't

think her legs could hold her. "But he don't do that no more," she said weakly.

Doreen took Lily's hand in hers and squeezed it. Looking in her daughter's eyes, Lily was startled by how old and hard they were. "Yes, he does. Barbara Jean's mama says it's hard for junkies to stop. They stop and start up again all the time. He ain't been working, Mama. He has to get the money from somewheres. Where do you think he goes every night?"

That night she waited for her son. Sat up in the living room after the eleven-o'clock news went off. After the late movie and the late late movie, until she finally heard him coming through the door. "Floydjunior," she said. Chills crawled up and down her back when she said his name.

"You still up," he said, coming toward her. He was grinning, walking a little wobbly, and his words were slurred. But it could be just liquor, she thought frantically; it didn't have to be dope.

"Floydjunior, there's some money missing from my drawer. Do you know anything about that?"

"No, ma'am," he said.

"You—you ain't on that stuff again, are you?"

"No, Mama. Who told you that?"

"Nobody." She didn't want to look at him. If she looked in his eyes she could tell whether or not he was lying, and she didn't want to know. She needed to believe him, to feel sweet relief surging through her. "It's late. You go on to bed."

After Lily closed the door to her bedroom, she went into her closet, pulled out the shoe box from the back, and looked inside. The white envelope with the money was right where she had put it that morning. She shoved the shoe box back into the closet, shut the door, and was in bed, feeling Doreen's warm body next to hers, before slow, quiet tears started falling. *Lordhavemercy*, she thought, *I can't trust my own child.*

She began to watch Floydjunior as he slept the mornings and afternoons away. He smelled bad sometimes, and she realized that he didn't bathe regularly. Nights, after eleven o'clock, she heard the front door open, and he'd disappear, returning two or three hours later. And when he came back he stumbled, he slurred, he sat on the sofa and scratched himself like a dog.

She didn't ask him where he'd been.

Other things began to disappear. The radio in her bedroom. The silver candlesticks Mamie got for her wedding. A pair of new shoes that she bought Doreen. Money from her wallet.

"He's stealing from us, Mama, to pay for that stuff. The heroin," Doreen said.

"Don't say that," Lily said, not looking at her daughter.

"Mama, he is. Shit. You gotta face the truth sometime in your life."

"But I don't know what to do," Lily wailed.

"Mama, put him out. Make him get the hell out."

Lily gasped. She backed away from Doreen. "I can't do that. He's my child. How can you say that?"

"Mama, if you don't put him out, there's gon' be trouble when Daddy gets back."

"Don't you love Floydjunior, Doreen?"

The girl shrugged her shoulders, and a look crossed her face that was both mournful and pragmatic. "Mama, he ain't there to love no more."

Lily went to bed early that night and didn't get up until late the next afternoon, and even then she dragged around the house as though weights were tied to her bare feet. She sat in the living room without bothering to dress or comb her hair, and smoked Winston after Winston until finally Mamie, who was watching *As the World Turns*, declared loudly that she couldn't breathe with all the tobacco fumes choking her. When Lily put away her cigarettes, she started crying, and Mamie said, "Oh, Lord. You ain't fixin' to go nutso on me again, is you?" Lily shuffled out of the room and got back in bed.

She wasn't accustomed to making decisions, and thinking about Floydjunior made her head ache. Doreen was right: There would be trouble if Floyd came home and found out his son was using drugs and had stolen his money. But if she told Floydjunior to leave, where on earth would he go? She thought about her brothers in Detroit, but she hadn't heard from them in years. There was no one who could take him.

Maybe, if she asked him, he would just quit.

She approached him one night soon after Halloween. The eleven-o'clock news had just gone off, and Floydjunior was about to walk out the door. Lily called him, and he sat down next to her on the sofa. She hadn't been close to him in a while, and now she was aware that his face was broken out and that he smelled awful, like some of those women in the welfare office. He was jumpy, too, and had been seated only a moment before he stood up and started pacing in front of her. "I gotta go, Mama," he said.

"Don't go right yet. I gotta talk to you, Floydjunior. You're taking that stuff again, ain't you? I know you are, ain't no need in lying." She lowered her voice. "You been stealing from us."

He slid in next to Lily. His voice was smooth as molasses spilling out of a bottle. "Mama, what are you talking about? I told you before, I ain't taking no dope. I do have a drink every now and then, but that ain't nothing. You worry too much." He didn't look at her as he spoke, or even when he gave her a quick, tight hug. He jumped up suddenly, hurrying for the door.

"Floydjunior. Your father is coming home in a few weeks. Maybe . . ."

"What?"

She could hear her heart pounding in her chest. She lifted her hands and then placed them softly in her lap. "Maybe you shouldn't be here when he gets back.

There's going to be trouble, Floydjunior. Because of that money you took."

Tilting her head a little, Lily gazed at her son, who was standing still, with his hand gripping the doorknob. There was a look of fury on his face that made her fingers flutter against her thighs. Then he began crying, which only frightened Lily more. "Mama, can't you tell him you spent the money? Just this one time. I'll stop. I swear I will."

"You got to stop, Floydjunior."

When Lily slid in next to Doreen that night, her daughter said, "He can't stop, Mama. Don't you know that?"

Floyd came home late the Wednesday night before Thanksgiving. Lily met him at the front door. He gave her a quick kiss on her cheek and said, "Where's the money?"

"Floyd," Lily said, as he was counting the bills and money orders, "we had us an emergency. I didn't want to write you about it. I been sick; I had to go to Dr. Mitchell three times."

He looked up at her, his eyes probing, suspicious. "What was wrong with you?"

"Female trouble," she said quickly. "I had to use some of the money to pay for the doctor. And I had to get Doreen some things for school. It ran near, uh, near a hundred dollars."

"What'd you get her?"

"Clothes. She needed clothes real bad."

"What kind of female trouble?" he asked, and Lily instantly regretted her choice of ailment.

"I was, uh, cramping."

"It ain't gon' stop you from having . . ."

"No," she said quickly. "No, it don't interfere with that at all."

Floyd didn't say anything. He pulled out a hundred-dollar bill from his wallet. "Here," he said, handing it to Lily. "Put it away."

Lily called the family to the table the next day at two o'clock. Mamie said grace and Floyd sliced the turkey and everyone agreed that the rolls were the lightest they'd ever tasted and that the bird was juicy. As everyone took helpings of turkey and stuffing, mashed potatoes and string beans and corn, Floyd told them about Jackson and the building he was working on, and Lily's eyes lit up when he said that he might be able to get a spot for Floydjunior. All her boy needed was a chance, and he would be all right, she thought. Watching everyone eating and laughing, Lily told herself that from now on there would be more good times.

After dinner, Mamie went to lie down, and Lily and Floyd sat in the living room and smoked and watched the news, while Doreen cleaned up the kitchen and Floydjunior had third helpings. Floyd put his arm around Lily and said, "If things keep going right, we'll have us a house soon." He put his hand inside her blouse and began squeezing her breasts. "Come on."

Hours later, Lily felt movement in the bed beside her. Floyd said, "What was that?" and sat up. Lily shut her eyes tight and didn't answer, didn't say a word as Floyd got out of bed. She stayed stiff and still until she heard Doreen's screaming, felt her frantic hands pulling on her. "Mama! Mama!" Lily opened her eyes. "They're fighting. Daddy and Floydjunior's fighting." When she didn't move, Doreen said, her voice like steel, "Didn't I tell you this was gon' happen?"

Lily ran from her bedroom to the living room, where Floyd had his son pinned against the wall and was punching his face. Floydjunior's lip was split, and blood was gushing out. "You goddamn junkie motherfucker!" Floyd screamed.

"Lordhavemercy," Lily said. "Floyd, stop!" She rushed behind him and grabbed his hand just as he was about to punch Floydjunior again.

Shaking her hand off, Floyd spun around and grabbed Lily by the wrist. "You bitch," he said. "You knowed he was shooting up all along, and you didn't do nothing. Female trouble! You let this junkie motherfucker steal my money." The slap cracked across her face like a heavy book slamming shut. Before he could hit her again, Doreen jumped on her father's back and began jabbing him in the head. "Don't you hit my mother, you jailbird asshole," she yelled.

Lily was so amazed she couldn't move or speak. She had never in her life thought of defending herself against Floyd, and watching her teenage daughter fighting for her, she was so overcome that she drifted into a daze and came to life only when Floyd tried to throw Doreen to the ground.

"Stop it, Floyd. Stop!" Lily screamed.

To her relief, he let Doreen go, but then he turned to Floydjunior and grabbed him by the neck. "You're getting your ass outta this house now," he said.

"I ain't got no place to go," Floydjunior whimpered.

"You go where the rest of them junkies stay," Floyd said. "I done all I can do for you."

"You ain't done nothing for him," Doreen screamed. The room got very quiet, and Mamie, who'd crept to the doorway, stood there trembling, her lips moving but no sound coming out. "You ain't done nothing for none of us," Doreen went on. "You never got anything right in your whole goddamn life, you fucking loser."

Floyd came toward her, his face twisted with fear and rage. "You shut your mouth, or I'll—"

"What you think you're gonna do? Kill me like you killed that nigger you was supposed to be protecting Mama from? The only person she ever needed protection from is you. You better not put your hands on me or her again, you son of a bitch, or I'll call your parole officer to come lock your ass up."

Floyd's face became pale. He stepped away from Doreen, who stood with her fists raised and her eyes full of fire.

He's afraid of her, Lily thought. The idea was so astounding, so expansive, that Lily's mind couldn't contain it.

A hollow-eyed Floydjunior left late that night to stay with friends, and three days later, Floyd returned to Jackson. After her father went away, Doreen got into bed with her mother and curved her slim body around the older woman. Doreen felt warm, solid, and strong to Lily as they cuddled together.

He's afraid of her. A girl.

The thought was as soothing as an old-fashioned swing, rocking her into a sound, peaceful sleep.

42

Delotha looked up when the door of the shop swung open. Before she could say a word, Lionel grabbed her in a tight bear hug. "Wydell in the back?" he asked.

Delotha nodded. "Where are you going in such a hurry?"

He grabbed Delotha by her arms and pulled her in for another hug. When he released her he was grinning, and his chest had expanded slightly. He held his head up. "My second boy's graduating from Howard on Saturday, and I've got a million things to do before we drive to D.C."

"That's so wonderful," she said, nodding at Wydell's cousin, but as much as she wanted to be glad, she couldn't smile as she watched Lionel rush to the back of the shop. As hard as she tried not to think of him, visions of Armstrong forced their way into her mind. Her church's twenty-year memorial for her son would be held later that year, and the prospect had set Delotha to thinking of him almost constantly. Now she couldn't help reflecting bitterly that if he had lived, he might have graduated from college also.

Delotha sighed and glanced at the clock that hung over the shampoo bowl as she applied the relaxer to Mrs. Banks's hair; she was an old woman, whose thinning curls required less than the minimum time the directions suggested for perms. It was four-fifteen; she'd rinse her off at four-twenty.

From the street there was a sudden barrage of car

horns honking and brakes squealing. Delotha looked out the picture window. A city bus rumbled by, on its side a billboard with a picture of a pretty black woman drinking a Coke. Dark, carefree faces plastered on the sides of public conveyances and buildings, their perfect smiles hawking cigarettes, sodas, and booze, still shocked her, as did the thin though widening stream of black men in suits and black women in high heels as they took the subway to office jobs in the Loop. Such dazzling progress was almost an affront to her. What would Armstrong have become in such miracle times?

"I see your little boy is being good today," Mrs. Banks said.

"What? Oh," Delotha said. She looked near the front of the shop, where W.T. was playing with the daughter of one of her customers. He was the spitting image of his dead brother at five years old. She told herself that she should enjoy the sight of her young son laughing and playing, but instead she felt tense and anxious. Worry, like a small gnawing mouse, crept out of its hiding place: *Suppose something happens to him?*

Delotha heard shouting in the street and looked out the window again. Behind the bus, a wiry comet of a boy, maybe fourteen or fifteen, shot through the crowded lanes of moving cars. As he ran, he looked behind in a desperate, fearful manner. Three other boys were on his heels, screaming curses and trying to catch him.

"Will you look at those little punks," Mrs. Banks said, peering out the window. "They aren't happy unless they're killing each other." She sucked her tongue in disgust.

The rest of the customers, those from the beauty parlor as well as some men from the barbershop, looked until the diminishing screams of the boys indicated that whatever carnage took place that day would occur on another block.

"It's getting terrible out here," one of the women said.

"What these little mannish boys needs is for their daddies to whip their butts," said one man.

"Where is the daddies?" another interjected. In the midst of the lively discussion that ensued, there was a howl of pain, coming from the front of the shop. Delotha and the other customers looked up just in time to see W.T. pushing his smaller playmate. The mother, a young woman with her hair in rollers, rushed to her child and picked her up. Delotha was about to go to W.T.'s side, when Wydell swept by her. As she watched, he wrapped his hand around his son's wrist. "W.T., you stop hitting little girls," Wydell said.

Hearing his father's gruff, firm voice, W.T. began to cry. Delotha dropped her curling iron and ran to the front of the store. "Why are you yelling at him?" she said to Wydell. "He ain't done nothing."

"I saw what he did," Wydell said.

"He knocked her down," the mother said.

"Well, she must have done something to him," Delotha said.

"Delotha, I'm handling this," Wydell said.

Delotha ignored Wydell. She turned to W.T. "What did she do to you, honey?"

"She didn't do anything to him. He knocked her down," the mother said.

"What did she do, W.T.?" Delotha repeated, her voice inching toward hysteria.

Pink rollers began hitting the floor as the mother snatched them out of her hair. She grabbed her daughter's hand. "I'm not ever coming back here," she said.

"Make sure you don't," Delotha yelled.

"You're wrong, Delotha," Wydell said quietly after the door closed.

"How am I wrong?" she asked. "Why are you siding with a stranger against your own child?"

"What W.T. needs is to get his butt whipped," Wydell

said. The boy flinched and pushed his face into his mother's lap.

"Don't you ever put your hands on him!" Delotha shouted, and in that moment when her voice was raised she remembered the old days when she and Armstrong waited for Wydell to come and he never showed up. More and more often, those memories plagued her, and why shouldn't she remember? Wydell had deserted one son. Did he think she was fool enough to trust him with another?

"You go in the back room and watch television," she told W.T.

He walked over to an empty chair and sat down. "I want to stay here," he said.

Delotha said to no one in particular, "He's all boy."

At that moment Mrs. Banks cleared her throat and asked Delotha if it wasn't time for her to rinse out the relaxer. It was four forty-five.

"Oh, Lord," said Delotha, rushing her elderly client to the sink. Too late. The rinse water contained most of Mrs. Banks's hair. The poor woman couldn't be consoled. Through her tears she managed to tell Delotha, "My lawyer will be calling you."

Wydell walked away from the intense rage and loathing he saw in his wife's eyes. Lately he'd begun to see things in Delotha's face that disturbed him. He went back to his station, where his cousin was waiting, and picked up his scissors. "She's upset," he said.

"I see she is," Lionel said.

For a moment the only sound was the metallic clinking of the scissors. Then suddenly Wydell's clear, angry voice shouted, "She doesn't want me to touch him!"

Lionel said nothing.

Three months later, Mrs. Banks settled out of court for five thousand dollars, payable in twenty equal installments. W.T. started school the day after Delotha made her first payment, and for the life of her, she couldn't decide which was more painful, writing that check to her former customer or watching the big brick school building swallow up her son.

Long after the children went inside and the crossing guard left, Delotha stood on the sidewalk outside the schoolyard, glad that she was the only person on the deserted street, so that no one would see her cry. She remembered walking Armstrong to his first day of school, so many years before. Standing in front of the ancient building, she was frightened in a way she hadn't been earlier. She didn't know then that there were forces that could take her son from her. She was innocent then.

Brenda and Karen brought W.T. home safely that afternoon, but Delotha was still worried. She couldn't sleep that night. Suppose someone grabbed the boy and kidnapped him from the schoolyard?

"He's so little," she told Wydell when they were in bed.

"He ain't no smaller than the rest of the kids. The boy will be all right, 'Lotha. You're doing too much for him. You fuss at the girls and let him get away with murder. Every time he calls, you drop whatever you're doing. W.T. ain't the only one who needs you, baby."

They were quiet for a little while, and then she felt Wydell's hands rubbing her shoulders. He laughed a little, brushed up against her, and held her breasts in his hands. "I need you too," he whispered into her neck.

For a moment she felt heat stirring between her thighs, and she wanted to pull her husband close to her, to feel him inside and drown in the pleasure that they created. But as Wydell began caressing her, she thought she heard W.T. calling her. She pushed her husband's hands away. "My baby wants me," she said.

43

Wydell and Delotha sat up in bed, their faces solemn as they listened to the presidential election returns. "We're in trouble now. The man don't want to help poor white folks, so you know he don't mean us no good," Wydell said, sighing.

"Black folks shouldn't be depending on Reagan or no other crackers meaning them no good," Delotha said. Wydell turned to look at her face; her mouth was drawn up sharp and angry.

Wydell wasn't a political man, although he did vote regularly and he knew his precinct captain. Some of his customers were teachers and businessmen, and a few lawyers and doctors came to him. He listened to their conversations, even if they did try to talk proper and thought they were better than everybody else. And now, as Walter Cronkite announced that Ronald Reagan was the new President, he felt a sudden emptiness, a sense of futility. "The man's got the power to appoint judges to the Supreme Court, baby. Who you think he's gonna nominate? Another Thurgood Marshall?"

"You think having Thurgood Marshall guarantees justice? You think anybody can guarantee justice?" Delotha's voice cracked and wavered from the anger in it.

Wydell could tell by the heaviness in her words that she was thinking about Armstrong. It was funny, he thought, the way they dealt with their memories of the dead boy. Delotha embraced hers and let them live inside her. Whenever thoughts of his first son threatened to overtake him, he tried to escape them in whatever way he could. Mostly he immersed himself in his work and his wife and children. At least that's what he used to do. Work was still there, but Delotha seemed to be pulling away from him, and his daughters were lost in their own world, to which he wasn't invited. He longed to be close to W.T., but the harder he tried to get to know him, the more like strangers they seemed to become. He realized that if it hadn't been for the shop, he would have been a lonely man.

When he turned to Delotha, she was crying. He put his hand on her shoulder, and she let it stay there for a moment. Just feeling her made him happy. So often she pushed him away. "I need you, baby," he said, squeezing her arm; she didn't move.

"Wydell, I'm sorry I've been—" Delotha began, then stopped as they both heard the noise. Their bedroom door opened.

"Mama, I need some money for school." At ten, W.T. was small for his age but with a pushy attitude that made him seem like a miniature adult. The boy looked like Wydell, everyone said so, but they didn't really know each other. When he had time to spend with the boy, Delotha usually called W.T. away. He was a mama's boy, and Wydell, seeing him standing in front of him, was surprised by the intensity of his annoyance.

"You know how to knock before coming into people's rooms?" Wydell said.

Delotha put her arms around the boy until he pulled away from her. "I need one dollar and fifty cents," he said, not looking at his father.

Wydell pulled his pants from the bottom of the bed and reached in his pocket. He handed W.T. the money. "Here. Now, you knock the next time."

The boy took the money silently but didn't thank Wydell. Delotha gave W.T. another tight hug and kissed his forehead.

"Why are you always yelling at him?" she asked as soon as the door was closed.

"I wouldn't have to yell if you'd stop letting him get away with so much."

"Don't tell me how to raise my son, Wydell," Delotha said.

"He's my child too."

"Yeah, he's your child until you feel like walking off and leaving him, like you done Armstrong. I'm the one he has to depend upon."

Her words burned into him like acid. He wanted to shout at her, scream that for nearly twenty years he'd been a good father and husband and now here she was telling him that all that time didn't count, that he was still the same trifling bum who walked out on her so long before.

Maybe he was.

By the time Delotha's soft snoring filled the room, Wydell had put on his clothes.

He drove around aimlessly for a while, overwhelmed by sadness. He remembered when his father used to beat him, how he called him "Dumbass." That was the way he'd been feeling lately, like he couldn't do anything right, like he wasn't needed anymore. He sighed. Delotha didn't have time for him; all her time went to W.T. Even Brenda and Karen didn't seem to want him around.

He passed the street where he and Delotha had rented a kitchenette when they first moved to Chicago. They'd shared a bathroom with three other families who'd come up from Mississippi. The area had been hit hard by the riots and had deteriorated badly. Now as he drove he was dismayed to see the avenue littered with papers, and abandoned buildings scored with letters that made no sense to him. Perched on every corner were young girls with bright-colored hair they couldn't have been born with, tracing their nipples on their see-through blouses whenever a car drove by. In the middle

of some blocks he saw young men walking up to slowing cars; the windows rolled down, and they stuck their
hands inside.

Stopping for a red light, he looked around and was
surprised to find himself across the street from the
Down Home Bar and Grill. He hadn't been there in
years, not since he and Delotha had gotten back together. They served good fried chicken in the Down
Home and used to play live music, Mississippi-style
blues. The real thing, not the watered-down, electrified
stuff people were now calling the blues. For a minute
he thought about going in; then he changed his mind. It
was late.

Just as the light turned green, Wydell heard tapping
on his window and looked into the face of a young
woman. She made a signal for him to roll down the
window, and against his better judgment he cracked it
just a little. The spicy odor of her perfume made him
choke.

"Hey, baby. You want a date?"

She was a girl, no more than eighteen and pretty,
with her eyes ringed in black and her pouting lips
painted a vivid orange. Her teeth were even and white
when she smiled, and her breasts, wide and soft as
homemade biscuits, seemed about to burst through her
blouse. She wore a tight black skirt, short enough to
reveal far too much of her thin, bowed legs.

Wydell chuckled. "I'm too old for a date," he said.
"You better go on back to school, little girl, before you
get too old."

She didn't laugh. Instead she leaned in closer and
turned her face toward him and pushed her lips so that
they fit neatly in the open space. "Mister, I can blow
your dick so hard it'll start whistling." She had a serious, purposeful expression as she raised her sweater and
showed him her breasts.

Wydell rolled the window all the way down. He
handed the girl a ten-dollar bill. "Pull your sweater

down, girl. Have some shame. Now you go buy you something to eat."

The hard line that was her smile crumpled a little. "Thank you, mister." She looked around quickly, then leaned into the window, so that her behind was jutting out; she smiled again. "The only place around here I can get something to eat is across the street, and the manager won't let me come in by myself. Please, mister."

Wydell looked at his watch. It was nearly one o'clock. He thought about Delotha's words, and he could feel the pain seeping into him.

The girl's name was Mikki, and her fingers were moist when she grabbed Wydell's hand and pulled him across the street and into the Down Home. As Wydell stepped inside, the odor of the fried chicken crowded his nostrils, and the music grabbed him in the gut. A dark-skinned old man was sitting on a stool in the middle of a tiny stage. He was stooped and frail-looking and wore sunglasses and a battered fedora that dipped down below his eyebrows. He was wailing blues so low down that the notes reached out and grabbed Wydell under both his arms and lifted him up. When the old man came to the bridge of the song, he blew into a piercing harmonica, and the notes seemed to stab Wydell right in the heart. "Sing the song!" he shouted. For a moment he couldn't move; then he felt the girl's thin, moist hand pulling him into the room. "Come on, Pops," she said.

The place was just as small, dim, and crowded as he remembered it, and when he peered inside, he recognized several of the faces, but he couldn't recall any names or recollect whether he knew them from the Down Home or from Mississippi. Standing in the doorway, looking around, he realized that he was smiling, that coming through the door he felt as welcome as if somebody was shaking his hand.

"You wanna sit there?" the girl said, pointing to a small table near the stage.

"That's fine."

The song had ended by the time they took their seats, and the singer nodded at the audience, basking in the glow of the whistles, hoots, and applause that suddenly filled the club. They had barely sat down before the bartender approached them. "You know you ain't allowed in here," he said, looking at Mikki.

"I ain't doing nothing, and he brought me in here," she said resentfully, grabbing Wydell's hand. "Tell him, mister."

Wydell was about to open his mouth, although he didn't know what he was going to say, but before he had a chance, the bartender waved his hand. "All right, since she's with you." He bent down and whispered into Wydell's ear. "Mister, you be careful with her; she's poison." Straightening up, he said in a louder voice, "We ain't got no pork chops or shrimp and ain't no potato salad left. Greens, neither."

"Well, hell, what do y'all have?" Mikki asked.

"Fried chicken."

The girl ordered a fried-chicken sandwich, and while she was eating, the blues singer began a song about a woman who left her man for another; the plaintive lament stirred Wydell. The man sang several more songs before he took his bow. He walked off the stage with small, slow steps, feeling the air around him and moving carefully. Wydell grabbed him by the wrist as he passed their table. "You sure can sing," he said, and the man nodded toward him.

"That motherfucker," Mikki said after the singer left.

Wydell shrank back from the venom in her voice. "Why you talk about that old man like that?"

" 'Cause he all the time be trying to get me busted, me and all the other sisters trying to make a living," she said, picking up the sandwich again. "Say, can I have a drink?"

"Listen here, girl. This ain't no date."

"Well, it can be one if you want it to," she said, smiling.

Wydell grunted, but in a way that revealed he was flattered. Mikki was pretty, even if she was a whore. "What you drinking, girl?"

"Whatever you drinking."

He shook his head quickly. "I don't drink."

"Gimme some Jack," she said.

Wydell ordered Jack Daniel's and paid the bartender. He put his wallet back in his pocket, stood up, and was about to walk out when he heard the first strains of the harmonica and saw that the blind man was onstage again. He sat back down.

He could feel the pain in the old man's voice, could reach up on the stage and grab it. There was grieving in his song, a mourning that was deep and profound. And when the old man was singing, it was as though his hurt entered Wydell, because how else could he explain the blues inside him, how else could he interpret his sudden tears?

Mikki's eyes were wide with sympathy. She slid her drink to him. "Have some. You'll feel better."

He hesitated for a second, then lifted the glass and drank.

By the time Wydell was able to unlock the front door, sweat was dripping into his eyes and he was laughing at his own foolishness. He put his finger to his lips to shush himself as he climbed up the stairs. He took slow, careful steps; he didn't want to stumble, to fall and wake up everybody. When he got to the bedroom, he took his clothes off in the same careful way, leaving everything in a heap on the floor, and climbed into bed. He wouldn't bother Delotha, he thought, but when he got under the covers, the whole bed was warm from her and smelled like her, and he put one hand on her breast and the other between her legs and rubbed for a little

while, enjoying the growing excitement for a moment
or two before he fell asleep.

Delotha stirred, feeling Wydell's hands, which were
stuck between her legs; they hadn't made love in weeks,
and his fingers on her thighs felt too good to ignore.
She opened her eyes. Looking down on her husband's
head, she felt sorry that she'd spoken such harsh words
to him. Why had she said such mean things? Wydell
had been a good man ever since they'd gotten back together. She would try to appreciate him more. She was
about to kiss him when the odor of bourbon rose up
from her cleavage and burned her eyes. Delotha moved
her husband's hand and rolled away from his face.
From the far side of the bed she observed him coldly.
She said softly, "Mama told me sooner or later you'd
do wrong."

When Wydell had taken his first drink after so many
years of sobriety, a dam broke; an insatiable need
surged forward, with nothing to hold it back but his
compelling desire for secrecy. Drinking again was like
finding an old lover and taking her to bed; Wydell knew
what to expect and where her secret pleasures were hidden. What he forgot was that he didn't know how to
control her. He constructed elaborate rituals to escape
detection and allowed himself to drink only on weekends. Every Friday night he bought a fifth of Jack Daniel's across town, near the Loop, and hid the bottle in
the trunk of his car. Sometimes he merely drove around
the corner and parked as far away from a streetlight as
he could before he drank. Delotha never said a word to
him about his drinking, but gradually Wydell realized
that she knew, and his steady alcoholic decline was
marked by feelings of dread for the inevitable confron-
tation with his wife.

He'd been drinking on weekends for two years the
night he visited the Down Home for the second time.
The blind man was still singing his blues, and the music

made Wydell emotional in a way he couldn't control. One minute he felt morose and bitter, and the next he was so wildly happy that he started dancing alone in the middle of the floor. He stayed until the place closed.

At almost three o'clock that morning he put his key in the lock, and the door swung open so fast he fell into the house and landed in a heap in the entryway. When he looked up he saw his wife's feet, wide and flat, shoved into soft-backed slippers. It took all the strength he had to look into her face. "Where you been, Wydell?" Delotha asked him.

He was so shocked that he couldn't think of a lie. "I been to the Down Home," he said.

"I know you been drinking," she said.

There was a noise at the top of the stairs, and they both looked toward the second landing in time to see bare feet running down the hallway. "W.T.," Delotha called, approaching the steps. "W.T., baby, is that you?" She had her foot on one step and was about to go upstairs when she turned to her husband, who still lay on the floor. "You better control yourself, Wydell. I'm not putting up with no foolishness."

As Delotha padded softly up the stairs, Wydell watched her, mesmerized by the swaying motion of her wide hips. When she disappeared, he tried to recall what she'd said, if he had in fact even seen her. Her words wove in and out of his consciousness in such a rhythmic pattern that he thought they'd come to him from a song on the radio. He sat in the middle of the entryway, humming to himself, laughing when he discovered that he'd composed his own blues.

As he lay on the floor, his head throbbing and his stomach churning, his knees aching from his fall, Wydell was horrified to imagine what Delotha was thinking. He resolved that he would stop drinking. And he would do better in every way: bring in more customers; take command of his home and his wife and the son who was a stranger to him.

When he thought of W.T. he felt weepy and confused. He didn't even know who the boy's friends were or what kind of games he played after school. He realized Delotha had taken charge of W.T. since the day they brought him home, but now, goddamnit, it was time for Wydell to claim him. He pictured W.T.'s smiling face for a moment. Then a strange thing happened. The image he held in his mind became fuzzy and then melted into the face of Armstrong, who was not smiling but crying. He closed his eyes tight until the vision disappeared, but when he opened them he could still make out the hazy outline of his dead son. Or was it his living son? In his hallucination they seemed to be the same frightening child, both crying, their fingers pointing at him. Wydell put the pillow over his head. He didn't want to think of either of them. All he needed to think about was that he wasn't going to drink ever again.

Wydell decided to stay home in bed the next morning; he called one of the other barbers and asked him to take his customers. During the morning he slept fitfully, dozing on and off until the telephone rang. When he answered, the woman on the line asked to speak with one of the parents of Wydell Todd. "This is Wydell you speaking to," he said.

"I'm referring to Wydell Junior," said the woman, who identified herself as Mrs. Eggleston, the vice-principal of William Dawson Intermediate School. "We need for a parent to come down to the school and take Wydell home."

"He sick?"

"Your son has been suspended, Mr. Todd."

As Wydell drove up, two black boys were fighting in the schoolyard, rolling around on the ground and pummeling each other senseless. Wydell sat and watched in mute amazement for a moment, until he realized that a crowd of kids were cheering on the fighters. He'd never been to his son's school before—Delotha was the one who attended to the teachers—and he had envisioned a peaceful, quiet place. This was like something out of *The Blackboard Jungle*.

W.T. was sitting on a bench inside the office. He turned his head when his father came in, and later, when they both sat inside the vice-principal's office, the boy kept his eyes low.

Mrs. Eggleston was white, and Wydell began to feel distrustful and defensive. Why should he believe some white woman, much as they liked to lie?

"So you see, Mr. Todd, your son has been warned on repeated occasions that this school will not tolerate fighting. And of course, this isn't the first time he's been suspended for it. I believe we had to take that same action several months ago."

Wydell blinked, and his head jerked involuntarily. The recent past was a blur, but he could remember Delotha bringing the boy to the shop with her for three or four days, saying he had a cold.

As Mrs. Eggleston walked Wydell and W.T. to the door, she said, "So many of our children don't have fathers in the home. Your son is a bright boy, but he's got to learn discipline. We have an after-school program that you may be interested in enrolling Wydell in. It's a kind of counseling program for boys we've identified as overly aggressive." She handed Wydell a form. "This describes the program, and on the back is the application. I think it would be a very good choice for your son."

"I have to talk with his mama about it," Wydell said.

They drove home in silence, but once inside the house, Wydell said to his son, "Was you fighting up at that school?"

The boy's eyes grew large, and even though his voice was subdued, he seemed pleased. "No," he said.

Wydell knew the boy was lying and that the white woman had told the truth. "Why you lying to me, W.T.?"

W.T. seemed surprised and wary. He didn't say anything.

"You think your mother and I send you up to that school to act a fool?" When his son didn't answer, Wydell continued. "Do you know that when I was a boy, I couldn't even go to school all year long. That's right. All the black kids had to pick cotton, and our schools stayed closed as long as there was cotton to pick. Some years I didn't go to school but four months."

"That sounds good to me," W.T. said.

"You think being treated like shit sounds good?" Wydell unbuckled the thin leather belt around his waist. "You know—you need your butt whipped."

"Mama said nobody is supposed to hit me," W.T. cried.

"Your mama ain't here."

"I'll tell her," he shouted, as his father grabbed him and turned him over his knee. Wydell had never whipped anyone before, and his first blows alarmed Wydell as much as they did his son. "I send you up to that school to learn," he shouted, punctuating each word with a blow. He paused for a moment, and when he got ready to hit his son again, the boy rolled off his knees and bolted to the far side of the living room.

"You don't send me to school, she does," he yelled, tears streaming down his face. "You don't do nothing for me. And you didn't do nothing for him, neither."

Wydell heard the front door open and then his son's rapid steps, running down the street. After a few minutes, he closed the front door, got in his car, and drove off in the opposite direction. Hours later, when he swerved into a space in front of his house, an empty pint of Jack Daniel's rattled around in the front seat. Delotha met him at the door, her arms folded across her breasts like steel-plated armor, her face like an iron mask; W.T. stood behind her. "Don't you never touch my child again," she said.

"The boy needed a whipping," Wydell said, his tongue thick and uncooperative. "The vice-principal told me he's up there fighting at that school. Fighting. And I know this ain't the first time, neither."

"You believe that white bitch over your own son? She's lying on W.T. She hates him. She hates all those black kids."

"She told me about an after-school program—"

"I'm not sending my child to no class where white folks brainwash him. The hell with them crackers. And the hell with you, you drunken fool!"

Wydell's descent took nearly four years. His weekend binges slowly melded into midweek forays into the liquor store and local bars. By the time Reagan was re-elected, Wydell was drinking every day after work. It was during this period of escalating binges that Brenda and Karen, who had moved away from Chicago after they completed college, came home at Christmas and were so appalled to find a drunken Wydell slumped over in a chair most nights that they cut their visit short and stayed with friends. After that holiday they rarely called home, and when they did they asked for Delotha.

Wydell started taking little nips at work during the day. Delotha discovered him passed out in the back room of the shop one afternoon when he had been gone for hours. Wydell woke up to find Delotha standing over him, screaming and cursing like a madwoman. When they both returned to the front of the shop, it was empty, except for her youngest operator, a loud, irreverent girl who didn't bother to lower her voice when she told Delotha, "Girl, you need to get rid of that fool."

That night W.T., lying in bed, listened to his parents shouting. He was tired of their arguments. In the darkness he got up and dressed quickly, and as his parents screamed and yelled, he crept down the stairs and out the front door.

It was nearly eleven o'clock, and the street was still

and dark. There were a few people on the avenue, but no one seemed to pay him any mind. He started running, taking the familiar route to his school. When he got to the yard, he peered into the darkness. *They didn't come*, he thought. Then he saw a quick flash of light, like matches, way in the back of the yard, near the monkey bars.

"What's happening, man," the boys said when they saw him. There were six or seven of them, standing around in the shadows. The moon revealed their black caps, the brims all pointed to the left. W.T. moved in close to them, and several made familiar gang signs with their fingers. "You got it," he said. One of the boys passed him a joint, and he took a long toke, then passed it back.

The older boys observed him silently. The one they called Alien chuckled. "Young homeboy be hanging. I told you the motherfucker was cool." The rest of them laughed.

"Yeah, he cool," another one said.

"Cool enough to handle this?" Alien asked. The black steel shimmered under the lamplight.

W.T. stared at the gun without speaking. As the first wave of the reefer hit him, he felt exhilarated and in control. Later for his mama and drunk-ass daddy. He had him some boys to hang with. Some brothers who would go down for him.

They called him Strong Arm, the backward version of what he told them his name was.

W.T. was suspended from junior high for fighting, twice the first year and three times the second year. Always for fighting. The first year Delotha cursed out the vice-principal and the teachers who reported her son. Toward the end of the second year Delotha attempted to talk to the boy, with a voice that was beginning to rise with increasing hysteria, but W.T. only smirked.

Once when Wydell wasn't in a stupor, he looked up

from the television to see W.T. walking out the door, a tiny glint of gold in his ear, his pants hanging loose and low off his narrow butt, his black cap tilted to the left, his arm pumping the air in a hard-core stroll like the hoodlums from Woodlawn. "What the hell was that?" Wydell asked himself, but before he could figure out an answer, he sipped some more Jack.

W.T. didn't come home until three o'clock that morning, and Wydell heard Delotha screeching like a banshee as the boy climbed the stairs. When Delotha got in bed she was crying. Wydell put his hand on her shoulder. "What's wrong, baby?"

She jerked away from him and slid to the other side of the bed. "I want you out of here," she screamed.

44

At twenty-four, Doreen was the Delta beauty her mother had been, but already the loveliness that clung to her had a fleeting, fragile quality, like that of a ripe peach just before it begins to spoil. There was a hardness about the set of her mouth and in her eyes, and a vertical line was etched between her eyebrows. The line deepened as she drove up to her parents' house; the last notes of "Thriller" were playing on the radio. For a moment she smiled, thinking of how her three-year-old, Melanie, started dancing whenever she heard the Michael Jackson song; but when she saw her father rushing out the front door onto the porch, his eyes wild and hollow and red-rimmed from drinking, her smile faded. She thought of her mother's hysterical voice on the telephone and then recalled her own tears when her ex-husband, Crosby, used to hit her. *Asshole,* she thought, looking at her father.

Floyd shouted at his daughter. "That nigger mayor in Philadelphia bombed a whole house full of niggers." He started to laugh. "They say *we* treat them bad." When Doreen didn't speak, when she kept walking, he ran and stood in front of the door and yelled, "Hey! Hey! You ain't got no business coming between a man and his wife. That's what's wrong with this country now."

"Mama!" Doreen yelled, and pushed right past Floyd, who stamped around on the porch and then sat down mumbling to himself.

"Lordhavemercy," Doreen said as she stepped over

beer bottles, spilled food, and empty plates on the living room floor. Three of the four kitchen chairs were turned over, pillows from the tattered tweed sofa were thrown all over the tiny room, and the one good lamp they had was broken. The inside of the house looked as though King Kong had used it as a dance floor. Lily was balled up in a corner of the sofa, crying softly. "Mama—" Doreen gasped when she saw her mother's eye.

There was ice in the tiny freezer compartment of the refrigerator, and Doreen picked out three cubes and stuck them inside a sour-smelling dishcloth. She put the ice pack on her mother's eye, which was swollen and darkening rapidly, then fixed them both a cup of coffee. "Mama," she said to Lily, "you can't stay with him no more."

"Doreen . . ." Lily began, wiping her uncovered eye, struggling to stand up.

Doreen held up her hand. As she held the ice over her mother's eye, she said, "Mama, he's an alcoholic, and he won't get any better, with you taking this kinda shit offa him."

"Well, I just don't believe Floyd is no real alcoholic," Lily said, her words coming out fluttery and soft as magnolia petals. "He's just been a little down ever since he had that accident. And he took it kinda hard when Mamie passed."

"It's been eight years since he got hurt, and Grandma's been dead for three. Mama, he's addicted to alcohol, and your not owning up to it just makes it easier for him to deny it. You're what they call a codependent. My girlfriend said they talked about that on *Donahue*." Doreen's voice was dull with fatigue. Lily pulled her daughter's hand away and placed the ice pack on the table next to her coffee; her black eye shimmered under the kitchen light.

Lily said quickly, "Now listen, sugar. Men are gon' always get drunk every now and then." She squeezed her daughter's knee with her palm and let out a little conspiratorial giggle. "Us women just have to put up with it as best we can and learn to stay out of their way."

"That's bullshit, Mama," Doreen said, and she instantly regretted the harshness in her voice; her mother looked as though she'd been slapped. She said gently, "Hasn't he made your life a living hell already? All that meanness he got inside of him, all that ugliness he can't control. What do you think he's gon' do with it? He will kill you. Just like he done that boy."

She could see her mother struggling with the twin fears: of being with her father and of being alone. Why couldn't she see that she'd be better off without him? Doreen reached across the table and picked up the dishcloth and dabbed at her forehead, then fanned herself, spreading the sour odor all through the room. Her mother's knuckles were scraped raw, probably from trying to crawl away from Floyd. The last time, he'd kicked her in her side and cracked a rib. Before that he broke her tooth.

"Floydjunior was by here yesterday," Lily said softly. "He looked good. He's talking about going up to Jackson or Memphis and getting a job."

Doreen pulled a pack of cigarettes out of her pocket and lit one. She stood up. "Yeah, he's always talking about working. How much did he hit you up for this time?"

Lily looked hurt. "Well, he's trying. Doreen, he's sticking with the program. He's gon' beat them drugs this time. You'll see."

"Mama. Mama. You done had faith in the wrong men your whole life." Doreen sighed.

"I'm not like you young girls. I was raised to trust men. All of them."

"Go get you some clothes. You're coming to live with me."

The fluorescent lights inside the Jitney Jungle were bright as a noonday sun; Lily had to step back and blink to adjust her eyes, but the chilled air felt good on her back. She wished that she could put that cool air in a bottle and carry it to the cramped, stuffy trailer that she and Doreen and her two granddaughters shared.

The store was pretty near empty. The only clerks, two young white girls with identical blond dye jobs, were gossiping with each other as though they were at home in their own bedrooms with the door shut, talking on the telephone. When Lily walked past, the smaller one was saying, "He ain't that good a kisser." Then Lily heard the taller of the two, her stage whisper rough as a Brillo pad: "There go Miss America, forty years later." Lily stood absolutely still. Forty years. She heard the two girls snicker, and she sucked in her stomach hard and held it for the minute or two it took to pass by them. By the time she reached the row of cookies and snacks, her belly was hanging out dispiritedly. Her rubber thongs slapped hard against the concrete floor, and she left a little trail of mud behind her as she walked through the aisles.

The meat was kept toward the back of the store. Lily didn't have any business even looking, and she knew it, but she stopped to examine the roasts and legs of lamb. The meat looked fresh and inviting. If she could have that roast, she would bake homemade biscuits and peach pie and make lemonade to wash it down. She'd smother her some cabbage and throw carrots and new potatoes in the pot. Then she and Doreen and the kids would sit down at the table and they'd light candlesticks and have music playing in the background. Her grandbabies deserved a nice dinner. Lily stared at the meat a long time before she reached into the freezer. She looked at the price: $14.89. Tears stung her eyes. Didn't make no sense. You could work like a goddamn slave and still not be able to have the kind of Sunday dinner you wanted for your grandbabies. Not even a little thing like Sunday dinner.

Lily stood at the short girl's register, behind a trim

black woman wearing high heels and a business suit,
who pulled three steaks out of her basket, a box of
Rice-A-Roni, a head of lettuce, some tomatoes, and diet
Thousand Island dressing. Seemed like everyplace she
went there were dressed-up black people, looking like
they were in a hurry. They even had them a couple of
mayors in towns right in the Delta, and there was a
black congressman, light-skinned, with sharp, white-
man's features. Lily forced herself not to stare at the
food; she didn't want to look at the checker, either, so
her unfocused eyes wandered around the store. When
the woman stepped back and bumped into her, Lily
froze, not out of pain but from the sheer panic that the
lady would turn around and look at her to apologize;
she didn't want anyone's eyes on her. But the woman
never said a word, which left Lily feeling outraged and
relieved at the same time. While the checker was ring-
ing up three packs of Winstons and a box of Pampers,
Lily read the headlines on the *Star*. There were photos
of Michael Jackson, showing the progressive changes
that plastic surgery had made on his face. Lily stared at
each face carefully, trying to discern exactly how the
surgery had altered the singer. Melanie, the older girl,
loved Michael Jackson. The checker rang up Lily's purchases and gave her eighty-three cents back. The gig-
gles started up again as soon as she walked away, but
Lily tried not to hear them.

She didn't miss Floyd, and it was shocking to think
that she could live with a man for all those years, have
his babies, go through all kinds of trials and tribula-
tions, and then just walk away and not feel anything but
relief. In the last two weeks she had had to ask herself
just why in hell she had always been so afraid of being
without him. She didn't even miss having sex, or what
was left of their sex life, which was pretty much nothing but huffing and puffing and fumbling around, her
looking off at the ceiling while he put his mouth on her.

And it was a relief not to have to listen to him talking

about niggers. It got so that all he talked about was how much he hated niggers, like that was filling the space that a job would have occupied. Talking about how he'd like to kill Jesse Jackson. How Bill Cosby and Michael Jackson were part of a plot for blacks to take over the world. And then the next thing she knew, all those mean-looking men, mostly young, were coming to her house, drinking beer and talking about the niggers. Such an assortment of tattoos she'd never seen in all her life. Just trash. And she could hardly believe it when Floyd started bragging to them about killing Armstrong Todd. And those bums egging him on.

Hating niggers was one thing, but being crazy was another, and that crew Floyd had joined, well, they weren't dealing with a full deck half the time.

She didn't even miss cooking for him, or talking to him, or lying next to him in bed, not even that. Now she slept with Melanie and cuddled her warm little body all night long, and that sleep was sweeter than any she could remember.

The trailer was even hotter than when she'd left for the store. Doreen was sitting on the sofa with the baby sprawled across her lap, and she was fanning her with a magazine cover and had her other hand soaking in a pot of hot water and Epsom salts. Melanie was sitting on the floor, drinking purple Kool-Aid and watching television. "You get Crystal's diapers?" Doreen asked.

Lily nodded. "Your hands still bothering you?"

"They hurt something terrible, and I believe my fingers will smell like catfish for the rest of my natural life."

"I don't see why you just don't quit that job, Doreen," Lily said.

"And do what?"

"Well, you could—"

"I'm not getting back on the county, Mama," Doreen said sharply. "I don't want Melanie and Crystal to grow up seeing me standing in no welfare office with everybody looking down on us like we're some kind of sewer-rat trash. Cleaning catfish for the New Plantation may not be the easiest job in the world, but it beats welfare every day. No offense," she added, noticing her mother's lowered eyes.

"At least your hands wouldn't be hurting you."

Switching the pan of water, Doreen said, "Don't worry, Mama. There's gon' be some changes at the New Plantation. You'll see."

The next morning, while Doreen was at work, Lily cleaned the trailer until it was gleaming, and later she started a garden, planted string beans, squash, cucumbers, lettuce, and tomatoes in the plot near the trailer. She put the girls down for a nap after lunch, and then she watched her stories. And when the stories went off, she turned on *The Oprah Winfrey Show*. How she started watching that was by accident. One time she was changing the channel, and she saw a black woman holding a microphone and crying. Lily hadn't heard anything about her, but she was so startled and comforted by the sight of the plump, brown-skinned woman crying that she sat down and watched the whole thing. She was amazed when it turned out that what Oprah was weeping about was the fact that her cousin had molested her when she was a child, and that all the women on the stage had been abused when they were children. And of course Lily sobbed too, and thought about her uncle Charlie. An 800 number for victims of child abuse to call came across the screen, and she wrote it down, but she never did use it.

By late August they were eating the vegetables from the garden. At the dinner table, Melanie sat close to her grandmother and Doreen put the baby in a high chair next to her. "I feel good for the first time in a long time," Lily told her daughter after dinner was finished

and they were sipping coffee. "I mean, I feel peaceful."
She lit a cigarette.

"You deserve peace, Mama."

Stinging tears sprang to Lily's eyes. "Do I? Sometimes I wake up in the middle of the night and I just feel so sorry, so sorry for everything."

The heat didn't let up until late in October, and some nights Lily would get in Doreen's Pinto and roll down all the windows and drive along the road as fast as she could, just so she could get a breeze. That was what she thought she wanted, but when she discovered that along with the breeze she got a heady sensation of freedom, she realized that she craved that even more.

Right before Thanksgiving, Doreen came home crying that her hands felt as if they were on fire. Lily had her soak them in Epsom salts, and rubbed them with salve, but nothing gave her relief. "You think you need to see a doctor?" Lily asked.

"I ain't got no money for no doctor," Doreen said. "I get so mad sometimes. Here I am aching like a mule and ain't even got no medical insurance. If one of the kids gets sick, what am I supposed to do? Them same people that own the New Plantation, they worked the niggers to death picking cotton. Now they're trying to pull the same shit. They work us all like dogs. That goddamn Reagan don't give a good goddamn if you ain't rich. I'da been better off with Jesse Jackson for President."

"Lordhavemercy!" Lily said.

"You figure it out, Mama."

"I told you not to work with them," Lily whispered. "They're making you crazy."

Doreen's eyes were red and tired-looking as she spoke. "Mama, either I work with them or I get in the welfare line with them, and you know how I feel about that. I was raised around here, and even though I went to school with them, I always felt like they was different from white people, like I was better than they were.

Hell, I was raised on that feeling, and I'll probably take it to my grave, but Mama, you know one thing: It's getting to where I just can't afford thinking like that no more. Them feelings just ain't practical when you work at the New Plantation."

They were all asleep, Doreen and the baby in the bedroom, Lily and Melanie on the daybed, when the phone rang late in January. Lily looked at the clock before she picked it up. It was after midnight.

"Lily," the voice on the other end of the receiver said. "Lily, it's me."

"Who is this?"

"Louetta."

She hadn't heard from her sister-in-law in several years. "Is something wrong, Louetta?"

"You know, I been born again, Lily. I wanted you to know that life has more meaning for me, knowing that Jesus Christ is my personal savior. Praise his name."

The way Louetta said "my personal savior" made Lily think of the Lord dressed in a butler's uniform, walking around picking up her dirty drawers and the banana peels that she'd thrown on the floor. She stifled a giggle and propped herself up on her elbow. "I'm happy for you," Lily said. There was silence on the other end of the line. "Louetta? You still there?"

"Amen," Louetta said. "Lily, I didn't know if you knew about the television program that comes on in February."

"What program?"

"You know how they done give the month of February to the niggers. All over the radio and television, everything is black this and black that. Black History Month. It's like niggers done got to be real people. You know about that?" she said, her Christian voice suddenly full of nails and vinegar.

"I think I heard something about it."

"In February they have right many of them programs

about niggers. Anyway, next Monday at nine o'clock they're gon' have a series on, and it's about when they integrated and all. And there's a part about Armstrong Todd. You're in that. I seen it in an ad." Her voice trailed off, spiraling down like a balloon that had been popped. When she spoke again she sounded old. She mumbled, "I don't know. Maybe you can sue them."

"Sue who?"

"The people who put on the television program. Maybe we can make some money offen it."

Lily tasted the words for a little bit, not just the part about the lawsuit or even the "we," but the fact that the whole confusion was going to start up again. Lily spoke slowly, so that Louetta wouldn't miss her meaning. "Somebody told me once that you can't sue if it's history. That makes it what they call public domain. What Floyd and John Earl done is history."

"Oh." Louetta paused for a moment, then sighed. "Well, anyway," she said softly, her voice turning girlish, "it's a five-part series, and it starts Monday." She got quiet, and Lily was afraid she was praying again. Then she said, "I didn't know that you and Floyd was separated. You know, I called over to his house. He didn't want to give me your new number. He must still be mad."

"Floyd stays mad, Louetta. That's what he does for a living." Louetta started giggling and then got louder and louder, until Lily had to either put the phone down or join in. She laughed.

"Don't it feel good, getting away from them mean ole men?" Louetta said. "Damn! It's like being let out of jail, ain't it? Lily"—her voice cut right through the last vestiges of her laughter so quickly that she sounded hysterical—"Lily, John Earl died last week."

Lily was surprised that she felt nothing. "How?"

"Cancer. He was at the charity hospital in Birmingham. They say he was bad off before he died." Her voice trailed away. "I just thought you'd like to know."

"I reckon I need to know it."

"Sometimes I sit and think about things that have happened. That night, Lily, that night when Floyd and John Earl went after that boy, we couldn't have stopped neither one of them if we . . . I was wrong, Lily. Loving us didn't have nothing to do with it."

"Louetta, I been figured that out."

The television program had bouncy theme music. She had watched Cosby and was just having the last laugh with Melanie and Doreen. She shooed her granddaughter to bed and turned the channel. She and Doreen sat in the dark, smoking Marlboros. Doreen placed her rough, fishy hands in her mother's, and Lily started rubbing them. "Mama, you sure you want to watch this?"

"I'm sure."

And then, halfway through the program, there she was, a pretty girl again, with a waist small enough for a man to put two hands around, a full, firm bustline, hair so shiny a boy could see his face in it.

She couldn't bear looking at herself. She could watch fat Judge Chisolm bellowing for the room to get quiet, and Phineas Newsome and Waldo Anderson admonishing the twelve stern-faced men. She could look at all of them, but when it came to seeing herself, she felt as if she was looking at somebody who didn't know she was about to be ambushed.

All that beauty she had had. Just squandered.

And then she was standing next to Floyd, holding Floydjunior, and the two of them were kissing and the child was squeezed between them.

They showed the niggers being interviewed. The men in suits at the table. The grandmother and mother, tearful and holding on to each other.

And Ida, looking like a young white girl in the black-and-white film. Ida saying, "He didn't deserve to die."

That was hard to watch too.

"Is that you, Grandma?"

Lily turned around, and there was Melanie, standing behind the sofa, her finger in her mouth.

"You get in the bed, Melly," Doreen said, scooping her up and taking her into the bedroom with the baby.

When Doreen returned, Lily said, "Ain't nobody ever loved me the way Melanie does."

"She does love her grandma," Doreen said.

"I don't want her to know about me."

Doreen patted her mother's hand. "Mama, some things you just can't hide."

Lily sighed. "I don't know why I set through that," she said. "The television made out like it was their story, like the whole thing belonged to them. Like they got all the heroes and all the victims."

The next day Lily was watching Oprah Winfrey interview women who were addicted to food, when she heard the sharp, sudden sound of banging on the front door. She peered out the window and saw Floyd. She crawled along the floor to the television and turned it down low. Her plan was to lie on her belly. That way she could still watch Oprah, until Floyd got tired and went away.

"I know you're in there, Lily," Floyd yelled. "You open this door. I ain't gon' hurt you none."

"Go away. I got sleeping babies here. You leave me alone."

The air around Lily was quiet for a moment, and then the knocking resumed. She ran to the door. "You go away," she yelled.

"Lily, open the door. I love you. I ain't never loved nobody but you. Things will be different. I won't hurt you no more. I love you, Lily."

She sat on the floor, holding her hands over her ears so she wouldn't hear Floyd's seductive pleading, but her arms started hurting, and after a while she took them down.

"Lily, I love you. Let me come in."

If he hadn't lost his job, he'd be sweet to her, like he used to be when he bought her perfume and lipstick. If only she didn't always make him so mad. "Please go away, Floyd. I want peace." There was a long, heavy silence, and then she heard his receding footsteps.

Doreen sucked her teeth when Lily told her that Floyd had come by. "Crosby tried that same bullshit after I put him out. I knowed that son of a bitch was lying. I told him if he kept bothering me I'd call the sheriff and have him lock his ass up. That's what I told him."

"Your daddy sounded right pitiful," Lily said.

Doreen gave her a sharp look and grabbed her wrist so hard Lily almost cried out. "Don't listen to him, Mama. You be strong."

The pervasive odor of fish was enough to make anyone swoon, but Doreen was used to the smell at the New Plantation. She stood in front of a long steel table that was covered with hundreds of catfish, ripping open their bellies—one every second; that was the requirement. Above the din of the electric head saws, she heard screams coming from the other end of the floor, where the women who chopped off fish heads were stationed. She looked around quickly to see if a supervisor was near, then put down her knife and ran toward the commotion.

By the time she got there, a crowd had formed. Pushing her way to the front, Doreen saw a huge black woman, Fannie, her hand slit from the wrist to the tip of her middle finger. Blood was dripping down her gray uniform onto the floor.

"All right. All right. Everybody back to your stations. The ambulance is coming. Get back to work," called Joe, the supervisor, a short, stocky white man.

"Yeah, but is she gon' have a job when she gets back?" a voice next to Doreen said. She looked up and saw Ida Long and smiled at her. Ida was always talking back to the supervisors and asking questions nobody else had the guts to ask. Now Joe, whose face was turning red from yelling, barked at Ida. "Get back to work. The excitement's over."

But the real excitement began two weeks later, when Fannie returned to work. This time the screams Doreen heard were filled with rage.

When she looked up, she saw Joe and his assistant grab Fannie, each white man taking hold of one of her tremendous arms and pulling her past the workers, who were watching the disturbance with growing agitation on their faces. Fannie broke loose just beyond the head-saw section and turned to face her adversaries, with sweat streaking her face. For a moment she didn't say anything but just stood silent before them, the flesh on her massive body quivering. The entire room was eerily silent, and then Fannie's voice broke over them all like a lightning bolt. "Y'all sons of bitches may think you done seen the last of me, but I'm getting me a lawyer and suing your asses if it's the last thing I do. I ain't taking this shit, you can believe that. You got us holed up in this stinking room working like goddamn slaves for bullshit money, walking around here feeling on our asses and trying to get some pussy, and then when one of us gets hurt on your goddamn machinery, you fire us. Shiiit! You can kiss my black ass. New Plantation can go to hell."

Doreen heard a sudden thunderous sound, like a herd of stampeding bulls, and when she looked around, to her amazement, the whole floor was applauding. The two white men, whose faces were like tomatoes, began turning purple. Someone shouted, "New Plantation can go to hell!" and suddenly the chant was taken up: "New Plantation can go to hell!" The women screamed the words over and over, until the helpless men walked away.

* * *

"A whole bunch of us who work at New Plantation are meeting over to Ida's tomorrow night," Doreen told her mother at dinner that evening.

Lily opened her mouth, but nothing came out. She swallowed and then tried again. "Ida who?"

"Ida Long." Doreen looked at her mother's eyes. "You know her, Mama?"

"I used to." Lily got up and began clearing the table.

"Yeah, well, Ida's an all-right woman. She's kind of our leader. There's gon' be some changes made at New Plantation. The sisters are coming on strong," Doreen said. She started grinning, and then she let out a war whoop and leaned her head back and started laughing.

"I can't believe you come outta me," Lily said, shaking her head. "You got such gumption."

"Aww, Mama. You got it too."

"No. I don't know what fighting back feels like."

45

Ida shifted her sign as she walked with the crowd of more than a hundred black demonstrators assembled in front of the Hopewell Senior Citizen Center, the former Busy Bee Café. Holding the placard, she thought about Sweetbabe and, as she did constantly, said a quick prayer for him. She was so glad he'd gotten away from Hopewell and was living in Chicago. It seemed like only yesterday that he'd graduated from high school and she'd put him on a bus for the army base in North Carolina. She'd never imagined she could miss someone so much. In a few weeks he'd be visiting with his wife and young son; Ida could hardly wait.

They were singing the second verse of "We Shall Overcome" when she saw the funeral procession for Stonewall Pinochet gliding down the street. One of the protesters laughed gleefully and said in a loud voice, "That's one cracker who is turning over in his grave before he gets buried." Ida didn't join in with the others, who chuckled heartily. As she watched the shiny black limousines slowly making their way down Jefferson Davis Boulevard, her head began to throb so that she could hardly lift it. She was engulfed by a sense of futility as the caravan disappeared on its way to Greenwood. She wanted to punish the white man who was her father, but how could she seek revenge from a dead man?

The sight of Barnes, the former sheriff, being pushed across the street in his wheelchair by a young black boy, his head lolling almost on his chest, his eyes vacant and pitiful, pulled Ida back into reality. The boy parked the chair on the corner, adjusted the sign around Barnes's neck, centered the cup in his hand, and then left the paralyzed man sitting alone. "God don't like ugly," one of the women in the group said. Ida raised her placard higher.

After McDonald's added a breakfast menu, the Busy Bee Café breathed its final breath, which was hastened by the deaths of Jesse, Clyde, Gilroy, and other regulars. The restaurant remained empty for nearly a year, until finally the owner donated the building to the city. A few months later, it was summarily christened the Hopewell Senior Citizen Center.

For a while, none of Hopewell's citizens knew what to make of the center. The building was unoccupied until the mayor and the city council of three septuagenarians, who had come up with the idea in the first place, decided to send letters to registered voters announcing the opening of a facility to serve the recreational needs of those sixty-five and older, and proclaiming that bingo games would be held every Friday night at seven o'clock. The place immediately filled with old people. At first they trooped in only to play bingo, but gradually, as the roster of activities expanded to include crocheting, knitting, bridge, senior exercise, and a singing group, and the county social services department sent out a geriatric social worker to organize the activities, the place was filled during the day as well. That is, until the center's cleaning woman noticed that not one black senior citizen was participating in any of the taxpayer-supported recreational activities; as it turned out, blacks had been systematically excluded. The furious maid informed her minister, and a community meeting was scheduled. The preacher had urged people to protest the segregated facility, but now, as Ida read the sign on the door of the center, which said "Closed for Repairs," she realized that they needed to do more than picket.

"Those white folks are just gon' keep that place shut

until we get tired," Granny Jones, an active sixty-year-old, said at the follow-up meeting held later that week at Mount Zion Baptist Church; called the new church, it had been erected after the bombing had destroyed the original building years earlier. "What good is marching around with a bunch of signs gon' do? They'll just close that place down before they let us in there. Just like they put sand in the city swimming pool when they knew they had to integrate."

"Well, what else can we do?" someone asked.

"Something similar happened in a town near the Alabama border. The city was running a day care center and wouldn't take in black children. Well, the black folks sued them. And they won," said Granny Jones. "We oughta sue them crackers. Then if they shut the place down, we got money to build our own center."

"That's if we win. We might end up owing the city," the minister said.

The church was silent, as everyone digested the idea of suing white people. What did they know about lawyers and courts other than the fact that neither had ever protected them in the Delta? But in the end, they all decided to give the legal system a try. And Ida volunteered to go to Greenwood and talk with Lucius Jacobs, one of that town's natives and, more important, the minister's third cousin, who'd recently opened a law practice after returning from Cambridge, Massachusetts, where he had attended law school and worked as an assistant district attorney.

"We don't have any money, Mr. Jacobs," Ida said as soon as she sat down.

Lucius Jacobs passed a bowl of popcorn to Ida, who shook her head. "Well, I hope you'll excuse me if I indulge. This is breakfast," he said, shoving a handful of kernels into his mouth. "Miss Long, I have a lucrative drug-dealing business. The law is just a hobby, so don't worry about the money."

Ida stared at him.

"That's a joke, Ms. Long."

"Oh." Ida smiled a little. The lawyer peered at her from behind thick glasses, and then he smiled. "I didn't expect to get rich coming back home," he said. "Listen, what you folks are talking about is a discrimination suit. To win, we've got to prove deliberate discrimination, and we've also got to show that people have been hurt. Can you get me that proof?"

Ida thought for a moment. "I think so."

"Well, good. Good." He smiled again, helped himself to more popcorn. He reminded Ida of Sweetbabe. Mr. Jacobs was about her son's age.

"None of us has ever sued anybody before," she said.

"That's all right. I'm a pro. This is America, even if it's Mississippi, and Americans are a litigious people. They sue for divorce, for child support, for loss of income, for car accidents, for malicious gossip, for taking a lover away. You name it, people sue about it." He stood up. "I'll be calling you and setting up a meeting with your committee. And don't worry. I'll take my fee out of whatever we recover." He reached over his desk and shook Ida's hand. "It's been good meeting you, Ms. Long."

"And it's been real good meeting you."

Clayton Pinochet's laughter startled his eighty-five-year-old aunt, who was riding next to him in the funeral limousine. The sight of the protesters had struck his funny bone. He thought the singing of "We Shall Overcome" was a fitting farewell to his father.

The First Episcopal Church of Greenwood was crowded. There were people from every part of the state, from Gulfport to Holly Springs. The governor was there, as well as several congressmen and both senators. Clayton nodded as person after person came up to him to offer condolences, so many that after a while he couldn't feel the hands that were clasping his. As the sleek mahogany casket was lowered into the ground,

Clayton felt himself consumed with curious elation, as though something was about to begin.

He spent the night at his father's house and, after all the guests had left, went to bed in his old room. He had just fallen asleep when the phone rang. It was one o'clock in the morning. He knew who it was even before she spoke. "Marguerite?" he said.

"Hello, Clayton. How are you?"

"I'm lonely."

"You can be free now, Clayton."

"What will I do with all my freedom?"

"You don't have to answer to anybody anymore."

"Marguerite, would you come back? Would you marry me?"

He heard her sighing. "Our time has passed, Clayton. You know that, don't you?"

"Yes. I do."

"The only thing you can't do with freedom is waste it. Take care of yourself, baby."

The following afternoon Clayton drove to the New Plantation Catfish Farm and Processing Plant, parked his silver Mercedes in the staff lot, and took the elevator up to the third floor of the building, where the boardroom was located. As he opened the door, the strong odor of coffee and cigarette smoke assailed him. Nine of ten chairs assembled around a huge oak table were filled. He slid into the empty seat, nodding at the men around him. After fifteen minutes of rehashing old business, Henry Settles, Jr., the new chairman, began extolling the virtues of the late Clayton Pinochet, Sr., in great and extended detail, until Clayton rose. "I hate to cut off our esteemed chairman when he's just building up steam," he said, pausing as the rest of the men laughed, "but since we all attended yesterday's ceremonies, I'm sure that my father's virtues are quite fresh in everyone's mind. In case they are not, I can capsulize his many accomplishments, his steady singleness of purpose, his leading role in the future of this great state:

He was one hell of a guy. And he owned a great deal of New Plantation stock. He was, in fact, the majority stock owner. Which brings us to the business at hand, gentlemen. I am now the owner of the majority of New Plantation stock, and as most of you are well aware, I am not the man my father was."

Around the room, eyes began shifting, there was stereophonic clearing of throats, and men reached into their pockets and pulled out cigarettes. Henry, his face reddening in slow, steady bursts of color, turned around toward a middle-aged black man in a white jacket and jerked his head violently to the side. The man lifted his eyes, a gesture both mocking and desultory, and didn't move until the chairman yanked his head to the side again, and then he glided forward with the coffeepot in his hand. After Henry had taken several gulps of coffee and some of the clamor had died down, he stood. "Now, Clayton, just what do you mean by that?"

"I mean, Henry, gentlemen," he said, nodding at the men assembled around the table, "that I don't know what I'm going to do with my stock."

Henry Settles, Jr., gulped down more coffee. "Well, Clayton. Clayton, that's why we're here. The board is prepared to make you a mighty generous offer for your stock. How does twelve million dollars sound to you?"

Clayton gently set down his coffee cup. Twelve million dollars. The amount was astronomical. "Very fair."

"Well?" Henry Settles, Jr., was smiling.

"I'm overwhelmed by your generosity. To tell you the truth, your offer is much more than I expected, but I'm not prepared to accept it at this time. Let me do some, uh, soul-searching and get back to you at the end of the month." He looked at his watch and said, "I have an appointment, gentlemen."

The door to the *Hopewell Telegram* office was unlocked when Clayton arrived. He stood just inside the threshold, looking quietly into the room, smelling the soft scent of bubble gum. His desk had been pushed to the center; behind it was a blackboard, and in front were ten smaller desks, their chairs now occupied by black teenagers who appeared to be sixteen or seventeen years old. There was a steady buzz of voices and an occasional giggle, combined with the flipping of pages and the scratchy noise of pencils as the teens read and took notes. Clayton cleared his throat, and the soft din evaporated. The students looked up, and smiles broke out across their faces. They sat up straight and waited as if under military order. Clayton walked to the desk and stood before them. He said gruffly, "The SATs are in three weeks. What are you looking at me for?" He didn't smile until all the black faces had disappeared and all he could see was the rounded tops of their heads.

Ida turned off 49E into a small, grassy yard and parked her car. Like many of the blacks in the area, she'd moved away from the crumbling shacks in the Quarters, having managed to scrape together enough money to buy a small house. While she was eating dinner that evening, Ida thought about the irony of poor black people suing the town. Everyone else on the committee was exultant, as though they'd already won the case, but the more Ida thought about the lawsuit, the more enraged she became. Suing the town should be just the beginning. She should file a lawsuit against Barnes for trying to rape her. The blacks ought to sue because the dilapidated schools hadn't taught them how to read or write. Odessa and Delotha could sue the Coxes for killing Armstrong. There weren't enough lawyers in Mississippi to give black folks the justice they deserved.

Ida went to bed angry, and when she woke up she was still furious. At New Plantation, she was short with everyone who spoke to her, and she ate her lunch alone. When Doreen asked her about the next organization meeting of New Plantation workers, she snapped at her, which she instantly regretted; in spite of the fact that she was Lily Cox's daughter, she liked the young white woman.

By the time Ida got home, she was feeling thoroughly evil, and washing the catfish smell off her body didn't improve her mood. She thought about running but decided against it and got into bed. Before she began leafing through the magazine on her nightstand, she reached under the bed and pulled out a metal box. She picked up the first yellowed piece of paper and read it intently. As she studied the four pictures, her head began to throb. She tossed the photos on the bed and began to pound the mattress with her fists. All those years of not knowing who she was. All the years people called her mama a whore. All the years she struggled, not knowing how she was going to make it. And all that while, her father, Stonewall Pinochet, had been living in luxury, never acknowledging her.

Where was the justice for his crime?

In life, the trick is to do what's necessary to keep on living. Willow had told her that.

Ida hesitated a moment, then picked up the telephone.

"Mr. Jacobs, this is Ida Long."

"Oh, yes, Miss Long. How are you?"

"I'm fine. I just want to ask you about something, and I was wondering if you had a moment."

"Well, if it's about the desegregation suit, I want you to know that I think we've got an excellent case and—"

"Mr. Jacobs, it ain't about that."

"Well, what's your question?"

"Mr. Jacobs, can you sue somebody if he's dead?"

Even as Clayton walked up the front steps, the tidy clapboard home seemed to proclaim itself as the abode of a single woman. There wasn't a speck of dirt on the porch, and the two chairs were placed neatly side by side. Ida had put her mark of orderliness on the place in a way that would have been impossible had other people lived there.

"You're late," Ida said, smiling as she opened the door for Clayton. "Sweetbabe and them been here for more than two hours."

She had no sooner said her son's name than a tall, dark, thinnish man, his hair cropped in a close flattop, his glasses balanced lightly on the bridge of his nose, loped into the living room. Clayton remembered standing with Ida at the bus stop when the boy went off to the army and how excited Ida was when he began attending college after his years in the service ended. And now he was a man. Sweetbabe grasped Clayton's hand. "It's good to see you, Mr. Pinochet," he said.

"It's good to see you too," Clayton said. He slapped Sweetbabe smartly across his back and then released him to greet his wife, Belinda, who was as tall and thin as her husband, with a perpetually smiling face. Clayton stepped back in mock surprise as a very young boy, no more than a year old, and the spitting image of Sweetbabe, toddled into the room. "And who is this handsome creature?" he said, picking up the child.

Sweetbabe grinned. "That's William the third," he said.

"Well, he sure is good-looking. Must take after his mother."

"Daddy would have just loved him," Ida said sadly.

The table was crowded with fried chicken, tamales filled with tomatoes and beef, macaroni and cheese, mustard greens, potato salad, and corn pudding. As Ida served generous helpings to everyone and Belinda propped her son on her lap to feed him, Sweetbabe cleared his throat. "I've got an announcement, everyone," he said.

Ida looked up. She'd just finished filling her own plate and was buttering a biscuit. She put down her knife. "What is it, honey?"

"I have accepted a position as a teacher at the Hopewell Middle School, and Belinda, Trey, and I are moving back here."

For a moment no one spoke. Then Ida said, "I thought you liked it up there in Chicago."

"I do like it, Mama, but it's freezing in the winter, it's expensive, crime is out of control, and I feel like I can do more good right here. Hopewell will be a better place for Trey to grow up."

Ida shook her head and looked at Clayton. "Never thought I'd see the day when black folks was leaving Chicago to come back to Mississippi. What is this world coming to?"

"Mama, it's not like Chicago is a million miles away. We can go up there for important occasions."

"Like what?"

"Like the Blues Festival."

"Honey, we got all the blues you want right here. I always wanted you to go away and be somebody. Never thought you could be somebody here." Ida wiped her eyes and looked up at Sweetbabe. "I'm glad you're coming home, son."

After the peach cobbler and coffee, Clayton was too stuffed to move, and he sat at the table talking for another hour before he finally stood up to leave. At the door, Ida told him, "I need to say something to you. You've been a friend to this family. A good friend."

Clayton waited, not knowing what to expect. Ida went on: "You know that things is bad at New Plantation. We've tried to talk with management, but they don't want to listen. So anyway, I know you're an owner now, but I want to tell you that the workers will be moving on getting those demands met. That's all I can say."

"I understand, Ida," he said. He turned to leave but felt her hands gripping his wrist.

"There's something else. Come into my room."

Ida and Clayton sat down on the bed; the rusty metal box was between them. She handed him the ancient letters and watched while he read them silently. Then she handed him the pictures and showed him what was written on the back. When he was finished, he put them all back in the box. He seemed dazed. "I can't believe it. My father and Susie had a child. I remember Susie," he said softly. "She worked in our house. She was beautiful. But where did you get this?"

"They belonged to my mother. Susie."

"Your mother?" Clayton gasped. "My God." He pulled out a cigarette and lit it and didn't say anything until he'd finished smoking it. "You're my sister," he said finally.

"Yes." Ida stood up.

He was silent again, and she held her breath. He began laughing. "I'm sorry," he said when he saw her shocked face. "I just don't think this family is classy enough for you." He started laughing again, and this time Ida joined in. "It's funny," he said, after they stopped laughing. "When I was little I used to wish that my father was married to Etta. She was my—my—"

"Your mammy. I knew her. She lived just up the road."

He nodded. "I think for a long time, until Marguerite, I loved Etta more than I loved anybody on earth. Only I was never allowed to say it, or feel it. I had to pretend she was just a servant, a glorified baby-sitter, instead of someone who taught me how to be a man. I think I'm more like Etta than I am like my own parents. I still miss her. I miss Marguerite. To my great astonishment, it seems that my father and I did have something in common: We both loved black women and we both dishonored them."

As Ida listened to Clayton and saw the sadness in his eyes, she fought the urge to put her arms around him. He seemed so vulnerable. He'd saved her child's life in more ways than one. She was grateful to him.

But she couldn't think about gratitude. She had to keep her future in mind, hers and Sweetbabe's and her grandchild's. That's what white people always did. They didn't let feelings get in the way of what was truly

important. And what was important was the money. She
cleared her throat. "Clayton, I have a lawyer. I intend to
sue the estate for my share."

She could see the astonishment flooding his eyes.
Why was it always so shocking to white people when
blacks asked them for what was rightfully theirs? Then
she saw his eyes turn cold, and when he looked at her
she was staring at a stranger. Clayton shook his head.
"The Pinochets own every lawyer and judge in this
state. You don't stand a chance."

"I'm suing."

"I'll give you some money."

"You'll give me what you want me to have. I want
what I deserve."

She could see it in his eyes, the fast figuring and cal-
culating. Their friendship was forgotten. All that talk of
his about wanting to see black people take their rightful
place in society was just talk. He didn't want to share.
"And just what do you think you deserve? What do you
really want?" She'd never noticed how hard his eyes
could be.

"When I was little I used to hear people whispering
that my mama was a white man's whore," Ida said. "I
didn't care so much about the whore part; I just wanted
to know which white man. They said I didn't have a
daddy. Well, I did. And I want everybody to know."

46

Delotha adjusted the towel around Maudine's neck and fastened the plastic robe that covered her client's dress as she guided her head back into the kitchen sink and squeezed the bottle of Clairol auburn number 109 into her hair, making sure that her gray roots were well lathered with the dye. Her own roots were showing a good two inches of silver, which Maudine pointed out to her that morning. "I don't go nowhere but to the store," Delotha told her friend. The fact was that she was no longer as meticulous about her grooming and dressing as she had been when she owned the shop and faced the public every day. Then, even after she'd gotten heavy and her wide hips spilled over her own chair, she wore Lane Bryant's finest pantsuits, which made her appear slimmer, and A-line skirts with slimming jackets. As her feet grew wider, she could always find a neat pair of comfortable sling-backs that didn't have her heels spilling out the sides. People who saw her had to say that she was stylish, even if she was big. And Wydell never complained about her weight. Wydell didn't like skinny women.

Now the business was gone, sold to Koreans who renovated the building and opened a grocery store. They were nice enough people, Delotha thought, although she wanted to sell to her own kind. The Kims had the right idea. The family lived upstairs—mother, father, kids, grandparents, uncles, and aunts, a horde of folks, and every one of them working in the store.

Sometimes she passed the place on her way to the doctor, and they were always bustling around. She got sad, looking in at the Kims, seeing their gleaming rows of vegetables. Sadder still when she drove between Thirty-ninth and Fifty-fourth and passed the giant cage of a housing project, heard what sounded like a million cicadas rubbing their wings together. She always kept her windows rolled up and her doors locked when she passed the project, even in broad daylight. Who knew what those crazy junkies would do for a fix? It was enough to make you cry, looking at that place. When did her people get so down-and-out? Hadn't they come to Chicago to do better? But who was she to talk? Unless she had a customer coming to the house, she sat around in her bathrobe in front of the television from morning to night, watching soap operas and smoking cigarettes.

She lit a cigarette while the dye was on Maudine's hair. She couldn't even remember when she'd started smoking again; she never smoked when she was working in the shop. Now, however, her most frequent errand and her only exercise was walking down to the corner store for a pack of Salems. Sometimes, lighting up, she felt good to be consumed by something outside herself.

While she was puffing on her cigarette she had a flash of Wydell's face. She hadn't seen him since he left, three months before. She knew from Lionel that he had rented an apartment just south of Hyde Park. She knew, too, that he wasn't working; and he was drinking. She got sad thinking about Wydell stumbling around drunk somewhere and her smoking cigarettes by the packs. What a pair! Lately she'd look in the mirror and become bewildered at the old woman she saw there. Her daughters called her up once in a blue moon, and there were such huge silences on the phone that she would get embarrassed and say goodbye. She couldn't figure out why she and the girls weren't closer, even though Odessa used to always tell her, "You don't never touch them girls; you save all your loving for that boy." Was that what had happened? Had she pushed her daughters away from her and held her son too close? Was her mother right? Well, Odessa was dead, so she didn't even have the comfort of arguing with her about how she had raised her kids all wrong. Wydell and the girls were gone. And W.T. was wild as a reindeer and way too strong for an old woman. And yet he still needed raising.

"Don't get me too red now, 'Lotha," Maudine said, fanning Delotha's cigarette smoke away.

"I'll rinse you right now."

"Girl, they was shooting right down the street from me last night. What do they call it? Gang banging. They took two or three of those boys to the hospital. I wish to God they'd taken them to the morgue. Almost every weekend, the same damn . . ."

The water drowned out Maudine's words but not Delotha's fears. Beneath the spritz of water, inside the rubber gloves, her hands were trembling.

"It's this damn new stuff these fools are buying."

"Crack," Delotha said, fear inching up her spine like a poisoned worm.

"Crack! Crack is gon' kick a lot of asses, you hear me. That there is some serious stuff. And these fools ain't got no better sense than to try it. Lordhavemercy. My people. My people."

Delotha could feel the warmth and pressure of the water as she rinsed Maudine's head. She squeezed her dripping hair, then dried it with a towel; she applied conditioner and put on a plastic cap and had Maudine sit under the dryer. The whirring noise was too loud for Maudine to talk over, so Delotha walked to the window and lit another cigarette. Then she turned on the tiny portable television that sat on the kitchen table.

A sea of black faces appeared on the screen. Delotha was confused for a moment, until she remembered that it was August and recognized the parade the local black newspaper sponsored to honor the city's black children. For the last five years she had ridden on a float that said "We Remember Armstrong," but this year she declined. She was just too tired. Watching the black drill teams make their way down State Street, she recalled how excited her children used to be when they went to the parade. She got into the rhythm of the marching band, and then all of a sudden there was a huge banner with the face of the deceased black mayor, and the whole crowd got quiet.

"Well, we won't see another one like him for a long time," Maudine said, turning the dryer off. "At least black people can say we pulled it off one time."

"Fighting that goddamn Polack and his buddies, that's what killed him," said Delotha. "That's what I think. Most of them white boys on the city council didn't want nobody black in there in the first place."

Maudine and Delotha were both silent until the DuSable High School drill team flashed across the screen. Then Maudine said, "If we could just keep these children off these drugs. That's the problem."

Delotha grunted. She didn't need to be told what the problem was, not with W.T. running the streets like a wild man. Words like "crack" and "gangs" stung like a thousand razor-blade whips, made her tingle with a fear that was almost sickness. Why did that boy love those streets so much? His rhythms matched those of the loud rappers who constantly screamed from the radio in his room. He moved fast and sure like those hard-legged young men from the projects. They were slim and brazen, with an inbred meanness clinging to their skins, and they'd slipped into his life, encroached upon her world, and now seemed to possess W.T. They were like lovers calling to him, those high school dropouts and troublemakers, boys with no prospects, boys from that cage of a housing project who carried guns and beepers. Where was W.T. right now, this minute?

she thought, staring out the kitchen window. And when she saw him, if she saw him, and asked him where he'd been, would he even answer her question? Or would he make his baby face hard and mannish and then walk away? She didn't know where he was, except that he was somewhere gravitating toward peril, dancing with it, embracing danger like a woman he paid for. Delotha sighed. All her life she'd been defending him against the wrong enemy; she would have to fight the streets to save him, and she didn't have the strength.

When Maudine left, Delotha sat at the kitchen table and pulled out a pack of Salems and began smoking. She went into the living room and watched the evening news on the big set. When that was over, she went back into the kitchen and began frying some pork chops, telling herself that W.T. would come home to eat with her. She waited and waited, until she felt a headache coming on. She put the food in the oven and lit another Salem.

He came home late that night, after one o'clock. The next morning, even before it was time for W.T. to go to school, the bell rang. When she answered the door, a police officer was standing in front of her. The cop, tall and sandy-haired, smiled when she opened the door. "Ma'am, do you have a Wydell Cox Junior living here?"

"That's my son," she said, clutching her housecoat around her.

"I'd like to talk with him."

"What's this all about?" she asked.

"I want to ask him some questions in connection with a robbery that took place last night."

"No," she said, "you must have the wrong boy. Not my son."

"Well, ma'am, if you don't mind, I'd like to speak with him."

She called W.T. down the stairs. He walked to the door slowly, with his head down, a swift, boyish walk, not that foot-dragging hoodlum stroll he affected whenever he left the house to go off with "his boys," that walk that was as savage as it was cool. This day there was more fear than bravado in his eyes. "You tell this officer," she said when he got to the door, "you tell him you didn't have nothing to do with no robbery."

He was innocent, she thought, as she listened to him deny any wrongdoing. "I'm not the one you're looking for," he said. His voice, his face, the way he stood, the tiny gold hoop in his left earlobe, everything about him was innocent. And no cracker was going to tell her anything else.

But the policeman didn't seem as convinced as she was. He asked specific questions. Where were you at this time, at that time, on this date? "I was home last night, wasn't I, Mama?" W.T. said slowly.

Delotha hesitated. Why should she tell this white man anything. She nodded. "He was home all night."

When the policeman left, he didn't say goodbye; he said, "Ma'am, your son needs to be careful about the people he associates with." And to W.T. he said, "You'll be hearing from me again."

While he was waiting for the policeman to return, W.T. went to school every day. He came home when he was expected and ate dinner with Delotha each night. They sat at the kitchen table and talked as they hadn't in years. Some evenings they laughed way into the night, and he didn't shift his body when she put her arm around his shoulders. He brought down his camera and took pictures of her. Once, when they were eating sweet potato pie, she called him Armstrong. She said, "Armstrong, you love you some sweet potato pie, don't you, boy?"

W.T. said, "What was he like?"

"Who?"

"Armstrong. You just called me that. You're always calling me by his name."

"I am?" Delotha lit a Salem and took a couple of quick puffs. She smiled. "He was a lot like you. You favor him. Same freckles. He was funny. He could make a mule laugh. And he was smart. He learned things real quick. And he loved making money."

"How old would he be?"

She didn't hesitate. "He'd be forty-seven."

"Damn. Old enough to be my daddy."

"That's because I'm old enough to be your grandma. I had him real young, and I had you when I was real old."

"Whatever happened to those people who killed him?"

She shook her head. "I don't know. I hope they're all dead."

"Y'all should have killed them crackers," he said. "I'd have gone down to Mississippi and smoked every last one of them motherfuckers."

"Don't you talk like that," Delotha said. She could feel the meanness coming out of him, and it frightened her.

He laughed, took her cheek between his fingers, and squeezed it. "Is Dad ever coming back?" He gave his mother a sharp look, and just when Delotha thought she could see something like yearning in his eyes, he got up and took out the trash.

Later she would think of that time as the week of calm, a period when she learned how to fall asleep again, when she sang with the radio and danced a little around the house. But after a few days, when the officer didn't return, her son's schoolboy walk disintegrated into his familiar swagger. She looked out the window one morning and saw W.T. driving down the street in her car. He had taken it without asking her. The school began sending home notices of his absence. He began staying out late at night.

One evening when she was waiting for him to come home, she went into his room. There were photographs everywhere, pictures of lean, mean-looking boys, and where there were no photos, the walls were covered with large posters of rappers, whose names all began with Ice. They stared down at her with practiced coldness. W.T. had that same look, she realized. Was that expression borrowed from the rappers, or did it come from somewhere within him?

His king-size bed was covered with clothes, and athletic shoes of all descriptions were all over the floor. Nikes. Pumas. Converse. Why hadn't these glorious sneakers made her boy obedient and happy? Why hadn't these magic shoes kept him at home, where he could be safe? When she bought them for him, that's what she thought she was purchasing. She cradled a brand-new pair of Reeboks in her arms and started crying.

The closet was an even bigger mess. He asked for Guess? jeans and he had Guess? jeans, jackets, shirts, everything. All the Guess? clothes were in a heap on the floor. She'd clean things up tomorrow, she thought, and was about to close the door when something bright and shiny caught her eye. Delotha reached up to the shelf above the clothes and put her hand on steel as cold and hard as a rapper's eyes.

She stared at the gun until the sheen on it had almost hypnotized her, and even then she couldn't look away. The gun was much bigger than her hand and heavy, a thing that couldn't be easily concealed, that would bulge in a pocket. Delotha sat down on her son's king-size bed, in the middle of a sea of dirty designer jeans and expensive athletic shoes, and holding the gun in her hands, she began to mourn as though she'd just buried someone.

Delotha wrapped the gun in an old towel and put it in the drawer where she kept her underwear; then she got into bed. She hadn't expected to sleep, but she was dozing when she jerked awake to the sound of voices in her house. For a moment she lay frozen with terror. Then she heard W.T. and some of his friends, but that recognition didn't dispel her fear. She sat up, listening to the boys rummaging in the kitchen. There were three or four of them. She could smell the pork chops they were heating up. She tried to calm herself. They were just hungry boys coming from a party or something. Why was she worried?

Because her son's gun was in the drawer with her bras and girdles. Because, as she sat in the bed with her hand over her heart, she heard her boy's voice, loud, eager, and vengeful, saying, "We ain't gotta take shit from nobody."

The first thing Delotha did the next morning was call Wydell's apartment. She hadn't spoken to him since he left, but he had sent her a letter with his address and telephone number on it. Every month a check for one hundred dollars arrived, "in case W.T. needs something," his notes said. The phone rang for a long time before she hung up. She called him at least a dozen times between seven and nine o'clock, before she realized that he wasn't taking a shower or sleeping hard.

She wiped her eyes as she dressed. If anyone had asked her, she would have said she was crying for a lot of reasons, for a lot of people, but at the moment she couldn't put any of those reasons into words. All she knew was that she had to find Wydell.

Lionel and Amelia's shop had just opened when Delotha got there. Over the years, the couple had purchased the buildings on either side of them, and their business had expanded to include a cleaner's, which the oldest son and his wife ran. Two other sons worked in the family business. The shoe shop was now divided into retail and repair. Above the counter in a neat row were the three college diplomas of the oldest boys. But Delotha barely noticed her surroundings as she dashed through the door. "What's the matter, girl?" Amelia said when she saw her.

Delotha wiped her eyes. "Sit down," Lionel said, taking her hand and leading her to one of the chairs on the retail side.

When Delotha attempted to speak, she started crying and looked at her husband's cousin and his wife helplessly. "Just take your time, honey," Amelia said, patting her back. She disappeared in the back for a moment and emerged with a cup of coffee, which she handed to Delotha. "Drink this."

Delotha took several sips, then placed the mug on the floor. "I'm all right now," she said, but she wasn't, and as soon as she began to speak, she started crying again. She spoke anyway. "W.T. is in trouble. I found a—a gun in his room. I took it, but I think he's gon' do something bad. I don't know what to do. I don't know how to stop him. I just can't handle him by myself."

"You want Lionel to go talk to him?" Amelia asked.

"No. No. I want you to help me find Wydell. Wydell needs to talk to him."

"Girl, isn't it a little late for that?" Lionel said quietly.

"Lionel," Amelia said. She put her hand on his arm. He patted her fingers.

Delotha glanced at Amelia quickly, then turned to Lionel. "No. Tell me, Lionel," Delotha said, watching them. "Say what you got to say."

"What I got to say is this: I got eyes; you pushed the man away. From the moment that boy was born, you made him feel like he couldn't be a father to his own son. Now the boy's in trouble, and you want Wydell to be his daddy again."

Amelia said quietly, "And I got eyes. Wydell let himself be pushed. You can't put all the blame on Delotha."

Lionel shook his head. "He's been drinking like a fish. He can't save his ownself, let alone somebody else."

Tears streaked Delotha's face. "All I ever wanted was for W.T. to be safe, for white people not to kill him like they done Armstrong."

Lionel said sadly, "The streets is killing more black boys than the white folks ever could. We always had more than one enemy."

"Oh, God," Delotha said, sobbing, raising her hands in supplication, "please save my baby!"

47

When Wydell walked into the Down Home early one Friday evening in November, the first thing that caught his eye was what everyone else noticed, a huge sign over the bar that proclaimed in bold red letters: "The All-New Down Home Bar and Grill." He stepped back when he read the words, and looked to his right and then his left, but as far as he could see, nothing in the place had changed. Except for the sign. He'd wanted to come back for some time but somehow hadn't gotten around to it, even though the blind man's music kept haunting him.

He sat down at the bar and ordered a Jack Daniel's, straight up. Several old men, with grizzled faces and gray hair or no hair, nodded a greeting. "What's new about it?" he asked, pointing to the sign, when the bartender, the same fat-cheeked, bald-headed man who'd waited on him when he came in with the young prostitute, handed him his drink.

"The white kids done discovered us. That's what's new," the bartender said. He told Wydell that his name was Sam, and the two men shook hands quickly. Then Sam leaned over the bar, close enough so that Wydell could smell the crisp, spicy after-shave he wore and the spearmint gum he was chewing. "Some entertainment reporter from the paper come in here last year, a brother, and he wrote an article saying that we had the best blues in the city. Which is true. Them white college kids read about it, and they been packing in here every weekend ever since. Most Friday and Saturday nights there's more white folks in here than black."

"That's why I don't hang out here on the weekend nights no more," a man seated three stools down from Wydell said. He wore a plaid shirt and a Bulls cap. "Ain't nothing worse than drinking with white college kids. While it's early, they all educated. By midnight, they done turned into the damn Klan and shit. They get drunk, they liable to say or do anything. Next thing you know, one of 'em done called you a nigger. If I'm in a situation where white folks is drinking, I be watching them. Soon as they faces turn red, shade number three, I'm gone. Shades number one and two are manageable. Number three is the turning point. They start looking like beets and shit. That's when the devil commence to possessing they souls. You know what I mean? What they want to come in here for anyway? They got they own music."

"But they ain't got no blues," said a light-skinned man, so thin that the veins in his temples seemed to bulge out of the sides of his skull.

"Yeah, they do," the man in the Bulls cap said. "That yahoo music. Loretta Lynn. Hank Williams. Willie Nelson. That's they blues."

"That ain't no blues," the light-skinned man said. He slammed his fist against the counter, and the ice in his drink tinkled. "White peoples don't sing no blues, 'cause they ain't got no blues. But they indirectly responsible for the music, 'cause they sure be giving black folks the blues." The man in the Bulls hat extended his hand, palm up, over an empty stool, and the light-skinned man reached out and slapped it with his own hand. "Now am I lying?"

"Yeah, you lying," said Sam. "Goddamn Reagan and Bush done gave everybody the blues."

"White folks ain't got no 'Willie Horton Blues,'" said the light-skinned man, and the others at the bar started chuckling. "They ain't got that damn Bush trying to make them look like animals. I'm not saying white folks don't get sad when their mamas die and all like that," he insisted, after the laughter died down. "Everybody gets sad. But the blues is deeper than sadness. See, I know, 'cause I am a blues man from way back. I know what's authentic. The blues is something in your soul telling you they ain't no hope, shit ain't never gon' be right. You know what I mean?"

"Aww, now you trying to get deep. Hell, everybody feels like that sometimes," Sam said.

"Don't listen to Sam; he liable to tell you anything, because Sam want that white money coming in here," the man with the Bulls cap said. "You want them white people's tips, don't you, Sam?"

"You damn right. Y'all wouldn't tip your mamas if they was pouring."

"I'm on a fixed income," the man in the cap said.

The others laughed, slapping one another's palms. Sam shook his head. "I got your fixed," he said.

"What are white folks doing in here anyway?" the light-skinned man asked. "If I tried to go to some redneck bar in Cicero to listen to that goddamn yahoo music, I wouldn't live to tell the tale. But white folks think they're supposed to be every goddamn where. Shiiit."

"It's their world, squirrel. You just living in it, trying to get a nut," said Sam.

"Michael Jordan could walk in one of those Cicero bars and they'd try to kick his ass," the light man said.

"Naw. They'd make Michael an honorary white man," said Sam.

"I don't care what you say," the light-skinned man muttered. "White people ain't got no blues."

"You want a sandwich, maybe some fried chicken?" Sam asked after he poured Wydell his fourth Jack Daniel's. Wydell shook his head.

"Say," Wydell said, "does that blind man still sing here?"

"You talking about Blind Jake? Yeah, he's the one they all come to see. He'll be on at nine o'clock."

Around eight-thirty, people began filtering into the club. Wydell looked around, and the light-skinned man and his friend with the Bulls cap were gone.

More and more people were filing in. Lots of white kids in jeans, with long hair and scrubbed faces. They smoked a lot, pulling out Marlboros and puffing away, the fellows looking as if they were playing John Wayne in some cowboy movie. Wydell watched a few young blacks coming in together, tiptoeing in as though they were walking on glass or nails in their bare feet, edging into the crowd nervously, as if not sure the Down Home was the right place for them to rediscover their roots. Crowded among the newcomers were the regulars, the old transplants from Indianola, Ruleville, and Greenwood, the ones with the gold teeth and the Jheri-Kurl juice dripping down the collars of their ten-year-old leisure suits. They saw the startled, slightly rosy white faces and the hesitant black ones as part of the night's lineup of entertainment.

Shortly after nine o'clock, the lights dimmed slightly and the stooped, jet-black man wearing his trademark dark glasses, the beat-up hat dipped down to his eyebrows, shuffled to the stage, and the spotlight found him. The white kids started pushing their way to the stage and screaming before he had completely pulled the harmonica out of his pocket. The girls were especially loud, shaking their heads and pulling on their hair in the same hysterical way as the teenagers in old clips of Elvis Presley and Beatles concerts, as though at any moment they might be swept up in a wave of pandemonium that would render them catatonic. Blind Jake craned his head from side to side. "How y'all folks doing?" he shouted, and the people in the front row yelled back their greeting. Wydell felt a twinge of recognition, seeing the singer, but by that time he was sipping his sixth shot of Jack and not too sure of anything.

Blind Jake put his harmonica to his lips, and a sound both sweet and tinny whined through the instrument, surged into the smoky air, and grabbed Wydell in his chest and then floated up to his temples. He saw a vision of juke joints and smelled pigs' feet, heard the sound of crickets on a hot summer night, saw the outline of tall cotton plants, the white tops sparkling in the moonlight, and for a moment he felt as though he were in a place where he could begin again. He let his mind drift back to memories of Hopewell and was startled when he heard the applause, saw Blind Jake nodding his head toward the audience, shoving into his pockets the dollar bills that the people pressed into his hand.

A white girl standing up front suddenly yelled out, "Sing 'Sharpen My Pencil, Baby!' " and the crowd began whistling and clapping as Blind Jake started shaking his sad head from side to side. He began a low, bawdy number laden with innuendo, rich with metaphor. "C'mon, sharpen my pencil," he sang, twitching his frail hips and pointing to his groin. The young white kids, already full of beer, their cheeks like beets, hooted and stamped their feet. "Sharpen my pencil, baby!" His voice was strong for such a skinny, hollow old man, a man who looked as if he didn't weigh more than 120 pounds and who needed a shave and maybe a drink. He was almost comical, singing his thinly disguised song about getting some pussy, gyrating his puny hips as though he was twirling a Hula-Hoop, nodding at the crowd he couldn't see, bending down when he heard the rustling of their dollar bills. "C'mon, sharpen my pencil, baby!" The more the people hooted, the harder he twirled his hips, too lean for his pants. He turned around, unbuckled his belt, and his pants began slipping and sliding down, revealing his scrawny, naked behind, until there was no music, just yelling and screaming as the old blind man stumbled around the stage, twitching and shaking his ass, with his pants down around his knees. The song ended, and holding the harmonica between his teeth, he pulled his pants up, then turned around to face the audience. As he leaned over to accept the bills that the men and women were pressing into his hands, his glasses fell to the floor.

And just that quick Wydell knew him, knew him with his begging hand out, his ass showing for Gold Coast tourists, Hyde Park yuppies, and college kids. Jake. Black Jake. Ugly as a snake. Eight shots of Jack were not enough to mask the rage that suddenly pulsed through Wydell's blood, not enough to winnow out his pain. When he stood up, Wydell felt his temples throbbing, the scream sprinting in his throat like a track star. He tried to move toward Jake, but the crowd was pressing in on him, holding him back with their hoots and hollers, their applause and their dollar bills, so that when he took his first step he realized that he was hemmed in, trapped in the tight and airless space between his stool and the bar.

"Wydell?"

He looked up, and Lionel was there, extending his hand, pulling him forward, away from the crowd.

"That was Jake McKenzie in there singing," Wydell yelled as soon as they got outside.

"I know," Lionel said quietly.

"Why didn't you tell me he was here?" Wydell shouted.

"For what? You ain't got time for revenge, Wydell. And you ain't got the strength."

Wydell didn't protest when his cousin drove to an all-night diner on the South Side. Lionel ordered two black coffees and two slices of pound cake. The two men sat stiff and silent until the waitress brought the food. "Cake's a little dry," Lionel said after he took a bite.

"Why you come looking for me?" Wydell asked.

"Delotha was asking for you, man. She mentioned the Down Home. You been to see your son lately?"

"She put me out."

"He's still your son. When's the last time you saw him?"

Wydell sipped his coffee and pushed the cake away. He didn't answer.

"W.T. is in trouble, Wydell. He's running with a gang. Delotha found a gun in his room. She wants you to talk to him."

"She do, huh? Well, I ain't got nothing to say to W.T., nothing he'd want to hear." He looked at Lionel steadily, without blinking. "How many boys you got, Lionel?"

"Wydell, I got me six sons. You only got one son left. You want to lose him too?"

"I can't save that boy. I ain't never been a father to him. It's too late to start now."

"You don't have to start at the beginning. Start in the middle."

"It's too late."

Lionel grabbed Wydell's hand. "Start at the end," he said.

48

Spring had officially begun, but the March winds blowing off Lake Michigan provided frigid testimony to the staying power of winter. W.T. blew on his hands as he and his homeboys cruised down Forty-seventh Street in Sonny's ride, a turned-out burgundy Cabriolet. Earlier, they'd all met in an abandoned building on the South Side and Alien had produced a glass pipe. "Yo!" he said, setting the pipe down on the concrete floor. He held out his hand, so that everyone could see the small white pellets he had in his palm. "This shit is the bomb, y'all. Check it out." Crack, he called it. And after W.T. smoked it, the feeling inside him was just like love. Now, as they zoomed with the top down, the radio blaring WGCI's top-ten rap hits all over the block, W.T. could think of nothing but the high he'd just experienced; he had to get some more crack. Then the shooting started. W.T. was sitting up front, and for a moment he was dazed, confused; then he felt Sonny's hand pressing his head into the seat. "Get down, Strong Arm, 'fore these motherfuckahs smoke your narrow ass." And then they were all ducking into their seats, crouching down low. They were trying to stay out of range but lifted their heads just high enough so that they could see who was shooting at them. Because there was definitely going to be some payback. W.T. heard Sonny saying, "That's C.J. and them Woodlawn motherfuckahs. We gon' find them motherfuckahs, and we smoking they black asses. You can believe that shit." Even while the shots were hitting the side of the car, sounding like a ton of marbles raining on them, fast and hard, they were planning revenge. "Hey, Sonny! Watch out!" *Bam!* They hit a pole, and the horn blared, as if Sonny was telling somebody to get the fuck outta his way. Everybody started jumping out of the car, not opening doors, just going over the side and hitting the ground running. And Alien, a fat boy with eyes set so wide apart that he looked as if he was from someplace strange, called over his shoulder, "Damn, Sonny. Lighten up on that horn, man." But Sonny didn't reply, didn't move. And W.T. stopped running, because nobody was firing on them anymore. Everything around them, except for the horn, was still. He stood in a daze, wondering what was up with the horn, until they saw the blood oozing out of Sonny's breathless chest, which was pressed against the wheel. The blood was a shocking red. The other times, W.T. had seen death from a distance. He shuddered. Then he sensed his homeboys watching him; he swallowed his fear. And the first thing W.T. said—and he was proud to be the first to say it—was, "We smoking them motherfuckahs."

His house was empty when W.T. rushed through the front door, blowing on his gloveless hands, rubbing his frozen ears. The stillness of the place surprised him; he was used to being assailed by the odors of hair preparations, the sweet subtlety of shampoos, the orangy scent of conditioners, Jheri-Kurl formulas smelling like the plastic caps that set the process in motion. When he walked in the door, he expected the hum of the blow dryer or the sharp hissing and clicking of curling irons as they rattled in his mother's hand. Slurred southern voices and cackling female laughter usually greeted him. As he stood in the living room, the silence of the house almost scared him, as when he was a little boy and he'd wake up in the dark and see the eerie shadows on his bedroom walls. Ghosts. That same yucky feeling played around his shoulders and in his gut, like nausea but not quite, maybe more like the shakiness he experienced as a child when he knew he was going to pee in his pants and that the other children would laugh. Only now, of course, he was too old for fear. Fear he could peel off like a scab. He shrugged his shoulders, as if to reinforce that he didn't care. He didn't want to admit, even to himself, that he liked coming home to a house full of his mother's cigarette smoke and hair creams, that he felt a little lonely standing in the living room knowing she wasn't there. "Mama! Yo! Mama!" He felt better just calling her name.

On second thought, it was good that his old lady wasn't around to hassle him. He had serious business to deal with. Serious! The thought of what he was about to do raced through his entire body like liquid mercury. His feet flailed, and he started dancing across the living room floor, the coins in his pockets jangling noisily as he bounced. His toes tapped against the hard wood, sounding like typewriter keys. When he stopped, he was too jittery to sit down. He took a quick look at his watch. In a little while he had to go meet his boys.

His mother had set a plate for him on the stove: fried chicken, greens, potato salad, and corn bread. He left the food and ran up the stairs to his room and opened his closet door. He reached up to the shelf and felt around. Then he grabbed the wooden chair from the desk his mother had bought him when he started junior high school. He pulled it over to the closet, stood on it and looked everywhere on the shelf, but there was no gun. Standing on that chair, realizing that his weapon was missing, what he felt was relief, pure and cold as a first snow. Now he wouldn't have to kill anyone. But the thought melted away immediately. Of course he had to kill. They had smoked his boy.

He pulled everything off the ledge until caps and clothes were all over the floor; he looked among the clothes. Where was his gun? Tears were stinging his eyes. He had to find it and smoke the guy, otherwise what was inside him wasn't the hardness of a man, just some bogus Mickey Mouse shit. He looked under the bed, in every drawer, in the wastepaper basket. Then it dawned on him that his mother had found it.

He ran to her room and stood at the door, looking inside. On her wall was a large picture of Armstrong, taken the year before he died. The photograph, so lifelike in its stillness, was the main reason W.T. rarely went into his mother's room. Now he gaped at the photo, his mouth wide open. It was like looking in the mirror. Same freckles and light skin. Same smile. Same full cheeks. He felt his brother's eyes on him as he began rummaging through his mother's closet. He looked under her bed and even under the mattress. Then he opened her drawers. It felt weird to touch his mother's underwear, her bras and girdles, almost as though he was touching her in the places the garments covered. He was about to close the drawer, when he felt something hard, covered with a towel: his gun.

He ran downstairs, and when he reached the bottom step, the front door opened and his mother came in. He slid the gun inside the waist of his pants and pulled his jacket around him. Delotha looked up and smiled without energy. "Hello, baby. You eat your dinner?"

He rushed past her. "I gotta be someplace," he said, running out the door.

"Wait a minute. Where you going? Armstrong! Where you going?"

Her instinct was too strong to ignore. Delotha climbed the stairs slowly, and by the time she reached her room she was out of breath. Her underwear drawer was still open. The towel was on the floor. "Oh, my Jesus," she said.

By the time the bus dropped him off in front of the project, it was almost dark and the temperature had dropped into the teens. A droning sound came from the cagelike structure, as if the place housed thousands of angry wasps. He ran the two blocks to where he had told Alien and the rest of the boys to wait for him. He kicked away trash as he made his way to the meeting place. Cars zoomed by, a few filled with white kids from Evanston, coming in for their weekend purchases; the neighborhood junkies were making transactions as well.

When he got to the corner, Alien and his boys weren't there. W.T. waited for about twenty minutes, trying to figure out what to do. When he heard the car he looked up expectantly; the ride was full of young, strong-looking black boys. W.T. started running even before he heard the shout, saw the flash of red caps, the fingers throwing gang signs. "Yo, nigger, what set you from?"

Just that quick, there was nobody on the street, no place to hide. He heard the first shots when he was half-way down the block, and he looked up to see a skinny boy with intense eyes, his body protruding from the car window, aiming a gun at him. There were more shots, and then he was running, running, as the car slowly trailed him. He passed two women, who cowered in their shoes and screamed faint gibberish as he approached. In the next block he ducked inside a store, filling the air with his hot, crazed breath. He could feel the fear all around him. "You get out," the man behind the counter said. He had round eyes, skin as dark as plums, and he was staring at W.T.'s waist, his open jacket. The man raised a gun and aimed it at him. "You get out now. I don't want no trouble."

W.T. ran to the door and looked out. He didn't see the car, but he eased out warily, hoping that the darkness would hide him. His heart roared in his chest, and his legs ached. There was a street to cross, a narrow alley between one side and the other. Sweat dripped down onto his collar. He raced across the street and felt hands grazing his shoulders, another hand on his arm. He struggled free and began running again. "Motherfuckah!" someone yelled. A gun fired several times behind him.

He ran for blocks, his heart pumping pure adrenaline and sending it to his feet. He was nearing the edge of his neighborhood when he began to slow down a little. He peered over his shoulder and didn't see anyone. Then he looked into the street, and there was a police car crawling beside him. "You there," the loudspeaker said. "Stop and put your hands up."

Without thinking, he took off again, down alleys and back streets. He heard brakes squealing, and his heart jumped inside his chest. He didn't know whom he was more frightened of, the police or the Woodlawn boys. His legs were screaming with each step he took, but he kept running, trying to stay in the shadows. He didn't know whether to throw the gun away in case the police caught him, or keep it for the rival gang that might jump him. He was five blocks from his house and he couldn't hear or see anybody. The street was deserted. As he ran, the gun jammed into his belly, making him sore. Then he heard a lone car on the street, slowing as it approached him. W.T. was afraid to turn his head to look. He was so tired; he felt he'd collapse if he took another step. The car stopped and a door opened. He heard footsteps running toward him, only he was too frightened and exhausted to move. Suddenly, strong hands were grabbing his arms. He tried to reach for his gun, but the hands, big and hard, yanked it out of his waistband and he heard it clatter against the sidewalk. A fist glanced off W.T.'s cheek. Then he was being dragged and pushed into the car, and it took off into the black night.

49

After Clayton dismissed his tutorial class, he sat in his office, going over some papers. Usually Ida would have brought him dinner by now, but he hadn't seen her since the week before, when she showed him the letters that were in the metal box and told him that she was suing his father's estate.

He missed Ida, her cooking and her conversation. He didn't realize how much he'd come to depend upon her. Halfway through the week, he started to telephone her, but he stopped himself. He didn't want to succumb to sentimentality; a great deal of money was at stake.

As he sat at the desk, he reviewed his strategy. He would call up Waldo Anderson, the family attorney, and inform him of Ida's intentions. Waldo could start lining up the judges and lawyers, begin asking for the favors they would need to smash Ida's case before she even got started. For years, he'd been at his father's beck and call. And now he was about to get his reward, enough money to buy the independence he'd always craved. And he deserved every penny of it. Friendship was friendship, but this was business. If he wanted to fund a scholarship program for black students he could do that, but he wasn't going to give away half of his fortune to a black woman just because she claimed to be his sister. He reached for the telephone.

"Clayton! I've been expecting to hear from you," Waldo said when his secretary put him through. "How have you been?"

"I've been fine, Waldo. And you?"

"Couldn't be better. Listen, I meant to call you this week. There's a meeting of the Honorable Men of Hopewell coming up next Tuesday night, and we're all expecting you to take your father's place."

Take his father's place, he thought, holding the receiver in his hand. His father had told him the Pinochet name and tradition must continue. And that's exactly what he was doing. Continuing the tradition. Why didn't he admit it? Stonewall had won after all. He had trapped him with his values and his money, finally put him in the cage he had been trying to escape all his life. Clayton remembered Etta's motto: "If they know you scared, you's already licked." Maybe his father had licked him.

"Clayton?"

He didn't want to be his father's son; he wanted to be his mammy's. "Waldo, I am not an honorable man," he said.

After he hung up, Clayton sat at his desk until the sky outside his office turned a deep purple. He closed his eyes and remembered the way Etta looked as she sang him to sleep when he was a child, and the way she looked when she died. He recalled the weight of Marguerite's dark thighs wrapped around his hips. He thought of all the babies they'd never had. I've lost so much, he told himself. And now, what do I have left?

It was dark when he left the office. And darker still when he parked his car in the small yard in front of the neat clapboard house. He could smell the cooking from inside. Fried chicken, he thought. He waited for a long time at the door before Ida finally opened it. When she saw him, she didn't speak. The light from the living room illuminated her features. Clayton stared at her for a long while and in his heart he acknowledged that the tilt of her nose, the curve of her chin, the way her eyes slanted had been undeniably marked by Stonewall

Pinochet. Their father. Finally he spoke. "I want to work something out."

Ida just stared at him.

His voice cracked. "I don't want to lose you. I couldn't bear it."

She saw the pleading in his eyes, but still she didn't speak.

"We'll go see my lawyer tomorrow. Together."

Ida opened the door wider. She said, "You're just in time for supper."

50

The purple and red flowers on Doreen's cotton shirt made Lily dizzy as she watched her daughter pick up several placards that read: "New Plantation Workers Demand Higher Wages and Medical Benefits." "Come on here, Melanie," Doreen called, and the little girl, her hair in two pigtails, ran to her mother.

"You ought not to be going up there," Lily told Doreen. She was sitting on the sofa, holding three-year-old Crystal in her lap and folding a mountain of clothes. Her forehead was crinkled with apprehension. She closed her eyes and tried to imagine her daughter carrying a sign, maybe yelling at the people who owned New Plantation. If the police came and arrested them, would she go limp, the way the niggers used to do during the unrest? She shook her head. The whole idea was unbelievable.

"Mama, that's where I work." Doreen was smoothing Melanie's bangs and didn't look at her mother.

"Yeah, but it's mostly them. Let them do it." The thought of her daughter carrying a sign and marching around the fish-processing plant with a bunch of niggers made her dizzy. Her stomach was rumbling and churning, and she wanted to scream and shake Doreen until she admitted that what she was doing was wrong, but Lily felt so tired, so out of breath, that she didn't think she could stand up. She was getting a headache from looking at the crazy flowers on Doreen's shirt.

"New Plantation is treating all of us like shit, Mama. I'm in the same boat as the niggers. I ain't scared of being raped by Willie Horton, Mama. I'm scared of not having medical benefits."

Doreen's words were true enough, but everything she said only intensified Lily's fears. "Well, why do you have to take Melanie with you? Ain't you afraid she might get hurt? You don't know what's gon' happen out to that place."

"No, I don't know what's gonna happen, but I'll tell you what: No matter what happens, I want her to know that she has to stand up for herself. 'Cause if she don't, won't nobody do it for her. I want her to have courage."

Lily's eyes almost met her daughter's, but at the last moment she looked away. Courage was what men were supposed to have: that was what she wanted to say. But the words froze on her lips. "Y'all be careful," she whispered.

The theme music from *The Young and the Restless* was trailing off when Lily finished folding the clothes. She worked around Crystal, who was sleeping in the middle of the sofa, in a space surrounded by her little shirts and dresses. Just as Lily was about to put Crystal's things away, she heard banging at the door, and her heart began to jump and fall inside her, because she knew it was Floyd. Floydjunior always rattled softly, a begging kind of knock. The angry fist slamming against the wood could only be Floyd. "Lily. Open the door, Lily."

He started shaking the door, and the sudden clatter made her realize just how flimsy the barrier between them was.

"I know that you're in there," he said. "Open the door and let me talk to you, Lily. I want you to come home with me. I love you, Lily."

"Go away, Floyd," she shouted, the words bubbling out of her mouth like soapsuds.

His lips were on the crack of the door. She could tell that he'd been drinking, from the sloppy way his words slurred, the whining in his voice. "You need somebody to take care of you. Doreen's a young woman. She gon' get married again. Then what?" He was quiet for a moment, letting the warning of her eventual abandonment penetrate.

He was just trying to scare her, she told herself, but the question remained: Then what? Where would she go if Doreen didn't want her? The notion of being totally alone was a chilling one. "Go away," she yelled, her words propelled by venom and fear.

"I'll take care of you, Lily. I'll protect you." Then his lips were on the door again. "Lily, baby, I know I done a lot of stupid things, but honey, everything I ever tried to do, it was all for you, Lily."

She rushed to the door, knocking half the clothes to the floor as she got up. She put her head to the door. "You ain't done nothing for me. Everything was for you. To make you feel good. Even that boy."

Floyd began screaming and pounding on the door so hard that the entire trailer seemed like an earthquake in progress. All the other times, he'd just yelled her name for a while and then left, but today he seemed as wild and excited as a madman. Lily ran to the small window above the kitchen sink and peered out. She watched as Floyd patted his pants pockets, then turned around and looked in the dirt, squinting until his eyes became two angry cuts in his face, then stooping with his nose almost touching the ground, like a rat sniffing for food. When she saw the rocks in his hands—two good ones, palm-size and smooth—she ran to where the little girl was sleeping. "Floyd, don't do nothing crazy. I got me a kid in here," she yelled. She heard the glass splinter behind her, and then she felt a sharp stinging on her chin.

Lily wiped the blood from Crystal's arm; it had dripped down from the cut on her chin. Crouching on the sofa, she held a rag to the cut. Crystal woke up and began crying. "Hush, baby," she said, patting her grand-daughter's back until she was quiet. She crawled to the kitchen and raised herself up, holding on to the sink until her eyes were just over the window. Floyd was standing outside the trailer in the dirt, passing a rock from hand to hand, looking at the window, waiting for Lily to come out. She started to say something, but she stopped herself and ducked her head down, because she didn't want to get him started again, and who knew what would set him off? She reasoned things out in her mind. The last time she called the sheriff about Floyd, he didn't come for hours. And what did they do when they got to her? The same thing they did the other times she called. Nothing.

Doreen was gone. There was no one to help her. He wouldn't ever stop bothering her, she thought wearily. For the rest of her life, he'd be banging on her door, calling her name, screaming way into the night, trying to drive her crazy all over again. She started crying and then bit down on her lip.

Then she remembered the gun in the drawer on Doreen's nightstand. She could go get the gun, she thought, just have it in her hand if he burst through the door.

Lily felt very calm as she crept into the bedroom, reached into the drawer, and palmed the cold steel. She crawled back into the living room and sat on the floor next to the sofa, pulling Crystal down on her lap. "It's gon' be all right," she said softly.

Lily stayed on the floor for at least half an hour, and then she placed the child on the sofa and crept to the window. She couldn't see him. Just before she opened the front door, she looked inside the gun to make sure it was loaded.

He was gone. The road was empty. Lily sat down on the concrete step, the gun in her lap, her eyes focused on the narrow road. She thought: *If they would only sing now, just this one time, to soothe me.* Her only answer was the wind whispering through the grass. For all her straining, she couldn't remember the words to any of the songs. Her palms itched, and she began scratching her hands, first one, then the other, until she realized that she was waiting for him, hoping he'd return, enjoying the gumption she'd found. If he came again, she wouldn't be afraid.

Clutching a rock in his hand and with several others in his pockets, Floyd ran down the road, looking over his shoulder, listening to the little girl screaming inside. His granddaughter. He couldn't remember her name or if he'd ever known it, and he thought that maybe she was born after Doreen stopped speaking to him. He tried to figure out if the kid sounded hurt, half thinking that the crying was a trick, something to throw him off guard.

If he could talk Lily into coming back, they could live off her check until things started coming through for him again. He could buy another car; his old one had stopped running several years before. He wouldn't be eligible for Social Security for a few years. What with the rains, there hadn't been much construction, not even very many odd jobs. When he went to apply at McDonald's, the manager asked him if he had ever been in jail, and he didn't even bother to lie. And when he was walking out of the place, whom should he see serving customers but some nigger. Even now he couldn't stand thinking about that: A nigger could get a job, while he starved to death. Niggers had the Supreme Court and the Congress looking after their interests, and who cared about his?

Floyd didn't see the man coming out of the woods until he was almost next to him, and then he almost missed him because he was dressed in green—green pants, green shirt, green baseball cap—and walking real slow. With his coffee-brown face, he looked like a slim old tree. Floyd took a quick glance around, and when he didn't see anyone else on the road he quickly caught up to him. "Hey," he called out.

Floyd laughed softly to himself as he watched the

man, who eyed him warily. He laughed harder when he threw the rock, aiming for the old man's belly. But he missed. He had more rocks; his pocket was filled with them. Suddenly the old man was running toward him with surprising vigor, and as he got closer, Floyd could tell that it wasn't a man at all, but a woman, more old than young, as brown as a pecan and with a braid dangling down her back and licking the wind as she moved. He couldn't explain why she scared him; there was nothing in her hand, no weapon of any kind, but when he saw her moving toward him he took off. The rocks weighed him down, and he stumbled and fell in the middle of the road. When he looked up, the woman was standing over him, holding a large rock in her hand. It crashed to the ground, inches away from his face. Her smile revealed a row of gleaming gold teeth. The woman's hands were empty, but he still felt as though she had a weapon aimed at his heart. "Trash," Willow Scott sang out, in a voice that was strong, almost triumphant. The word struck Floyd like a bullet that would remain lodged inside him forever.

51

When W.T. felt the strong hard hand on the back of his neck, the fingers spreading around to his throat, and then the other hand pushing him into a car as dark and frightening as the belly of a whale, he thought he was about to die. He waited for death, which he had always expected to be as quick and dramatic as any in Arnold Schwarzenegger's movies, only his breath kept coming in fitful spurts and the fear gripping him was deep and cold and real. Suddenly both hands released him. He stopped trembling and looked beside him, trying to make out his captor in the dark. But before he could see him, he heard his voice. "You must want to die real bad."

W.T. smelled the liquor before he had a chance to even make out his father's features. He hadn't seen the man in three months, and he stole a look at him as they drove down the street. "Where are we going?" he asked finally.

"You and me is taking a trip."

"Where?"

"Down home."

His father's profile looked worn and harried under the passing lights, and the longer W.T. looked at him, the angrier he got; all the fear that he'd been feeling all night long turned into rage. Who the fuck did this old man think he was to be taking him anywhere? He showed up anytime he felt like it, and W.T. was just supposed to drop everything he was into and get in a

430

car with the dude and go wherever he said to go. Shiiit. "Let me out," W.T. said, his voice as flat and hard as asphalt.

"You keep your ass right in this car, boy. I told you, we taking a trip." Wydell reached over W.T. and pushed down the lock on the door. "Put your damn seat belt on."

By the time they were forty-five miles outside the city, V103 began to sputter, until the radio station was nothing but static. Wydell reached into the glove compartment and pulled out the first tape he put his hands on. He slid it into the cassette player. "You know who this is?" Wydell asked when the music began playing.

The boy shook his head.

"You don't know ole Muddy Waters, huh? That's a damn shame. He's singing blues. You know about the blues, don'tcha?"

"I heard of 'em."

"Sure you heard about 'em. Everybody's heard about the blues."

W.T. realized that his father was still a bit drunk from whatever he'd been drinking earlier. He thought back to when he was little, when his father never touched alcohol. That time seemed far away, as though it had slipped down a dark tunnel and would never be retrieved. "Well, we going to the home of the original blues. Mississippi. That's my home."

"Mississippi! What the hell are we gonna do there?" W.T. asked. Shiiit! Damn if he was going to some country town. His dad was tripping. As they sped down Interstate 55, W.T. wondered about his boys, why they hadn't shown up, why they left him hanging the way they did. He leaned back in his seat and closed his eyes for a second, trying to recall his entire harrowing night. Why hadn't his boys been there for him? That was cold, them not being there.

"You gon' see me and your mama's home, that's what. We still got relatives down there. Friends too. We never took you before because, well, you know what happened to your brother. Me and your mother had such bad memories of the place. But you need to see it."

"Why do I need to see it?" W.T. asked irritably.

"You just do. It's just something you need to see."

"Are you and Mama gonna get back together?" He didn't know where the words came from, or even that he was thinking them, and he was surprised at how frightened he felt, listening for the answer. Scared like a little kid.

"I don't know. Why you ask me that?"

"No reason." W.T. leaned back against the seat and closed his eyes.

When he woke up it was light, and warm air was coming through the open window. He looked around, and everything he saw was green and flat, as if someone had slammed a frying pan down on the world. "Where are we?" W.T. asked.

"In Mississippi. You slept through Memphis. You hungry?" Wydell asked.

W.T. nodded.

Wydell pulled into a McDonald's and ordered two breakfast trays. They ate quickly, without talking. Wydell carried his coffee with him to the car and drank it as they drove off.

They began to smell the fish way before the lush green fields of cotton and milo gave way to the manmade ponds. "I heard they turned all this plantation land into fish farms," Wydell said. From the highway they could see the beige building, the large gold block letters on it: NEW PLANTATION CATFISH FARM AND PROCESSING PLANT. Around the building they saw people, mostly black women, but some white ones too, marching and carrying signs. There were television cameras and reporters from a Jackson station. "What's going on?" W.T. asked.

"I don't know. Progress, maybe."

They parked the car on the shoulder of the road, right